Praise for Song of the Seals:

"Like Alice Hoffman, Christy Yorke makes the best kind of magic. What a richly woven and rewarding novel."

—Carrie Brown

"Christy Yorke writes about matters of the heart with pure poetic justice. A lyrical and spellbinding writer. An exquisite storyteller."

—Deborah Smith

"A thought-provoking look at the perils of life and, ultimately, of the hope that follows tragedy."

—*Booklist*

Praise for the novels of Christy Yorke:

"Peopled with sympathetic characters, adding to the charm of this often ethereal exploration of the complications of love."

—*Publishers Weekly* (starred)

"Fabulous, delightfully unique. The real spell is cast by Christy Yorke's lyrical voice and stunning characterizations. Haunting and evocative, it will hold the reader spellbound until the very last page."

—Kristin Hannah

the secret lives of the sushi club

CHRISTY YORKE

BERKLEY BOOKS, NEW YORK

THE BERKLEY PUBLISHING GROUP
Published by the Penguin Group
Penguin Group (USA) Inc.
375 Hudson Street, New York, New York 10014, USA
Penguin Group (Canada), 90 Eglinton Avenue East, Suite 700, Toronto, Ontario M4P 2Y3, Canada
(a division of Pearson Penguin Canada Inc.)
Penguin Books Ltd., 80 Strand, London WC2R 0RL, England
Penguin Group Ireland, 25 St. Stephen's Green, Dublin 2, Ireland (a division of Penguin Books Ltd.)
Penguin Group (Australia), 250 Camberwell Road, Camberwell, Victoria 3124, Australia
(a division of Pearson Australia Group Pty. Ltd.)
Penguin Books India Pvt. Ltd., 11 Community Centre, Panchsheel Park, New Delhi—110 017, India
Penguin Group (NZ), Cnr. Airborne and Rosedale Roads, Albany, Auckland 1310, New Zealand
(a division of Pearson New Zealand Ltd.)
Penguin Books (South Africa) (Pty.) Ltd., 24 Sturdee Avenue, Rosebank, Johannesburg 2196,
South Africa

Penguin Books Ltd., Registered Offices: 80 Strand, London WC2R 0RL, England

This book is an original publication of The Berkley Publishing Group.

This is a work of fiction. Names, characters, places, and incidents either are the product of the author's imagination or are used fictitiously, and any resemblance to actual persons, living or dead, business establishments, events, or locales is entirely coincidental.

Copyright © 2005 by Christy Cohen
Cover design by Rita Frangie
Text design by Tiffany Estreicher

PRINTING HISTORY
Berkley trade paperback edition / August 2005

Library of Congress Cataloging-in-Publication Data

Yorke, Christy.
    The secret lives of the Sushi Club / Christy Yorke.—1st ed.
      p.   cm.
    ISBN 0-425-20275-5
    1. Fiction—Authorship—Fiction.   2. Female friendship—Fiction.   3. Women novelists—
Fiction.   4. Betrayal—Fiction.   I. Title.

    PS3575.O634S43   2005
    813'.54—dc22

                                        2004058317

PRINTED IN THE UNITED STATES OF AMERICA

10 9 8 7 6 5 4 3 2 1

For my dad, Rocky,
who made mountains seem like the safest places on earth

Acknowledgments

"When are you going to write about Idaho?"

This is a question I've heard often in the fourteen years I've lived here, but I knew I had to wait. On the surface, Idaho is a state of homogenous views and people, but as a novelist, what lies on the surface doesn't interest me much and in most cases it isn't the truth. Idaho is a spectacular, complex, often conflicted state. Its generous, strong-minded people warm the heart; its majestic mountains and rivers astound the senses; its politics and prejudices often boggle the mind. I waited until I felt I had some hope of capturing these complexities. Even then, it was both a challenge and an awakening to go inside the minds of people I might not agree with. It's an experience I highly recommend.

Many Idahoans played a pivotal role in the making of this book. First and foremost, I could not have written a word without the help of my personal jet boat captain, Mel Reingold. Mel and his wonderful wife, Beverly, took my family down the Salmon River, an experience that not only gave me firsthand knowledge of the canyon for this novel, but was a life-changing trip. If you have any opportunity to get to the Salmon River, do it. The only way I can describe it is a soul place. A place where, if you haven't been breathing right for a while, within an hour or two, you will. Mel knew every nook and cranny of the canyon, knew all the hidden trails and caves and people who call it home, and better than that, he let my son drive the boat. Beverly and I had an instant and otherworldly connection that continues to this day. I consider them both lifelong friends.

Back in Boise, Shawna Shearer is always there when I need her, for marketing support or, even better, long conversations over wine. Magical and astonishingly devoted, Shawna gave me the best and most unexpected gift—a best friend at my age.

Highlands Elementary parents and teachers: Thank you for your enduring support. And to the book club—Jane, Sharon, Michelle, and Andrea: Don't be alarmed. Your secret lives are safe with me.

Life feeds my books, and my books influence my life. While writing this novel, rivers took over. After an exhaustive search of all things wet, I finally found an old, electricity-less cabin in Lowman, Idaho, set on a crest between two streams. I want to thank my husband, Rob, and children, Claire and Dean, for enthusiastically coming along for the ride.

As for those outside the state, my heartfelt gratitude goes once again to my stupendous editor, Leona Nevler, for her genuine kindness and for doing everything she can to make my work a success. Bill Johnson took a remarkable amount of time and care editing the first pass of this manuscript. My agent, Natasha Kern, goes far beyond the call of duty. It is a privilege and a joy to work with her.

Finally, this book is dedicated to my father. Dad, you led me to mountains, which turn out to be the only place I feel at peace. Thanks for the directions.

the secret lives of the sushi club

Christy Yorke

Once, they called this river Lorelei. Spoke of her as an enchantress, a wild thing, liquid, cold, and blue. Curvaceous, tantalizingly acrobatic, Lorelei lured young, gangling brooks to her sparkling depths and consumed them. She devoured canyons and made love to stones.

But creeks began to bore her. She became enamored with the ocean, and bedrock was no obstacle, the cities people put in her way no more than a day's inconvenience while she flooded a path to the sea. Like any force of nature, or teenager in love, she hurt and terrified those who valued things they could predict.

So she was chained.

Shackled to dams, forced to watch her awkward sweethearts tamed with concrete, her limbs cut off to feed lawns and farms.

The river churned her fury, then fell into a slackwater of despair. Even on a flat surface, liquid will meander back and forth, curling around invisible obstacles and up against itself like a body in search of warmth. Water requires a mate.

At best, Lorelei had disregarded the men who rode her back, screaming or laughing; at worst, she'd sunk them. Now abandoned, bound, alone, she found the only one worth noticing, a man who loved her as much as she loved the sea. She reached out a watery hand and pulled him down, but the man fought. He spoke of a woman, pleaded for his life. Spurned, the river granted him his wish, failing to tell him that when a man nearly drowns in her waters, he can never live happily on land again.

What rose from the river that day was neither man nor fish. Gills erupted beside ribs; a warm heart turned out unnaturally cold blood; fingertips glistened with silver scales. The fish-man haunted the riverbanks, gasping for water, becoming better acquainted with salmon than with men. When his wife finally returned for him, her body couldn't warm him. His slick arms slid right through her fingers; she had to let him go.

The man returned to the river, heartbroken, and the river welcomed him sadly, her heart broken, too. It is said that he's still there, a silver glimmer beneath the rapids, a ghost among the trees.

The river left him his voice so he could tell you: Be careful who and what you love.

—legend told at camp by Salmon River guides,
after a few rounds

1

The River of No Return

In her dream, of course, he lived.

They fell overboard together into a cauldron of foam. The river's brutality was more shocking than the cold; Zach was up-ended and slugged, Jina dragged along jagged boulders and gravel beds, but they came up laughing. They found their footing in the rapids, and Zach held out his arms.

He presented her with an oyster overflowing with pearls, the star-shaped logo of an electronics company stamped on its shell.

It was the triviality of the vision that woke her—the print design that had eluded her for weeks, one more ultimately unimportant piece of her other life, her unchosen life. She reached out to slap away the oyster and touched only bedsheets. It shouldn't take death or pain to create something beautiful, but later, when the design won accolades, she'd remember that the way things ought to be is often a far cry from the way things actually are.

Jina Woolridge woke bruised, though when she rolled over in bed she knew she'd been ignored rather than abused. Mike had already left for the office, remade his side of the bed so tightly he seemed to be making the case that life would be a neat and tidy thing without him. She squeezed her eyes shut again, but that brought visions of the way he'd held his breath when she came to bed last night, as if he feared she might ask him to marry her for a second time. As if it was better to go without air than to not love someone enough.

She opened her eyes, flung back the covers.

She had to wake her son twice for school. Though Danny's childhood nightmares had abated, he still woke bleary-eyed and grumpy most mornings. He was eleven, but she often found his light on at night. The tardy bell had rung by the time she dropped him at the front gate, though she knew she wouldn't have gotten a kiss or backward glance anyway. She watched him enter the school like a soldier in enemy territory, checking the gaps in the junipers, eyeing the shadows behind the flagpole. She bit her lip and drove home, read the newspaper from front page to back, finally drifted into the bedroom she'd converted into an office. She delayed the inevitable by checking her e-mail, playing Snood, but at noon she gave up and re-created the oyster. She didn't bother with a cover letter, almost rooting for the design to fail, but two days later she got a rousing endorsement from her finicky client, the assurance that a check was in the mail.

The creation of rivers and art is a violent thing.

It was easy enough to avoid water; in Danville, it was stopped, stored, and recirculated through underground pipes and resin fountains made to look like stone. At the entrance of new subdivisions, there were crystal-clear, chlorinated waterfalls, lined ponds full of lethargic, listing fish. Art, on the other hand, was more insidious, even in the suburbs. Though her neighborhood had gone for years without an outbreak, a few blocks over someone had put out a garden sculpture and, one week later, another challenged the covenants in order to paint her house green. As a child, Jina had thought she could be anything—a teacher, scientist, or pilot—but by high school, she'd already quit three real jobs in favor of drawing caricatures at the street fair, volunteering at the art studio and as a contributor to highway murals. By eighteen, she'd already gotten into the habit of taking jobs that didn't pay.

Two of her three best friends were just like her. Irene Goddard was still waiting for her big acting break, despite the soap-opera role that had made her almost famous and a body that had been cut, tucked, and starved to perfection. Then there was Alice Aberdeen, whose fourteenth novel would certainly have been her last, if it hadn't met with such success. A high six-figure advance; foreign, book club, and audio rights; an option from a movie producer at Miramax—all bestowed upon the novelist before the book's publication, all for an author nobody had heard of, who had been dumped by more publishers and agents than Alice would care to admit.

The book party was this Friday. At San Francisco's Avante, paid for by Viking, whose top editor had snatched the book in a

three-house auction. This was all Jina knew, the most information she could gather from Alice in a series of rushed, excited
phone calls. Jina dressed for lunch, then drove across town to
Zutto's, where Irene had already ordered "the rainbow"—an
assortment of California rolls, tuna, eel, and squid. Beside her
sat Mary Bonelli, who had joined the sushi club nine years earlier, after Jina did an advertising layout for her law firm. As a legal aide, Mary was the only member of the sushi club who
seemed capable of holding a steady job. Jina had first seen her
sitting behind her desk, typing at a fantastic speed, until she was
asked to go out and get everyone caffe lattes. Jina had asked her
out for her own caffe latte that afternoon, an invitation that
caught Mary so off guard that she stopped typing, and the
lawyers in the room turned and stared.

Alice had too much publicity work to meet them for lunch,
though she must have known that in her absence she would be
discussed almost exclusively.

"I don't get it," Irene said as soon as Jina sat down. She
reached for the squid only she dared to eat, adding extra wasabi.
"How could this book be that much better than the others? Her
novels are the reason I don't read, you know. The plots are all
over the place. The characters are either crying, screaming, or
having sex. I mean, are they romances or fantasies or what?"

Mary looked away. Her condominium was filled with books,
and silent as a library. She was always the first to finish Alice's
novels, and often suspiciously failed to show at Zutto's after
publication, leaving Jina the task of making up praise.

"Right before she got the offer, John asked her to come work
in his insurance office," Mary said in a whispery, girlish voice

that contrasted drastically with her middle-aged face. When she asked the waiter for more sake, he had to lean close to hear, a situation that made her blush. "She was crying all the time. Can you imagine Mike or Naji putting up with that? John was at the end of his rope."

Jina could tell the sushi club anything, but this time the words about Mike wouldn't come. It was bad enough to be turned down; worse was admitting she hadn't seen it coming. The third time's a charm, people said. She'd put her two disastrous marriages behind her and focused on security and what her son needed, on a good man. She knew her three-year relationship with Mike wasn't perfect, but she'd reached a point in her life when it had to be good enough. If the admission ever came, it would be a whisper: At a certain age, love lost its glorious ambitions and grew careful, finite, small.

It was a relief to lift her sake glass. "To the stuff of dreams," she said.

Irene flashed a dazzling Hollywood smile. "Or ruins."

"Irene!"

"Believe me, I've seen it happen enough. It's bad karma to get too much at once. One too many cars in the garage and a person goes batty. You'll see."

"I think she deserved it," Mary said quietly.

Irene drained her sake and looked Jina in the eye. "So do I."

Jina kicked Irene under the table. Her friend smiled innocently. It was obvious that Irene could have done without Alice and Mary entirely, but thankfully nothing was ever said. Jina loved their foursome, loved meeting once a month for sushi and a celebration of the smallest things—a fight-free afternoon with their children, a new show on HGTV, the loss of a pound. She thought of them as an impenetrable fortress, each taking a corner, keeping the little things safe.

"What do you think it was like for her?" Mary asked. "Getting that phone call from her agent? Having everything change?"

Having imagined her own success enough, Jina had a pretty good idea. In her case, a wealthy, connected client would launch her into galleries, make the eleven years she'd toiled as an underpaid graphic artist count for something. In her dreams, success actually made her taller, stretched her from her childishly petite frame to the height of a supermodel. And it did wonders for her bobbed hair, tinting it to the shade of amber displayed on the dye box instead of the sepia color that had actually come out.

Alice's metamorphosis must have gone like this: One night, she went to bed poor and miserable, her sixteen-year writing career as limp as the pajamas she wore to work, every sentence she'd written that day contrite and careful, filled with fear. To fall asleep, Alice toyed with giving up writing; in her dreams, she went into bookstores without hunger, she told strangers she used to be an author, then laughed out loud. First thing in the morning, she giddily yanked the computer's cords from the outlet, put her hard drive out by the garbage cans. Which was the moment when the phone rang and her agent's first words were: "Are you sitting down?"

"I've had calls like that," Irene said. "When I got the soap, I was euphoric. You remember, Jina. I thought I had everything I wanted. And I did. That's the whole problem. You get what you want and have nothing else to yearn for. You make up things, just to want more."

Jina sat back. "Has she talked to either of you about the plot?"

The women shook their heads and right then, in the middle of Zutto's with her best friends in the world, Jina felt her first ripple of dread. "Don't you think that's strange?" she said. "We usually hear every detail. I don't even know the title."

"With the kind of money she got," Irene said, "it's got to be a love story that ends tragically. Mark my words, the hero will get killed."

They finished the rainbow, spent another half hour trying to guess the storyline. Alice had asked them to wait until the party for their first glimpse of the book, but by the time they paid the check, they all agreed that was crazy talk.

"Let's go to Rakestraw Books," Irene said. Mary gathered her purse, coat, and briefcase full of case files she'd be working on well past the hour the lawyers went home. "The owner said he'd order a dozen copies. He's great with local writers."

Jina shook her head. "You two go. I'll treat Danny to the Walnut Creek Barnes & Noble. He likes hanging out in the music section."

They hugged good-bye, and Jina watched her friends cross the street. Mary had to struggle to keep up with Irene, whose five miles a day on the treadmill kept her in terrific shape. They were nearly the same age, in their late thirties, yet Irene's bold, platinum-dyed hair swung exuberantly like a teenager's, while Mary's dull blond curls seemed to weigh her down.

Jina did errands until three, then waited at the obscure parking spot Danny had requested outside his elementary school. She had a partial view around trees and a telephone pole as Danny trudged slowly from the school. Joe and Aaron, who had come over after school nearly every day last year, ran past him without a word and hopped into Joe's mom's minivan. Danny hesitated, and Jina nearly broke their bargain and rushed to his side until she saw that he was just reaching into his backpack for his Game Boy. By the time Peter and Eric tried to mow him down on mountain bikes, he'd bent his head so low over the small screen that he hardly flinched.

Jina did. How long had it been since there'd been boys in the house? Three months? Six? She missed the stomping feet, the machine-gun sound effects, the forced bodily eruptions followed by gales of laughter. Their house used to be known for unsupervised Nintendo, popcorn on the couch, and an unkempt yard perfect for army-man wars. Lately, its only claim to fame was quiet. Danny wasn't afraid to be alone in his room anymore. He'd stopped screaming at night, and she'd been so relieved that she hadn't prodded the silence once. Hadn't dared to know what it was made of. Why *was* Danny's light on at night?

Her son got into the backseat without a hello, and greeted her with the irritating synthesized music of Super Mario World.

"How was your day?" she asked, knowing he'd only shrug. "I thought we'd go pick up Alice's book. I'll even set you loose in Barnes and Noble."

Danny had already cleared level one, and he managed a grim smile. His red hair closed around him and the Game Boy like a curtain.

Jina knew he wasn't getting along with the kids at school, but she had one last hope. Charlie Grimes, who had lived next door until a couple years ago, when his mother followed a boyfriend to L.A., was moving back to Danville this summer. Jina vowed to invite him over, let the boys tear up the backyard the way they used to, turn Danny's bedroom into a circus tent.

She drove through the steam-cleaned streets of Danville, past the bakery and their favorite Blockbuster and the Safeway she shopped at most Mondays. As a dreamy teenager, an ambitious young wife, a river runner, she never would have believed she'd end up in a San Francisco suburb where taupe was the only recognized color and dull, sophisticated lives flourished. She had a house here, devoted friends, a front yard that met the neighborhood's stringent C, C, & R's. She'd done better in Danville than she could have imagined—better, she realized, than she would have liked.

She headed out of town into larger, more sprawling Walnut Creek. She pulled into the parking lot of the gargantuan Barnes & Noble, where Alice had occasionally done signings for crowds of three. Danny began a new level with Princess Peach just as she cut the engine. He pulled out every last vegetable while she waited by the door, but when he lifted his bloodshot gaze and saw where they were, he turned off the game and followed her to the store. Two years ago, he went with Charlie to the skateboard park; this year, he talked to himself in the aisles of Barnes & Noble. His interests had dwindled to video games and music; today, music won out. He moved toward the headphones, where he'd sample CDs to sing back later, his eleven-year-old choirboy voice at odds with the gutter lyrics of rap.

She promised to be back in fifteen minutes and headed past

the espresso bar and the seven aisles of self-help, and stepped up to the information booth.

"I'm looking for the new novel by Alice Aberdeen," she said. She expected the usual click of the computer, the lost records, sometimes even the revelation that the buyer had failed to order copies altogether, even though Alice had lived in the east bay her entire life, and could at least sell out five copies at the local Barnes & Noble. Instead, the young saleswoman, dressed more for a backpacking expedition than bookselling, smiled widely.

"Ohmygod," she said, her speech bunched together like a train wreck. "Yougottareadit. Imean, the VirginMaria. It'ssupposedly basedonatruestory, butcomeon! Elainewiththeshooting? Andthat-patheticwoman, allwrappedupinaguywhocouldn'tevensurvive! I-stayedupallnighttofinish. Ihaven'tdonethatsincecollege."

Which apparently hadn't been that long ago, or all that successful.

"Where can I find it?" Jina asked.

"Where can't you find it? I mean, look around."

For sixteen years, Jina had been buying Alice's books from dark corners and bottom shelves. She ordered as many copies as she could afford to pump up her friend's sales numbers, added glowing reviews to Amazon.com. She read everything Alice wrote, from romances to fantasies and westerns, and always found something to praise, even if it was just a line or two in the first efforts, one sparkling metaphor that made up for the rest of the awful prose. She blamed agents for bad reviews, encouraged her friend to go on when Alice was dumped by not one, but three major publishing houses due to lackluster sales.

Which was why, when Alice had begun to talk about the buzz surrounding her new novel, when she'd mentioned dollar amounts and trips to New York City, national tours and NPR interviews Jina had, ashamedly, thought it all a lie, a writer losing what little grip she had on reality in favor of entering one of her more pleasurable, unrealistic plot twists.

There was a pecking order among women, among friends, that no one talked about. Jina had never imagined Alice as a success.

Until she saw the dumps.

Three of them in front of the new hardcovers. Fancy, cardboard bookcases, the edges curved to represent a woman's anatomically impossible hourglass figure, with Alice's name in large, glittery red letters. And on the already sparse shelves, two dozen hardcover copies of the novel, the title in scintillating script: *The Secret Lives of the Sushi Club*.

Jina glanced at the clerk, who was on the phone now, then down to the lonely end of the romance aisle, where Alice's paperback originals had once languished. She laughed, latched on to the idea that the title was a gimmick thought up by the sales department or an ambitious junior editor. She was certain, until the last second, that a secret between friends was the most valuable thing on the planet. A treasure set behind fortress walls.

Hesitantly, she approached the dumps. It was nearly impossible to imagine Alice sitting at her computer, typing the words Jina had barely gotten out, words that choked her, that made them all cry. Even if the crudest acts and a neighbor's quest for a husband were now events fit for TV, in actual reality people were almost always more honorable than they were given credit for. Devotion undermined greed. She was nearly sure of it.

She picked up the book, opened the cover, and saw the contents page, the novel divided into four sections: The River of No Return; The Virgin Maria; Just Breathe; Sex, Lies, and a Smoking Gun. Jina closed the book abruptly, took one deep breath, but it felt gurgly, as if tears had slid to the base of her throat and formed a pool, an eddy that with stealth instead of violence was as dangerous as a Class V rapid. She walked quickly to the checkout line, steadied her hand as she reached for her credit card.

She bought the book.

She found Danny beneath headphones in the rap section, red hair bobbing, which did not bode well for what she'd hear later. He swayed and, still without hips, his baggy jeans scared her. She tapped him on the shoulder and, still under the spell of the music, he smiled. Twelve years, two states, a third of a lifetime spent out of the water, yet when she saw that hair, that smile, she still felt saturated and cold. When she'd crawled out of Idaho's Salmon River more than a decade ago, ice had formed on her lashes. There had been no way to go but up. Up, somehow, over black granite cliffs. Up where a plane might spot her. Where someone might still be looking. Continuing to move was the hardest thing she'd ever done. Not because of the cold or the nearly impassable terrain, but because all the things that could have been were lost in the river.

Danny removed the headphones, tossed them on the hook. "You find the book?" he asked, his first words all day.

Jina clutched the bag to her chest. "Yep. Let's go."

"Can I get the new Eminem CD?"

"No."

"How about Nas? Last nigga alive."

Jina couldn't make the necessary comments about the offensiveness of rap lyrics. She moved toward the door and Danny followed, halfheartedly sulking, already humming a song with words that he hopefully wasn't taking in.

"Hey," he said when they stepped out into another perfect California afternoon, the skies clear, the air seventy degrees. "Is it a mystery? Roger thought it was. He said his mom was a mess while she was writing it, pacing all the time, like she couldn't figure out how it would end."

It was nearly as hard to get to the car as it had been climbing the mile from river to rim. And afterward, when she'd returned to art school, restarted a life she'd forsaken, each act on land seemed to erase another sliver of the adventure she and her husband, Zach, had faced on water. Danny was born, and Devil's Teeth Rapid became a whimper, she bought the house in Danville and couldn't recall just how abrupt the horizon line of Salmon Falls really was. The only link to the past that didn't crumble was Danny's nightmares—first his screams, then the crying, then an almost irritated insistence that the man was there, *right there*, can't you see him, hear his feet squishing across the carpet, see those puddles where his red hair drips? She'd bathed her son's sweat-drenched body in cool cloths, bit her lip to keep from asking him how he knew this when she'd never told him about the river, never told him what happened to his father at all.

She slept on the floor of Danny's room in the early years,

though she knew she wouldn't be haunted. Zach's life had been stolen, but she was the ghost.

Her legs buckled only after she'd gotten in behind the wheel.

"Mom?" Danny asked, his voice soft now, quiet.

"It's a love story," she said.

2

Even poison can be withstood if an immunity has been built up.

Jina read the book in five-minute spurts, read until her skin grew hot. She put the novel away until she could control her breathing. She felt as though she was back in grade school, snubbed by her best friend, nearly immobilized by hurt. She had barely been able to tell the story, had never granted Alice permission to write it down. If she had, she certainly wouldn't have agreed to Alice's portrayal of her as foolish, self-absorbed, and cruel. So unsympathetic, Jina couldn't even root for herself. The novel was overrun with maudlin love scenes, a stupid disregard for the danger of rapids, pages and pages of river philosophy neither she nor Zach had had time for. A story of fools.

Jina shoved the book in her desk, pictured Alice's neck in

the way as she slammed the drawer, imagined a bloodcurdling scream. She wished a good imagination was enough to soothe her, wished revenge and violence really worked. She tried to work, but for two hours all she produced were mundane designs that hadn't come to her in dreams. For a caterer, she created a letterhead and menu bordered by fruits and vegetables; for a landscaping firm's web page, a river, along with the kinds of plants that grow along streambeds—reeds and pussy willows, yellow irises and blackberries.

From the other room, she heard the steady explosions and coyote reincarnations on Cartoon Network, Danny's occasional laugh. When he got bored, he would play Nintendo. Once he'd blown up the Death Star, or snowboarded down a virtual cliff, he'd do his homework, no questions asked. He was gifted, his sixth-grade teacher had told Jina, but a little strange. Could a teacher say that? Wasn't there some law that prohibited an educator from calling a mother's only child a weirdo? "He thinks he sees things," the counselor had said gently. "Have you noticed? He talks to someone who isn't there."

"Of course I've noticed," Jina had snapped. Her boy's best conversations started when he went to bed alone; he asked questions and laughed at the silent response. "So what?" After seeing the way the kids in his class treated him, ostracized him, could anyone blame him for creating someone kind? He wasn't *crazy*. He was small for his age, mathematical and nonathletic, a gamer; his potential was a complex calculation still being solved in his head. It was a phase; he'd grow out of it, the way nerdy kids outgrew their awkwardness and went on to become com-

puter millionaires, physicists. Some people squandered their al-
lotted happiness in childhood, but not Danny. *He was biding his
time*, Jina told herself. Waiting for the swift justice of the SATs
or a class reunion where all the jocks are divorced and fat. He
was preparing to be happy later.

The front door slammed. She heard Mike's voice, the happi-
est reply Danny had managed in days. She thought she might be
sick. The roof of her mouth tasted bitter. She had no idea what
she and Mike could possibly say to each other now. Are there
any words after the pronouncement that you are not loved
enough?

"We could have an autumn wedding," she'd said to Mike over
dinner last night. "Maybe at one of the Napa vineyards."

She'd felt ten years younger as she closed her eyes to imagine
it—a real wedding this time, the gown, the music, the dusk sky
the color of burgundy grapes—so she missed the full range of
shock and dismay on his face. By the time she looked at him,
Mike had sunk forward as if marriage was a cliff you either
soared from or fell off. He looked as if she'd shoved him.

"Jina," he said. "I didn't expect . . . Is three years enough
time to know? With your other marriages, I thought you'd be
more cautious. Let's not mess up what we have. There's Danny
to consider. There's so much to lose."

She had nodded, a stupid smile stuck on her face. Too surprised to offer a rebuttal, and wondering, perhaps, if she'd been
too soundly loved before. Apparently, she did have a lot to lose.
Her optimism, for one, her pride, her certainty about a man
who had, until that moment, seemed easy to read. She'd always

believed that any action, however reckless, was better than surrendering to fate, but maybe there came a time when that was no longer true. Maybe growing up meant realizing that from now on, very few things should and would happen to her.

She had taken the rejection the same way she'd offered the proposal—within reason, not bursting into tears or launching into a tirade. She'd stopped short of begging or ordering him out, the two things she might have done before, the two things that would be difficult to take back later. It would have scared and insulted her, in her twenties, to know just how careful and dignified she would one day become.

Now, Mike came into the bedroom, loosening his tie—smiling, normal, silent. Last could have been a gruesome detail of a case. Too horrible to mention.

"Hey, hon," he said.

She walked to the window. Outside, a meadow had engulfed her backyard. She'd tried to weed at first, but discovered she didn't have the heart for it. She liked wild things.

After Danny was born and she graduated from art school, she used the money from Zach's life insurance to buy this house, a tiny bungalow tucked like an afterthought between grander, remodeled ranch houses. There were no rivers nearby to haunt her, but the neighbors on the left spent eighty thousand dollars on a fake stone waterfall that ran day and night. It should have hurt her to listen to it, but instead Jina opened the windows and let water do what it always did: trickle, slosh, gush, gurgle, and gently drown the silence; gracefully, relentlessly make her think she wasn't alone. Water always rewards those who wait.

"Good day?" she asked stiffly.

Mike dropped his tie on the bed, sat, and slid off his polished shoes. "The usual."

He was not allowed to talk, which of course meant she imagined worse things than the truth. Terrorists on every street corner, plans he'd discovered on some madman's computer for blowing up Danny's school. She knew by the way Mike checked the windows at night what kind of people he was paid to trace and profile. He'd been an active FBI agent once, but had lost his partner. He decided he could do more behind the scenes, profiling terrorists via computer. Their library was a competitive mix of Jina's art books and Mike's biographies of serial killers. Even the evening news divided them; he called the office after the brutal headlines, while she only waited out the tragedies for the weather.

"Mike," she said, "we have to—"

"I read it," he said. "Alice's novel. John sent me a galley."

He continued to undress, while she dropped her hands to her sides, heard her own heart racing. He went to the closet, changed into a pair of gray sweatpants and a T-shirt from his alma mater, Stanford. He turned around, his hair cut so short she could no longer make out the color, his soft green gaze lowered to her face.

It had taken her four chapters to realize that he wasn't going to be in the story. Alice had changed the names of the sushi club to Elaine, Jeanne, Maria, and Abby, tried to veil it all in a glitzy L.A. setting. But every storyline was painfully familiar, from Irene's tabloid past to Mary's virginity to Jina's flight from Maryland, that alarming, electric escape that set up everything to come, that doomed her. Alice had even outed herself, devoting two chapters to her depression and flirtation with suicide. Everything was there, except for Mike. He wasn't mentioned in the novel at all.

She saw herself in the mirrored doors behind him, tiny even in reflection. Her dark hair arced over her left eye and stopped abruptly at her chin in a straight line, like the water's edge. She'd worn the same pageboy hairstyle since high school, dressed in the same slender pants and large men's shirts. Not in an attempt to keep things the same; what thirty-two-year-old, twice-married woman wouldn't, in her right mind, change everything? But because, next to wishing Danny happy and hoping for a man who would jump, she wanted comfort most of all.

Mike held out his hand. She turned away, wouldn't be taken in by all that empty tenderness. He was good to cats and old women, too, a yearly subscriber to public radio, a sucker for Girl Scout cookie sales. His reluctance to get married was just the tip of the iceberg; he was so universally nice, he could have fallen in love with anyone else just as well.

On the other hand, he was the only one who could have made her take that leap again. She loved to tell the story of their first date—a trip to the hospital after the bus she'd been riding in lost its brakes and met the side of a warehouse. Mike had leapt from his car to calm the hysterics of a little girl and bandage the head wound of the bus driver. He had spotted Jina cradling an arm she feared was broken, and rode with her to the hospital, talking the whole way to take her mind off the pain. He was planning to rid the world of bad guys, he had said, run a marathon, watch his son get married, even though he sat behind a desk now, his waistline had expanded to a 36, and he was still childless. Three hours later, when they had bandaged her arm and gave her Tylenol with codeine, it was clear he knew his dreams were hopeless, and this mattered not a whit. He was devoted to all kinds of optimistic unlikelihoods, and she'd fallen for his happy endings. Her future felt safe with him, which made his rejection that much worse.

"Tell me the truth," she said now. "You believe a woman who betrayed me, who tore apart her best friends *in print*, over what I've told you about me and Zach. You think—"

"I don't know what to think. Apparently, I didn't know the half of what you went through."

"It's not how she makes it seem."

He nodded. "I imagine not."

"She put in all kinds of things that never happened. You can't survive Salmon Falls in an overturned scow, believe me. That scene was ridiculous. She made us seem . . . I don't know . . . doomed from the start. When actually it was thrilling; it was the greatest adventure of my life."

He ducked his head as if she'd hit him. As if who and how much she'd loved before was a double strike, a jab. She imagined what she'd never heard, his voice raised, cruelly honest, full of fears she couldn't soothe and desires she could, imagined herself becoming not everything to him, but enough. She imagined him a different kind of man, and for a moment he looked as if she'd spoken out loud, looked forlorn, lost. That man, they both knew, was gone.

She stepped forward instantly, but he'd already smiled to cover it. He put his arm around her like the exemplary, composed man he was. A man prudently afraid of bad guys and the water and promises, anything that could come back to haunt you.

"Danny doesn't know any of this," he said. "What happens if he finds out?"

"He won't," she said, but her throat had gone dry.

"He'll want to know everything about his father."

"You're the only father he's known," she said, but she didn't look at him. The sweat she'd wiped from her son's brow during his nightmares had been river-cold and blue.

"I didn't want you to . . ." He let go of her, ran his hand down his neck. "I thought I'd be the one to propose. I was looking forward to it. You know, Jina, things come in their own time. They don't have to be forced because of some . . . some need in you to prove you'll never grow up."

She blinked back tears, couldn't believe his nerve. "Oh, I'm a grown-up all right," she said. "Doesn't a grown-up take care of her son, buy a house she can hardly stand, forget the things she once wanted? Doesn't a grown-up go on instead of dwelling on what she's lost?"

"Yes," he said heavily. "And now what you've lost is stacked twelve copies deep in the window at Rakestraw. It's everywhere now."

She shook her head. Over the years, Zach had come with the dark, with Danny, and she was no fool. She was lonely, exhausted, dating men who didn't compare, and she took what she could get. She was loved in dreams at least, until Mike came into their lives. Then she began staying up late to talk to him, waking early to make love before he went to the office. She had such full days, she forgot her dreams.

"The past is dead."

It was too bad he was trained to spot liars.

Jina fixed grilled cheese sandwiches the night of the party and got into her pajamas at six o'clock. When Alice left her seventh message of the night, she disconnected the phone. Just a week ago, she'd spent an hour discussing the latest pointed-shoe fad with Alice, but now she couldn't settle on the last word she would say.

Mike and Danny turned on the GameCube, began a hockey game that Mike consistently, good-naturedly, lost. At seven, Jina ignored the doorbell. She sipped her second glass of Chardonnay and reread a newspaper article on a ski lodge she had no desire to visit.

"Hon?" Mike said, but he'd already set down his controller. He was in the entry, his hand on the knob, when Irene shoved open the door.

"Where is she?"

Irene swept into the room, her red dress, when not clinging to surgically enhanced curves, swatting Mike's legs, the wall, and finally the kitchen table. She'd applied eye shadow and lipstick like war paint, wore dagger-shaped earrings, and the wedding ring Naji had given her that could, if swiped at just the right angle, cut skin.

She eyed Jina's pajamas, the half-empty bottle of wine, and

leftover sandwiches on the counter. "Oh, no," she said. "You're not wimping out on me. Get dressed. We're going to that fucking party."

Danny turned down the volume, ecstatic at the presence of an adult cusser.

"I'm not wimping out," Jina said. "I don't know what I want to say to her yet."

"Who said anything about talking? We'll shoot her in front of all her hoity-toity editors. Trust me, I can aim now. I'll put a bullet right between her eyes."

"Oh, Irene," Jina said. "Not again."

Danny straddled the back of the couch. Mike, at least, made an attempt to look away from Irene's breasts, which Naji had enlarged two cup sizes before he married her. Danny didn't have Mike's control.

"Go brush your teeth," Jina said to her son.

"It's seven o'clock! On a *Friday*. Anyway, I thought Alice just wrote some stupid romance."

"Romance is not stupid, young man," Irene said. "Alice is."

"Irene, please." Jina grabbed her friend's arm and led her down the chilly hall. She'd left the bedroom windows open and, along with a cool burst of jasmine, the tumult of the neighbor's waterfall poured into the room.

Irene put her hand on her hip. "Did you read it?"

"Of course."

"It's bullshit. You know I'm all for scandal. That attempted-murder garbage only helped my career, but did you see the way she wrote me? I come off like a fucking sex maniac. The affairs are in there, Jina! If Naji finds out—"

"He won't. He only reads medical journals. He's in his own world."

"If he finds out, he'll leave me. His lunatic brother will have me stoned. Did she bother to mention everything that's happened in the seven years since? I haven't looked at another man, you know that. That . . . bitch knows it. What the fuck was she thinking?"

"Bestseller," Jina said quietly.

Irene shook her head. "I say we kill her."

Jina smiled despite herself. "Your answer to everything."

"Mary's already getting calls, you know. It's not difficult to figure out who Alice based her characters on, and she's getting calls from perverts who want to be the first."

Jina closed the window. "Is Mary going tonight?"

"Who cares? She won't be any help. She'll hide in a corner and scream if a man comes too close."

"You're too hard on her," Jina said.

Irene waved her off. She stomped to Jina's closet, ransacked the clothes with obvious dissatisfaction until she found a slinky blue dress that Jina hadn't worn in years. She picked black pumps, searched the drawers until she came up with a pair of fishnet stockings that Jina didn't even know she owned.

Then, as if she was acting in one of her old commercials, plugging courage the way she would dish soap or panty liners, Irene marched across the room and took Jina's chin in her hand. "You," she said, "are made of sterner stuff."

And just like it happened twelve years ago, when Jina stood to face her first rapid and her husband shouted over the thunder that she could do it, Jina rose up to what someone else thought of her. She squared her shoulders and, as if it were a magic trick, became brave.

Avante was on the top floor of a converted warehouse south of Market, ten thousand square feet of art deco design and surprisingly delicious nonanimal entrées. The four of them rode the mirrored elevator in silence. Danny sulked, torn from the most challenging peak in SSX Tricky 3; Irene piled more gloss onto lips that were already the color of blood. Mike hadn't said a word, in protest or otherwise, since she'd announced that they were going to the party after all. Which made his quiet words in the elevator sound like shouts.

"I thought no one fell in love the way we did. On the spot. So *adamantly*. Then I find out you did the same thing before. With both of them."

He'd been betrayed, too. Stripped of his version of the truth, introduced to a woman in print who had little in common with the one who had said she loved him. Jina had told him about Zach, succinctly, the way you told any new love of an old one. "He was my second husband," she'd said. "He died on the river. It was years ago."

This was the moment when something ought to pass between them, a look that cemented the past in its place, a smile that made their future not just possible but necessary. But hurt made her childish, stubborn. She'd lost the courage to speak first.

"Jina?" he said.

"Is it a crime to fall in love fast?" she asked.

"No. But it seems untrustworthy. She wrote that you still loved Zach."

"Alice called our scow a *raft*. Nothing she wrote can be trusted."

They emerged on the top floor into a riot. Two hundred people they didn't know, New Yorkers flown in on expense accounts, already drunk and flirty. The music blared something circa-1970 with a danceable beat.

"Just for the record," Irene said, "Alice is the one who goes to the grocery store in her pajamas. She freaks out when she has to speak in front of the PTA."

"She always dreamed of being successful," Jina said.

"Honey, this ain't success. This'll be packed up and cleared out tomorrow. When her next book bombs, people will turn away when they see her coming. I kid you not."

Jina squeezed Irene's arm. In the pecking order of the sushi club, Irene had almost always been on top—a popular soap-opera star, the spokeswoman for Colorfast Detergent. For years, Irene flew to the daytime Emmys and ordered champagne at dinner, and not one of them begrudged her success. Irene was made for money: She bought presents for friends; dinners for strangers; ugly, extravagant statues to keep starving artists alive.

Then her part was written out of the soap opera, the detergent ads were canceled, and she'd gone five years without a job. She was thirty-five years old now and called back only for small parts in Viagra ads, nonspeaking roles pitching dog food. Her husband, Naji, made a stratospheric salary as a plastic surgeon, but Irene had given up champagne, as if the real luxury was not what you drank but what you felt you deserved.

They walked slowly into the room, adjusting to the strobe light above the dance floor. Danny spotted Alice's nine-year-old son, Roger, who had a new PlayStation and considered Danny a genius. "I'll be over there," Danny said, already gone.

Mike started to follow him, but Jina grabbed his arm. If she gave up rashness now, who was going to fight to make it work?

Before she could speak, he removed her hand from his arm, followed Danny.

Irene clapped her hands. "All right," she said. "Now we attack."

Irene started across the room, and a few people must have recognized her from the soap opera she'd been on years ago, because they began whispering "Sondra." Irene threw back her shoulders and stuck out a chin that Naji had slimmed and elongated. Jina glanced at Mike's stiff back, then started after her. Alice's high-pitched laugh came from the corner, and they both turned. Mary stood on the outskirts of the crowd, nursing a black-cherry soda while everyone else drank gin.

Mary had come in her work clothes, a brown wool skirt, white blouse, flat shoes. Only her curly hair rebelled, a few dirty-blond corkscrews wiggling themselves loose from the bun.

"You came to support her?" Irene said loudly enough to be heard over the music. "I can't fucking believe it."

A woman turned to her husband and said, "I knew it was her."

"She called me," Mary said, crossing her arms around her waist. "She was worried none of us would come."

"Oh, we're fucking coming all right."

Mary backed away, blushing. She always apologized in advance to the other diners at Zutto's whenever they arrived.

"Does Naji know?" Mary asked, looking around. "Is he here?"

"He's on call. And Naji doesn't read for pleasure, which doesn't mean I won't kill Alice anyway."

"What about you?" Jina asked Mary. "Irene said you've been getting calls."

Mary blinked, her brown eyes filling with tears. "Strangers," she said. "Men. They call late at night. They want . . . It's horrible, those voices. The way they . . . breathe."

Jina put her arm around Mary. "You need to change your number. Right away. Stay unlisted."

"And you," Mary said, beginning to cry in earnest now. "Everything you told us about Zach. I can't believe she used that. I can't believe it."

Strangely enough, Jina couldn't cry. Her eyes had gone dry the moment she read the first line of Alice's book—the only line that was, without question, true.

He never thought about what would happen to her if he died.

"Would your boss take the case if we sued?" she asked Mary.

Mary blanched, stepped out of the embrace. "Oh. I don't know. Don't you think . . . well, if we sue, then we're admitting it's true. Right now, no one in my office really believes it. That I could be so, you know, unloved."

Jina turned to Irene, saw the steel in her eyes, the smile that always crept out when she was picturing bone damage, scars even Naji couldn't fix. Jina linked an arm through Mary's, the other through Irene's, and the three of them pushed aside Alice's entourage. Alice stood by the back wall, holding court with a dozen New Yorkers, her champagne glass etched with the title *The Secret Lives of the Sushi Club*. Her shoulder-length brown hair had been dyed a golden blond, styled into shiny waves. She wore a silver dress that accentuated her tall, slimmed-down frame, hoop earrings, and a new, fat ring.

When Alice saw them, she flinched; the champagne in her glass toyed with the rim. Then she smiled widely, set her champagne glass on the table, and held open her arms.

"Girls!" she said. "Can you believe this?"

Irene's body practically hummed with bloodlust, but Jina moved first. She grabbed Alice's arm, squeezed until she produced a squeak. Why hadn't she noticed that Alice's eyes were sometimes green, sometimes gray, sneaky in and of themselves? She whittled down all the words she'd planned to the only three that mattered.

"I trusted you," she said.

Irene pushed her way forward, dragging Mary with her. "You fucking lying bitch!"

Conversation stopped. Mary bowed her head, stared into the bubbles of her black-cherry soda.

"Irene," Alice said. Amazingly, she still held a smile. "It's just a book. *Fiction*. You know that."

"All I know is you're a backstabbing thief. If I'd wanted those stories in print, I'd have written a memoir, and you can bet it would have had more style than this drivel. My life was not for sale to some two-bit novelist."

"You don't have to insult me," Alice said, her voice high but firm. "What I've done is perfectly fair. I've been to the lawyers.

Didn't you read the disclaimer? Any similarities between my words and real life are coincidental."

"But Alice," Jina said. "You put *Zach* in there."

Alice shook her head emphatically. "The character's name is Jack. And you'll notice he was wearing a life jacket when he died on the Salmon. It was the impact with the rocks that killed him, not stupidity. You can't compare the two."

Alice's rare cruelty was bad enough, but the familiar voice behind Jina spelled disaster.

"Mom?"

Jina turned to find Danny's hands balled into fists, his red hair as uncontrollable as Zach's had been, his body thin as a book but all muscle, like his father's.

"You mean my dad?" he said. "He died on Grandpa's farm. Right?"

Alice's husband, John, looking miserable in a tuxedo, walked past Alice without a word and stepped onto the balcony. One of the New Yorkers mumbled something about a lawsuit. Jina wondered who had turned off the music.

"I say we shoot her," Irene said, and some of her old fans applauded.

"Mom?" Danny said.

3

The seven-hour drive from the farm in Kimberly, Idaho, to the river town of Salmon was more dangerous, Jina was certain, than the rafting trip that lay ahead. They followed the dizzying switchbacks over Galena Summit and came within inches of hundred-foot drop-offs past Stanley. Once, when Zach took a turn above Sunbeam Dam a little wide, Jina thought they might hit the water early. A portion of the trailer, with the twenty-by five-foot scow inside it, hovered gleefully in the air above the Salmon River, until Zach hit the accelerator and yanked it back onto the road.

They emerged from the forested canyon into the eerie, Mars-like desert around Challis. With relief, they met up with the river again along Highway 93 and pulled into Salmon before midnight.

They filled up at the Exxon on Main Street, pulled into the empty parking lot of St. Charles Catholic Church. "We can spend the night here. It's still a two-hour haul to Corn Creek."

The late-September night was flawless, cold, and clear. Jina put on one of Zach's sweaters while he lined the bottom of the scow with sleeping bags. Aside from the dance floor, a five-foot-square platform where she and Zach would man the giant sweeps, the floor of the scow was flat, solid, and surprisingly roomy. Like a wooden sleigh bed, minus the fluffy mattress, at one of those couples-only hotels in the Poconos—which seemed fitting, since this was their honeymoon.

Jina snuggled into the sleeping bag, laid her head on Zach's shoulder. She was twenty, so it was rare to recognize her own happiness, not to want one thing more. She tried to stay awake to savor the new sensation, but the breeze that swept off the Bitterroots was thick with pine dust, as soporific and yellow as sand.

Her newlywed dreams were not as sure. A baby starred in one scene, only to be erased in the next; Zach kept changing the color of his eyes. All stories eventually dissolved into the roar of a river. She and Zach were running their first rapid, and because she'd never done it before, she dreamt the waves three stories high and sharp as dinosaur teeth that quickly devoured them.

When she opened her eyes, the moon was gone and the sky had turned as ruddy as the faces of mountain men. A dozen of the real thing stood around the scow, the older ones in overalls and cowboy hats, the forty-year-old-boys in baseball caps and jeans, all eyeing their craft with the condescension and smugness of anyone prophesizing another's doom. They poked the metal toes of their boots at the pine planks, tugged without success on the two wooden sweeps, each of which was twenty feet long and one hundred and fifty pounds. Zach explained about the lead shot he'd used to counterbalance the weight of the water, the handles of old oars he'd attached to make the grip comfortable. While cumbersome and awkward to transport on the ground, the sweeps were supposedly as easy as oars to move in water.

Zach leapt out of the scow, oblivious or perhaps challenged by the skepticism. He showed off his caulking technique, answered every incredulous question. Yes, he knew what he was doing. The Salmon was a scow river—low flow on a medium gradient. Little or no pool and drop. No, he wasn't a fool; he'd run the Salmon all his life, on guided trips and later solo. He knew every feeder creek and riffle. Jina never lost him in the crowd: a big Idaho boy, red hair hogging the sun, his jeans dusty and soft, the sleeves of his chambray shirt rolled up twice, showing off blond, downy hair and freckles on his forearms.

"Cap Guleke did it," Zach said, walking the length of the scow, checking the deck screws they'd used on the one-by-ten planking. He ran his hands over the rough-cut pine the way, she hoped, he'd run them over a baby. Once she told him.

Zach nudged an old man with his elbow. "The old-timers came down spring and fall, low water and high. Didn't worry about flows. Johnny McKay owned this river with his sweep."

The old man stiffened. "Son, Johnny McKay was a broken man. Heartsick. He was just waiting for the river to take him. He knew who owned whom."

Zach's response was a smile, as dazzling as the sun that had inched up to shine in Jina's eyes. A marriage license and two months of near-constant contact had not curbed her desire for him. She liked the idea that because they'd met on a ship, they were destined for a lifetime of romance. Who cared that they'd both been on the San Francisco–to–L.A. cruise for fiscal reasons—Zach to meet a sugar-beet buyer, and Jina hoping to sell a few of her paintings on the ship. When she'd first seen Zach on deck, standing straight through the deepest swells, an incongruous hunting knife slung through his belt, she had lost all interest in money.

Not that she'd been a financial whiz to begin with. She'd gotten from Maryland to California on less than a hundred dollars, threw her only asset—her gold wedding band—into the bay without a moment's hesitation. What she'd cared about was feeling things—looking at a rugged stranger and feeling all ninety-five pounds of herself growing taut as a sail in a hurricane, feeling herself begin to fly.

On that ship, she had tilted back her head to get a good look at him. She was used to looking up at men. By fourth grade, it was apparent that she wouldn't get any taller. Barely over five feet, she had the opportunity to peek at a number of tender spots. Pale necks, quivering Adam's apples, the hairs beneath the chin missed while shaving. This man was tanned to the shirt line, but when he breathed deeply, the way he did when she moved toward him on deck, smooth, pinkish skin peeped out.

The fog had surrounded them; the captain did a long, slow turn, as if getting his bearings.

"He's going too slow. Can't be timid about it, or the tide'll sweep him back in."

His voice had almost spoiled it. It was gritty, deeper than the voices of the boys she'd known back east, less smooth than Earl's, who had honed his on poetry. But a man this tall, six feet two at least, and gorgeous, made it easy to overlook it.

"You know about boats, then?" she'd asked.

She had been close enough to smell his breath—coffee, she thought, and something sweet to go with it—and when his hand didn't come close enough, she moved her own toward him. His eyes were a crayon color a child would use to draw in the sky, a blue too good to be true. He'd smiled, and she knew the rest was merely formality. The introductions, the histories, the courtship—all ritual, but unnecessary. You fell in love with the man who moved you.

"Yes," he'd said. "I know about boats."

She never made it to her room that night. When she woke in Zach's arms and he asked her to come to Idaho and marry him, her mind skipped past the art classes she'd just started, the apartment she'd made her own, all the things she'd vowed never to give up for a man again. She wasn't giving them up, she told herself as she kissed him. She was getting more. Every artist has some great love story to tell, a masterpiece that arises from passion, not technique. How could she not marry a man who fell in love the same way she did, who took one look at her and *knew*?

On the way to Idaho, she would mention that she needed to get a divorce first.

She expected to love Zach's farm, but she'd imagined it greener. Only the rows of sugar beets and potatoes were pretty; the earth between and around them was rock-hard and gray. The scent of sagebrush was everywhere; one step, and her ankles were stabbed with arrows of the prolific cheatgrass. One step, and she began to cry. Zach made excuses to his father, called her "dreamy" and "overly poetic," but she knew land like that was made for silent men and big, practical women—people who ate cows they'd named and potatoes still smelling of Metribuzin and sulfuric acid. People who did what had to be done and didn't think too much, except about the pointlessness of those who did nothing and thought about it all the time.

She was relieved to discover that he hated it, too. On their wedding night, in the room Zach had grown up in, he kissed her neck, the dark hollows beneath each breast. She bit her lip to keep from crying out.

"Sometimes we don't break twenty degrees until April," Zach said. "You plan your vacation, then the tractor needs a new transmission, half the horses die. Dreaming's futile on a farm."

She put her hands on either side of his face. He was so beautiful, so different, so charged, she felt electrified wherever she touched him. She imagined wonderful and terrible changes being wrought beneath her skin, organs moving, her blood turning blue. She wanted him to alter her very form, make her taller. She willed him to say more; once he'd gotten out the basics—the proposal, the future expected of him on the farm, his mother's early death and his father's silent, relentless work—he'd said very little. She was surviving on a subsistence diet of him, mostly body language, glances, the way he kissed, things a good artist could build a sketch around, but that a woman, from lack of better information, often makes into more than they are.

Zach turned his mouth into her palm, sucked the moisture. They heard footsteps in the next room, the creaking of the bedsprings, a sad silence.

"Gotta do all your living in summer," Zach said, pulling away. "That's the way I see it. To hell with the crops. The work's endless; the river season is short. My father's used to me leaving by now. The Snake in the early season, the Salmon in July, even if it's a circus. Four companies, a hundred people at the put-in every morning."

He sat up, ran his fingers through his hair. "The Salmon's touted as the last great wilderness, but once you get past Black Canyon, it's a suburb. If you're not camping over cigarette butts and pop bottles, some jet boat's screaming up a rapid you've just tiptoed down. Some moron's hiking the canyon walls not for the view or the exercise, but to get reception on his portable television."

She kissed him, ran her fingers down his arm; she wanted to talk, but not about rivers.

"Some people don't know how to relax," she said. "They need a trip to Hawaii, a week with nothing to do. What do you think? We could go there for our honeymoon."

He turned to her suddenly, pinned her with his steady gaze. "I've been reading about the scows, the first boats to make it down the Salmon. They built them out of wood scrap. Just planks and nails, like magic. A scow takes castoffs, both wood and men, and turns them into something more."

"Zach—"

"*That* could be our honeymoon, Jina. Not a summer circus,

but an autumn retreat. You've got to see the place, feel it for yourself. Maybe it's the weight of all those people who came through before, who lived and died there, but I'm telling you, there's a living, breathing soul to that canyon."

She wanted to turn away, wanted to state the case for Honolulu—white sand beaches; pink, frothy drinks with pineapple garnishes—but when he looked at her like that, her words seemed frivolous, almost with no point at all.

"I've never rafted before."

His shoulders relaxed. "No problem. I've been down the Salmon dozens of times. Of course, there's always a risk, but that's the thrill of it. You like thrills, Jina. I saw that in you from the start."

He stroked his thumb across the back of her hand, and she thought of Earl, her first husband, how close she'd come to thinking that a life in the suburbs and a man she used to love was the most she could hope for.

She put her hand over his. "Go on."

He smiled. "We'd wear life jackets, take every precaution. Believe me, it's not the out-of-control death ride you see in the movies. Guides know what they're doing. *I* know. Mid-September or later, the flows will be low. Rocks that would tear apart a raft are inconsequential to a scow. The canyon will be quiet, the rafting parties gone. Most of the homesteaders leave until spring. And if we're lucky . . ."

"If we're lucky what?"

He dropped her hand. "It's understood I'll take over the farm. Just understood, without anyone asking me what I want.

I'm not planning on letting my father down, but if it happens . . . Let's say I build a scow. I could take people down the river fall and winter, till it ices up. No girls in bikinis. No volleyball or filet mignon. Just solitude. History. Peace. Something like that could take off. You never know. We could go and never come back."

He sat back and smiled. Wiggled his toes like a happy boy. Of course, he hadn't had time to consider what *she* wanted. He hadn't asked, but that was her fault as much as his.

"I'm going back," she said. "I'm finishing art school."

She didn't look at him. Somehow it had been easier knowing Earl would simply hit her; she could prepare for that, stay low, never doubt that she deserved better. Zach's silence undercut her certainty, made her consider just what art school would be worth without him.

"Ah," he said.

"Not right away," she hurried on. "Just at some point. Someday."

He took her chin, tilted her up to look at him. He was smiling again, a farmer's son for sure, seeing no sense in worrying past tomorrow, treating somedays like pies in the sky.

"Sounds good," he said. "My little artist."

He kissed well, so she overlooked the "little" part. He pulled her beneath the blanket, tucked her against him.

"Did you know the Nez Percé Indians named the river Natsoh Koos, or Chinook-Salmon Water?" he said.

She played with the hairs on his chest and forced herself not to sigh. "No. I didn't know."

"The Shoshones call it Agaimpaa: Big-Fish Water. Once, you could walk downstream on the backs of sockeye; the river turned red when the salmon spawned. Last year, only one male sockeye made it through the Snake and Columbia dams to spawn in Redfish Lake. The salmon are expected to go extinct in the next twenty years. Sooner, if the ranchers bring in any more cows. So many graze the banks, the river is a sewer after the spring rains; the salmon eggs suffocate in the runoff. The whole corridor is being ruined."

She glanced up. "Why should we run it, then?"

He looked out the window as if seeing water, not acres and acres of furrowed, dry land. "It's a *river*," he said, his eyes shining with such devotion that she felt even smaller than she was, and jealous. "It will win."

They built the scow while Reed Woolridge looked on in silence. When Zach's father left for the fields, they made love on the dance floor and christened her Splinters.

Two months later, Reed stood on the porch to say good-bye to his son. The irony of Idaho was that for all its rough work and wilderness, men emerged from it tame. There were pieces of an old motorcycle in the barn, photographs of a long-haired, panicky-looking youth on his wedding day, but Jina had never seen Zach's father anything but calm. He wore a suit on Sundays, whether or not he went to church. His neatly trimmed beard was pure white. He would never tell his son he needed him.

Zach bent over the hitch on the trailer. Jina walked to the porch, took her father-in-law's callused hand in hers.

"It's only a seven-day trip," she said.

He nodded, though they both knew Zach hoped it would last a lot longer than that. Long enough to create a buzz around their boating venture. Long enough to erase him from this farm.

Reed turned to her. "You can manage the sweeps? If you need to?"

"I can manage. You'd be surprised."

He studied her tiny frame, her hands. "Maybe I wouldn't."

Now, in a parking lot near the Salmon River, Zach was right about one thing: This late in the season, the boats, rafts, and pontoons were gone. Thanks to another drought year, the rafting companies had stopped running the river in late August, when the flow levels at Corn Creek plummeted below the shoes, which meant even fish got a bumpy ride.

"The river's flowing at just over two thousand," one of the Salmon boys said. "You're not thinking of running it *now*?"

Jina stepped from the scow, met the gaze of the old men—hunters, trappers, retired fishermen, farmers. All the young, Democratic, Teva-wearing river guides must have migrated south and east, back to their parents' houses and the winter desk jobs they loathed.

"We're putting in this afternoon," she said.

Zach smiled at her, while the men started in with an onslaught of dire predictions. The river was ungodly low. You couldn't send a shoe down Devil's Teeth without damage, let alone a two-ton scow. It would require better than expert maneuverings to avoid the exposed rocks; this late in the season, a number of rapids would have to be lined. There was already snow on the northern slopes. A storm was heading in. They'd never make it through Gunbarrel Rapid, the first minor hazard past Corn Creek, and there'd be few people around to help them should they have trouble.

Jina hardly listened. She didn't pretend to be logical. With Earl, a poet, she'd been in danger all the time, but with a thrill-seeker like Zach, she felt perfectly safe. All the scary stuff was behind her—Earl's drinking and his fists; the need to escape, even erase, him; the protestors she had to get past to reach the women's clinic and the surprising kindness of the doctor who sat with her afterward, talking softly of a book he'd read, his herb garden, other joys. She wouldn't tell Zach *that*; he was as open-minded as any man she'd met, but there was a limit to how much a rural Idaho man could accept.

She brushed a thumb across her navel; she was on a lucky streak. Zach didn't want children yet. He always wore a condom, but apparently that was no barrier for a child this relentless. A child who would come whether they both welcomed him or not. Who would offer as many chances as it took.

"We're putting in today," Zach said, his smile gone.

The oldest man took Zach's measure, finally held out his weathered hand. "Ellis Cantor," he said. "I run the Red Salmon Lodge between Gunbarrel and Rainier. You'll need to take Gunbarrel on the right this time of year. There's no other passage with the water this low. You make it through, you're welcome to come for dinner."

Zach shook his hand, and Jina watched the stiffness in his shoulders subside.

"What happens if I go left?" he asked.

Ellis stuffed his hands in his pockets. "Oh," he said. "You wouldn't want to do that."

In the middle of nowhere, there's a traffic jam. A caravan of trailers, buses, minivans with sticky windows, crying children, drunkards, dogs. Wide-eyed men thinking about never leaving and palefaced women with no idea why they've come. A forty-six-mile highway of anticipation and taillights, fear and washboards and dust.

The last time Zachary Woolridge had arrived at Corn Creek, the campground was hosting a Harley-Davidson reunion and the sound of gunned engines was all he heard. He'd put in his raft alongside ten other inflatables, a fleet of kayaks, and a jet boat with a grizzled captain who'd been running the river longer than most of the floaters had been alive. Zach had seen everything, or so he thought, until he and Jina drove through the rain, past the old mine in Shoup, and realized they were the only car on the road. Late September in the Salmon wilderness was exactly as he'd hoped—dark, cold, and empty. One lonely pickup sat in the parking lot of Duncan's Outpost.

Rain pattered the windshield as they crossed a flimsy, one-lane bridge. This last narrow gorge led to the end of the road, the launch site. He drove carefully, though Jina was sitting forward, straining to see around every turn. She came from the East Coast, and that scared him. The Continental Divide separated not just east- and west-running rivers, but people. Cynics and settlers on the right, optimists and adventurers on the left. He didn't know if anyone could really change sides, but he tried not to think about it too much. He'd been raised where the reservoirs sometimes dried up overnight, where winter could last until May. It didn't pay to imagine the worst.

He saw the campground. A mob scene in July, there was only one SUV in the parking lot this morning. Two men were tying a deer to the grille of a Jeep while a third kept a fire going with copious shots of lighter fluid. Zach backed the scow to the put-in and got out to unhitch the trailer. The hunters, dressed in flannel with bright orange vests, came over to gawk.

"Looks like a coffin," one of them said. Zach glanced at Jina, but she was already in the boat, checking the dry bag containing her camera, charcoals, paper, and diary.

Zach declined their offer of a beer, went over his provisions. Jina had sealed the meat, canned the potatoes and carrots; he'd packed a Coleman stove, propane, crates of peaches, beans, and tomatoes, a rifle, three cartons of bullets, and roofing tar— should the scow sprout holes and need to be recaulked. The scow had a vast supply of storage space, and because everything was riding on Jina enjoying her time in the wilderness, pulling out in Riggins wanting more, he'd added luxuries he'd never consider on his own. A two-room tent and 0-rated sleeping bags, blankets, pillows, a solar shower, and two comfortable camp chairs with built-in cup holders. It was a far-fetched hope, but he warmed to it: Maybe she'd never want to leave.

It was no small feat to drag the scow from the trailer. The hunters helped, though they looked at the boat suspiciously when it touched water, as if wood had never floated before.

"What is this thing?" the coffin man asked.

"A scow," Zach said. "First thing they ran on this river."

The hunters looked over the craft dubiously, burrowed deeper beneath flannel and insulated coats. "First rock you hit, you'll split in two."

Zach smiled. Let them think he was a fool; he knew the truth about scows and rivers. He was a farm kid who, in every spare moment, had searched out scum ponds, irrigation streams, culverts. His happiness was slippery, obtainable only through water. He practically lived on rivers each summer, first on rafts down the tame Snake, then in kayaks and wooden dories on more adventurous stretches of the Payette, Clearwater, and Salmon. He'd thought he'd mastered it all until he came across a sweep boat on the Middle Fork of the Salmon. Zach's raft and the sweep shoved off from Boundary Creek at the same time and, seeing as everything on water is a race, within seconds the other guide called out, "Sweep! No brakes!" The sweep boat lunged past him, faster than the river itself.

When Zach finally caught up on Black Hound Beach, the guide, hauling the gear for a ten-man raft trip, showed him the simplicity of the craft. "The old scows were just wood boxes and two giant sweeps," he said. "A little caulk, if they had it. We use inflatables, and we're smaller than the old scows. Only twenty feet, with steel sweeps. A perfect fit for the Main and Middle Fork. Low flows are best. No pool and drop or you're toast."

"You were going faster than the water."

"Good thing. That's sweepage, and it's the only time you've got control. Slow down and you're just wrestling water. Big waves, you've lost sweepage. Wind'll do you in, too. You gotta be an expert guide. Drag on a rock and you'll stop dead, probably go overboard."

The most important moment of Zach's life, next to meeting Jina, came when the guide let him steer the sweep down the Middle Fork. One bullet-train ride, a boxing match with a boulder, a short ride in the water, and Zach was hooked.

He was also careful. He'd researched the scow, charted its history of stoutness through low-flow, rocky courses, its surprising maneuverability once the heavy sweeps were laid in water. He'd mapped the canyon they would travel. Despite its growing popularity, the Salmon River corridor remained a remote and unparalleled hideaway for recluses, criminals, geniuses, and ghosts. Beyond Lantz Bar, the trail left the river. A few steps beyond the white-sand beaches where the rafters camped, creeks disappeared into inaccessible canyons and a man could, if he wanted or needed to, turn his back on family and friends and take up residence with black bears. The banks and cliffs practically hummed with the souls of men who'd done just that; a few had left gravestones and markings, including John McKay's numerous inscriptions at Barth Hot Springs.

McKay was one of the earliest boatman on the Salmon; his first trip down the rapids occurred in 1872. Every spring McKay would build his wooden scow in Salmon City, load it up with months of supplies, then work his way slowly downriver, stopping to pan for gold at sandbars and side streams. Sometimes, he'd build a hut with the lumber from his boat and winter in the canyon; other times, he'd sell the whole rig for scrap, and by spring he'd be back in Salmon City, ready to start the process again. He ran the river twenty times, no small feat in a coffin in 1872. No small feat for a man who never wore a life jacket, and who had witnessed his young wife dragged to her death by the mill machinery he'd built.

Then came the others: Harry Guleke, probably the finest boatman the Salmon would ever see, charging a thousand dollars a ride, a fortune in 1900, and Monroe Hancock and the Smith family and the men of today who couldn't hold jobs or mow the grass to please the neighbors but who were perfectly capable of living without electricity and company for years on end. All gentle wild men, in love with rivers. Enamored with starlit skies and red fish and one man-made thing—the strength and beauty of a hand-built scow. For them, for Zach, the wooden boat was more than transportation; it was kitchen, bedroom, observatory, safe refuge, and escape from a mediocre life on land.

"Remember that kid?" one of the hunters asked. "Jesse something or other. Died in Gunbarrel last spring. Water was at forty thousand."

"Yeah," one of the others said. "They say he was spooked by Neal Allen's ghost. Son of a bitch got even meaner after he killed himself."

"And didn't someone die in Rainier in July?" the first hunter asked.

You couldn't avoid the stories. You made it through one rapid only to hear about who'd died in the next. Zach glanced at Jina and was relieved to see her rolling her eyes. For a moment, he forgot about rivers, or perhaps got her confused with one. He began to think her the answer to everything.

The hunters ran out of drowning stories and watched Zach park the car his father and sister would come for later. His sister would drive back to Kimberly, while his father took Zach's truck to Riggins. He'd pick them up at the takeout at Vinegar Creek, seven days from now.

Jina held the life jackets. Zach helped her put hers on, tightening the straps around her middle.

"Not that authentic, huh?" she said.

He put on his jacket. It was true, most of the early scow men had eschewed life jackets, thinking them too constrictive. They figured they'd have a better chance swimming.

"They didn't use deck screws on their scows, either," he said. "We're aiming to survive."

She smiled even as she shivered. He offered to get her heavy coat from the scow, but she glanced at his light wool shirt, the sleeves rolled up to the elbows, and shook her head. She took her place on the dance floor by the rear sweep, the way they'd practiced in the barn. The hunters helped them shove off, and as Zach hopped in, they raised a beer in salute, said something about luck, and laughed. Zach took his place at the front sweep, placed his hand on the slick, cold handle.

He'd steered, or tried to steer, the inflatable sweep boat on the Middle Fork, had practiced with the scow in dry dock. But nothing could have prepared him for the first turn of the sweep, when the scow responded so enthusiastically, Jina tumbled off the dance floor, landing with a thunk on a crate of peaches. The hunters hooted.

Jina looked up at him angrily from the floor of the boat. "How am I supposed to stand in this thing?"

He took her tiny, ice-cold hand in his and helped her to her feet. He showed her how to stand almost sideways to the river and keep the handles waist-high. He demonstrated the way to spread her legs, bend at the knees, rise and fall with the current. "Learn fast," he said. "In two miles, we hit Gunbarrel."

He looked through the rain at the river running at less than three thousand cubic feet per second. At such low flows, many rapids would be considered unrunnable, a challenge he couldn't resist. He'd have to read the water, react to it with strength and artistry, like liquid itself. Portaging was impossible. They could line the rapids, though trying to hold a rope with a two-ton scow at the end of it was a fool's job. One tug of the current and the scow sprung from your hand or, worse, dragged you into the river after it.

But these potential problems were miles ahead. For now, the river was slow and more welcoming than the sky, which had turned to slate. They neared Killum Point, where Jack Killum, after suffering a nervous breakdown, brought his wife and five children to homestead. Jack's younger sons, Hugh and Marvin, often walked all the way to Salmon, carrying calypso orchids they'd sell for eight cents apiece, eventually earning enough money to buy a Mother's Day present. At the ages of fifteen and thirteen, the boys lived alone in the canyon.

Zach swore he heard them sometimes, sword fighting with sticks up on the bluff, shouting, though the Killums were long gone. He never talked about the things he heard—not because he feared embarrassment but because he wanted the magic to last. It wasn't often that a kid from Idaho stood at the center of extraordinary things.

Zach glanced at his wife standing sideways, holding the sweep so tightly that her knuckles glowed white.

"I hear Gunbarrel," she said.

He turned forward. In the distance was the crashing of water on rocks, the sound of jet engines, panicked herds, avalanches. His heart accelerated; he regripped the sweep. A couple years ago, he'd guided an eight-man raft through the rapid at a mesmerizing high of 65,000 cfs, and would have had them all in the water if two of his fellow passengers hadn't high-sided the craft, jumping on the rising side to keep the boat from flipping.

Today, the rapid ought to be tame—technical but safe. First Gunbarrel Creek came in from the right; then the rapids, named for a rifle left by a tree, kicked in. As they rounded the bend and the whitewater came into view, he quickly assessed the current, the rocks, a narrow funnel to the right between an obstacle course of boulders they had to avoid. He turned once again to check on Jina. She'd bent a little more at the knees, and her eyes were wide with excitement. He didn't have the heart to tell her the little whitewater and foam of Gunbarrel were nothing compared to what they would encounter later.

"Here we go!" he shouted. "We'll go in on the right. See that channel? Remember, a little movement of the sweep is all you need."

She nodded, crouched down farther, looking so tiny and fierce that he wished he had a moment more to tell her what this meant to him. Her coming. This unquestioned trust.

But the current had them. Zach turned forward, felt the exhilaration he always felt at the beginning when the river caught him, took control, sucked him past the point of no return. The road had ended behind them, and there was only one way to go from here: straight through the heart of a wild thing.

They were set up on the right of the channel. Too far, he saw right away.

"Left," he called, and Jina dug in the sweep. Too hard. They began to turn sideways to the current just as the rapid picked up. "Not so much!"

But the left side of the scow had already dropped over the first plunge, and a wall of water shot over them. Zach dove backward, but by the time he reached the high side of the scow, it was empty. He looked up in time to see his wife cast perfectly, sideways up over the river, so as not to alarm the fish. Like a well-tied fly, she hit the water almost without a splash and rested on the surface for a moment before sinking.

4

The Virgin Maria

The people in the office were bound to figure it out. Mary Bonelli had talked up her friend's novel for weeks, encouraging the lawyers to buy a copy for their wives and attend the book signing at Borders. She'd laughed when coworkers asked if she was in the story somewhere, embarrassed but not entirely averse to the idea that she might have inspired a character, a hard-working legal aide whose modest life is rewarded in the end.

The title didn't scare her; if anything, she feared she'd have no place in the book. She had no scandalous secrets, no sexual escapades she'd let slip over a glass of wine. She bought the book and got into bed to read. It was midnight before she realized the unattractive spinster in the story was herself.

It was like hearing her voice on tape and being stunned to discover that she spoke with a lisp. How could she be so unappealing and not know it? In Alice's novel, she was called "the Virgin Maria," a prickly, sexless, ridiculous waste of a woman. Obviously, for nine years Alice had only been pretending to applaud Mary's reticence on dates, her complicated screening process that had so far eliminated all eligible men. Underneath, Alice had been laughing.

The phone startled her, thankfully made her lose her place on the page. Mary hadn't even said hello before a man asked, "Why didn't you tell me? If I'd known——"

It was Henry Silverstein, the lawyer she'd dated for three weeks until he'd come into her bedroom one night while she was getting dressed and put his tongue on her neck. She'd jerked so abruptly that she'd knocked his chin with her shoulder. He called her skittish when he broke up with her, and a little violent to boot.

"If you'd known what? What difference does it make?"

Mary meant the words, but at thirty-nine, her voice still squeaked like a little girl's. The slightest bit of fervor made her sound hysterical, despite the fact that until now, not much in her life had warranted panic.

"None," he said. "It just caught me off guard is all. When we broke up, I thought . . . You're, what, almost forty now? You have to admit it's unusual to go that long without . . . I mean, to never have been with a man. Or a woman. Is it a religious thing? Were you saving yourself? Maybe saving yourself for me?"

Mary rolled her eyes, stretched out in bed in her flannel pajamas. She pushed the book aside, tucked her feet beneath the warm belly of Frisky, her tabby. Smoky purred beside her, pressing his white-tipped paws into the fleshiest part of her stomach in pure contentment. He seemed to like her flaws best, her soft belly and lack of willpower when it came to the dairy group. Smoky had miles on this man, who had mirrored the inside of his courtroom briefcase. Too bad a woman couldn't fall in love with a cat.

The proliferation of relationship books and reality dating shows proved only one thing: People couldn't stand their own company. She, on the other hand, had been raised by a woman who was so self-contained that once she got pregnant, she never kissed her husband again. Mary's mother taught kindergarten for forty-two years, ran triathlons before people knew what they were and before it was customary for women to do anything more athletic than the laundry, and cringed at the sight of her stonemason husband's rough hands. She never drank, except when Mary's father came across the hall once a month. Afterward, she let Mary curl up on her lap and they snuggled like sunken ship survivors, like two people who would never feel entirely safe again.

"Find a man with smooth hands," her mother told her. "With a college degree. And friends and hobbies of his own. And money."

Mary laughed, but later she wondered if even words you disregard and scorn sink into your skin. If the things people say flippantly, meanly, carelessly, slither down to bone and build who you are. She passed thirty without meeting Mr. Right or even Mr. Good Enough, and instead of panicking and settling for less, her standards went up. At thirty-nine, she wanted kindness in addition to good looks. Not only brains but nobility and a sense of humor. She didn't want to jerk when a man touched her. People pitied her for all her self-defeating self-respect; even the sushi girls thought her a tragic mixture of mouse and snob, incapable of luring a man and snubbing the few who approached of their own free will. Perhaps she did sabotage the few chances she got, but not for religious reasons. Not because of closet lesbianism or to save herself for the perfect man. She was still a virgin because she'd never been offered a good enough reason not to be. She hated her voice and her freewheeling hair, but there was one thing about her she would protect.

"Forget it, Henry," she said. "Go to sleep."

But Henry didn't forget it, and no one else did, either. In the next few days, word spread rampantly, giddily, through the office until one of the secretaries told her sister, who worked at KDZY. On the drive to work one morning, Mary heard Alice's name on the radio and nearly bumped the taillights of the car in front of her. She pulled to the side of the road in front of the crowded entrance to Starbucks.

". . . local writer Alice Aberdeen's number-one bestseller for two weeks now. So, of course, we're latching ourselves on to a winner," Bob, of "Bob and Sue in the Morning," was saying. "Can you top the Virgin Maria? Nearly forty and not entirely heinous-looking. There's that lumpy body, the electrocuted hair, but, heck, I can close my eyes."

"Bob!" Sue said, followed by the sound effects of a drumroll, crazy laughter.

"Oldest virgin to call in the next ten minutes gets a KDZY

T-shirt," Bob said, "and an entry into our drawing for a year's worth of escort services. You calling in, Sue?"

"Yeah, right. On my fourteenth birthday. From the back of a Chevy."

Mary glanced at a man getting into the Hummer in front of her but quickly looked away when he turned. Laughter spilled from Starbucks, and she thought it entirely possible that she'd been pointed out.

She turned off the radio, pulled back into traffic. At the first residential neighborhood, she pulled into a cul-de-sac and cut the engine.

"Don't cry," she said out loud.

She shook her head, made fists. She forced herself to look at the new beige houses, some as large as her entire condominium complex, and their surprisingly unattractive landscapes of bubble-shaped shrubs and bark. She took a deep breath and glanced in the rearview mirror. Staring back at her were all those could-have-been-beautiful features Alice had taken such pains to describe—the nose a dent away from smooth, perfectly arched eyebrows too blond to see, a bow-shaped mouth, chapped and ruined from lip chewing. A mismatch of imperfections adding up to nothing, a face forgotten the moment it passed, a highly strung, middle-aged body not worth the effort of unwinding. And no lesbianism, no religion, no quirky traits or scandalous behavior to compensate.

A tear leaked out but, unlike Alice, Mary could control herself. She might be living a life "completely without meaning, utterly devoid of warmth," yet she wasn't a basket case. She dried the tear, fixed her smudged mascara. She'd be late for work if she didn't pull herself together, and Alice was right about one thing: Mary's uninspired job as a legal aide at Bowen, Bowen, and Taft was the only constant in her joyless life.

She turned on the engine and headed to work. No one at the office had said anything yet, but they'd probably start trying to set her up again. Years ago, coworkers had fixed her up with single attorneys until it was obvious nothing was going to happen, until the word *frigid* was bandied about. They began to roll their eyes when Mary said this one was self-absorbed, that one touched her too freely in public. When a man was gentle and patient enough to keep, it was only a matter of time before Mary was dumped. She was sweet, they all said—always a relationship killer—but a bit nervous. On dates, they found themselves talking about uninhibited ex-girlfriends, the possibility of reconciliation. Mary had been the maid of honor at six weddings.

Mary's mother told her she was proud of her. Mary ignored the sadness in her father's eyes. It was still possible that she'd find someone, and if she didn't, she made decent money and had cats, a condo, and T-ball games featuring the children of her friends. She'd be forty this year, and it wasn't until this moment, when she swore a perfectly coiffed woman in a Mercedes looked at her and laughed, that she began to feel like a freak. Maybe what she'd called an existence was just the line to get in, just the waiting. Maybe all that mattered was that she hadn't been loved.

Her cell phone rang, and she lapsed into oncoming traffic, trying to pick it up off the floor. A man sat on his horn, shouted something as he swerved around her, and a high-pitched cry started emanating from the back of Mary's throat. She broke out in a sweat, the car smelled awful, the bottoms of her soles burned. She kept missing the talk button and the phone still rang, that horrible playground melody. She slowed to a crawl, finally pulled to the shoulder of the road, and pushed talk. She'd never get to work at this rate.

"What?"

"I'll pay good money," a man said. "Five thousand. For one night. That first night."

His voice was querulous, nearly as girlish as her own. Last night, she'd gotten a call from a man in Japan who'd heard about her on the Internet. In his country, apparently, deflowering a virgin was considered a great honor. Someone else had e-mailed her and told her the color of her bedroom curtains, what time she went to sleep.

Mary rolled down the window. For a second, maybe two, she considered what she could do with the money. Then she hung up. Before she started up the car again, the man called back, his voice more strained than before.

"Seventy-five hundred."

She turned off the cell phone, just like she'd unplugged the phone at home. She had stopped going out at night, but neither could she bear to watch television. Apparently, the payoff for sex was now a million dollars and a man who would leave the second the cameras were turned off. Eleven-year-old girls were thinking about doing it; cartoon characters got more action than she did.

She got to work half an hour late, didn't leave her cubicle all morning, then raced out to lunch alone. She walked the eight blocks to Wendy's, where she prayed she wouldn't run into anyone she knew. Despite her perennial diet, she ordered a cheeseburger, large fries, and a chocolate Frosty. She took the food to a corner booth and ate everything, even after her stomach began to hurt. She undid the top button of her skirt and went back for ice cream. The missed calls were piling up on her cell phone. Her only concern was that one might have come from Jina or Irene.

She decided to risk it. As she turned on the phone, it was already ringing. Mary didn't answer until the newborn in the next booth began to waken and his mother glared at her.

"It's me," the caller said, and though it sounded like a woman, Mary couldn't be sure it wasn't the same breathless man, offering his life savings or a shiny, new Corvette.

"It's *Alice*," the caller went on, but Mary still had her doubts. First, the Alice she knew wouldn't have the guts to call any member of the sushi club ever again, and second, this voice belonged to a person of substance, a woman who hadn't spent a good portion of the last seven years either whimpering or on vacation in her head.

"Oh," Mary said. "Hi."

Mary had every right to be furious, but somehow hysteria and binge-eating were all that came out. On her, anger looked too much like shame. Irene's and Jina's secrets had been exploited, but at least they were *characters*; they had plots, tension, tragedy, climactic scenes. Alice's chapters were the dullest in the book, pages and pages of what never happened, and the worst part was, it *wasn't* fiction. Mary's life had been a series of hasty retreats, little gasps of fear. Everything in that horrid novel was true.

Even the chapters about Alice herself—her depression and suicide attempts—weren't melodrama; Alice had always been a mess. Driven but despondent, relentlessly hopeful and, thus, perennially disappointed, Alice was no overnight sensation. She'd been writing for fifteen years, and it showed. Her makeup drawer was pitiful, her clothes a travesty of elastic-band pants, oversized shirts, and pajamas. Every bad line she'd written was a wrinkle around her mouth, every rejection and hurtful review a pockmark or gray hair or unhealthy mole. She'd begun to take on the paleness of untouched paper, the stiffness of a book spine that had never been cracked.

Mary had been in a bookstore with Alice when a woman opened one of Alice's earlier novels, read less than a paragraph, and tossed the book back on the shelf with a snort. Just like that, a year's worth of work and a soul offering were discarded, ridiculed. Mary had put her arm around Alice, but her friend shook her off, cried only halfway home. Most people buckled in the face of total humiliation, but somehow Alice, who had never been encouraged by anyone to go on, had kept writing. She'd been miserable nearly every day of her life, but at least she'd gone on.

The cell phone crackled. "You understand, don't you?" Alice said.

And the sad thing was, Mary did. Unhappiness preyed on some people. Mary's father, for instance, hated his rough hands as much as Mary's mother did. He cringed at the look of panic in his wife's eyes whenever he stepped toward her, clueless about how he'd earned it. Sometimes, Mary thought, you were given the wrong life, you woke up with strangers. Mary wouldn't take even the slightest bit of devotion for granted. She'd forgive her friends anything; she didn't care what it was.

"I know why you had to write it. How much you needed . . . something good to finally happen."

"All I ever wanted was some sign that I was meant to do this," Alice said. "That this ridiculous overload of feeling had some point . . . some place. Suddenly, it was right there in front of me. The story of a lifetime. These rich, complicated characters. My friends. Until the party, I didn't realize . . . When I saw Jina's face . . . It didn't feel like a betrayal until then. Honestly, Mary. It felt like a gift."

"You could have asked," Mary said.

"I didn't think I had to. I pull ideas from everywhere. From friends, newspapers, places I've visited, conversations I've over-heard. I always fictionalize it. They're just words."

Mary could have pointed out that she'd used the same line on Alice two years ago, when she'd visited her in the hospital. She'd taken Alice's hand, the one with the bandages across the wrist, and said, "They're just words, Alice. My God."

But it was hard to connect that pale, suicidal woman with this fast-talking creature on the other end of the line. Mary wondered if Alice even saw the terror in it, this transformation caused not by herself but by the world's reaction to her. If she worried at all what the world would think next.

"Have you talked to Jina?" Mary asked.

Alice paused. "Not since the party. Irene sent me my book in shreds. How's that for maturity?"

"Naji left her," Mary told her. "Last night. His brother, Ahmad, gave him the book. You know how he's always hated Irene. Naji read it in one sitting. You should be proud it's so hard to put down."

Alice was silent, but in the background Mary heard the clicking of the keyboard. Was Alice writing *now*? Jotting down reactions and repercussions for a sequel? What did her husband, John, think? It was no wonder he hadn't said a word at the book party. He'd been exposed as woefully devoted and boring in bed.

"Alice?" Mary said.

"*I* didn't have those affairs." The clicking of the keys went on. "*I* didn't sleep around, then expect everyone to forget about it. Are there no consequences when you're a soap-opera star? You get to run around and fuck whoever you want, and everybody smiles and says it's your fiery, artistic nature? There are always prices to pay for our actions. Maybe Irene forgot that."

"What price are you paying?"

The typing stopped. It was almost painful for Mary to be mean, and she was beginning to wonder why. Apparently, it was all the rage.

"Honey," Alice said.

"I've got to go."

"Wait," Alice said. *"Please."*

Mary closed her eyes. She'd eaten too much. She felt bloated and loveless and ugly, and she couldn't blame any of that on Alice. They were just words.

"I couldn't bear it if I lost you over this," Alice said, the keyboard silent. "The sushi club is my only . . . I couldn't have survived without you. You know that. Can't you see the book as a compliment? You know how we always joked about it? The secret lives of the sushi club. How it would make a great title. You all laughed. Don't you remember that, Mary?"

Who wouldn't laugh after four glasses of sake, and all their scandals and tragedies made humorous, bearable? Who didn't feel publishable in the company of friends?

"We thought we'd be heroes," Mary said softly. "We're not heroes in your book."

She hung up and gathered her empty wrappers, stuffed them in the trash. The newborn had gone back to sleep, and the mother appeared on the verge of it herself, her hair dangling precariously over her chicken sandwich.

Alice was right about one thing. Every action has a price; every inaction costs something. When you stand perfectly still, your undisturbed life pools around you and takes you down. Mary stepped outside, an afternoon of speed-typing ahead of her while the sun shined, and teenagers ditching school shrieked in their cars in the drive-thru lane. She closed her eyes and didn't move; how could she? She was drowning in an unlived life.

Later, she would recall only a few events of that afternoon. She called her father, not her mother. She took off the plaid jacket she'd always hated and stuffed it in the trash. She realized that Alice had started her story too soon, before the plot really got going.

Beyond that, it was hard to remember which bridges she burned first and which last.

By the end of the day, the Virgin Maria had quit her job, put her condominium up for sale, and, with tears in her eyes, gave Frisky and Smoky to a cat-loving neighbor. By the end of the day, everything Mary had built in two decades had been demolished, as if a fearful life has all the strength of a tower of cards. In Alice's sequel, Mary imagined she'd sleep with the first man she saw, but in real life, just recognizing that she had the power to change everything—for good or ill—was enough. She stood outside her condominium, staring at the FOR SALE sign, and cried just a little. Just enough to make it all real. Then she drove to Jina's, her future unclear except for one thing: It would not be the same.

She found Jina's son, Danny, on the front stoop, surrounded by magazines: *Outside* and *Wilderness* and *Rivers, United*. In his small hands, he held a deluxe color brochure of a river company that guided trips down the world's great whitewater—weeklong adventures on the Salmon and Colorado, fourteen-day treks through the Amazon.

"Hey Dan," she said.

She sat beside him, swore his body emitted a high-pitched hum. She thumbed through one of his magazines, was struck by the vibrancy of color on the glossy pages, not just the blue of the water but the variety of greens in the trees and brush, the lavender lupine swamping the banks, a splash of red as a kayak cut through a wave. As if wilderness inhabited another, more colorful planet.

"It was a total lie," he said. "All that stuff about a heart attack on the farm. Just bullshit."

He was nearing puberty but still cried like a little boy, with hiccups and singular, perfectly formed tears. Mary put her arm around him. He was built with sticks, hot to the touch. He smelled like dirt. And it hit her hard, in the pit of the stomach, that waiting for the right man had probably denied her the right child. The worst part was not going unloved, but living without someone to adore.

"It was terrible for her," she said. "She lost the love of her life."

"She's got Mike."

Mary said nothing. She heard Jina through the screen door, putting something on the stove, turning on the five o'clock news. Mike was not mentioned anywhere in Alice's novel, and Mary considered this a terrible oversight—not on Alice's part, but on Jina's. Mary was an expert on the things she didn't have; she knew who her friends ought to love. The right man for Jina had never been the one who took off his life jacket on a raging river; he was the one whose entire life's work was to keep her safe.

"She won't tell me anything," Danny went on. "Just that it happened on the Salmon. She was pregnant with me. She never would have told me if the book hadn't come out."

Mary couldn't argue. Reckless teenagers become the most cautious parents, suffering daily from memories and imagination. Jina wouldn't let Danny play after dark; she turned on

Cartoon Network while his friends watched HBO. Jina had never said it out loud, but her mandate was obvious: She wasn't going to risk anyone else. As if such a thing was within her power to control. It was terrible to be ignored, but Mary imagined it might be worse to be suffocated. She could almost feel Danny willing himself taller, older, stronger, willing himself away.

"You want to hear something weird?" he asked.

Yesterday, Mary would have leaned away, laughed off his intensity, made an excuse to flee into Jina's cozy, childproofed kitchen. Today she imagined Danny's dirt smell might linger on her fingers for days, that she could still adore someone who wasn't hers.

"Absolutely," she said.

He looked around cautiously. "He smells like a garden. Like mint. The first shoots of peas."

Mary stared at him, felt the hairs along her arms rise and tingle, as if brushed by wind. "You mean those dreams you used to have about your father?"

"They're not dreams. And I still have them."

"Danny—"

"I want to go there," Danny said, his face determined, like Jina's was when she had to defend him. "To the Salmon. I want to raft down the same river he did. Try to convince her, okay?"

And Mary Bonelli, who'd held the same job all her life, who'd never risked loving a man, let alone running a river, noticed that the hairs on Danny's arms stood on end, too. They were eleven years old and thirty-nine, and each of them was just beginning. She turned her palms over and found sweat in the crevices of her lifelines.

Then she squeezed Danny. "I will."

"Absolutely not," Jina said.

She'd spent the last two hours slicing and parboiling squash for Danny's favorite shish kebabs, knowing full well that he was on a hunger strike. As of midnight last night, he'd refused all food, though she'd noticed a dent in her soda supply and a pile of crushed Pepsi cans in the recycling bin.

"Why not?" Danny asked, elbows on the counter, his voice reverting—consciously, she was sure—to that little-boy alto she could rarely resist. "School's out in a week. There's nothing stopping us."

Jina looked at Mike, his head bent to the salad greens he was chopping carefully, slicing away every blackened edge. Here was a valid occasion for caution, an arena where he could really shine. "Mike?" she said.

He smiled at Danny. "Let's not get crazy."

"Why is it crazy?"

These last words came from Mary, who'd been sitting at the counter, sipping sparkling water spiked with gin. Quiet, responsible, wine-drinking Mary, who had, apparently, taken up hard drinking and a life of leisure all in one day.

"Because I have a job," Jina said, probably too harshly, but she had eight skewers of vegetables that probably wouldn't get eaten, a man who couldn't commit to her, and friends who were changing form daily.

"No one's asking you to quit," Mary said quietly. "It's a *vacation*, Jina. These trips take, what, a week? You fly in, camp your way down the canyon, then fly out. *Voila.*"

Jina picked up the tray of shish kebabs. She ignored Danny's pleading face, the redness in his eyes from reading so many of those damn magazines. They'd started showing up the day after Alice's book party, and they accumulated quickly. On the floor of the bathroom, splayed across tables, twisted among his bedsheets. She knew it was impossible, but she swore she smelled the river whenever she entered his room. She hadn't heard Super Mario Brothers music for days, and now she pined for it. Anything to cover up that waterfall, the incessant whitewater-like roar in her ears. At Blockbuster, all Danny would look at were river adventure movies. *The River Wild, Snowy River,* the old Marilyn Monroe flick *River of No Return.* He wouldn't speak to her unless it was about his father.

"It's only a week," she said to no one in particular, "if you survive. Otherwise, it takes longer."

She went outside, put the skewers on the grill. From the patio, the neighbor's waterfall sounded as though it was taking out entire hillsides. She sat at the wrought-iron table, feeling as weightless as she had when she and Zach headed sideways down Gunbarrel Rapid. It had been thrilling, the first physically dangerous thing she'd ever done. The soft spots in her body vanished; she stretched into the taut shape of a daredevil. Zach was directly below her; as they plummeted down the face of the wave, her foot grazed his hair. She screamed for joy, even as she fell overboard.

Mike came out with two glasses of wine and eased himself

into the seat beside her. He said nothing, but she knew his back was hurting him. He chalked it up to an old racquetball injury, never let it slow him down, though by evening each night he had trouble walking. She rubbed it for him sometimes and also said nothing, as if they had made a pact to steer clear of discussions of past injuries and pain.

"Acheron is the river of pain in the Underworld," she said.

"Are we discussing mythology or Zach?"

She was surprised at his directness. Perhaps, once he'd turned her down, he'd realized it wasn't all that difficult to be cruel. A man could get used to it fast.

She stared at a piece of lint on his shirt, his wide shoulders. Her left foot went numb while she looked at him, as if she was already turning something off.

"I just think it's interesting that they named a river after it," she said. "Not an ocean or lake. A *river*. Something that looks the same but is always changing. A work in progress." She paused, watched his shoulders rise and fall. "I've never asked anyone to marry me before."

He went to turn the shish kebabs, but not before she saw his mild eyes flare. "And doesn't that strike you as the slightest bit suspicious?" he said, keeping his back to her. "You can't wait for me. You need to get married now, before you start having Danny's dreams, imagining Zach around every corner. Before you admit who you love and who you don't."

Jina tightened her grip around her wineglass. "Danny would be devastated if you left."

He turned around slowly. When she had returned from Idaho, she painted the river gods. Alpheus was her favorite—

the river who fell in love with a huntress so reluctant to marry him that she changed from a woman into a spring. Alpheus, undaunted, mingled his water with hers, a love story if it had ended there. Instead, Alpheus went on to marry another. There was no loyalty in myth or nature.

"I know," he said, his eyes no longer a true green but more like the edges of a river, murky. "But I don't know if the same is true for you. I can't tell if you proposed because you wanted me to say yes, or because you knew I wouldn't. You seem to expect me to take chances."

She rose quietly, took off the shish kebabs one by one. He'd been married once before, in his early twenties, to a woman who wanted a career more than children. They still exchanged Christmas cards, and Jina wanted to know how this could be. Why didn't he revert to a vengeful, greedy, adolescent lover, wanting someone's whole heart or nothing? What did he know about being swept away?

"Obviously, neither of us is taking chances anymore," she said.

When they returned to the house, they found Mary and Danny at the kitchen table, hunched over another of Danny's brochures.

"Listen to this," Mary said, and Jina wondered just how much gin she'd had. Mary was jiggling in her seat, her corkscrew hair dancing. Her voice was high but also fervent. Like someone making a wish. "This company brings along a chef from New York. First night's course is filet mignon, steamed asparagus, Caesar salad, and French cabernet. They offer streamside facials and massages."

"Mary—"

"It's a life experience," Mary cut in. "They're not just taking you down a river for a few thrills. They want to change your perspective, help you get in tune with nature and yourself. They want to *alter* you, Jina. Change your life."

Mary pushed back her chair. Jina had known her for nine years, had seen her overweight and addicted to diet pills, mothering other people's children and pretending she didn't mind sitting at home alone. She'd never seen her like this. Brown eyes lit to the color of amber. Smelling of joy.

"I'm doing it," Mary said.

Mike set the shish kebabs, already growing cold, on the table. "You're what?"

"I'm rafting down the Salmon."

"All right!" Danny said. "Mom, if you won't go, Mary can take me."

Jina was saved, or thought she was, by the slamming of the front door, the appearance of a disheveled impostor. Instead of her usual suede and silk, Irene stumbled into the room in an old pair of blue jeans and one of Naji's shirts, a size thirty-four, powder-blue Oxford. She hadn't set her hair or put on makeup of any kind, unheard-of oversights for Irene, and unadorned, she looked eighteen. Rickety and miserable.

"I can't sleep," she said. "I mean it. Since Naji left, I can't bear to close my eyes."

Mary had trouble keeping her eyes open as she helped herself to the bottle of gin, pouring it straight now.

"I'd like to kill that psycho brother of his," Irene went on. "Ahmad gave him the book; since Naji moved in with him, he won't put him on the phone. They're probably joyfully discussing all the ways they torture unfaithful wives in Saudi Arabia."

"Irene—"

"And that awful Maxine in his office won't let me past the waiting room. They all think I'm poison."

Jina put her arms around Irene, resisted the temptation to flinch at her prominent ribs. Irene was fanatical about her weight, attending daily kickboxing classes and eating celery for lunch to stay under one hundred and ten pounds.

"Jina, you've got to help me," Irene said. "Call Naji for me. Explain."

Jina stepped back. Naji had been in the United States long enough to speak nearly perfect English, but she still doubted he would understand. His wife had never expected their marriage to last. Before Irene met Naji, she caromed through men who wanted her for her looks or fame or money, content that at least she had something people wanted. At least she heard compliments. She hopped on the bandwagon, married Naji Saleh for his money, and when he stood before their guests on their wedding day, praising her vivacity, her boldness, her thorough Americanness, she cocked her head as if they were reading from different scripts. For a year, she tested him by coming to bed with mascara beneath her eyes, by threatening to quit the soap opera and take up palm reading, by a few increasingly self-defeating affairs, and for a year he smiled at her as if she was a colorful bird, there to entertain and delight him. Who had known he would delight her, too?

"I don't think he'll listen to me," Jina said.

"Bring him to the Sha . . . Salmon River," Mary said. "Ideeho. Land of blondes and Tater Tots, hey Dan?" She was fully drunk now. Swaying.

Irene raised an eyebrow. "Mary Bonelli. Is that you?"

Mary took up a dance with the draperies. "I quit my fucking job," she said.

Even makeupless and devastated, Irene clapped her hands. "Oh, honey, that's wonderful." It was unclear whether she meant quitting or Mary's first profanity.

They detached Mary from the curtains and guided her to the couch, where she promptly began to cry. "I quit my fucking job," she said into her hands. Jina hadn't even noticed that Danny was gone until he returned with a suitcase, which he placed by the door.

"He wants me to go," he said. "That's what he's been trying to tell me."

"Who?" Irene said. "Naji?" She was patting Mary's shoulder, but she'd also gotten ahold of one of Danny's brochures.

Danny challenged Jina with his steady gaze. "He haunts that river," he said.

"Danny." Jina tried to hold him, but he pressed himself to the wall. "We see what we want to see sometimes," she went on. "Not what's really there."

Danny blinked. "You think I'm making it up? You think I'm crazy, too?"

"No!" Jina said adamantly. "Of course not. It's just . . . things get stirred up. We want something so badly we think. . . ."

"I *saw* him," Danny said, getting that look in his eyes, Zach's look, the one that said *I'm right. I don't care what anyone says.* "His ghost lives on that river, and if you stop me, I'll run away. I'll get there one way or another."

Jina stared at her son. She'd been so dazed with sorrow when he was born, she sometimes slept right through his crying. Eventually he gave up whimpering, and after that he never gained weight the way an infant should. He remained in the tenth percentile for his weight, and she never forgave herself for that. She'd marked her son not with abuse but with the things he lacked: pounds, tears, a mother's undivided attention. The necessities other boys didn't think twice about.

"I'd have to check the flows," she said. "They might be too high this early in the season."

"Jina! You can't seriously be thinking of this." Mike stood, and she realized she had not only forgotten about him, she didn't want him to come. Earl had forced her to cruelty; Zach erased her ambition; Mike made her feel old, unsure. Love is like a man who doesn't know his own strength; he means well, but sometimes he crushes you. Only one man had brought out the best in her, and he was eleven years old, standing in front of her, hardly breathing.

She looked at Danny and smiled. "I guess I am."

Mike shook his head. "Don't be ridiculous. There's nothing to see there but a river, a hundred other rafters. It's not some mystical wilderness; it's Disneyland. Besides, I can't get off work now." He glanced at Irene, who was slipping Danny's brochure into her purse.

"Then I suppose you won't be able to come."

They ate shish kebabs in silence. Even Danny didn't dare to gloat. After dinner, Irene left a message on Naji's brother's answering machine that Jina could scarcely bear to listen to.

"I . . . I can't sleep, Naji. I don't want to dream of you and wake up alone. I'm thinking of going on a rafting trip in Idaho with Jina and Mary and I hope . . . will you come? Will you come and listen? There's a difference between truth and fact, didn't you say that to me once? Please, Naji. Please."

After dinner, Irene drove Mary home, and Jina put Danny to bed. She tucked the blankets beneath his chin, and he yanked them down to his waist. His normal body temperature had always been above average; every morning he was thinner than the night before.

"You mean it?" he asked. "We can go?"

She sat on the edge of his bed, something he rarely allowed her to do. "I used to dream of him, too. It made me feel better. But this . . . this might make us both sad."

He shook his head, apparently oblivious to the tears at the corners of his eyes. "No, it won't. You'll see."

She looked around the room he cleaned by jamming everything beneath his bed or into the closet—at comic books and action figures and spy equipment littering every inch of floor space, leaving little room for a ghost. "You really see him?" she asked.

He looked toward the window. "I'm not dreaming, Mom. I open my eyes and it's like I'm there. I can smell the pines, the river. You think it's heaven?"

Jina took his hand. "I think it's where he would have lived, if given the chance."

Danny blinked. Once, twice. "Alice said in her book he was dumb on the water."

She shook her head. "He wasn't dumb. He was born to run rivers."

"Did you love him?"

Fantasies, dreams, were for darkness. By day, she'd kept busy, found happiness through work, friends, through Danny. Maybe her heart had scarred, and she'd loved Mike with a little less of it, but she'd done the best she could. Everyone makes concessions. The luckiest people don't have more; they have enough. Yet every once in a while, a recollection stabbed her. She saw Zach's face in perfect, minute detail, down to a scratch on the cheek, the beads of water still clinging to his chin. Her chest flooded with pain; a river ran through her.

"Oh, yes," she said.

"Did he know about me?"

She closed her eyes. "No. I didn't get the chance to tell him."

Later, Jina walked down the hall and found Mike at the kitchen table, the brochure folded in front of him.

"I don't know how to be with you now," she said. "I don't have anything else to say."

"I see."

"This'll give us both time to think. Maybe you were right about that."

"Oh, I was right," he said, not looking at her.

She picked up the brochure, walked to the phone. She dialed the 800 number, expecting a recording with information about office hours. Instead she heard a cough, an old man's voice.

"Oh," she said. "I'm calling for information about Salmon Adventures? I was wondering if any trips are still available in the next couple of weeks."

"Hold on," he said. "You're lucky you caught me with the satellite phone on. I'm in my home here. Let me get the schedule."

She heard papers and a clunk, followed by a string of curses. The man came back to the phone.

"Sorry," he said. "Goddamn paperwork. My son, Drew, usually does this, but he's out of town. Call back if the phone goes out."

"I shouldn't have bothered you so late."

"Doesn't matter. I don't sleep."

She heard him thumbing through papers. "June twelfth through the twentieth. Drew's got an open raft. How many in your group?"

Jina stared at Mike's stiff back. She realized that aside from taking steaks and shish kebabs to the barbecue, he never went outside. He ignored the weeds, the overgrown shrubbery, as if avoidance could make a thing disappear.

"Three to start," she said. "My son, a friend, and myself. Maybe more."

"We need at least four to book the raft. And a deposit for half. We'll try to fill the other seats, so you might have company. You want me to pencil you in?"

Jina heard the waterfall. She was never going to get away from it. Maybe she didn't want to.

"Yes," she said. "The name's Jina. Jina Woolridge."

The man was silent. She imagined him writing her name,

perhaps making a few notes, or even that the satellite phone had cut them off.

"You there?" she asked finally.

The man breathed deeply. "You *that* Jina Woolridge? The one came down the river with her husband all those years ago? The one we found?"

She felt cold again, and weightless. "Ellis?"

"Ah, hell," he said. "Come see me if you get through Gunbarrel. I think we need to talk."

5

He caught her by the heel, though Jina didn't feel his fingers gripping her or appreciate the strength it took for him to lift her back into the boat. She was laughing when she came up. Laughing and shaking. By the way he looked at her, squeezed her shoulder, she wondered if she was acting slightly hysterical. If so, there was no time for comfort. Zach grabbed both sweeps, tried to wrestle control back from the river, but by then they were rudderless debris, a waterlogged two-ton leaf.

It probably took only seconds to clear Gunbarrel, but they were on river time now, which ran backward in foul weather and rapids, and sped ahead when the current and scenery were good. Zach strained at the sweeps, and Jina found she couldn't remember yesterday or pinpoint what, exactly, she had hoped would happen next. Out here, memory and desire were as pointless as trying to paddle by hand. There was only the roar of the river, one plunge after another, until Zach pulled them into an eddy and let go of the sweeps. Jina's laughter sprouted tears. She sunk to the bottom of the boat.

Zach crouched beside her, touched the side of her face. His skin was on fire despite the rain, the river, the freezing wind.

"Well," he said, "we got that out of the way."

She managed one more laugh, swiped at her tears. She might have to start faking smiles in order to satisfy him, and that unnerved her more than the dunking. They'd already reached their first divide.

"I doubt it will happen again," he went on quickly. "We've got the feel of it now. I'm not happy with that life jacket, though. Should be more buoyant. We'll switch."

Her teeth began to chatter; the cold seeped in. Pain began along her jawline and raced up the apples of her cheekbones. She leaned forward, pressed her head against Zach's chest. He was wet, too. Saturated from the river spray and rain.

"Jina," he said.

Her mother had rarely met her father's eye, as if she could only continue to love him when she didn't see him clearly. Jina leaned back and met Zach's gaze. Perhaps he had expected her to cower because for a moment, his eyes were unguarded, panicky.

"I won't let anything happen to you," he said.

They moved in circles, round and round the eddy. She marked a spot in the river and watched the scow pass it once, twice, three times, seeing only water at first, then a tree limb, finally some kind of river weed. Nothing ever really changed; you just looked at it differently, noted what you'd ignored before.

"I know you won't," she said.

Zach smiled boyishly. They exchanged life jackets; he cinched hers tight to fit. Then he grabbed the sweeps, spent twenty minutes trying to pry them from the eddy. By the time they burst back into the current, he was sweating.

For the next few miles, there was calm water. "That's Horse Creek," Zach said, pointing to the stream flowing in from the right. "In the 1880s, two trappers set their horses free on the hillsides. Then one of them got a little greedy and shot the other."

There were no stallions roaming the hillsides now, nothing but dripping pine boughs and an amorphous mist climbing the slope. Not even a hawk graced the sky, as if the case was being made that this was wilderness, and from now on they were on their own.

"Neal Allen had a cabin at the end of the Horse Creek bridge," Zach went on. "He was the one those hunters mentioned. Meaner than the bears he hunted with a switch. Killed himself in his cabin. The canyon will do that sometimes."

"What? Drive you crazy?"

He shook his head. "Introduce you to who you really are."

He pointed out the Indian pictographs on the bluff above Legend Creek. In Maryland, elementary-school children celebrated Thanksgiving by pinning feathers to their heads and painting cardboard tomahawks. The library book on Native American creation myths was always available, which was why Jina knew that the Nez Percé, who first populated this canyon ten thousand years ago, believed they were formed from the heart of a monster. After the monster devoured nearly all the animals, Coyote slew him by jumping down his throat and cutting out his heart. Coyote sliced up the monster's body, flung the pieces across the land, and wherever a fragment landed, a different tribe emerged. When Coyote squeezed the brave blood from the monster's heart, the noblest of all the tribes, the Nez Percé, was formed.

"This is the beginning of the primitive area," Zach said. "The Forest Service has burned most of the old cabins. Nothing else can be built."

She imagined the whole place to themselves, no one to call if something went wrong, but also no one to come between her and Zach. But when she scanned the right bank, there was someone there, aiming a rifle right at them.

She screamed, but Zach merely laughed, waved an arm. The man lowered the rifle, and Jina recognized the old-timer they'd met in Salmon, the one who'd invited them to dinner should they survive that long. The structure he'd called a lodge stood up a sandy trail, encircled by ragged ponderosas. She made out a series of mismatched buildings, each one smaller than the one before, ending in a pair of outhouses. It appeared he'd built the structures out of whatever floated downriver, nailing logs to tin, boat hulls to mining debris, plywood to bright plastic scraps. The result was ugly, uneven, and strangely artistic.

Zach pulled hard on the sweep, maneuvered them to the sandy beach where Ellis Cantor tied them off. The old man ignored the hand Zach held out and put a foot in the scow. He must have noticed Jina's oversized life jacket, as well as the fact that she was drenched and still shaking, because he offered his hand.

"Come on now," he said softly. "Helena's got coffee on."

. . .

If it had been up to Zach, they'd have had a cup of coffee and gotten right back in the scow. They could have made a flawless run through Rainier to buoy Jina's confidence, camped at Lantz Bar, then gone deep into Black Canyon, where the granite cliffs rise so high and straight, the river looks like the easiest way out.

But Jina smelled roasting chicken. She loved the lodge. The armory of shotguns on the porch, the glassy-eyed bear in the living room illuminated by hissing propane lights, rooms that smelled musty and foreign, like treasure chests of silk and spices just recently unearthed. She raved over the luxury of a propane-heated shower, complimented the mismatch of plywood and rough-cut pine floors and walls as if they were works of art.

Ellis's wife, Helena, brought out a pot of coffee. She barely cleared the doorway, as tall and solid as Jina was petite. She had the most amazing hair Zach had ever seen, a waist-length skunk's tail of blacks and whites. Jina touched the ends as Helena poured her a cup.

The percolated coffee was unusual—spiced, Zach thought, with cumin. It left a strange but pleasant aftertaste in his mouth. Jina was still trembling from her fall in the river, and Ellis and Helena had a guest bed with down blankets. Outside, beyond Lucky Creek, stood a pungent but functional outhouse. Jina was already leaning toward the guest room, and he reluctantly agreed to one night. First thing in the morning, he'd get her back on the scow and the adventure would really begin.

But in the morning, Jina slept until ten, then went with Helena to pick huckleberries. Zach found her wet clothes hung on a line out back now that the storm had passed and the sky was an icy, clear blue. The temperature gauge on the porch read thirty-nine degrees, even after the sun came up. Zach paced the porch like a trapped bull, breath steaming from his mouth, until Ellis took pity on him.

"Don't tell the Forest Service about my generator," the old man said, "and I'll let you watch my movies."

In the basement, behind a false wall, Ellis proudly showed off his illegal propane generator. The lodge had been built before the river was designated a wilderness area, which saved it from destruction, but forest officials came by twice a year to make sure he didn't ruin it with luxuries like electric lights and toasters. Power tools would spoil the nature experience for the rafters.

"They took out all six of my mature cherry trees," Ellis spat. "Said they weren't native. Helena's not allowed to plant flowers at all. Goddamn liberal pansies. Twenty-year-olds, most of them, California rich kids with nothing better to do. I could shoot 'em if I wanted. Bury their bodies up the creek. No one would know."

He smiled then, looked twenty years younger, boyish and just out for a little fun. He fired up the generator.

"Just doing their job, I suppose," Zach said cautiously.

"Job," Ellis muttered. "I'll tell you what a job is. Keeping the river clear of strainers, for one. Piping three miles for spring water, building that stone hot tub up near Barth, one boulder at a time. These kids are on a perennial summer vacation, thinking they're gonna shoot the rednecks and save the salmon, all in one fell swoop. Couldn't look me in the eye when they confiscated my first generator. *Bah!* I boated in another right under their noses, hid it down here. I only use it to run my movies." He smiled once more. "And once in a while, Helena gets a hankering for a smoothie, and we power up the blender."

Back upstairs, Zach took a seat on the couch; Ellis put a blanket over the window. Zach prepared himself for a dull travelogue, but within minutes he was on the edge of the seat. Ellis had shot twenty rolls of the river, each in different years, at wildly varying flows. Ellis would take his jet boat downriver, then turn around to film the rafts. He seemed to have picked the most inexperienced guides to shoot. Fifteen of the twenty boats flipped.

Jina came in during the worst of it, when a raft took the wrong channel through Salmon Falls. They hit a hole and were maytagged, trapped between two opposing currents. Water flew into the hole at such high velocities that the raft was stuck there, in an endless agitation cycle. The men and women tried to throw themselves from the boat, only to be slammed back into the cauldron.

"That one was a little dicey," Ellis said. "We didn't get them all out."

Jina breathed deeply, then walked into the bedroom. Zach knew he should go after her, but what could he say? The river was magnificent and cruel; this was what he had counted on. This was why he was here. Kimberly had lulled him; danger woke him up. He watched until the screen went black.

"You gotta have a certain mentality," Ellis said, turning off the

VCR. "You gotta be arrogant, sure you're gonna survive. As soon as you get scared, it's over. That's when I stopped running. Lost two boys in Big Mallard, and couldn't find my way through water after that. Went up No Man's Creek. Stayed there eighteen years."

Zach leaned forward. "No kidding? How'd you survive?"

Ellis shrugged. "Had a garden. Fruit trees—apples, plums, cherries. North shore's sunny, great for vegetables. Gotta divert water from the streams is all. Beans and peas in the spring, tomatoes and squash in the summer, enough to store all winter. I mined a little, but it didn't pay. Turned the copper plates into utensils, dinnerware. I fished. You ever see how catfish dig holes in the bank? You can pull them out easy. I charged admission to the rafters who wanted to see an actual eccentric. That paid for ammunition, a few trips to Riggins."

Zach wanted to hear more, but a thump from the bedroom stole his attention. "I should go see her," he said, standing.

"Son, best thing you can do is let her be. Give her time to figure things out her own way. Not everybody takes to the place; not everybody should. The river asks a lot."

"Let me just see how she is."

Zach knocked on the bedroom door but got no answer. He entered to find Jina at the table, her paper and charcoals laid out. She'd already sketched the mountain and meadow outside the window, but had ignored the obvious sliver of stream that winded its way past the lodge.

He walked across the room, leaned down to kiss the exposed hairs on her neck. She was so fragile, he felt a bone beneath his lips. He often had to hold back when they made love for fear of crushing her. Maybe it was marriage in general, or it could have been just them: Either way, he could no longer do exactly what he wanted.

"Let's stay here another day," he said.

She blinked. "Don't do me any favors."

He stepped back, confused at the anger she showed when he gave her what she seemed to want, frustrated from trying to figure her out. He thought briefly, guiltily, of running this river alone, in total, luxurious silence.

"Ellis invited me hunting in the morning," he said. "I won't wake you."

She picked up one of her charcoals and stabbed at the paper.

The next morning, Zach woke, as always, without an alarm, as soon as the sky lightened from black to steel blue. He turned away from Jina's warm back, quietly put on his jacket and boots. He found Ellis on the porch, dressed in camouflage, rifle in hand.

"There's no shortage of elk this year," Ellis said, stepping off the porch. "Drought pushed them north."

Zach retrieved his rifle from the scow. In Kimberly, he'd taken out the rabbits that riddled the fields with holes, some from a distance of two hundred yards. He knew to aim high; bullets fall from that far a distance. He followed Ellis along the narrow path up Lucky Creek. The vegetation was thick along the creek, a dangerous mass of brambles, wild raspberries, and poison ivy.

"Keep a lookout for bear," Ellis said. "We've had a young one in the area."

This was the kind of statement that filled a city man with fear, but it invigorated Zach. They walked a mile uphill, where the elk grazed after leaving the river. Ellis set up behind a thicket of chokecherries.

"Elk steaks for dinner," Zach said.

Ellis turned to him. "We're not shooting today."

"What's that?"

"Just wanted to show you something." Ellis paused, turned back toward the meadow. "Elvis."

For a moment, Zach nodded the way he would to an expected answer. "Elvis? This a friend of yours?"

"An elk."

Zach laughed. "You named an elk Elvis?"

Ellis snorted. "*I* didn't name him. What do you take me for?"

"Then—"

"He's an eight-point bull now. That's rare. Proud and gaudy as all hell. You can't miss him, though I tried to when he was wiggling his fat hips in Vegas."

Zach scratched his chin, looked down the slope. "Just for the record. Are you saying Elvis Presley is now an elk?"

Ellis smiled, and Zach realized what it was that made him look so boyish. His teeth were a mountain range of zigzags, the adolescent Sawtooths in his mouth.

"Let me tell you something, son," Ellis said. "When you live on this river long enough, you go one of two ways. Either you start depending on God to tell you what to think, or you stop believing in everything. I took the latter route. I've met some of those Sierra Club vigilantes, and, believe me, they're out of their drug-induced minds. This canyon's not dying. No one's hunting the wolves to death. No twenty-year-old with a pony-tail and flip-flops is gonna convince me the dams on the Snake are killing the salmon. I catch my own fish for supper. I know what's in that water, and I ain't worried. The wife I chose took my son and left me for a strip mall in LaLa Land, while the one I ordered from Russia has stayed by my side every minute of the last eight years. Believe me, I'm not some goosey-eyed young-ster spouting romance and reincarnation at you. I'm just telling you Elvis Presley lives on the Salmon now. I've seen his eyes, the wobble of his knees. I know."

Those teeth stopped Zach from laughing again. His mouth twitched a little, but it'd have been stupid to do more than that with fangs and a loaded rifle staring at him. Men went crazy on this river all the time—stopped wearing clothes, cleaned their cabins from top to bottom, then shot themselves in the head. You went into the wilderness and met yourself. Sometimes the introduction was unbearable. That was the chance you took.

Other times you learned things you never would have guessed. That you believed in more than you thought you did. That you were brave when someone else was in danger. If you were hungry enough, you'd kill the hero of a Disney movie; you'd eat bugs, if that's what it took to survive.

"Don't think I don't know it's crazy," Ellis said, turning away. "I know."

"It's a bit far-fetched," Zach said delicately. "What makes you so sure?"

Ellis shrugged. "First saw him when I was up No Man's

Creek, a couple years before I sent for Helena. I was hunting, had my rifle out, locked in. From fifty yards I heard something. One of those melodies I'd forgotten I'd loved. The kind of song that makes people stay where there's radios. I heard his voice like he was standing right next to me, crooning. It was a hell of a lot to take in at first. But he kept coming back. Kept coming this close to me shooting him, just to sing me those songs from my youth. Remind me I used to dance once. Keep me from feeling so lonesome."

Zach nodded. What else was there to do? It wasn't fact that mattered but how much you needed to believe.

"He comes back every year," Ellis went on. "Stays around the cabin. It's not such a stretch. Eight points. That's an imperial. A king. No one bothers him."

The grass below them crunched as a monstrous bull elk stepped into the clearing. The beast was magnificent, his back easily five feet high, his shoulder fur thick and black, his rump white. His breath steamed when he looked at them. Of course, it was just the power of suggestion, but Zach swore he heard something un-elklike. Not a rutting bugle but a deep laugh. One smooth note, the grand finale of a love song.

Elvis lowered his head to graze. Ellis hummed. Zach wondered what a woman from Russia thought of a place like this, of a husband who believed in nothing and in everything, a lover who worshipped an elk.

The bull lifted his head, looked right at their hiding place behind the brush.

"Come on now," Ellis said to Zach. "He wants us."

Ellis emerged from the chokecherries. Zach followed more slowly, his rifle clutched tightly in his hand, the barrel aimed at the ground but ready to move at the slightest provocation. Moose were the most unpredictable animals in Idaho, but elk had been known to charge. This one merely flared his nostrils and took in the scent of him. Elvis lowered his head, shook it a little, until his fur fell over one side. Zach wasn't about to read too much into it, though his heart was racing like crazy. He was hearing things he'd never admit out loud.

The elk swiveled a knee as he turned and sauntered out of the meadow, away into pines.

"Imagine that," Ellis said, smiling again, showing off those teeth. "Elvis Presley likes you."

Jina would have lingered over pancakes and Helena's wonderfully strong Russian coffee. She'd have hunkered down in the cozy living room and read ten-year-old fishing magazines, but Zach had already loaded the scow. He'd made a copy of Ellis's river map, where each rapid was rated not with the Class I through VI system most rafters used but with a 0 to 10 graph of Ellis's creation. A 0 signified flat water; 10 was a rapid that was not only life-threatening but changeable: rocky one day, riddled with dangerous horizon lines and undercuts the next. There were twelve 10s between them and Riggins. Three of those had an additional asterisk and notes about who had drowned and why.

Zach came into the kitchen, stood by the door. Jina could de-

mand they stay; she could tell him she was going back to San
Francisco the moment they pulled out in Riggins, that his vision
of a scow business was nothing but a boy's daydream, implausi-
ble. She could ruin it for him, and instead of feeling drunk with
power, she decided to be careful. He had more to lose, that was
what it came down to. He'd have to give up his dreams for her,
while she only had to give up comfort temporarily, do without a
soft bed and security for a week.

"I'm ready," she said, standing.

He breathed out, relaxed a fist. "We'll clear Rainier, then
head down to Lantz Bar. The original blacksmith shop is still
there. The house burned, but Frank Lantz's friends helped him
rebuild. He was well liked, Frank. Johnny McKay may be the
soul of this river, but Frank was its heart. His cousin Coy is
buried there. I'll show you the grave."

He hurried down to the scow. Jina took her plate to the sink,
where Helena stood, watching her. "Thank you for everything."

"Wait on the porch," Helena said. "I have something."

Helena came out a few minutes later with a small, black velvet pouch. She untied the string, revealing a polished chunk of
turquoise, its edges worn and smooth.

"Rare in my country," Helena said. "For safety, yes? Your Indians know. I brought it over on the boat. You take."

Jina reached out to touch the cool stone, then drew back.
"No, I couldn't. It's too precious."

Helena shook her head, stuffed the turquoise back into its
pouch, and jabbed it at her. "Yes, yes. You take. Write what you
hope and put inside with stone. Keep dry. Get there safe."

Jina realized she was squeezing the pouch. She loosened her grip, tried to laugh but it came out all wrong. Loud and scary. She put her hand over her mouth, and Helena touched her shoulder. There was a permanent line of dirt beneath the woman's nails and blue scars along her knuckles.

"You have to go?" Helena asked. "No choice?" She didn't wait for the answer but nodded, as if a woman's desire and intuition were often overrun by a man's plans, his need for advancement and action. This was still the West, after all.

"Yes," Jina said softly. "I have to go. I want to."

Helena smiled softly. "Me, too. Have to. Boat, train, Ellis." She drew herself up like a giant bear and growled. Jina laughed. "This place," Helena went on, wrinkling her nose. "Four seasons, they say. Oh, sure. Bugs, mud, fire, snow. But soon I understand. It's a soul place."

She looked toward the river, her gaze turning tender when it fell on Ellis playing with the sweeps. Zach paced the beach, kicking the sand impatiently.

"Thank you," Jina said.

Helena hugged her hard. With that kind of strength, Jina had no doubt Helena could run the scow perfectly, guide them all to safety. "Write what you hope," the woman said. "Get there."

Jina slipped the pouch in her pocket, stepped off the porch. When she reached the beach, Ellis took her hand. Zach was more than impatient now. Bordering on whiny.

"Jina, let's go," he said.

Ellis ignored him, held Jina's hand tight. "It's a bad year for the river. Drought conditions all winter, and the year before.

Lowest flows ever recorded. I'm telling you this not to scare you, but because it's your life, too. He's a decent kid; he loves you, anybody could see that. But he's got blinders on when it comes to this river. Thinks it's got feelings. If it does, I'm telling you, it'd just as soon drown him."

Jina felt the scars on Ellis's hand, flesh as rough as sandstone. It hurt her just to hold it. "We can do it," she said.

She let go of his hand and walked to the scow. Zach gave her his life jacket, strained his way into hers. He helped her into the boat, met her gaze long enough for her to see that he craved adventure but loved her more. Long enough to know that he would stop whenever she said so, and he was terrified that she would ask.

"One second," she said. She heard him sigh as she reached into her dry bag. She ripped a page from her diary, wrote quickly as he stomped around the scow, nothing left to do. She took the velvet pouch from her pocket, stuffed the paper inside. She replaced the whole thing deep in her dry bag, though she thought perhaps she ought to toss it in the river, let it try to make its way past a host of lethal dams to the sea like a sockeye, or a message in a bottle.

Keep Zach Safe.

The stomping stopped. Zach stood behind her, waiting.

"Let's go," she said.

He hooted as Helena came down and Ellis unhooked the rope.

"You take care," Ellis said.

Zach nodded, his gaze already downriver toward Phantom

Creek and Rainier Rapids, which Ellis's system rated as a 5. Jina's stomach tightened, and she gasped. It was movement, as sure as a ripple in the river. A quickening.

The scow slipped into moving water. Jina watched Helena and Ellis recede. "Earl would have run from this river," she said.

Zach nudged the rear sweep, pointed them effortlessly downstream. "That so?"

"He might have written a poem about it once. Now he'd just call us fools."

She put a hand on her stomach. Some right decisions become terribly wrong at a later date. Earl was perfect for her the day he proposed—valedictorian of their Baltimore high school, poetic, confident his would be a romantic, bohemian life. Four months after their wedding, none of his poems had sold, they were still living with his parents, and Earl was mean. Drunk by noon, immobilized by the unromantic practicalities of adulthood, he stopped writing poetry and hit her when she brought up the possibility of entering art school in San Francisco. She covered her bruises with makeup and slept on the sofa, but by then it was too late.

Earl welcomed the news of her pregnancy. "Maybe a baby's what we need," he said. "We'll get our own place. I'll get a job. It'll be real poetry. A romantic life. Better than anything I could have written."

She looked around his parents' frumpy house, with its molting green sofa, the angry wing chairs with their backs to each other in the corner.

"I'm not ready," she said. "Forgive me, but I'm not."

He looked at her in horror. "You don't have any choice."

But, of course, she did.

He beat her to try to stop her. For the last acts of their marriage, they each damaged something beyond repair. When she arrived at the clinic, they had to set her broken bones and stitch her up before they gave her the abortion, and by then she had convinced herself that her life was the most important thing.

Jina heard the roar of the rapids ahead, glanced at the whitewater, then at Zach. He was looking at her, not the run.

"You ready?" he asked.

She took the rear sweep. Zach turned forward, held the front sweep firm. She saw the narrow channel on the right that they were already aiming for.

"Just a little left," Zach shouted over his shoulder.

This time, she did not dig in. She barely dragged the sweep in the water, and the scow turned beautifully. They took a mild course just left of a giant hole and, like magic, like nothing, sailed smoothly through the rapid. Jina whooped. Zach dropped the sweep and kissed her soundly as the boat passed gently, harmlessly, past Otter and Eagle creeks.

"I love you," he said.

She pulled back, eyes moist. It was the first time he'd sounded sure.

6

On their wedding night, Naji told Irene about the jinn. They are not fallen angels, as many in the West believe, nor do they bear any resemblance to the playful genies portrayed in Disney movies and on TV. Created from a smokeless flame of fire, some have wings; others take the form of snakes and dogs. They live in a world parallel to mankind and are invisible, yet they tell the future and can possess the souls of people and trees. Like humans, the jinn choose to be good or bad, and, like humans, evil tantalizes them. Plain and simple, some jinn are out to get you.

The strongest are called *afreet*; the evil jinn are known as *shayateen*, or satans. In Saudi Arabia, where Naji was born, no one breaks free of the devil. Every person has a partner jinn who stalks his every move. There could be one in the corner right now, he told Irene, watching her.

Back then, Irene had laughed. She didn't even bother to look over her shoulder. Who needed a troublemaking jinn when she did such a good job screwing up her life herself? Even managing to land in jail at the age of fifteen. She took Naji to the movies and told him that, in the United States, the *shayateen* got jobs in Hollywood. Evil here was obvious. Violent and stupid, accompanied by guns instead of imagination. Utterly devoid of myth.

Tonight, though, sitting on the damp curb in front of Naji's brother's row house, Irene was not so sure. One of the Muslim hadiths warns people to close their doors and keep their children close at night so the jinn can't snatch things away. *That* was certainly true. If you weren't careful, you could lose everything. You could wake up in the morning with far less than you'd had the night before.

She looked down the road at complicated weavings of electric lines and gingerbread trim, then out toward the San Francisco Bay. Five years ago, Naji's brother followed him to the United States on scholarship to Berkeley. Ahmad was now an electrical engineer who worked twelve-hour shifts at a computer terminal, then another three hours in his foreign-looking garden. Ahmad's tiny yard was overflowing with plants that shouldn't grow in the fog and damp—the Abyssinian banana, red bird of paradise, giant cup-of-gold vine. Even the soil was different—nearly black and ashy, while everyone else planted in sand. He was converting the land one desert plant at a time. He'd spoken more words to his flowers than he had to Irene in the eight years she'd been married to his brother. In the last few days, he had not allowed her to approach his front door.

She strained to hear Naji's voice through the window, but the street traffic was heavy, a constant, low rumble. She'd already called his machine a dozen times just to hear his ancient, endearing message, the one he'd made while still learning the language—"Name thank you. Please number. I call back"—Just to believe, for a moment, that he would.

She heard footsteps and jumped to her feet. But it was only Ahmad. At eleven o'clock at night, he wore pressed dark green slacks, polished shoes, a starched shirt and tie. He walked as if still in the office, hunched forward, clicking his tongue against his teeth.

He came to her side, smelling delicious as always, of spicy cologne and Arabian cigarettes. He was small and refined, only two inches taller than she was, but the truth was, he gave her the heebie-jeebies. Whether she joked or insulted him, he responded identically, with a cold stare. He had skin like old wood, smooth and almost gray, and large, brown eyes set deep and wide. He was handsome and completely unknowable, a jinn perhaps, a creation of another world. Naji had come to the United States because he loved all things American—baseball, blondes, 250 choices of cereal he insisted on counting each time they went to the supermarket. Ahmad came, it seemed, to prove he could live amid American depravity and not be tainted, to withstand gluttony, optional faiths, and women like her. He prayed five times a day, and even that did not seem like enough.

He held a brown cigarette between his forefinger and thumb, pulled a second one from his shirt pocket. She narrowed her eyes, but at this point she wasn't about to refuse even the smallest gesture of goodwill. He lit it for her.

"He wants you to go," he said.

She'd heard him talking to Naji in Arabic, but when he spoke English, he overpronounced, as if Americans misspoke their own language. She had half a mind to pretend she couldn't hear him, but for now he was the bridge between her and Naji—unfortunately, her only hope.

"I'm not going," she said.

He stared at her through the smoke. "He won't take you back. Muslim men do not tolerate infidelity. We are not weak."

"No. You're murderers."

She intended the preposterous stereotype, wanted him to strike. She had a blue belt in karate, and she was dying to use it. Just give her a reason. But surprisingly, Ahmad only smiled.

"Warriors," he said. "*In Sha' Allah*. If God wills."

She glared back at him. "You don't scare me."

He tossed his cigarette into the garden. The butt landed in a stack of spring debris—leaves, deadheaded hyacinths, and lilac blossoms, their petals parchment-dry. He watched her as the pile smoldered, probably trying to curse her. Naji had told her stories of snake charmers, too, and she had the feeling that at any moment she'd go limp and Ahmad would tie her in knots. Upon meeting her, Ahmad had immediately told Naji he was risking hell with marriage to such a woman—someone who flaunted herself in lingerie on television, who thought she could improve on God's design, at least around her breasts, eyes, and bottom lip. Naji had asked her, in his quiet way, to temper herself around Ahmad, to respect his sometimes irrational but fervent beliefs. She'd only laughed. Respect a man who believed her husband ought to hit her if she dissatisfied him in some way? Respect a man who took full advantage of American money and opportunity, yet seemed to wish for the downfall of the country that supplied it? Who watched the news in the days after 9/11 with thinly veiled delight? No way. She'd always figured if Ahmad didn't like what she was doing, it meant she was on the right track.

A strand of petals ignited.

"Ahmad," she said.

He only smiled. The flames inched toward the trailing vines of the cup-of-gold. Irene stepped forward, but Ahmad put out his hand. He had gardener's palms, callused and rough, with a burn mark beneath his knuckles.

The fire slowed when it hit a mound of cool soil. The flames winked, then went out.

"Better than compost," he said. "You'd be amazed what can grow in ash."

The door opened, and Naji stepped onto the porch. Irene raced to her husband's side.

"Naji," she said, then could think of no more. She'd blurted it all out on his answering machine, told a stinking cassette tape how much she loved him, how sorry she was. Before the machine cut her off, she tried to make him understand how different she'd been when she met him. She'd had no practice with honest men. She'd been trying to swim around sharks, all right? She'd lowered her expectations—perhaps even of herself.

"Go," he said. "This is already decided."

He was taller than Ahmad, nearly six feet, and slim. He had soft hands and softer eyes, round and amber-colored, eyes you could drown in. She'd met him on a consultation. He'd examined her breasts completely without ardor, drawing rings around her nipples where he would slide in the silicone and hide the scars. He was kind, darkly handsome, and, most important at the time, rich.

She asked him to dinner six times before he accepted. He wouldn't touch her until her breasts had healed. Over wine, he surprised her by ordering oysters—like any shellfish, an Islamic taboo—and seemed capable of nothing more than staring. She single-handedly carried the conversation, and little by little, Naji's palms unfurled. He realized exactly how little would be required of him, how long she could talk and act for them both. She told him the story of her first audition, which went so badly that she lay on stage and refused to budge. She was given the part of a corpse. Naji laughed at last, reached across the table, and pressed two fingers to her chest.

"A hummingbird's heart," he said. "Boom-boom-boom-boom-boom-*boom*."

She should have known, right then, how much she would grow to love him.

But his worth, along with his words, were softly spoken, and at the beginning of their marriage, she needed declarations, passionate speeches, shouts. She'd had a series of lovers, both before and after Naji, each one more theatrical than the one before, so the quiet adoration of one man hardly registered, an oversight she regretted to this day.

Bill Brandon, a college boy, had been her first, and she found almost instantly that she was good at it. At fourteen, she was limber. She arched her body this way, moved a leg like that, and Bill acted as if she'd handed him the Earth on a platter, as though he'd never find fault with her for as long as he lived.

Within days, she started encouraging him to take up mountain-climbing, to jump off the Karawatee bridge just to see if it could be done.

When she wasn't handing him the Earth, Bill was unbearable—a sports freak, a beer drinker, a dunce. He was either passing out, sucking on toothpicks, or talking about the professional football team he was sure he'd make, despite his small size and poor running speed. *Blah, blah, blah*, she began to say in her head while he made love to her. *Blah, blah, blah*, until she told him they were through. When his eyes got all bulgy and he came at her like the linebacker he'd never be, she almost laughed. What did he think she was, some unprepared, whimpering schoolgirl? She drew her father's gun from the shelf. It wasn't her fault he kept on coming and grabbed her hand. It wasn't her fault, she told the judge, that the gun went off.

While she sat in jail, Bill failed to die, which she took as an apology. Bill's mother wanted her tried as an adult, but this was her first felony, and the victim survived, so she merely got a year's worth of juvenile detention. The day of her release, she ditched her beleaguered parents and hitchhiked west. She lied about her age in order to marry a commercial producer with a mansion in Pacific Heights. He beamed when he showed her off at parties, puffed himself up introducing her to his show-business friends, until he found out she was only sixteen. The marriage was annulled, but by then she was getting bit parts, one as the sweet-but-stupid daughter in a pilot that wasn't picked up, another as a cheerleader in a toothpaste commercial. She took up nude modeling to pay the bills and met Jina, who ignored the broken arm she'd gotten from her husband and enrolled in art school. Irene suggested that Jina throw her wedding ring into the murky waters off the Embarcadero, and Jina convinced her to leak her criminal record to the press. It was the start of great things for both of them. The day Irene's crime story came out in *Variety*, she got the part on the soap.

Irene didn't believe Naji's marriage proposal at first. She searched it for some angle, wanted to know what he expected in return. On their wedding day, his stilted, seemingly heartfelt vows stumped her. Wasn't she the actor here? Naji couldn't tell the difference between her made-up face and her plain one. He couldn't see a gray hair if he tried. He lived beside her without ovations, without fuss, and at first she took this as an obvious sign of indifference—practically an invitation to cheat. It was only later that she longed to know who he saw when he looked at her. Wanted to be introduced.

Naji was so busy with his practice that it was easy to sneak around. At first, she ignored the queasiness in her stomach when she met some pretty boy for a quickie; she chalked up her reservations to the higher moral standards being written into her dying character on the soap. But after a few weeks, it was clear she'd get sick whenever she let another man in the house, and she blamed Naji for this. She turned his home office into a walk-in closet, threw parties on nights that he'd rather go to sleep early, agreed to a seminude layout in *Vanity Fair*, all to no avail. She loved him. At her ugliest, she felt prettier with Naji than she did with any stranger.

She took one last lover—Jacques—even though she couldn't stand him. They were writing her out of the soap at the time, and no other offers were coming in. It was vital, as an actress and a woman, not to back herself into a corner. It seemed plain foolish to love just one thing.

"Silly girl," Jacques told her when she cried every time he kissed her. "Go back to your husband. You're no good to anyone else."

After that, she had trouble sleeping. Naji kissed the circles beneath her eyes, rubbed her shoulders. He bought her the ugliest flannel robe she'd ever seen, and told her she would sleep like an angel in it. Which, surprisingly, she did.

Now Naji said, "In my country, you could be stoned to death."

"Then let's go there," she shot back. She threw down her cigarette, but it didn't spark the way Ahmad's had. The end merely smoldered; a wisp of fog put it out.

"Did you get my messages?" she asked. "I want you to come to Idaho with me. On this rafting trip. You have to give me a chance to explain. Our marriage deserves that much. One week, at least."

"Idaho." Ahmad stepped from the shadows, sneering. "My brother is not going to some wasteland."

"It's not!" Irene said. "The pictures are beautiful. Jina said—"

"This is bad enough," Ahmad said to Naji, ignoring her. "Seeing you here. This is as much as I can stand."

Naji shook his head. "You should have gone home a long time ago, Ahmad. You don't decide for me."

"Are you telling me you'll give her another chance? You'll let a harlot, a devil, into your bed? She shames you."

"No. I shame you. I picked a woman you can't stomach, chose a career you can't abide. I love this place, and you hate it, yes? That's the shame."

"We can go home," Ahmad said. "Let's go home, Naji."

It was the desperation in his voice that got Irene's attention. As if he'd been pleading for weeks and no one had heard him.

Naji turned his back on her to face his brother. Whenever Naji argued details of the Qur'an and jihad with Ahmad, he forgot about her. He rarely agreed with his brother, yet they fought in a disturbingly similar manner, both quoting the Qur'an to support their positions, neither listening to a word the other said. Sometimes Naji looked up, surprised and dismayed to see her still standing there, as if he'd expected her to slink away the way his mother and sisters had when the men got to talking.

"This is my home," Naji said.

Ahmad bowed his head.

"Naji," Irene said, pulling his arm, turning him toward her. "Come with me. One week is all I ask. You can do what you want at the end of it."

He stared at her, and she felt unsteady, felt she was looking into a stranger's eyes, starting all over again. And she had less to offer now, not even the confidence of her youth, the sheen of fame. She was an unemployed, aging actress. A woman he couldn't trust.

He waited an eternity to answer, and when he did, he spoke to Ahmad.

" 'Surely Allah causes those who believe and do good deeds to enter Gardens wherein flow rivers.' "

Ahmad stepped forward. "So you do remember your Qur'an."

"Only the parts that help me."

Ahmad shook his head, laughed. "That's a start."

Irene stared at them, hating both their arguments and their ease with one another, wanting in.

"Naji?" she said.

"I will go if Ahmad comes with me," he said.

Irene stepped back. She really did feel like a hummingbird. Her heart slammed into the bones of her chest; at this speed, she wouldn't last long. For a moment, she wanted to take it all back. She'd never feel comfortable on the river with Ahmad there. He'd hated her from the start; somehow, he'd find a way to sabotage her efforts with Naji. Jina's rapids didn't scare her; she'd always known it was people who weren't safe.

Yet what other choice did she have? It was now or never. It was both of them or none.

She turned to Ahmad, bowed her head. "Please," she said through clenched teeth.

When she looked up, he was staring at the last of the smoke in his garden. "Perhaps I will," he said.

. . .

Irene packed her plainest clothes, the ones Naji liked best. Just before she left, her agent called to tell her she'd lost out on another part, and the sting lasted only a moment. She'd play any role listlessly, like a lovesick girl. In a way, she was lucky: Nothing but Naji registered. It might be months before she summed up everything she'd lost.

When she arrived at Mary's, Irene found her friend at the kitchen table, a full-price offer for her condo in hand.

"I've made a huge mistake," Mary said. "I'm not signing."

Irene took a pen from her purse. "Oh yes you are."

Mary ignored the pen. "What will I do when I come back from the river? I've got no life now. No home, no cats, no job. I've got nothing. Do you realize what I've done?"

Irene sat beside her. "You've done what everyone dreams of and no one has the guts to do. You were on the wrong path, and you blew up the rest of the road." She forced the pen into Mary's hand. "I've never been so proud in my whole fucking life."

Mary smiled hesitantly. "So I'll come back and start over? People do that? They really change?"

Well, Irene thought, but she nodded. "You can't go backwards. That's all I know for sure."

Mary signed the real estate contract as the airport shuttle van pulled up.

When they arrived at Jina's, they found Danny sitting in a bare spot on the lawn, and a boy with twice his muscle slumped against the oak tree. The boy's fashionable haircut—short on the bottom, long on top—covered his eyes.

Jina came down the steps, looking nervously toward the

guest. "That's Charlie," she said. "He's just moved back to town. I thought Danny would like . . ."

Danny pulled tufts of grass from the lawn, apparently not liking much of anything.

"We had all those extra seats on the raft," Jina went on. "The river company said they only filled two of them. It seemed like a good idea to invite him along. He and Danny were great friends before."

Charlie kicked his backpack toward the van.

The great friends didn't speak in the van or at the airport, but on the flight to Boise they argued nonstop. Irene sat in the row in front of them, suffering kicks to the back of her chair.

"You play Mario all the time?" Charlie asked.

Danny's Game Boy beeped. "Not all the time," he said.

"Do too. That's a wuss game. In L.A., everyone's into M ratings. Mature."

"Don't look then," Danny said. "Take a walk."

"Maybe I will. I'll walk right off this fucking plane. That'd show my mom. I was taking surfing lessons, you know? Down at Zuma every weekend. Next thing I know, I'm in some cruddy U-Haul heading north. Home, she calls it. *Right*. Like I won't remember you were turning into a freak even before I left."

"Why don't you go fu—"

Irene reached over the seat, yanked the Game Boy from Danny's hands.

"I'm going to leave it on the whole time," she said with a smile. "Let's see how long the batteries last."

Actually, they lasted through twenty-seven games of Super

Mario Bros., which were more entertaining than Irene would have guessed. She mastered the art of flinging vegetables and got clear to level five. Not bad for her first time. Her thumb ached as the plane descended toward the Boise airport, and she finally looked out the window at a landscape as dull and monochrome as Mary's wardrobe. Wrinkled brown hills, dried-up fields, stunted sandstone high-rises. Only a small swath of green in what they called the City of Trees. It was blazing out. The tarmac sizzled as they landed; the plane rolled up to the gate over a shimmering mirage. Every face pressed to the windows in the terminal was white. She hated the state on sight.

She gathered her purse and carry-on, getting no help from Naji, who had refused to sit next to her, no matter what his ticket said. He'd asked a young man on his way to a job interview at Micron Technology to swap seats with him, and had moved beside his brother.

She always wore silk when traveling, and the moment she stepped into the terminal, she saw that she was the only one who'd dressed up. There'd been a run on zippered exercise pants and neon Lycra shirts, the kind of clothes worn cycling or skiing. The whole town apparently cycled and skied, and that only made her hate it more. No one should be enjoying their exercise while she suffered through two hours of kickboxing.

Down the terminal and into the rotunda, a high-school band was massacring "America, the Beautiful." Red, white, and blue banners were hung to welcome home a troop of National Guardsmen. Channel 7 news was there, along with a smiling governor. It would have been merely a podunk memory to take back to California if a few of the guardsmen hadn't cut their hugs short when Naji and Ahmad appeared.

Irene had to admit that they were the darkest people there, so obviously different that you couldn't help but look. Still, that was no reason for silence. There was no call for people to look scared. Ahmad gave her the heebie-jeebies, but she was just as dangerous, probably more so.

"Is there a problem?" she shouted.

The governor hastily began his speech; Naji studied the compass etched into the terrazzo floor as if it would lead him home.

Their charter flight to Salmon didn't leave from the main terminal. They had to pick up their luggage and head to a hangar near the freeway. Her suitcase was X-rayed again, her .38 revolver, the gun she'd carried ever since Bill came at her, examined, matched with her license, and finally returned to the pocket. An attendant led them through an unmarked door, across the blazing tarmac to a Happy-Meal-propeller plane. Naji knew her fear of small aircraft, but he never glanced at her. He took the seat across from Danny.

Charlie sulked in the row behind them. "No peanuts?" he said.

Naji strapped Danny in. "The bumpier the better," he said. "What do you say, Dan?"

Irene survived the hour-and-a-half flight with her head between her knees. She noticed every loose carpet fiber and a torn scrap of paper with a somehow ominous note scribbled across it: *There is much I'm not telling you, Samantha.* She heard Mary's girlish voice getting louder as she sipped the gin she'd smuggled onboard, and Charlie talking about the great food in L.A., but she concentrated on keeping her breakfast in her stomach. She felt every lurch of the plane, jumped at the slightest change in pressure.

Ahmad finally leaned across the aisle. "Put your feet flat on the floor," he said. "Think of it like a road. A few potholes. A couple dips. No problem."

She raised her head slightly. He was looking out at a landscape she did not understand. Nothing but mountains, pines, and the streak of a river. Nothing to draw the eye. Nothing man-made at all.

She flattened her feet, which did make her feel slightly more secure. They touched down roughly, bumping up and off the runway a few times before finally, thankfully, coming to a halt.

"That was awesome!" Danny said.

"We have jets in L.A.," Charlie said. "They land right on the beach."

The boys elbowed each other to reach the door first, and Charlie, the taller, more athletic boy, won. Danny rubbed the bruise in his side where Charlie had jabbed him with an elbow. The pilot opened the door to late-day sunshine. A blast of warm air, scented with pine, swirled into the plane.

"Thank God," Irene said.

Mary stood in the aisle, smiling drunkenly or giddily, Irene couldn't tell which. Years ago, she'd written Mary off as dull; she'd skimmed the chapters about her in Alice's book, and she was beginning to think both were miscalculations. Mary might have the most interesting ending of them all. Irene hadn't been lying when she'd said she was fucking proud of her. How had she done it ? She was a woman with no career, no ambition, no man, and she'd still taken center stage. Gone from invisible to electrifying, just like that.

"I-dee-ho," Mary said, then stumbled from the plane.

Irene looked out the window. The airport was little more than a short road, a couple of metal hangars, and half a dozen single-engine planes parked on the lot. A fortysomething man sporting water sandals and a deep tan stepped out of a red van to greet them. A tiny gray terrier leapt from the van and ran in circles.

Irene waited until they'd all left, then gently unwound herself from the seat. She took the mirror from her purse and swiped at her smeared mascara. She dabbed on fresh lipstick, took a deep breath, then stepped gingerly from the plane.

"Thought we lost you in there," the man called out. "I'm Drew Cantor. I'll be your guide for the trip. Welcome to Salmon."

Irene raised her hand to shield the sun going down directly behind him. There had to be a town around here, but she saw only farmland, a stack of foothills, and beyond them, the flanks of the Bitterroots.

"We're staying at the Riverside Hotel tonight," the guide went on. "That's about halfway to North Fork, then we've got the two-hour drive in. We'll need to get up early. Let's wait here for the other two in your party, then we'll be off."

He moved out of the sun's path, and she finally got a good look at him. An aging hippie, handsome, blue-eyed, with long, blond hair going gray. He had the legs of a twenty-year-old, brown and well-muscled, brushed with curly, bleached-blond hair. He smelled of coconut suntan lotion. Another day, she would have moved in for a deeper whiff. The terrier ran in circles around him, yipping with happiness.

"This is Jake," Drew said. "Official lunatic river dog."

"Do you know the other two who are coming?" Jina asked.

Drew nodded, smiling widely. "Absolutely. So do you. Alice Aberdeen, the writer, and her husband. She's setting her next novel on the Salmon, a story about a couple running the river. That's the kind of publicity I've been waiting for."

Irene felt the blood leave her face. There was no way Alice was getting on their boat. No way that woman would come within two feet of her. She glanced at Jina, who had gone still. From the moment they'd met in art class, when Irene dropped the robe and Jina winked, Irene had felt a streak of devotion she rarely did with men. Here was a woman with enough flaws to be endearing, enough strength and charisma to admire. The rarest thing: a woman like her, a woman she truly liked.

"Don't worry," Irene said. "If she sets one foot on our raft, it'll be a bloody one."

"Whoa," Drew said. "I thought you were all friends."

"Friends!" Irene said. "Hah. The woman's a first-class bitch."

"I talked to her on the phone. She seemed all right to me." He smiled at Mary, revealing a boyish, lopsided grin at odds with the wrinkles around his eyes. Mary tentatively smiled back. "This is our only boat. It's not like there's anywhere else to put her."

"How about over the side?"

Jina shook her head. "What can she be thinking?"

"She doesn't think," Irene said. "She writes. It's a major problem."

They heard the plane in the distance, sounding wheezy and exhausted as it approached. The pilot circled once, then touched down gingerly, as if mountain soil stung. Mary bit her lip; Drew squeezed her shoulder as he passed, then hurried to the plane. Alice was first to emerge, her newly gold hair limp, a black pantsuit Irene had never seen before wrinkled and damp with sweat.

"Think I could push her in front of the propeller before anyone stops me?" Irene asked.

Jina laughed, and some of the tension slipped from Irene's shoulders.

Jake the terrier leapt into the air as Drew introduced himself to Alice. "It's great to meet you. Your book's all over town. You have no idea how excited I was to hear you wanted to write about this place. I can only do so much from here. Educate the few people who come through. But you, you could write about the plight of the salmon. The toxins being dumped into the river every day. You could actually change minds."

They spoke as Alice's husband emerged from the plane, fumbling with two heavy bags. His tie rose up to slap his face in the wind.

Alice finally turned from Drew, raised her chin. Despicable but brave, Irene had to admit. Acting her way out of a dead end, which Irene admired—though courage wouldn't help her much when she was dead.

Alice headed across the tarmac. The truth was, Irene had never wanted Alice or Mary in the sushi club at all. Jina had invited them in, and Irene had watched carefully for signs that they had more in common with Jina than she did. Like a jealous wife, she suffered every time Jina asked Alice to dinner or met Mary at the movies for a matinee.

You put four grown women into a room together, and they regressed to eight-year-olds. Alliances were made, best friends taken, gossip gleefully exchanged. You put four women in a room together, and someone was bound to get hurt.

Irene stepped forward, but Alice spoke first. "You can say what you want but I won't go away. I won't let it end like this."

"It's already ended," Irene said. "You've got some nerve."

Alice turned from her to Mary. "You understand. Tell them I didn't mean to do any damage. Tell them I never expected this."

But Mary was looking at Drew, who bounced when he walked, much like his happy terrier. Irene found the man unnerving, like a spot of color dancing in the corner of her eye. What kind of man did a boy's job? Still spent all his time outdoors?

"You can just take her bags back," Irene shouted at him as he loaded Alice's luggage into the van. "I mean it. One of us goes, and it's not going to be me."

"Irene," Mary said. "Let's not make a scene."

"A scene? You're worried about a scene? Your whole life has been turned into a joke and you're worried about what I might say in front of some river guide? My God. This woman deserves a lynching! Do you hear me? Don't you dare forgive her now."

When Irene stopped, it was dead silent on the runway. The propellers had stopped; there wasn't a rumble of traffic from the highway. Jina was crying without making any noise at all.

"No," Irene said. "Don't."

"We've got no choice," Jina said. "We're here. She paid. You don't have to talk to her. No one has to be nice. But please, Irene. I can't take much more. Honest to God, I'm having trouble just standing here."

Alice wrapped her arms around herself. Aside from Drew, the men looked miserable, staring at buildings, planes, anything inanimate. Irene wanted to stomp her feet, but instead she stepped toward Alice, jabbed a finger in her face.

"You've made a huge mistake," she said.

Near the van, the boys were oblivious. Jake the terrier had come over to play, and Charlie had responded by putting a foot on the dog's flank. He laughed when Jake squirmed but couldn't get up.

Danny kicked him in the shin. "Jerk."

Charlie released the terrier, stepped toward him. "What did you say?"

"That's enough," Jina said harshly, and Irene could see that it was. Jina walked toward the van, her face drawn. She looked at the mountains as if they were haunted. "Get in the van now."

Mary's shoes had filled with rocks, and she kicked them off, followed the boys to the van barefoot. Irene had her hand on the door when Alice came up behind her.

"You've made mistakes, too," she said.

Irene turned around. Alice had spilled all their secrets but one, the one nobody talked about: All four of them were for sale. Jina for one more whiff of the past, Mary for a different future. There is a price at which every person will sell her soul, and for Alice and Irene it was heartbreakingly low. Just a bestseller and a part in a soap opera, then they were left with nothing but yearning, with the devil, a jinn, inside them.

"Go to hell," she said.

7

Alice had always set her sights too high. As a child, she could have settled for one or two equally odd, well-suited friends, but no, she wanted to be a popular girl—one of those light, giggling creatures whose feet, she swore, never touched the ground. Like them, she wanted to hover above it—winged, dainty, immune. A popular girl's biggest despair appeared to be the wrong color of nail polish or a teacher who bored her, while Alice worried that no one noble ever went into politics, that children were starving, that whales were dying, that poetry was dead. She spent hours alone in her bedroom, crying over the plight of the spotted owl, writing impassioned letters to senators, erudite essays that elicited snickers from her classmates and A's from her teachers. She never ate lunch in the cafeteria—empty seats filled when she approached—and she took her sack lunch to the football field, popular at least with birds.

She was even too weird for the smart crowd. They sighed whenever Thoreau or Yeats were read in class, knowing she would weep. She wanted to tell them it was the precision and depth of the words that moved her, not sorrow, but by then someone had taken her to the nurse, told her to stop embarrassing herself. She knew she was talked about. She was never told secrets.

So she made them up. She wrote love stories the dainty girls put under their mattresses in the hopes that the endings would come true, impassioned pleas for old-growth forests that the *Sentinel* published on their op-ed page. Writing made her briefly popular and, even better, sometimes changed minds. She wrote about what would happen if everyone tried harder, about fairy girls and packs of boys that swarmed like bees across the playground, about lightheartedness and joy that stuck. She wrote happy endings, wrote about everything but herself. She wanted no record of that.

Her grandmother, the poet Norma Meyer, disagreed. When she wasn't in some hospital having her stomach pumped, or dumbed down with mood stabilizers, Alice's grandmother often checked the tear streaks on Alice's cheeks. She counted the crumpled papers and held her hand. One afternoon, she arrived with a journal.

"It won't save you," her grandmother said. "But at least you'll be able to look back and see what went wrong."

Alice filled thirty pages in one night; it was like pricking her finger and letting the poison leak out. She bought another journal, and another, and crammed the pages with things only freaks know—how it feels to hate not only your baby fat and glasses but also how you breathe, how you think, the way your arms swing. How it feels to walk into a room that suddenly goes quiet. She wrote of the feeling that she was made up not of blood and bones but of sharp objects—glass shards, blades, metal edges. Every step that she took hurt.

After high school, she became even more prolific. In college, after John Aberdeen dumped her, Alice filled an entire journal with how idyllic their life would have been. They both carried Greenpeace membership cards, had met at one of her grandmother's poetry readings. John's hair was bleached blond and long then; it grazed her cheek every time he bobbed his head to her grandmother's dismal beat. Alice invited him backstage, where Norma was holding court, laughing with that horrible glint in her eyes, the one Alice knew meant that she was screaming inside and, as soon as she was done, would drink herself into a stupor. He took Alice out for coffee, hoping for more insight into the great poet, wondering how Alice thought her own writing compared to her grandmother's.

Alice hid her work from him until he dumped her two months later, then she graced him with one line. One line that demonstrated just how disciplined a writer she could be when she tried. One line that said it all. She mailed it to John, and he arrived the next day, his eyes and body eager, his mind bent around her words.

I'll do anything.

Which she did, until he married her and outgrew causes and

poetry. Until he became a busy insurance agent, read only Tom Clancy, and asked her to be happy—the one thing you can't ask of anybody. You can love them or leave them, but you can't tell them how to feel.

After the wedding, Alice dropped out of college to write full-time. She dabbled at poetry, mostly because people expected her to follow in her grandmother's footsteps, but she needed the length of a novel to see her characters through. Norma Meyer, whose most celebrated poetry was a series of gloomy sonnets written just before her suicide, would have been horrified to know that her granddaughter insisted on happy endings. But Alice was adamant. Her characters started out like her—odd, insecure, melancholy—and she saved them. She gave them popularity *and* nobility, love and a chance to save the world. Joy was as tangible and finite as the tape at the end of a race. You broke through and were done.

She finished her first novel the year she gave birth to Roger. At first she thought she could shield her son from her own peculiarities, that her melodrama would stop once she became a mother. But, in truth, Roger made things worse. His infant smell penetrated every corner of the house. Tending to him day and night gave her her greatest joy and a sense of sinking. For months, she was too tired to write; all her stories felt soggy, preverbal, confused.

The doctors told her it was postpartum depression. She went to a psychiatrist who, ironically, gave her the same antidepressant her grandmother had been on when she killed herself. Alice could have predicted that the pills wouldn't work. She wasn't hopeless; she aimed for too much. She wanted to never make a mistake with Roger, wanted mothering to be enough, or at least writing well to be its own reward. She wanted nothing but Roger's happiness one minute, the recall of the antienvironment governor the next. She wanted hordes of friends, then solitude, a bigger house, then no house at all. She wanted different things every day; sometimes, she didn't know what she wanted, but she was certain she didn't have it. She lived in a constant state of desire, her blood always a degree or two too warm, her shoulders hunched, her neck tight, her palms sweating when she tried to do the simplest task, a task any normal woman could do easily, even happily, like giving her own baby a bottle.

After Alice's grandmother shot herself, Alice's mother replayed the torment of being the daughter of a *poet*, while Alice suffered with shame that her grandmother's death felt inevitable and almost like a relief. They went through all the stages of mourning, plus the part no one dared mention: The children of a suicide are given another option—a horrible but effective way out.

Three months after the antidepressants failed to work, Alice walked into her garage. She turned on the engine of the car but should have known a house of such mediocre quality would not have an airtight seal. She got sick but didn't even pass out from the carbon monoxide. She ran inside to vomit, and was back in bed, her usual haunt, by the time John got home, and apparently she always shook that way because he said nothing. He fixed himself dinner, didn't comment on the fact that she'd left the car running in the garage. When she said in a whisper that she was fine, he smiled, wanting to be fooled. He'd married a woman he thought he could make happy. He loved Alice's writing and believed she would be a success. His loyalty was nearly unbearable.

Yet, in the end, he was right. On a Tuesday morning, Alice's Ohio agent, the only one who would take her on, called to announce a $3,000 offer on her first novel as if it were a million dollars and a movie deal—which it felt like at first. Alice and John made love for the first time in months; she cleaned the kitchen, got a stylish new haircut, and wrote furiously once again. For a while, happiness really was as simple as getting what she wanted.

Until critics called her a talentless hack. Until only five thousand mass-market originals were printed, and half of those were returned and stripped. Until she became the freak of the publishing world, too. She changed agents, this time to one in Pennsylvania, and four more books sliced from her soul were put out with horrible covers and no marketing, giving them a three-week shelf life at best. She realized there was only so much she could do, and if no one gave her a chance, there was nothing she could do. She had another child, Sue, and worried that a girl was the most likely to take after her mother in mood and misery.

Like many mothers, she faked bliss. She laughed when Sue yanked her hair, gave up on the absurd notion of a toy-free living room, stopped wondering what childless women did with all their time. She wrote when Sue napped, then took her children to the park, pushed a stroller around the mall to no purpose, put on makeup even when she'd be seeing no one but toddlers that day. She watched purple dinosaurs with her daughter and sang about friendship, but she didn't believe it until three women hung around after a book signing at Rakestraw. One of them, tiny as a pixie, touched her softly on the arm.

"I had to meet you. Your characters . . . I loved how they persevered. They were beautifully written. They sang."

Alice looked from her to the woman she recognized from TV, to a third who stared at her shoes. She started crying. The pixie put an arm around her.

"I'm Jina," she said. "This is Irene and Mary. We're going out for sushi. Why don't you join us?"

In the beginning, they laughed and called her "the emotional one." It was only later that Alice noticed Irene rolling her eyes. That Jina stopped calling so much.

The trouble with ambition is that it leaks. It trickles from work to relationships to bodies to home repair, until nothing you have is in the shape you'd like it to be. Ambition, more than time and hard living, ruins the complexion, alienates family and friends. It depreciates the value of houses, spoils lazy summer afternoons.

Every day, Alice taught Sue how to write the alphabet or worked up a sheet of subtraction facts for Roger. She went on a new diet or painted a bedroom, despite the half-completed wallpaper in the bath. She forced herself to write one page more than the day before, and her notes spilled from her office to the hall to the kitchen; manuscript pages commandeered the dining table, and the family had to eat on the floor. The computer hummed day and night; bills for books and paper became astronomical.

Roger stopped bringing friends over. It was embarrassing, he said. She was always in her pajamas, revved up on some project, wide-eyed. Other mothers fed their kids apples, not Hershey bars. They decorated with chintz instead of purple paint.

The result of her relentless work was three novels in one year, all of them rejected by her publisher. She was dumped once more and, though her agent found her another house six months later, by then she was dreaming unhappy endings, species that couldn't be saved, stories that went nowhere. To friends and family, it seemed sudden and incomprehensible when she slashed her wrists. She'd seemed so energized, so dedicated to her work! Her mother was horrified, the sushi club shocked, and Alice hated them for not seeing the obvious: She could no longer save even fictional creations. She didn't know where to begin with herself.

The hospital psychiatrist told her she hadn't really wanted to kill herself; if she had, she'd have dug in the blade. John said he couldn't live without her, her children told that Mommy had suffered an accident but would be fine. It was the sushi club who enticed her from that bed, who sent a card that sowed the seeds they would regret later: *Who will write our story?*

She was hopeless: Even in the hospital, doped up, the skin on her wrists still raw, the ideas slithered in. The Virgin Maria. The River of No Return. Sex, Lies, and a Smoking Gun. Snakes, each of them, that stared her down, refused to budge. She squeezed her eyes shut, tried to sleep, but her dreams were all surprise endings, plot twists no one had used before. The middle of a book sapped her confidence; endings, in some way, always disappointed. But beginnings were nothing but anticipation and potential, and maybe that was happiness. Maybe a start was all anyone could ask. She begged for a computer, asked John to take her home.

On the porch of the Riverside Hotel, Alice looked down at the Salmon River—so slow and mild, it could have been a backyard canal, one of Roger's hose-created puddles. Beyond the lazy stretch of water was a red-rock cliff and periwinkle sky. She sipped Fume blanc from a southern Idaho winery, listened to the last strains of a Bach concerto coming from the piano player in the lodge's great room. It was like a hotel plucked out of Danville, dropped down into better scenery. If Irene hadn't been lurking around, glaring at her, it would have been perfect—something she hadn't thought about in a while, something worth saving. The starting point of her new book.

She glanced down the porch, where John sat on a cedar rocker, not drinking, though he could certainly use a pop. He'd hardly spoken since they'd dropped the kids at her mother's. He'd looked out the window of the plane and refused to respond to her comments about the flight attendant there to serve only them, the delicious canapés, and homemade ice cream. He'd been as thrilled as she was when the buzz about this book began to grow, when the movie offer came in, when their bank account grew so quickly that they couldn't find enough things to spend the money on. He'd been with her every torturous step of the way and had always called her his poet. He'd taken a job in insurance claims, a job he didn't particularly like, so they'd have a steady salary coming in. So she could do what she said she loved.

He deserved some reward—not just a week to bask in the sun but the opportunity to see that she could step out of her stories once in a while. She could swim and roast marshmallows around a campfire; she could be real. So far, he hadn't taken much advantage of the offering. Like Irene, he seemed stunned that she could expect so much, that a person of her age and experience hadn't yet figured out the difference between what we want and what we actually get.

She crossed the porch. In front of the lodge, a meadow stretched to the river. Danny and Charlie threw a baseball, though Charlie seemed to be aiming for Danny's head instead of his arm, and Danny threw like a girl. It had taken every ounce of courage Alice had to show up here. She'd known Irene would explode, but she'd imagined winning her over with arguments for forgiveness and with poignant, well-spoken verse. She'd envisioned the scene like a mass-market writer would, in fast-paced clips, with characters she could transform in a heartbeat. She'd always been better on paper. On paper, she hadn't been cruel. While she'd been writing the novel, she'd hurt *for* her friends; she wrote their stories and wrapped herself around their pain. *The Secret Lives of the Sushi Club* reminded her of those stories she'd written in grade school, the ones about someone else. For the first time in years, writing wasn't a solitary profession.

Alice looked away. She literally ached for her children—felt Roger on the left beneath her heart, Sue like a tug on her right shoulder. She'd left them at her mother's, and neither had given her a kiss on the way to Grandma's candy jar. Roger hadn't squeezed her hand the way he might have a few months ago, or asked if she was all right. In his mind, thank God, the success of the book had cured her. She got dressed in the morning now, put healthy snacks in his lunch box, and that was that. He'd started inviting friends over again, and nothing in the world would make her ask him to turn down the music or stop stomping around in his bedroom. Nothing in the world should make a child worry what his mother would do.

She took the chair beside her husband. The piano music stopped, and the sound of the sluggish river quickly filled the void. A hawk circled the meadow, and Danny got distracted. The ball hit him on the knee hard.

"Hey!" Danny said, blinking so he wouldn't cry.

Jina got to her feet, but Danny shook his head fiercely. Charlie ran for the ball and flung it toward a tree. The boy cheered when bark went flying.

"Good dinner," John said.

She nodded. Leg of lamb, spinach fresh from the garden out back, grilled asparagus, double-chocolate cake in the shape of an Idaho russet.

"You don't think I should have written it," Alice said.

John stiffened. His once sun-bleached hair was brown now and receding, his stomach more lump than sinew, and she loved him better this way. He read her novels from start to finish in two days and never found a single flaw. He was a terrible editor but a lovely fan, a better husband than she could have written.

She reached out, and she chose to believe he didn't see her before he got out of his chair. He stepped to the railing, watched the first star come out.

"No, I don't think you should have written it. I don't think you should write anymore."

For one moment she knew he was right. She curled forward, assumed the posture of those who do what makes sense but not what fulfills them. Then she set her wineglass on the porch and stood.

"How can you say that? Didn't you always want me to succeed?"

He turned. She'd wished for everything to change, which was the worst wish in the world—the wish of teenagers and fools and the unimaginative, anyone who doesn't realize that there can be worse things than what you've already got. Catastrophically, her wish had come true. She now loved John more than when they started, and he loved her less.

"I've only wanted you to be happy. That's not the same thing."

Alice's eyes welled up, but even better than the money and notoriety of a bestseller was the way it held her together, as if victory was made of glue. There was no way she'd make even success unbearable. She took a deep breath, stopped the tears.

"When did persistence become a dirty word?" she said. "When did it become a sin to want recognition and security and even, yes, a little fame? What is so terrible about wanting to feel good about myself, just for once? I could use the money to help save the whales or stop old-growth logging, all those things that used to eat me up inside. I can do something now, John."

"Writing isn't good for you," he said. "Surely you see that."

"Having children hasn't been especially good for me, either. Was I supposed to stay childless so I'd never get worked up? Face facts, John. Sometimes you have to do exactly the thing that will hurt you. Sometimes that's what life is."

The door of the lodge burst open, and Drew strode onto the porch. Irene, with that same glare, Naji, and that quiet brother of his followed him out. Drew called Jina, Danny, and Charlie in from the meadow.

"A couple of announcements," the guide said. His sunglasses still hung on a string around his neck, his teeth glowed like the first stars. He seemed inordinately happy, as if he were another species. "We'll leave at seven in the morning. Have a safety lesson, get you fitted for life jackets, hit Gunbarrel by ten and Dad's lodge by noon. You'll have some thrills, but more important, you'll stay safe and leave your worries behind. When we take out at Riggins, you'll all be different people. I personally guarantee it."

Irene raised an eyebrow. Most likely, there was nothing about herself that she wanted to change. Yes, her career had slid in recent years, and she had no real hobbies or talents to fill the void, but she was still recognized on the street, her husband was ludicrously rich. While writing the book, Alice had tried to get inside Irene's skin and understand why a woman would cheat on a good husband, risk such a blessed life, but Alice admitted that she might not have made the character Elaine entirely sympathetic. Elaine was the first heroine whose story ended unhappily—Alice left her in a tiny apartment in Phoenix, all alone except for a mean-spirited cat. She wasn't proud of it, but during the course of the book, Alice might have even chuckled a time or two in glee.

They locked gazes for a moment, and Alice felt stung by the obvious: Even before the book, Irene hadn't liked her. What an accomplishment, a tremendous feat of acting for them both: They'd been pretending to be friends for years.

"I've got a bit of an agenda, as my dad calls it," Drew said, laughing. He passed out leaflets. "I can live with that. At least I'm not making widgets anymore. I wake up every morning and have a chance to *do* something. How many people can say that?"

The blue brochure documented the life of a salmon from egg to smolt to sockeye, the problems the fish ran into from predators, spoiled habitat, and, mainly, from dams. The Snake River dams were particularly suspect, built during the Cold War as a show of strength for the Soviets and, surprisingly, offering no flood-control storage. According to Drew's pamphlet, all four Snake River dams were virtually worthless as sources of hydroelectric power, generating only three and a half percent of the region's energy and turning just one or two turbines at a time in contrast to the ten turning on the Columbia River dams. But when those turbines did turn, they shredded salmon to bits, drowned them in slackwater. By 1986, all coho salmon traveling through the Snake River corridor had become extinct.

At one time, these dismal facts would have sent Alice to her room in tears; maybe the trouble wasn't crying too much but outgrowing the need to weep. *She* had been dying, that's what she wanted to say. She'd been trying to save herself.

"Fifty percent of your fare goes to the Salmon Conservation Fund," Drew said. "I haven't taken a salary in three years. You picked a great time to come. We're getting the wild spring salmon runs, and the flush from the hatcheries. An incredible sight. Salmon swim backwards, if you can believe it. They have incredible homing devices that lead them thousands of miles, over years at a time, to the sea and back to their birth river. They're not just fish. They're spiritual creatures."

Irene rolled her eyes, but the others were listening. Mary had moved forward until her arm brushed Drew's sleeve. He smiled at her.

"The trouble is people," Drew went on. "We can't take a step without ruining something. I can't speak for the other companies, but I'm adamant about keeping the canyon pristine. We leave it how we found it. We try to make no impact at all."

"Will we see any wildlife?" Mary asked, and Alice heard the tremor in her voice. She had goose bumps on her arms, even though the wind was warm.

Drew turned to Mary. "We almost always spot deer and elk, wolves and bear if we're lucky. Once in a blue moon, Cal Shroeder will come out of his dugout. Men are the wildest things we get in the canyon."

Charlie perked up. "Yeah?"

"There's one trail down in Black Canyon I warn people not to take," Drew said. "There's a woman at the end, Pearl. She's got a son who's slow, and she's protective as a grizzly. Probably would have mauled someone by now if it wasn't for her husband, Zach."

For a moment, there was no sound. Even the river seemed to hush. Alice looked across the porch at Jina, who gripped the railing.

"Pearl's the extreme," Drew said quickly. "Most people come here for the quiet, a shot at a different kind of life. They're a little strange, maybe, but they won't bother you. I grew up in

L.A., took jobs everywhere but here, so I heard the same horror stories you did. The white supremacists up north, the anarchists in the woods, the antigay, antiabortion, antieverything far right. Believe me, I wouldn't have come here if there wasn't hope. We're a magnet for extremists, probably because we've got so many hiding spots, and we don't interfere. Most Idahoans think people should have a chance to come to their senses on their own. We'll shield fools, if all they need is time."

Irene asked Drew something about the campsites, and Alice took the opportunity to cross the porch to Jina. She'd always dwarfed her, but the difference in their heights seemed more substantial here—as if they'd arrived with shadows.

"He'll be everywhere now," Jina said, her voice worse than Irene's. Not angry at all, but on the verge of panic. "You've resurrected him."

Mary walked across the meadow, blades of grass tickling her bare knees. Though it was well after midnight, it was rush hour—a whizzing, zipping, crackling mad dash. Ordinarily, she'd have retreated indoors, gotten into bed, and sealed herself off to the neck, but tonight the skimming of wings across her T-shirt and neck charmed her, as if she was being welcomed and fussed over, drawn forward by the barest of tugs.

All night, she'd been imagining herself as one of those people you read about in the newspaper or listen to over sushi. A daring, if foolish, woman who, on her first adventure, meets tragedy on the Salmon River. She marveled at how the idea of this transformed her in her own mind, made her thinner, stronger—doomed perhaps, but also a better read. She was stunned by how jealous she'd felt of Jina all along.

Mary reached the trees along the river, sighed when her bare feet touched sand. She didn't think there was much chance she'd die on this trip; the brochure had stated emphatically that the Salmon Adventure Company had seen no serious injuries in ten years of guided river trips. Flows were high in June, which meant fast water but easier maneuvering. Drew had seemed more concerned with stocking their favorite wines than first-aid kits. She was paying $1,300; of course it was safe. But some combination of risk and Drew's smile made her feel giddy nonetheless.

Drew. He was as exotic as this place. Every time he looked at her, her heart raced. She forgot her timidity, forgot who she was exactly. She met the river's edge, tested the water with her toes. She leapt back, not at the iciness, but because it was alive. Mary knelt down to scoop the water, came up with a handful of two-year-old silver smolts. Thousands of Idaho sockeye were swimming backward, their eyes looking toward their mountain home, as if anguished to part with it. She ran her hand down their glossy skins, imagined liquid silver sliding through her fingers. Gently, she returned the creatures to the river, where they shimmered around her feet like silver anklets.

At first, she mistook the figure in the center of the river as a swarm of them, then she saw the toes pointed downstream, a muscled arm thrown out for balance, a slick but human torso.

She'd have fled in another life, but that was the beauty of wilderness and strangers. You could be whomever you wanted in front of them. You could make someone up and become her.

She stepped forward, up to her knees, her shins, the hem of her shorts.

Drew came to his feet like a river king, naked. "I was hoping I'd see you," he said.

She held her breath so long that she made herself dizzy. She felt tender to the touch; the slightest breeze stung her. The chirping of the crickets was deafening. She kept her gaze above Drew's waist, where he was hairless, all sinew, like a piece of river himself.

She opened her mouth and the words spilled out. "I hoped so, too," she said.

She was stunned at how calmly she stood there. How little difference could be detected after everything had changed.

"Amazing, isn't it?" he said. "They're heartbroken, but they go anyway. Just babies, but they'll try to swim to the ocean. Most don't make it, but the few who do put in another ten thousand miles at sea. They throw themselves through turbines, actually transform their bodies to adapt to seawater. And a couple years from now, if they've survived predators and fishing lines and dams, they'll turn around and come back, knowing it's fatal. If they reach their mountain streams, they'll lay their eggs and die."

It was like catching fire internally. Like being torched, devastated, and no one knew. Mary's fingers burned; sweat broke out behind her ears. She searched for a safe topic of conversation, experiences they might have shared, and felt oddly invigorated at her lack of ideas. Wanting him was like stepping onto a new planet, smelling and feeling things she'd never known existed.

He scooped a rock from the river, turned it over in his hands.

With an effortless sideways swing, he skipped it across the surface of the water once, twice, three times.

"You see that?" he said, smiling like a little boy. "Three skips and you get a wish."

His optimism shocked her more than his nudity: At his age, at her age, he still believed his wishes could come true. "Aren't you cold?" she asked.

Drew laughed. "What's a little discomfort for a chance to be with them, feel their energy? It's a rare honor in this day and age to be in the company of creatures with purpose. You should try it."

She stiffened, knowing she'd been identified as a woman with no point, called out by a man who, most likely, had never been able to hold a desk job. "I don't know that fish are worth dying for."

She expected him to get angry, to spout statistics, environmental mumbo jumbo. But he only smiled and stepped forward. Desire felt so much like fear—a bubble in the stomach, hairs raised on the back of the neck—that she wondered if she'd misread her mother's tears all those years, if they'd both been confused.

She glanced down, didn't need moonlight to see him clearly.

"What is, then?" he said. "I asked myself that question when I came here five years ago. What matters to you, Mary? That's what I want to know."

He folded his body back into the water, pointed his feet toward the slight whitewater ahead. The river carried him and, at the first rock, swept him harmlessly, tenderly, around the danger. In a few minutes, most of the sockeye had gone with him.

A single smolt lay on the riverbank, gasping at the toxic air. She bent down, cradled the tiny salmon in her hand, looked where it looked. She pictured an alpine stream, the water so clear you could see the rocks on the bottom, a mound of sun-colored eggs, an obvious purpose. She still heard her name on his tongue.

She dropped her hand in the water, nudged the last smolt downstream. Perhaps it wasn't as impressive a journey as the salmon's, but for Mary, deciding to sit in the sand to await the return of a river king would do.

8

It's said that the Salmon's first river runner, Johnny McKay, met Satan and knocked out his teeth with a sweep. The excised molars became Devil's Teeth Rapid, which Jina and Zach ran easily on the left. A little tug of the sweep was all Jina needed. She looked upriver at the daunting teeth poking through the whitewater and stood in the middle of the scow.

"You see how I handled that?" she said.

Zach smiled, the lines around his blue eyes crinkling. "I saw it."

The sparse, brown hills were giving way to grand fir trees and water-loving understory plants like bluebells and twinflowers. Jina saw a bank of gargantuan, tropical-looking ferns, and a waterfall halfway up the slope; it seemed they were entering a remnant of lush, primordial forest. The air was humid, rich;

she breathed so deeply that she hardly noticed their passage through Little Devil's Teeth Rapid, an easy glide.

Two miles later, Zach pulled the boat to a white sand beach littered with river debris—gray logs, rusted Coors Light cans, pieces of shredded orange rubber. On the bluff above them, trail plants and pines surrounded a tiny, derelict cabin.

"Johnny Briggs's old place," Zach said, tying up the scow. "There's something I want to show you."

They hiked a steep path, the stream beside it engulfed by wild raspberries. Within minutes, Jina was sweating beneath her wool jacket and gloves. Zach walked briskly and didn't look back. He took no breaks, and she refused to ask for one. They hiked for an hour over scree fields and through groves of ponderosas that had been ravaged by wildfire but somehow continued to thrive. Their bark was like body armor, taking the scorching while the inner wood remained safe.

They climbed above the tree line, across a tricky moraine. Jina watched her feet, though what really unnerved her was the silence. Zach said nothing, and she couldn't hear the river. She saw nothing except the tops of trees. It was enough of a challenge to survive the river; next time, she would contemplate the 2.4 million acres of wilderness surrounding it.

Halfway across the moraine, the wind picked up, low-pitched, rumbling, like argumentative men. They reached the summit, then without pause descended into the next valley. Jina's legs ached in her effort to keep up; her lungs burned. Around a turn, Zach caught a glimpse of her and touched her arm.

"Not much farther," he said. "Come on."

Not much farther was a half mile to the edge of a cliff. She saw nothing there but a dead ponderosa, its trunk hollowed out and home to owls, and endless sky. Zach skirted the tree and started down a terrifyingly steep path. She followed sideways, one hand clinging to the crumbling soil above her, a foot stretched out below, trembling as she tried to glue it to the mountain. She didn't see the steam until she was nearly in the water.

Zach smiled triumphantly. Beneath them, perched on a narrow ledge with a hundred feet of straight descent beneath it, was a perfectly formed natural hot spring, its water as blue as the turquoise Jina had hidden in Zach's bag.

"I thought you might like a bath," he said.

Jina rested her cheek on his arm. She saw that with him everything would require just a little more than she wanted to give; with him she would stretch. She might not end up like herself at all, and the thought was more dizzying than the elevation. She sat to remove her boots, pulled off her sweat-drenched shirt. She'd left her hairbrush at Ellis's lodge, but luckily Zach preferred her this way—unshaven, unbrushed, her smell becoming indistinguishable from the river.

Zach went off exploring while she scrambled to the granite tub. It was almost too hot to stand, but she sunk down anyway. The rock bottom was smooth, the water neck deep. Someone had cut a bench seat on one side, carved out an overflow where the steaming water fell in a narrow waterfall to the creek far below, sparking all kinds of strange, orange vegetation.

She closed her eyes for a moment, and when she opened them, Zach stood on the ledge above her, naked as Pan, dotted with yellow poplar leaves and pine dust. She imagined a child growing up in this wilderness, running barefoot, holding a gun before he learned how to read. She imagined herself with hair like Helena's, down to her waist, river-washed.

Zach let out a "Bonzai!" and she moved aside, expecting a splash. But he just laughed, walked down the trail with the surefootedness of a mountain goat, and eased himself carefully, one inch at a time, into the water, more wary of comfort than anything else.

She took his hand, which flared red at the sudden heat. She imagined that the child inside her, conceived in summer, cradled in heat, might be born seven months from now with freckles already on his skin. With no fears at all.

She could tell Zach. Right now. His answer would become another breeze, a whistle of delight or a long-winded argument. She could fight for the other side this time.

Or she could stay alone with him a little longer.

Zach stretched out his long legs, closed his eyes. There was an angry bite swelling above his temple, a cut along his cheek. His red hair was a mess, far beyond a comb, yet she saw what he must have wanted her to see, what he'd been telling her all along. As long as the view was good, the people beside you looked fine.

"We're making terrible time," he said. Without opening his eyes, he put a hand on her knee, slid it upward.

She closed her eyes. Zach's hand found her stomach, the sensitive line between rib cage and breast. She hummed, not a song at all but a monotone chorus like the river, all the notes blended into one. He moved over her, pinning her with hands on either side of her hips. She leaned back against the smooth rock that was slowly being eaten away by mineral water.

"That's what we'll tell them," he said, kissing her eyelids, her lower lashes where sweat had already beaded. "When we don't show up at Vinegar Creek. When we evade the search party and stay here another year, maybe two. We'll tell them we just made terrible time, lost track of the days. We slept through winter, woke up with leaf garlands in our hair."

The water was slick, oily. He slid inside her easily. She opened her eyes but couldn't see his face through the steam. There was only the wind's squabbles, the echoing debates, the wilderness making love to her.

Afterward, she lay on a rock by the spring, her flaming skin impervious to the forty-degree air, the slap of the breeze. She rested her hand on her stomach, which was still flat but harder. As if she was growing a shell first.

"Zach," she said.

But he was already dressed again, moving up the trail, hopping from ledge to ledge to check out every precipice and view. She stayed silent, gave him what Earl had refused to give her— a little more time to himself. She would tell him about the baby when they were in sight of Riggins. The news would be the next great wilderness to face.

"We'll be heading into Black Canyon today," Zach said after breakfast. "Most humbling scenery on the planet."

Jina rinsed their plates in the river, still bleary-eyed. She'd come to bed after him, was sitting beside the campfire when he crawled out of the tent. She might have tossed and turned all night; he wouldn't know. Whenever he was by the river, he fell asleep the moment his head hit hard ground.

He took the plates from her and stored them in the scow. "After that," he said, "civilization will start creeping back in. The Allison Ranch is being transformed into a Christian retreat. The Whitewater Ranch has a landing strip, guest suites."

She touched her stomach. She'd grown fond of the gesture, and he prayed that she wasn't thinking of starting a family yet. There was plenty of time to settle down, far too much flat land to do it on. This was no place to begin a life; it was where you ended it or proved its worth. There wasn't a cliff or bar that wasn't marked with warning signs, child-sized graves. Coy Lansbury at Lantz Bar, Rose Cook and her stillborn child at Campbell's Ferry, and just beyond them, poor five-year-old Norman Wolfe, who slipped out of his father's hands into the swollen river. He wondered if he should mention these tragedies, scare her just a bit. Or at least say that after twenty-five years on a farm he wanted time to be responsible for no one but himself. Maybe that wouldn't sound as bad to her as it did to him.

She put on his life jacket, and he triple-tied the straps to cinch it, laughed at her tiny arms dangling out the sides. It wasn't pretty, but it would keep her afloat. He squeezed into the vest he'd taken from her. The edges bit into his shoulder; he could get only one buckle snapped. They shoved off, floated past Corey Bar. Black Canyon didn't officially begin until Arctic

Creek, but the cliffs were getting ready, leaning in over the water. Like vultures, patiently waiting.

They floated into shadows, wouldn't see the sun again until the canyon walls receded close to Barth.

In a mile they hit Arctic Creek, the Smith place up on the left, Salmon Falls roaring just beyond it. Whitewater sprayed upward, then disappeared over an edge. Zach dug in the sweeps, pulled the scow to the still water on the right above the falls. He tied off on a large boulder. He'd always known this was coming but still hadn't planned what he would say.

Years ago, the rapid was called Black Canyon Falls, and even Guleke had had trouble with it. To stop the drownings, it was repeatedly dynamited, and over time it became a relatively easy run if you had water. Today, Zach noticed the sound of extremely low flows—like fists on bare flesh, like a beating.

"I need to take a look," he said. "At low water, it's a difficult run."

He hopped out of the scow, made his way from boulder to boulder to the edge of the falls. At high water, the rapid was fast and washed out; today it was a minefield of rocks. Technically, there were three slots to run, but at this point in the season none of them looked possible. Jina didn't have the expertise to steer through even the widest run without damage. He'd have to take both sweeps on his own, maneuver perfectly.

Jina met him on the rocks. The skin on her face was windburned, ruddy, but when she saw what lay ahead, she went pale.

"Look at that," she said. "We'll have to line it."

He stiffened. Ellis was a good man, but his lodge was a problem. There shouldn't be mattresses in the wild, or men telling you to take care with a rapid that Cap Guleke had faced when it was even harder.

"We don't have to line it," he said. "I can do it."

Jina looked at him, then out to Salmon Falls. She slid her foot outward on the rock, almost to the edge. She had more chance of falling in here than she did on the river. There were a thousand more ways to die on land than in water.

"Zach, look at it," she said. "There's so little water. It's all rocks. We'll break apart."

"No. Not over there. See that? The left slot? We can slip through. It would take us half a day to line, and you have no idea how hard it would be. The scow is waterlogged. You really think you can hold four tons, with that rapid trying to steal away your line? We'd have to edge along the bank, and you tell me if there's anywhere we can get a solid footing. If we run it, we're done in a few seconds. We're through."

She looked past the falls to the beginning of Black Canyon, ebony monoliths rising two hundred feet straight up on either side. One damn thing after another, rafters often said, and he was glad. There was no point in being scared; it was vital to recognize, on a daily basis, how small and fragile a human life really was. That was why that Christian retreat they were putting in was superfluous. Rivers taught you how to pray.

Jina returned to the scow, took a seat with her back to him. He ran his fingers through his hair. He felt beat-up, torn, as if he'd battled Salmon Falls already. He walked back along the rocks, grabbed the line. He began fashioning handholds, knots, anything that would aid the grip.

"We'll still need to get to the left side of the river to line it," he said, not looking at her. "We'll walk along the shore as best we can. You can't let go, Jina. I don't care if you're not strong enough. Even if you slip into the river, you can't let go."

She looked up, blinked. Of course it was a lot to ask of her. He expected her to run every rapid, never show fear. Of course it was too much, but it was what he needed. He saw that now. He was a terrible lover—narrow-minded, demanding, harsh. He'd love only one kind of woman: the kind who could survive.

Abruptly, she yanked the rope from his hands. Immediately, the scow was swept into the grip of the current, heading out toward Salmon Falls without him.

"You better get in!" she shouted, and he hopped into the scow just in time and took both sweeps in his hands.

It was an incredible feat of steering. Zach strained at the sweeps, used every ounce of strength he had to hold the scow above the falls until he could guide them to the left side of the river. He positioned them above a channel only two inches wider than the scow. He said nothing and never took his eyes from the horizon line of the falls as the current took them forward.

They fell over the edge. Whitewater engulfed them; Jina couldn't be sure Zach was still there. She might have screamed, but the sound was a whisper in the torrent. They were a pebble in the surf, one moment on the crest and the next scraping river bottom. She heard the horrible grinding sound of rocks against wood, a terrifying crack on the flank. She imagined the boat breaking into pieces, wood splitting and shattering, the two of them thrown or swallowed up, then she heard Zach holler. The boat spun, suddenly evened out. She raised her head, found the scow safe below the falls, ensconced in an eddy. Zach wrapped her in his arms. He was shaking from head to foot.

"You imbecile," she said.

He kissed her hard on the mouth. She touched her stomach as the scow circled the eddy. The baby ran it, too, and much later she would notice he had no fear of water. He'd learn to swim when he was two, open his eyes underwater. He'd love all things wet.

She cried from jubilation. There were not enough rapids left to prove what she could do. They'd have to start over again.

"Next time I'm steering," she said.

Zach touched her cheek. He'd been crying, too, probably through the whole ride down Salmon Falls, and she wondered if he had any idea how much he needed her, how little this would have meant if she hadn't been here to witness it. She put her hand over his, vowed never to tell him, to let him go on thinking himself a hermit, mountain-tough and immune.

A sliver of light whittled through a slot in the cliffs. Moist, southern clouds had rolled in, and the temperature must have risen to fifty. It felt like summer. Zach unclasped his life jacket, took it off.

"God, it's killing me," he said, tossing it aside. "It's all flatwater from here to Barth. You can have another soak."

They kissed awhile, then pried themselves loose from the eddy. They floated through the canyon's masterpiece—sheer, black granite cliffs dotted by an occasional aerie, a brave eagle on a narrow perch. Zach sat on the lip of the scow, dangling his feet in the water. Jina lay on the dance floor, watching the mammoth walls and a narrow slice of gray sky go by. She hummed again, louder this time because the river was mild, like backup singers. She'd grown so accustomed to the nuances of water that she'd know when the current was picking up, well before any rapid was coming.

Which was why the slamming of the scow against a rock was so unexpected, and Zach's grunt and splash as he went overboard so strange. They were still in calm water, pinwheeling around a rock that had been invisible until the last moment. Jina leaned over the side, expecting Zach to come up, laughing, at any time. She had only a split second to deny the vision of his body sliding around a curve up ahead, facedown, then she dove in.

The scow flew past her. Jina reached for it, but her mistake was obvious as soon as she hit the water. She was now at the mercy of the river, unable to see if Zach washed ashore or sped downriver, unable to make out anything except water and rocks.

The water was low, but still taller than she was. Occasionally, a submerged rock struck her knee, took a bite from her thigh. She tried to get her legs out in front of her, but the river kept twisting her. The channel narrowed and swept sharply left; she began to pick up speed. Zach's bulky life jacket kept her above water but made it impossible to move or swim. She hit her head on a fang-shaped boulder that marked the outside turn. For a moment she lost consciousness, but the water slapped her awake. The cold began to seep in.

She struggled to raise her head, to search for Zach once the river straightened and slowed. He had to have come to by now. The cold would have seen to that. He was a good swimmer. Even without a life jacket, he'd be able to float with the current, keep his head up. Once they hit slack water, she'd find him. The trouble would be finding a way out of Black Canyon. They'd never catch up with the scow.

The river flattened and went nearly still. Fighting the over-sized life jacket, Jina swam for shore. She dug her feet into a floor of pebbles and found her footing. There was no sign of Zach. She had no idea when it had begun to rain.

She stood knee-deep in the water, bruised, shivering, in shock. It seemed impossible that ten minutes ago she'd been floating peacefully down the Salmon with her husband. Getting braver by the minute. Victorious. As if she'd passed some test the river set out for her, and water could be trusted now.

Later, when Irene demanded details, Jina would have a better sense of time. She'd be able to calculate how long she stood there, dazed, in the shallows of the Salmon River. She'd tally it at nearly thirty minutes, an eternity, the time it took for a man to float away, to be lost. Irene would remind her that she'd probably been suffering from hypothermia, that Zach had brought her to the river and it wasn't her fault, but none of that would make any difference. Jina stood there and let Zach go.

Eventually, she summoned enough sense to get out of the water. She stumbled to the bank, her clothes saturated and hardening against her chest, Zach's life jacket like a wet animal around her neck. She'd had no idea water was so heavy. She un-fastened the life vest, took off her wool jacket, dropped them both on shore. She forced her mind to attention, looked through the light rain for primary colors, a lock of red hair, a yellow collar, blue eyes. Her fingers began to lock up, but her eyes moved relentlessly from earth to rock to water. It would be months before she'd use natural colors in her paintings, before her landscapes became anything other than surreal fairylands of pinks, purples, and blues.

She knew her feet ought to feel cold, but instead they burned. Fire streaked across her soles, licked her ankles. It was the heat that got her moving. She clung to branches along the shoreline, stumbled downstream. There were only cliffs above her, at times a forlorn tree or two. She waded through the shallows, lost her footing on the pebble floor. She dug her fingernails into the slick, black cliffs to keep from being swept away in the current.

The skies darkened as she searched. Rain came harder, colder, slid into her eyes. She thought, once, that she saw Zach far ahead, a green shirt twisted in shrubbery, a mat of red hair brushed with sand. She lurched through the water, met a cliff in the river that blocked her path. She shouted her frustration, climbed a narrow crevasse with all the strength left in her arms. It took hours, she thought, to get up and over, and by the time she came down the other side, where the walls of Black Canyon finally drew back, the shore was empty. She screamed for Zach, a terrible sound in the canyon, a plea that no one heard. She shouted again, determined to add human sounds.

She fell to her knees where she thought she'd seen him, clawed through the shrubbery, ran her fingers over an indentation in the sand that could have been made by anything—by a rabbit, an eagle, a rat. She tore at the shrubs, cursed her imagination. The blood that dripped from her palms was the only sign of color.

The black cliffs turned north, framed a picturesque meadow that had probably been photographed and camped in a thousand times by happy floaters. There appeared to be a path through the grass, a narrow slot through the cliffs, but it was past dusk. The pain started in her head and worked downward, like she was being crushed. She stared sightlessly into the water, which was calm here—green and pretty, like a ribbon in a little girl's hair.

The rain fell until dark, then suddenly relented. The clouds raced eastward, as if fleeing the cold. The black sky lit up, magnificent, like a planetarium with its friendly ceiling of stars. She found Taurus and Auriga, the autumn constellations, and Cassiopeia at its highest point in the sky. She found new clusters, one so square that she named it Potato Field, and another she christened Bubbles, in honor of an old teddy bear. She kept her hands from her stomach. Her wet clothes had stiffened to the consistency of cardboard. She didn't know how to start a fire, couldn't remember when they'd been due out, when Zach's father might get worried and start looking. It hardly seemed to matter; if Zach had survived, he would have come for her. She wouldn't survive the night.

She imagined that she felt the baby move, though at two months she knew it was too early to feel it. Still, there it was. A flutter, an impatient tic. Just like a boy, incredulous that she'd sit around thinking when it was time to *go*.

She struggled to her feet, turned her back to the river. She tried to find the path she'd seen earlier, but in darkness it was impossible. She picked a line toward the meadow, but she was clumsy. She kept falling, sliding backwards. When the sky began to blush, she was less than fifty yards from the river. A crow flew overhead, a plane hummed somewhere, far off.

The cliffs of Black Canyon ringed the meadow, less vertical now but still daunting. She reached the first flank, chose the flattest route upward, and managed little better than a crawl. On all fours, there was nothing to do but creep up—up where that plane, or another, might spot her. Up, up, up, her palms slicing open on granite, and the bleeding welcome, warm. She jammed her feet into tiny toeholds, wedged herself into cracks. After a while, her fingertips blistering, her pace nearly stalled, she stopped looking up.

She had no sense of time when she cleared the first ridge. It could have been afternoon or evening, one day gone or two. The ground steamed and a thick forest stretched to the next, more ominous cliff. She knew the pines would conceal her, yet she stumbled toward the warm, flat woods, thankful for the feel of soil, not rock, beneath her feet. She dug at a camaslike plant, its flower long gone. Some of the bulbs were edible; others were death camas, twice as toxic as strychnine. She dug up the bulbs, ate them with relish. Either result was fine.

The bulbs made her sick, but apparently they weren't poisonous. She drank from a dirty puddle and fell asleep in the cradlelike roots of a tree. When she woke it was night again, and she started planning heaven.

She'd have two children. She'd play games and look them both in the eye; there would never be a word of blame. Zach would marvel at what she did with water; the way she breathed it, bent it in any direction. She made cliffs that rose and fell according to a woman's desires. She plotted cities and amusement parks in darkness, designed Ferris wheels at dawn. She wished she was weaker; at this rate, she could plan heaven for days.

The baby was impatient again. If given the chance, he'd probably become a cross-country racer, a man who can run forever because in his mind he's running only a few steps at a time. "See the tree?" he'd say. "Just reach the tree. Pass the tree. See the boulder? Reach the boulder. Pass the boulder. See the rock?"

She got to her feet, saw the tree, passed the tree, saw the boulder. She heard the wind through the tree limbs, an elk bugling. She listened for a plane, knew she had to be out of the trees when it came.

She picked up her pace. On the edge of the woods, a moraine spilled down the cliffs, impassable. She stepped out gingerly, felt rocks slip out beneath her feet. She put a hand on her stomach.

"See the cliff," she said. "Reach the cliff. See the sky."

She weighed less than a hundred pounds, walked as lightly as she could. She did well. She managed ten steps on the unstable moraine before the loose rock gave way beneath her. She was lucky; she didn't trigger a full-scale avalanche. She took only a narrow band of debris with her as she fell thirty feet. She came to a stop in a lifeless, rocky bowl, her leg twisted painfully inward, obviously broken. The pain shot up her leg, bullied away the cozy hypothermia.

When she finally cried, it was more from fury than sorrow. Helena's turquoise hadn't protected anyone; Zach had promised to see her through and he'd failed her. Even with the best of intentions, no one's word could be trusted.

She cried until her tears turned to flecks of ice, which was when Elvis appeared.

The elk Zach had told her about stood a hundred feet away, on the opposite edge of the moraine. He appeared impervious to the cold, and a little scornful of her predicament. He tossed his head, stepped back as if directing her to get her act together and start moving.

When she laid her head on the sharp rock, he bugled. She jerked and the pain shot up her leg.

"Shut up, Presley," she said.

When she looked up he was still there, swinging his head back and forth, uneasy. Finally, he stepped onto the unstable moraine.

A bull elk can easily weigh one thousand pounds. She waited for him to tumble, for his carcass, and hers, to become easy meat for eagles. But he had the lightest step she'd ever seen. He moved each leg deliberately and precisely, like a lifetime entertainer, and didn't dislodge a single pebble. He reached her side, and she saw a scar under his left eye, irises indistinguishable from the sky.

She'd called Zach's story of the Las Vegas elk ridiculous, and now she realized that was not only a cruel remark but a shortsighted one. People never knew when they would need to believe in something. Better not to scorn something you might one day have to depend on.

"I'm tired," she said.

He snorted, his breath forming warm clouds above her head. She was in agony, but exhaustion won. Much later, when she woke, the elk was still there, his black, spiky fur standing on end against the cold, his eyes at half mast, a back leg shaking from fatigue. Dusk or dawn was coming. The baby had stopped running. She no longer felt the urge to go on, no longer believed a plane or rescue would come.

Still, the elk stood there, and she began to grow delirious. She imagined music playing. Nothing silly or campy, nothing like the Elvis she'd seen on TV—the bloated, rhinestone-studded Las Vegas crooner. She heard perfection—a pure, young voice. A voice like an undiscovered river.

"You say you want me, and music I hear. Touch me, my darling, and clouds disappear. The sky is bright above, and cares have flown. And we're in a world of our own."

She was falling asleep again when the voice got gritty and split into two. She opened her eyes as Elvis bolted and Zach's father and Ellis shouted her name.

9

The night Jina left, Mike had the dream again.

He and his partner, Ben, were days, maybe hours, from nailing the mastermind of a terrorist cell they'd been after for two years. There was only one more witness, a jilted girlfriend, to talk to. She'd been around during the statehouse bombing, and was more than willing to talk.

In the dream, Mike went in first. He saw the girl, the explosives strapped to her chest, her eerie smile and hysterical eyes. Instantly, he returned the gun to his pocket, reached out his hand. She was shaking. She was nineteen years old, and some bastard had convinced her that it meant more to die than to live. Mike didn't care what religion you practiced; that was idiocy. The noblest thing you could do was go on, change things instead of making them worse, find a hole in someone *else* and fill it.

How desirable could heaven be if it was populated by a bunch of quitters?

In the dream, she lowered her head, took his hand.

He woke to the roar of the neighbor's waterfall and a relentless memory of what really happened that day. For the first time in his career as a field agent, he hadn't gone in first. He'd been twenty feet behind, taking a call from the office on his cell phone, when Ben Harvani opened the door. Ben had been a relative rookie—four years in the Bureau, six years Mike's junior. The explosion killed him instantly and shot Mike clear across the street. He broke a rib and his tailbone, which still ached to this day. He never knew what Ben saw when he opened the door, or if there had been any fear in that girl's eyes. For all he knew, she'd had her back to him or was praying. The autopsy said she was nineteen, born in the United States to an upper-class couple from Boston. Blond-haired. Blue-eyed. You never knew.

Mike glared at the clock—3:06 in the morning, an hour that, unfortunately, often found him awake. He got out of bed stiffly, tried to straighten his spine but reached only a quarter-to-six position. Sometimes it took him a full hour in a scorching shower to manage a straight line. He hobbled toward the kitchen, made a pot of coffee that was stronger than Jina liked. This side of the house was silent. He pulled up the blinds, blinked to adjust to the glow of the streetlamp. Unfortunately, the neon-yellow Post-it on the counter was the first thing to come into view.

He fumed at the sight of the hastily scribbled phone number, along with Jina's postscript that the satellite phone in the middle of nowhere rarely worked. She'd left her gold bracelet in the candy dish, along with the ruby earrings he'd given her last Christmas, when she'd probably been hoping for an engagement ring. Maybe the Salmon River was no place for jewelry, or else she was practicing good-byes. All he knew for sure was that she hadn't bothered to tell him anything about the trip, where they'd camp, which rapids they'd tackle, who else was going, whether Irene had convinced her husband to accompany her. When he'd asked her about Idaho, she'd actually looked alarmed, as if she hoped he'd confuse it with Iowa, disregard it as flat and mild. As if she could keep it all to herself.

He tossed the Post-it in a drawer, flicked one of the earrings against a stack of Game Boy cartridges that Danny had left behind. Mike picked up one of the tiny game chips, felt the anger slipping out of him. Already, he missed Danny—his sulkiness and catatonic Nintendo stare, both of which could be bested with ice cream or a bike ride in the park. Danny, who'd been the biggest and best surprise. Jina worried over the boy's peculiarities and unpopularity, but Mike had seen enough punks to know what real trouble looked like. Danny's oddness was like one of his video games, seemingly insurmountable now but sure to be overcome with time. Danny would be just fine.

Mike tapped his fingers while the coffee percolated. He was notoriously impatient with machines. He took his paperwork to the one-hour printer rather than stand over that tortoise of a copy machine in the office; he'd spearheaded the drive for new, faster computers. Thanks to him, all the analysts now had DSL. A click of the mouse, and the world's most wanted men appeared instantly on the screen. Mike tracked them exclusively from computer now, gathered staggering amounts of data, then sent the information on to the field agents who'd taken over his position, the ones who opened the door.

Finally, the coffee drizzled its last drop and he poured himself a cup, black. Outside the window, a tabby cat he didn't recognize stalked the bushes. Down the street, a trash can stood at the curb three days after pickup; hadn't Jina mentioned something about a messy divorce? It was three in the morning, and Mike realized it wouldn't have mattered if it was three in the afternoon. He didn't know anyone on this block. He'd moved in with Jina, but he'd always lived alone.

With two busy doctors for parents, at an early age he'd become an expert on bus transfers and canned soup. While training for the Bureau, he rarely saw his shoebox apartment, and when he married Lois, a young prosecuting attorney, they both worked such long hours they never unpacked all the moving boxes. It was surprising that they even had time to divorce. After Ben died, Mike refused visitors, shunned condolences. He holed up awhile, then quietly asked for a transfer to a desk job. He got a private office; he knew when to pull back.

Then a bus crashed not twenty feet from his car, and it all came rushing back—the panic, the adrenaline, the agony of someone else's pain. He leapt from his car, ran from victim to victim, shredded his sleeves to tie makeshift tourniquets. By the time he took Jina to the hospital, he was covered in blood and goose bumps; it didn't matter that she was a stranger—he was going in this time. He noticed the freckles across her nose, the childlike haircut, her tiny hands, and he felt almost weightless, unconnected to anything in the room except her. She thought he stayed from kindness, but he really stayed for himself. She felt woozy in the emergency room; he felt something frighteningly close to need.

Finding Jina was like receiving a threefold increase in salary; within days, he couldn't fathom how he'd survived on so much less. He waited for proof that she felt the same intensity. He waited and waited while they settled in together, and he thought that sometimes she seemed surprised to see him in the morning, like she'd been expecting someone else. She said the right things, but he was an agent; words couldn't always be trusted. More telling was the way she cried in the shower, where she assumed she couldn't be heard, the way she slipped out of his embrace right before she fell asleep and stayed rigid in her dreams. She'd been married twice before, so he'd assumed she'd be cautious. He'd been all set to grant her time, which was why her marriage proposal not only shocked him but made him doubt she loved him at all. Was she proposing to him, or just proposing? Relishing the sound of her own romantic voice? Words that should have thrilled him came across as an insult. She ought to have some fear in her eyes.

He walked to the office they shared and turned on the computer. Seconds later, one of her designs leapt onto the screen. Another river, this one meandering through a meadow, its water thick and green with pussy willows. He punched a few buttons, turned her background black, and connected to the Internet. He could work. There were always bad guys. He'd learned early on how to deal with that knowledge: Forget the odds, just take them down one at a time.

He had six new cases this week, two new terrorist cells in his region alone. He'd never told Jina this, but he also had files on

Naji Saleh and his brother, Ahmad. They were law-abiding citizens, but they were Arabs. He never pretended it was fair. Their records were spotless, but from the things Irene had said about Ahmad's anti-Americanism, Mike had kept the files active. It was the worst part of his job: not being allowed to trust decency, always doubting that things would turn out well.

Mike worked for an hour, e-mailed his updated files to his boss, then walked into the backyard. He'd never complained about Jina's fondness for weeds, though he preferred a more minimal, well-tended garden. He'd moved into Jina's house for Danny's sake even though his house had been bigger, grilled shish kebabs, and seemed, for all appearances, content—the way most people seem from across the street, when you don't look any closer than the trash can at the curb. The graying cedar wall that divided their lot from the neighbor's offered no protection from the racket of that waterfall, which sounded more like a busy airport than a soothing stream. All this time, he'd been listening to something he couldn't stand. He'd been living with things he hated.

He walked to the fence, gripped the post. He was six feet tall, a hundred and ninety pounds, and his back spasmed when he lifted his right foot. But he'd hopped fences before, chased bad guys through alleys and down embankments. He remembered that as soon as he got moving, pain either stopped or seemed less important. After the first spasm, his left leg followed easier. His back actually curled the way it should. He was up and over the fence in seconds.

The neighbors had never invited him over, and Mike was stunned at how much they'd overbuilt—not only a waterfall cascading down massive fabricated boulders, but koi ponds, Japanese bridges, color-coordinated gardens, a gazebo, a putting green. The covered flagstone patio was decorated with upholstered furniture, the kind that would have to be taken in whenever it rained, and lit by a crystal chandelier.

The stonework alone must have cost tens of thousands, and Mike couldn't think of anything more pointless than spending money on the ground beneath your feet. He preferred dirt, or a little soft moss if it was available. As a teenager, he'd camped for next to nothing—just the cost of a nylon sleeping bag and a can of beans. He'd never owned a tent; he was as particular about ceilings as he was about floors. On a perfect summer night, all his dreams turned blue.

He realized even if he'd wanted to go, Jina had never invited him to the Salmon. He had turned her down without considering how he would live without her.

He glanced at the neighbor's dark bedroom windows. He had no idea what he was doing here. He had no idea who he was and, strangely, this gave him the first pleasure he'd had all day. Though he hadn't realized it for ages, apparently he was still capable of anything. What more could he ask for than that?

He climbed the phony concrete boulders to the top of the waterfall. He had visions of tearing apart the streambed, but every fabricated stone was mortared in place. Unlike nature, nothing here would change. He was on the verge of a headache. Pain radiated from his poorly healed tailbone to his legs and feet. What a sad state he was in, to not even have realized he was living in agony.

He saw the cord in the low-voltage outlet behind a spiny blue juniper, and ripped it out of the socket. The waterfall slowly subsided. The last trickle sank into the lower pond and sloshed over the rim. There was one final gurgle, the splash of an agitated fish, then nothing but the hum of the streetlamp.

Mike stood there, appalled that he'd trespassed, appalled at how little he could do. The neighbors would come out in the morning, mop up the overflow, replug the pump, and the waterfall would crank up again. Anyone in the Bureau could tell you: You can't change anything, and you have to try. He plugged in the pump again and heard an angry motor, the roaring of the water up through the pipe to the top of the falls. He was appalled, and he realized this was an improvement over just standing there, hurting. He hopped the fence once more, and when he landed, the jarring was hardly distinguishable from all the other pain.

He finished the coffee, a full pot by six-thirty, but it wasn't the caffeine that energized him. By dawn, it was clear that he was running out of things to blame for his unhappiness. His partner had died doing what he loved. His job focused on the worst in people but often brought him into contact with the best. Mike had been waiting for something unequivocal from Jina, and God only knows why he couldn't believe her marriage proposal was it. She'd lost her partner, too, and it shamed him to realize he'd never wrapped his arms around her or told her he was sorry. Maybe he was her second, even third, choice, but wouldn't it be something not to care? To love a woman so well that she didn't care, either?

He ought to be getting ready for work, but instead he stood by the window and watched the woman with the trash can race to her car. She waved to someone in the window, and Mike wondered how many kids she had, if she'd hired a babysitter or if she now had to leave her children alone while she worked. The least he could do was offer to bring in her trash cans. He headed to the door, had it halfway open when the phone rang.

He sighed, returned to the kitchen.

"Mike," his boss, Patrick Bergowitz, said. "Good work on the Yousef case. We've got enough to give it to Jacoby now. I e-mailed you the itineraries from LAX. Looks like it's a slow travel week."

Mike watched the woman drive away. "Good," he said.

"Jina might get some good insights this week. We'll take a look at that."

Mike had been heading toward the refrigerator; now he stopped. "Excuse me?"

"It's like a freedom frenzy. Guys like that come here and re-alize they can say whatever they want. Ironic, huh? They con-demn the first country that allows condemnation. As far as we can tell, though, none of the cells will have him. He's too obvi-ous. Too much of a wild card."

"I'm not following," Mike said, but he was.

"Jesus, Mike, don't you and Jina talk? Naji Saleh went with her to Idaho. He took his brother along."

Mike grabbed the back of a chair. "Oh God," he said. "Ah-mad."

It was so changed, it could have been a different river.

Corn Creek Campground was hot and dusty, a parking lot for

SUVs and orange buses. Standing in a dazed line on the wooden dock were dozens of white-legged tourists sporting brand-new river sandals and billowy hats to cover their ears. Some shifted nervously, others were silent, a few laughed too loudly when one of the guides announced he'd never run a river, either, and was looking forward to seeing whitewater for the first time.

Jina stepped gingerly from the van, her bones aching from the two-hour ride over gravel washboards. She'd been astonished at the change in scenery along the road—new subdivisions going in near North Fork, a remodeled patio and saloon at Colson Creek, five bed-and-breakfasts before the old mining town of Shoup.

Jake the terrier, dove over the front seat, let out a joyful bark. Two black Labradors with red bandanas tied around their necks greeted him enthusiastically, sniffing, circling, then taking off for the water. Gone was the rain, the hunters, the silence. A group of campers had a boom box and blasted a tune from Sheryl Crow. The air smelled not of pine but of coconut suntan lotion and insect repellent. The first raft in line launched to cheers and a child's wail. The next guide lifted an oar above his head, and a hush fell over his group. He began giving safety lessons.

Drew approached two guides from the Salmon Adventure Company—one to drive the van back to Salmon, the other to paddle ahead and station supplies at each camp. There was a ludicrous amount of supplies to load into the rafts—food, tents, sleeping bags, chairs, utensils, pots, toiletries—and the three of them worked with alacrity and good humor. Charlie climbed over their neatly stacked boxes to get to the stash of root beer. He rummaged through a carton of snacks, and Jina resisted the urge to yank him by the ear and humiliate him with a time-out. In the two years he'd been gone, Charlie had gone from an endearing Hot Wheels enthusiast to an obnoxious brat, but every time she opened her mouth to reprimand him, Danny looked as if he'd rather take a beating himself. It was obvious their kindergarten friendship was over, yet apparently they honored some boy code to protect the enemy, to band together against interfering adults. At least, Jina thought, her son was part of a team.

Except for Naji, they all left the van. Still in slacks and a starched, long-sleeved work shirt, he sat, reading, while Ahmad stood by the door and laughed.

"He's afraid of boats," Ahmad said.

Jina looked toward the rafts. She understood that.

"There is nothing to fear," Ahmad said, softer. "Invoking the name of Khidr ensures a safe sailing. He's the patron saint of sailors and travelers. We'll be fine."

Ahmad headed up toward the campsites, the few shady places beneath the trees. Jina left Naji in the van and walked slowly down the concrete ramp, maneuvering around a group of shirtless boys kicking a Hacky Sack. She found Irene on the docks, didn't look at the river gauge at their feet. There had been plenty of snow this winter; the spring was abnormally hot. The water was running high; there was no point in knowing more than that.

"I can't do this again," Jina said.

Irene nodded. They both knew she couldn't, and they both knew she would.

"There are more than forty rapids between us and the take-out," Jina went on. Mary came over to listen. Naji lit a cigarette, peered out the window of the van. "We'll drop close to a thousand feet, an average of twelve feet per mile. At such high water, rapids like Big Mallard will be washed out, but Gunbarrel might be hellish."

She looked upriver, where there were rafters, too. Now there were companies that ran trips from North Fork to Corn Creek, then bused you back out, mocking the river's nickname. You could return if you wanted to. The jet boats carried you backward. One fired up behind them, took off quickly to gain enough speed to plane on top of the water.

The stories Jina had told seemed unlikely now, nothing but good fiction for Alice's book. These days, there were too many people, boats, and safeguards for anyone to be lost. Dogs and babies ran the Salmon; how could it be dangerous? Each bank was a city with phone lines, satellite dishes, and enough beer to keep everyone calm. Ahmad looked as impatient with the campground as Mike did with machines. He walked from campsite to campsite, trying to find a quiet place, some of the wilderness he'd been promised.

Jina hadn't said good-bye to Mike. She'd left him only a spotty itinerary, and she wasn't sure if that was because she didn't want him to find her or because she feared he wouldn't bother to look. She'd left her jewelry on the counter in a huff, but that fury was slowly being eaten by despair. She couldn't begin to formulate what she'd say to Danny if she and Mike couldn't work things out. The best part had always been the family they made. The three of them. Holes filled. The circle completed.

She and Mike had never really been alone together at all.

Drew approached the group, put his hand on Jina's arm. Jake's Labrador buddies had departed. The terrier whirled around them, a blur.

"My dad said you might be a little spooked, coming back."

Jina glanced at Danny, who bounced on the balls of his feet. What spooked her was not the river but how different it seemed, not like what she'd been remembering at all.

"This place gets ahold of you," Drew went on. "God knows I didn't think I'd stay. Came to tell the old man off five years ago, and I'm still arguing my point. Who knew I had so much to say?"

Another raft set off with a large, quiet family, all slathered in multicolored suntan lotion and gripping the handholds on the sides of the raft. Danny's feet sported sand between the toes, grit on his water sandals. Jina had coated him in suntan lotion, but freckles had already broken out on his cheeks.

"So this is it?" he asked. "This is where you and . . . Dad started?"

It was ninety degrees and hard to imagine, but she nodded. Danny leaned forward, as if wilderness was sloped and required extra balance, more care.

"He's here," Danny whispered. "I can feel him."

When Charlie snorted, Jina stared him down. She'd tried to let them work things out for themselves, but she'd be damned if she'd let some punk scoff at the truth. She grabbed Charlie's shoulder, squeezed hard enough to let him know she was done now. She wanted him quiet.

"I know," she said. "I can feel him, too."

. . .

After instructions and a safety lesson, Drew happily announced that just yesterday a six-man raft had flipped in Gunbarrel. No one had been hurt, but a forty-five-year-old Chicago lawyer hadn't been able to stop crying, even after his life jacket carried him into shallow water. A guide retrieved him, but the man refused to get back in the raft. They had to flag down a jet boat to get him a lift back to Corn Creek. Word was he spit on the runway before he stepped on the plane. Called the land unforgiving, the rivers a death trap, which any Idahoan will proudly state is the truth.

Irene claimed the front of the raft; Alice and John took the seats farthest away, in the back. No one had seen Ahmad for half an hour when he came bolting down the slope.

"We were ready to leave ten minutes ago," Drew said.

Ahmad shrugged, climbed into the back of the raft. Jina ordered Danny and Charlie into the middle of the boat, an arrangement neither of the boys appreciated.

"This blows," Charlie said. "I can surf, you know."

"Look at Jake," Danny whined. "He's, like, two pounds and he gets to sit in the front."

The terrier, indeed, had his back paws on Irene's lap and the other two draped over the bow. His tail wagged furiously.

"Trust me," Jina told them, "you'll see plenty from here."

Drew stood on shore, one foot on the back of the raft. "All right," he said. "I'll see you." He pushed them off.

Jina stared at him in shock, then picked up a paddle. Drew laughed and jumped into the raft.

"I love to do that," he said, smiling.

As soon as the boat was free of the ramp, Danny stretched

from side to side, thinking every riffle a thrill ride, having no idea what lay in wait.

"Are those rapids?" he asked.

"Not yet."

"How 'bout those?"

"Shut up, freak," Charlie said.

Jina turned to the sandy-haired boy beside her. "What did you call him?"

Charlie squirmed. "It's just—"

"It's nothing, Mom," Danny cut in. "Let me paddle."

Drew held out an oar, but Jina waved him off. "Not yet. He needs to get a feel for the raft first."

"*Mo-om*. If you haven't noticed, there are no waves here."

"This is not a video game," Jina said quietly. "You don't get more than one life."

Danny glared at her, but his sulk didn't last. Already, the scenery was better—pine-covered bluffs instead of camper shells. Blue sky instead of exhaust smoke. A hundred yards from the campground, they no longer heard Sheryl Crow.

"Paddle right," Drew said, and those on the right put in their oars. The raft quickly shifted toward the center of the river. They sloshed over a gentle ripple, listened to the gurgling of the water beneath the raft. Around a turn, mountains boxed them in, stretched to all four corners.

"And off we go," Drew said.

Naji looked ridiculous in his white shirt and slacks. Jina hoped he'd brought shorts; one way or another, the river would have its way with him. It would strip him to his boxers before long. Ahmad glanced over his shoulder, smiling for once, as if the beauty of the place had disarmed him. "Khidr the Green Ancient was my companion," he said softly. "He taught me the Great Name of God."

There had been no way to tell Ahmad he couldn't come. He was Naji's condition for making this trip, and Jina would do anything for Irene. Still, she wasn't sure what to make of him. She'd seen him only a few times before, at Irene's house, and he'd always kept to himself. When they drank, he left the room; when Irene cursed, he left the house. She didn't like to admit it, but it was easier to like Naji, who drank wine and prayed in private, who made some effort to adapt.

Ahmad gazed at the last plume of smoke in the distance, then leaned toward Jina. "Islam is the only religion not associated with any person or place. It is the religion of the universe, of natural law. Everything from the sun to the Earth to the trees is created by and subject to Allah's laws; thus, everything is Muslim. You are Muslim."

"My parents would be shocked to hear that," Jina said, smiling.

"It is no joke," Ahmad said. "Islam stands for complete submission and obedience to Allah. Those who deny God are called Kafir. Concealers. They hide from the truth. They rebel against nature and become tyrants."

Jina leaned back, but Naji merely laughed. "My brother," he said, "goes by the book."

The lines around Ahmad's mouth softened. "While you make things up as you go."

"Who is Khidr?" Jina asked. "I've never heard of him."

"The tyrants hide our stories," Ahmad said. "Khidr is the Green One. A mystic, an immortal, the guide through the wilderness. When Moses declared himself the most learned man on Earth, God did not like his conceit. He sent him to find Khidr to learn the subtleties he missed. To chip away at his arrogance."

"My brother likes to think himself a modern-day Khidr and me a wretched Moses," Naji said. "He chips away at me. Chip. Chip. Chip."

Ahmad laughed. Jina liked how his face looked when he did it. His serious eyes were obscured by wrinkles; she glimpsed his teeth, which were endearingly crooked.

"When we were boys," Ahmad said, "I played, you studied. Do you remember? I would sneak out, you'd flash the light from your bedroom to let me know when it was safe to return."

Naji shook his head. "I remember it was rarely safe."

"Everything changes. Now I study and you play with your fancy car, take trips with your wife's movie-star friends, attend her ridiculous parties. You're fortunate Father isn't here to beat you for your excesses."

Irene slapped her paddle into the river, splashing them. "I can hear you," she said.

"You would never cry when he beat you," Naji said, ignoring the water on his brow. "You would never do anything until . . ."

In the silence, Irene turned around. "Until what?"

Naji ignored her. "I never agreed with what you did to him, but what came after was worse. You said you wouldn't let him win, but I think he did."

The brothers stared at each other. " 'The penalty of the blazing fire,' " Ahmad said softly. " 'We have prepared the doom of flame.' " Then he bowed his head. "I was confused. Angry. Father was a good Muslim. That is something a rebellious, headstrong boy cannot understand. He surrendered to God, as is required; he expected no less from his children. He wanted pious sons. He did not bet on the right one."

Naji shook his head. "You stayed with Father too long, Ahmad. You became him."

"And you betrayed him by coming here. It is my duty to bring you back."

"Your duty is to yourself. To your God. As for me, America suits me fine. So this place has another point of view. So what? As you say, we are all Muslim. 'There is no God but Allah, and Muhammad is his prophet.' Nothing else exists."

"Except money," Ahmad said. "The latest celebrity to thank you for her new lips."

"Speaking of which," Irene said pointedly, splashing once more to make sure they were through, "have you seen Meg Ryan? I swear she's had hers done."

"Why would anyone leave Dennis Quaid?" Jina asked. "That's what I want to know."

"Oh, come on. Russell Crowe. I wish that had worked out."

"Do you remember how Dennis stood up for her when everyone started saying she was a bad mother?" Alice asked.

It was the first thing she'd said all day, and Jina watched Irene's back straighten, Mary look out over the water. Alice had been brave to come with them but not very smart. Irene might throw her overboard. Even worse, Alice would have to admit that the conditions here were harsh; there would be no forgiveness.

They were silent for a terribly awkward minute, until Drew said, "Paddle back."

They put in their oars, paddled against the current. The raft slowed, and Drew used his oar like a rudder to steer them around a rock.

Jina turned to Alice. "I'm surprised you came."

Alice bowed her head. "It seems more surprising that you did."

After an hour of calm floating and no sign of turbulence, Jina let Danny and Charlie take an oar. Charlie had a sure, strong hand, while the current nearly snatched the paddle from Danny's grip. He grimaced and held on tighter. Charlie paddled ferociously and the boat turned left. Danny slammed in his paddle and they veered right. The boys' arms strained; their silent competition zigzagged the boat down the Salmon.

Killum Point was occupied by a camping group of thirty. Nothing was as Jina remembered until she heard the roar of Gunbarrel.

She grabbed the back of Danny's and Charlie's life jackets and yanked them to the center of the raft. Charlie grumbled and Danny looked ready to argue, until he got a look at her face.

"Don't be scared, Mom," he said. "It'll be fun."

To prove the point, Jake leaped fearlessly to the bow, tail

wagging. Irene stood up beside him. "Look at that fucking thing!" she shouted over the roar. "Naji, will you look at that?"

But Naji was looking at her, her curves lost beneath the unflattering orange life jacket, her hair windblown and wild.

"Sit down," he said, the first words Jina had heard him speak to his wife this whole trip. "Hold on tight."

Drew hooted when he saw the whitewater. Alice dropped her paddle between her knees.

"Everyone forward paddle!" Drew shouted.

It was a totally different ride in a raft. Bumpier, bouncier, more like a roller coaster than a fight for survival. Aside from Alice, who sat frozen in fear, they all paddled at Drew's command and flew down the right side of the torrent, through a seam between two waves. Danny screamed joyously, Charlie raised his arms above his head, and when Jina saw that they would make it, that even with all their weight the raft was as buoyant as a leaf, she took a deep breath and smelled the canyon for the first time. River, pine, and humus, air so clean and familiar that it stung.

"Oh my God!" Irene shouted, laughing as a wave plunged over the front of the boat and slammed her backward. She fell on top of Naji, who caught her and might have even cracked a smile. Danny sailed up and into Jina's arms, as if the river had a mothering streak after all, a soft spot. When the raft unfolded and everyone found themselves alive at the bottom of Gunbarrel, Irene stood again, her hair drenched and hanging in her eyes. She lifted her paddle above her head.

"Queen of the river!" she yelled.

Alice began to cry. John put his arm around her, told her she'd done fine. Mary turned around to see the torrent they'd come through, then looked up at Drew, her face radiant.

"Please," she said. "Can we do it again?"

Jina let the boys paddle to the lodge. Danny sat on one lip of the raft, Charlie on the other, each dangling a leg in the water. Still high on excitement, they forgot to battle and worked in sync. Every ripple delighted them, they cheered for the tiniest bounce, and she saw what she had never noticed before. Her son had survival instincts. He could fight when he had to, outlast a bully. He was kinder than some friends deserved.

Ellis and Helena stood on the beach, exactly where she'd left them twelve years ago. Time meant so little on the river, they were unchanged—still old and solid, wearing blue jeans and flannel shirts. Ellis scanned the faces in the raft, his gaze finally settling on her.

Irene stepped out first. "Well, that seals it," she said. "I'm moving in."

Naji helped Alice from the boat. She was still green, though her tears had dried. She'd worn polyester pants, which now clung to her legs. It was hot out, probably close to ninety-five, but she was shivering.

Helena moved to her side. "Come," she said. "We warm you up."

Ahmad didn't greet his hosts or offer to help unload. He spent a moment getting his bearings, then disappeared on a path through the trees. Maybe he truly believed he was Khidr; perhaps he was psychotic. That was all they needed, Jina thought. In addition to bad memories, failing marriages, and bullies, they'd have Kevin Bacon on the raft.

John helped Drew secure the boat while Danny asked, "When's the next rapid? Where will we camp? Are there bears? Mountain lions? Any chance I can have my own kayak?"

Drew laughed. "Hold on there," he said. "One question at a time." He hoisted Danny onto a rock, politely pretended he had all the time in the world to answer an eleven-year-old's questions, when in actuality he had to unload supplies, get lunch started, do the dishes, prepare dinner, and pitch tents. Steering the boat through the world's greatest whitewater was the least of what a river guide had to do.

"Why don't you all go on inside?" Ellis said. "Look around. Helena will show you the rooms we've got, if you want to stay in the lodge."

Irene's smile faded as Naji walked right past her. Jina would have offered a few words of comfort if Ellis hadn't gotten hold of her arm.

"We need to talk," he said.

The buck, Elvis, had undergone two more resurrections. In this life, he was now a three-pointer, young but strong. In the meadow above the lodge, he raised his head from grazing and eyed them curiously. He turned a back hoof outward, jiggled a knobby knee.

"Never expected to see you again," Ellis said. "After everything . . . had no idea you'd come back."

"It seems like yesterday," Jina said. "That's what's scary."

"You know how hard we searched for you both," Ellis said. "It started snowing right after we found you. Never ran the river so low before. I was out every day. I tried . . ."

Jina put a hand on his arm. "I know how hard you tried. You couldn't have done anything more. The river took him. There was nothing to find."

Ellis shook his head. "That father-in-law of yours wouldn't give up." He smiled, revealing a gap where he'd lost two teeth on the bottom—the mark of a kindergartner to show how he'd aged. "Stubborn as all hell. Said you'd survived, why shouldn't Zach? He would have made a great river runner. How is he?"

"Zach's father is dead," Jina said. "Years ago."

Across the meadow, Elvis pawed the ground, nibbled, shook. She remembered only bits and pieces of those days after Zach went under—the woods, the moraine, Elvis Presley keeping her alive.

Ellis breathed deeply. "I wish . . . Jina, there's something you gotta know."

She stepped away quickly, hurried over to Elvis, who watched her unconcernedly, as if they were old friends. Ellis approached slowly, as if she were the elk and he didn't want to spook her. He'd been an old man before, and must be ancient now. She couldn't guess his age. Yet he didn't stumble; he was heartier than she was.

"There's things you've gotta listen to," he said, "even when you don't like the words."

She laughed harshly. She'd heard them all. How her husband's body would never be recovered. How the state of Idaho declared him dead, gone. How the next man she loved wouldn't have her, as if she was tainted. Cursed.

"My son wants to run the river his father died on," she said. "That's all I can handle right now."

"Jina—"

She heard a heavy step behind her, figured it was Drew coming to call them to lunch. Instead, a woman in a pink party dress and work boots stepped from the trees, wearing a ragged pack on her back. She was of an indefinable age, dressed for a prom but obviously careworn, her amber hair full and wavy, her skin rough as slate. She had gray-green eyes that never glanced at Ellis, never left Jina's face once.

"Hello?" Jina said, thinking her some lost, crazy thing, a mental patient who'd taken a wrong turn at Challis and kept walking.

The woman said nothing. Her red, chapped hands were fists in front of her.

"This is Pearl," Ellis said. "She lives downriver."

"I'm Jina." She smiled, but the heat from Pearl's stare withered it.

Finally, Pearl turned to Ellis. "We're overrun by spinach." She took off her backpack, which was stuffed with glossy, green leaves. "Think Helena can use it?"

"Are you kidding? The gophers got ours. Poison didn't faze 'em."

Pearl turned to Jina again. "I hear you have a boy. You taking him down the river?"

She'd forgotten that about this place: Before you'd even realized you had a secret, someone downstream had spilled it.

"Yes," she said. "I'd better get back."

But Pearl stepped forward, caught her by the wrist. Her hands were rough and callused, her fingernails crescents of dirt. She smelled of dirt and pine and fish—not bad smells, but more like the woods than a woman.

"Our place is in Black Canyon, up over Corey Ridge," she said. "I don't mean to be rude, but my son's afraid of company. I'd appreciate it if you didn't take the trail."

Jina nodded dumbly, twisted out of Pearl's grip. Ellis avoided her gaze, and Jina felt strangely betrayed. She stomped across the meadow, down the trail. She made so much noise that she almost didn't hear Pearl's voice.

"Goddammit!"

Out of sight down the slope, Jina paused, though she knew she ought to keep going. She shouldn't strain to listen over the beating of her heart.

"I told you not to come," Ellis said.

"I had to see her."

Go, Jina thought, but even the thought was quiet. Waiting.

"Ah, Pearl," Ellis said. "Promise me you didn't tell Zach she was here."

10

Just Breathe

"Jump!"

In their dim room in the lodge, Charlie leaned over Danny's shoulder, his breath like dung. "B button!" Charlie shouted. "*B!* Look out for that . . . Jesus, freak. This game is like so easy. You're totally lame."

Danny cranked up the backlighting, hunched over the screen. He was unsure of his next move, even more puzzled at how he and turd-breath had ever been friends. Sure, Charlie had lived next door, and the L.A. sun had yet to bake him into a troll, but it seemed impossible now that Danny had been inconsolable the day Charlie moved away. He'd buy him a ticket south this instant, if he could afford it.

Danny was unsure about most things, except this: He could

play. He'd put up with Charlie's taunts and put-downs, but this was Game Boy they were talking about. Danny had beaten every fire-breathing boss and alien army created. His mom hadn't even let him bring the really tough fighting games like Mortal Kombat and Sonic Battle. Super Mario's ice mountains and volcanoes were like easy rapids, Class III's. He could whiz through them in his sleep.

Charlie still had the nerve to scoff. "Come on," he said. "Don't go that way. Shit. Jump!"

Danny glared at him, then intentionally led Mario over a cliff.

"Game over," Charlie said. "Totally lame, freak. Gimme it."

Danny was a freak at school, a regular in the gifted and talented program, so he had practice avoiding fights. Who knew he could also start one? He chucked the Game Boy at Charlie's chin, where it rewarded him with a nasty clunk and Charlie's bellow.

Charlie leapt to his feet, a giant for an eleven-year-old, but at this point fear seemed as much a choice to Danny as which trail to take. The little bit of whitewater they'd faced had gone to his head, and he was itching for more danger. Last night, his toes reached the edge of the mattress for the first time. He was growing so fast, he woke up every morning and nothing was in the same place.

"Excuse me?" Charlie said, stepping forward.

"You're a jerk."

The matter-of-fact way Danny said it, as if it was common knowledge, stopped Charlie in mid-stride. For a moment,

Danny thought he might escape without damage. Then Charlie came at him.

Even as he was getting creamed, Danny transformed the beating into a Nintendo game. Once upon a time there was a boy who was weak and soft, until he began to think like a river. He looked mild, but deep down he harbored an undertow. He only appeared to take everything that was dished out. In the game, the mild river chews up sewage, erodes dams, innocuously floods cities on its way to the sea. Once there, it swims across the ocean and starts all over again on the other side. It's the first and only game that never ends.

Between punches, the smack of fists against skin, Danny heard the river, a gust of wind through the trees. Even when the blood slipped from his nose and Charlie got an ugly smile, Danny wondered how he'd ever lived anywhere else, how he could ever go back.

He swung wildly, hit air, and prayed the adults stayed down by the river. He didn't want anyone to stop them. Once, like a miracle, his fist landed solidly on Charlie's nose and there was a wonderful cracking sound.

Charlie crouched over. "Freak," he spat with a mouthful of blood.

Maybe Danny was, because he didn't mind the pain in his chest and ribs and eye so much. It felt good to hit a troll, an admission that would kill his mom, that only Mike would understand.

"Come on," Danny said. "A button. *Fight.*"

They went at it again, but Danny had never realized how exhausting a fistfight could be. He had trouble holding up his arms; Charlie hung on him like a fat Muhammad Ali.

"Get off!" Danny said, using the last of his strength to shove him.

They glared at each other. Danny's mom would surely see the blood on the floor, the new angle of Charlie's nose, the bruises over most of Danny's body. She was bound to go ballistic, but Danny found he didn't care much. Every bone in his body hurt, and the pain felt spectacular, as if a new level of sensation had kicked in.

He went to the mirror. His left eye was already swelling. There were cuts across his cheeks and neck. He dabbed at the blood, grinned at himself. He was stunned to see that Charlie looked worse.

The troll sat on the bed, winded, curled up like a snail. Maybe no one in L.A. had dared to fight him. Danny was no popularity king, but at least he didn't scare people into being his friend.

"Hey," Danny said, and Charlie spit at his feet—a thick, bloody glob of phlegm. Danny narrowed his swollen eyes. "I'm outta here."

He opened the door, crept down the musty hall. He saw Naji and John on the porch, sipping beers. There was no back door, so Danny tiptoed across the living room, eased open the screen. If he was quick, and as invisible as he was in school, he could duck behind them and hop the porch railing. He could disappear into the meadow before either man noticed he'd been there.

They helped with nonstop conversation, a discussion about the delights of Danville. Starbucks and Safeway and the new sushi place the women had been going to on Main Street. How much they missed thirteen-hour work days, their comfortable Volvos, the overcast that protected them from sunstroke, from seeing too much.

"No amount of showering is going to rinse off this dirt," John said.

Naji looked out over the river. "She expects something to change here," he said. "But Ahmad is right in this. The past is set. Here or there, we must own it."

John swatted at the dust on his shorts, the tops of his shoes. "I'm sorry for all this."

Danny ached to run, but he forced himself to inch along the wall of the lodge. He reached the railing, silently lifted one foot over.

"Mr. Cantor will take me back to Corn Creek," Naji said.

Danny had never heard either of them talk so much. Whenever the families of the sushi club got together, Danny and Roger fought over video games, the men found a television and gratefully crowded around some obscure sporting event, Danny's mom and her friends forgot anyone else existed. The women drank and laughed and chattered like birds, one on top of the other, beautiful and kind of scary at the same time. Danny hadn't even noticed what the men looked like until now, hadn't known, for example, that John Aberdeen was losing his hair, that Naji Saleh had puppy-dog eyes, round and brown and sad—eyes you didn't dare look at, unless you were willing to take him home.

"What does Alice say?" Naji asked.

John shook his head, sighed. "Alice." It seemed he might

leave it at that, but as Danny straddled the railing, the man went on, his voice clipped and grainy, like every word was a stone in his throat. "Maybe writing is her only choice. Maybe. She's worked harder than most people can imagine. Day and night, pouring her soul into the books, struggling to keep the disappointments from the children, from me. She deserves success, yet . . . she might have been better off if she'd given up years ago. Is it so horrible to downgrade expectation? You get more of what you want."

Danny quietly brought his second leg over, leapt to the ground. One step. Two. Almost out of sight.

"Not too far now," Naji said.

Danny turned back, looked right into those forlorn eyes. He knew about Naji Saleh, or at least the parts Alice had put in her book. A month ago, Danny read nothing but Yu-Gi-Oh! cards, but when his mom wouldn't turn over her copy of Alice's novel, he used his entire savings to buy one himself. He was only interested in the parts about his dad, but there was no resisting those sex scenes in Irene's section—Irene's character doing it with men in the shower, in restaurant bathrooms, buck naked at midnight in the middle of public parks. Doing it with strangers and men she'd known all her life, with everyone but her husband. It was like getting the porn channel his mother hadn't known was coming through the cable for a whole thrilling week. Danny had read the chapter eight times, memorized the parts about how a woman's genitals looked and smelled like flower petals, and how she'd scream if you kissed her there, before he forced himself to move on to the chapters about his father.

In the book Naji was a fool, but in real life he looked at a kid's cuts and bruises and didn't say a word. John, too, merely glanced at Danny's swollen eye and turned to the river. Danny got a funny feeling in his stomach, as if he hadn't appreciated until now how many men there already were in his life.

He glanced at the meadow, but escape didn't feel quite so urgent. "Do you believe in ghosts?" he asked.

Naji sat forward in his chair, placed his small, dark hands on his knees. "Do you?"

Danny had been holding his breath, and now he let it out. It wasn't clear, until someone believed him, how many people did not. He walked to the porch steps.

"My dad . . . He came to my room each night. I'm not making that up. He was there. He showed me things about this place."

Naji stared at him, then finally nodded. "In general, Muslims do not believe in ghosts. A man's soul is not free to roam at will or settle business he couldn't finish before death. When you die, you are cut off completely from this world, yes? You are restricted within Allah's custody."

Danny picked up a stick, broke it into pieces. "That sucks."

Naji looked at John, smiled. "Well. I say in general. We have the jinn. They live on Earth in a world parallel to ours. Like humans, they have the choice to be good or bad. They are invisible."

Danny perked up. "Invisible? Cool."

"The jinn possess not only people but also animals, trees, a river perhaps. For most people, they're frightening. They prey on our worst fears and instincts."

"Do you believe in them?"

Naji looked to the tops of the trees. "Allah creates everything from specks of dust to magnificent galaxies. He has a much greater imagination than I do."

"Maybe Irene was possessed," Danny said. "I know Charlie is."

Naji touched his arm, careful to pick one of the few places not sporting a bruise. Danny felt that strangeness in his stomach again, an unexpected warmth.

"We are all possessed by something," Naji said.

The sun glimmered off the cliffs like a beacon, a fairy light. Ghosts, jinn, Danny's father, whatever. Since he was already a Muslim, according to Ahmad, Danny decided to be one of the lucky few who believed in ghosts. Life seemed to get more interesting the more things you believed in.

"I won't go far," he said.

Naji and John watched him, silent. He waved nonchalantly, like he was any ordinary kid off to explore. But he felt anything but normal as he approached a trail he swore he'd seen before. His heart raced as he reached a boulder his father had leaned against in Danny's dreams. He pressed his hand to the rock and found it warm.

The lodge was out of sight now, but the large ponderosa up ahead would be marked, he knew. Notched four feet up, to show the trail in snowfalls. There was a smaller rock on the left, what looked like an unmarked gravestone. Sweat trickled down his back. He shouldn't know that the Lymonds had a cabin a half mile from where he stood, that in a pinch he could take the trail along Horse Creek clear to Gattin Ranch or follow the fire road along Long Tom Ridge. Nothing made sense, and that was wonderful. He was all for it. If these woods turned everything up-side down, then it stood to reason he'd be happy here.

He smiled, might have messed around trying to find other things he already knew about if he hadn't heard the crunching of twigs behind him, a club-footed approach. He balled his fists and turned.

It was the troll, looking worse for wear. Charlie's rock-star hair was limp, his nose a glorious shade of purple. He tried to hide a grimace with every step.

"Bin Laden sent me to find you," Charlie said.

Danny stepped forward, surprised when Charlie moved back.

"Don't call him that," Danny said.

He turned his back on Charlie, but the familiarity he'd felt a moment ago was gone. Who were the Lymonds, anyway? The notch in the tree could have come from anything, from an er-rant ax throw, from an angry bear. He had no idea which trail to take, and as long as Charlie was tagging along, he didn't want to follow any of them.

"You smell that?" Charlie asked.

Danny didn't answer. It was just wood smoke, the scent of a campfire.

"That's no campfire," Charlie said, as if Danny had spoken.

Charlie limped to a small ridge. The smell wasn't coming from the lodge behind them, but from somewhere up the draw. Danny looked for signs of smoke, saw nothing but a clear blue sky, a blue he hadn't even known existed. Yet the smell was get-ting stronger. More than a few logs were on fire.

Danny nearly turned back. At a moment like this in Danville, he'd go into his room and shut the door. But this wasn't

Danville, thank God. Out here, a forest fire could sweep right through the lodge and take him out. There wasn't any use in hiding; fear found you either way.

"Come on then," Danny said.

He headed off trail. It was a terrible idea, the singular bad decision that always leads to children being lost in the woods, existing for a brief while on roots and puddle water, until they become carrion. Nevertheless, the farther he walked, the calmer he felt. A hundred yards in, his heart stopped hammering. Under the dense shade of trees, Danny stopped sweating. By the time they'd hiked for an hour, over a cliff, into a second valley, then a third, he was on a mission. The Boy Who Became a River: Level Three.

"I don't smell anything," Charlie said. "Come on, freak. We ought to go back."

Nothing could have made him move faster than the squeak in Charlie's voice. Danny only wished he had a tape recorder; he'd play it day and night. The harder Charlie stumbled, the faster Danny went. He didn't know where he got the energy, and he didn't care. He was better at something, even if it was getting them lost.

He crossed a stream on a precarious log. Charlie crumpled to his knees, drank so much water Danny could hardly contain his giddiness imagining parasites in his bloodstream, all the agonizing symptoms of giardia. He looked up the next rise, realized the sun was behind him, not on the left as he'd thought. The smell of smoke was gone.

He stood straight. For a whole minute, he didn't panic. He looked back the way they'd come. From here the path was clear, but once he slipped among the trees, he might lose his way. He could go up the second ridge instead of the first and end up in an entirely different valley.

Charlie caught his breath, looked up. It was obvious from the widening of his eyes that he knew they'd gone too far. Danny concentrated the way he did when he was finding his way through a video-game maze. He tried to memorize every rock and stump in the path they'd taken, clues he'd have to look for later. He was so intent, he almost didn't notice the jinn.

The spirit materialized on a ridge less than fifty yards away. Black hair, black eyes, a smokeless flame of fire before him. The jinn raised his arms and flames shot up after them.

"Shit," Charlie said. He turned and ran.

Danny couldn't have moved if he tried. The jinn held him spell-bound while red sparks leapt from a bush to a twenty-foot ponderosa. Flames raced up the bone-dry trunk and crowned. If the wind shifted, as it often did in the afternoon, this whole valley would go up.

The jinn stared at him, but from this distance, Danny couldn't make out his face, didn't know if he even had one. Very slowly, Danny backed up. He didn't run until he was well within the cover of trees.

His heart hammered as he leapt over unfamiliar rocks, dashed through an aspen grove he knew he hadn't seen before. He didn't dare slow down to find the landmarks he'd picked out. He didn't care where he was headed, as long as it was away from the devil, back where the sky was still blue.

He was sure he was being followed. The hair on his neck prickled; he nearly crashed trying to look back. He imagined the devil coming after him or, worse, Charlie emerging from the woods, laughing hysterically, telling him he was not only a freak, but a wuss. Danny fought for breath, finally stopped, turned. He imagined being torn limb from limb, but saw nothing but a chipmunk running as fast from him as he'd run from the jinn.

He shook from head to foot. He tried to move, but his feet wouldn't agree. He'd have sat down and wept if he hadn't heard the singing.

It came from the wrong direction, he was sure, but at this point he'd follow anything human. He forced his feet to move, stopped when the voice stopped, corrected his direction twice. Finally, he stumbled into a clearing. In the middle of a thicket of raspberries, a girl sat, picking fruit, apparently without a care in the world. She had straw-colored hair that fell just past her neck, the narrowest shoulders he'd ever seen, like she was less than half a person. Danny blinked, but the apparition remained. She rocked up and back, turned slightly in his direction, and he realized his mistake. The child was fine-boned, delicate, but definitely a boy. Probably no more than eight. And somehow Danny knew his name.

"Andy," he said.

The boy turned, eyes wide for a moment, then welcoming. His mouth spread into a grin.

"You help," he said. "Daddy likes raspberries."

It was all a dream. Danny was at home in his room, dreaming this the way he'd dreamed Andy's snug cabin with its chunky log furniture, the woodstove in the corner, a garden out front, a wood pile stacked past the roof, a woman known for her wariness of strangers and her aim.

A good dream, though, certainly better than the jinn, so he went with it. He got torn up a bit maneuvering through the thicket, picked raspberries until the boy's basket was full. When they stood, Danny realized he'd misjudged both the boy's size and age. Andy was taller than him, and older—twelve or thirteen at least. He just looked childlike because he was simple—what Charlie would call a retard.

Andy smiled at him happily, apparently with no intention of heading home.

"Is your cabin around here?" Danny asked.

The boy shrugged. He was singing again. "Pearl, girl, used to twirl, heidi-hee, Andy free. Zach, black, dead and back, heidi-hee, Andy free." He repeated the lines over and over, delighted with himself.

"Look," Danny said. He'd read *The Hobbit*, played *Lord of the Rings* excessively on the GameCube. Maybe there were such things as wood elves and fairies. Maybe an unexplainable world was not fantasy but the reality of life as you grew up. "I should go."

But he didn't. Andy offered him raspberries and he ate some. They were nothing like the store-bought variety but were smaller and sweeter. He asked for more. Soon the two of them were sitting on a bed of pine needles, devouring the whole basket.

"Andy!"

Danny jumped to his feet, but Andy laughed. A woman in a

pink dress emerged through the trees, her hands on her hips. She was as tall and muscular as Mike. Her long, thick hair, the color of pine, was tied back in a ponytail. Her skin reminded Danny of a well-used copper pot, dulled but still beautiful; the lines around her eyes were like intricate folding fans, works of art. Danny rarely looked at girls, and never at other people's mothers, but he thought she might have been pretty once.

She shook her head at the empty basket, then turned to Danny.

"What are you doing here?"

He opened his mouth, but nothing emerged. The other thing he remembered from *The Hobbit* was that not all things in the woods are nice. Some tie you up in nets; some eat you.

"My friend," Andy said. "My friend."

The woman stared at Danny a moment longer, then sighed. She pulled Andy to his feet, brushed the pale hair from his eyes, wiped raspberry juice from his mouth. She smiled tenderly, and Danny was sure she'd been more than pretty. She'd held boys' hearts in the palm of her hand.

"Now what will we have for dessert?" she asked.

He laughed, and she tousled his hair. Her eyes, the same gray-green as Andy's, crinkled at the edges, until she turned to Danny. She said nothing, but he stepped back. He had practice with hatred. It burned from a hundred feet away.

"You need to go back," she said. "Do you know the way?"

He nodded. He was completely lost, but he didn't need a father to warn him that some people could not be trusted.

He stepped backward, tripped over a tree root, and went sprawling. Andy laughed as Danny got to his feet and ran. He heard the woman calling him back, but he wasn't about to stop. He knew he was going too fast, not watching for trails or vistas he might recognize, but too much was already familiar. He wasn't liked here, either.

By the time the stitch in his side dropped him to his knees, the forest had surrounded him and he had no idea where he was.

He actually wished for Charlie. He'd even settle for the reappearance of the jinn. He sniffed for smoke and smelled nothing, looked to the sky and saw an eagle circling.

"Shit," he said, curling up. "Carrion."

11

Situated on the lee side of Parker Mountain, over a fat, slow section of the river, guests of the Red Salmon Lodge feel safe and serene when, in fact, they've never been more at risk. The meadow is flood-prone, wolves roam the area, fires have swept through five times in the last twenty years, taking out cabins, the outhouse, and, unfortunately, Ellis Cantor's renowned moonshine still. In an emergency, there's no way out but the river.

Jina had yet to return from her walk when Irene sat in a green plastic chair, overlooking the river, a glass of surprisingly good wine in hand. She'd never minded being trapped. At the height of her celebrity, she'd welcomed swarming crowds, day-long benefits and interview sessions the producers insisted she attend. If the road led to riches, she had to take it; there was no sense worrying about other routes she might have traveled or what else might have been.

Naji leaned against Ellis's jet boat, a step from leaving her, and the remarkable thing was how the world didn't spin, how many birds chirped in the face of her sorrow. Even her own body went on; she breathed, took a sip of wine, decided, if it had to be this way, she would be the one to move out. She'd once thought she ought to live in L.A., closer to the work, but she'd never seen this color of light before—pure blue above the tree tops that melted into amber along the canyon walls. She'd never imagined herself in the mountains, and if she loved this place, what else might she adore? Small towns? Solitude? Anonymity?

It had never occurred to her that she might outgrow fame.

John sampled the hops-rich beer that Ellis brewed in his basement while Mary took a seat beside Irene. Alice walked up from the river warily, but Irene held her tongue. When Alice slipped into a chair beside Mary, she saw how much she shook. Watching Alice go to pieces on the river had been nearly as satisfying as tossing her overboard would've been. Irene couldn't wait to see what a Class IV rapid like Bailey would do to her.

Ahmad returned from his walk and went into the lodge to prepare for the Salat-ul-Asr, the mid-afternoon prayer. Irene had teased him once that he spent more time fixing himself up than she did, and had gotten only that hard stare in response. He would first wash his hands, then his mouth, nostrils, and face. He'd scrub his forearms and feet, and repeat the same ritual five times a day. Fifteen minutes later, he came out of the lodge, sparkling clean, and crossed the meadow. He narrowed his eyes when Irene poured more wine, and she glared right back. She couldn't deny his faithfulness, but she preferred the devotion of Jake, the terrier, who'd worship anyone who threw a stick, who wasn't so picky.

Ahmad turned east, brought his hands to his ears, palms forward. *"Allahu Akbar,"* he said.

"So I thought I'd start the new book in Salmon," Alice said. Irene stiffened. The woman's voice was like nails on a chalkboard. How did John and the kids stand it? "Really play up the luxuries of that B-and-B, so when the characters hit the river, it'll seem like they're entering another world."

Alice reached for the wine bottle, and Irene leaned back, made sure their fingers, even their exhalations, didn't touch. She rolled her eyes at Mary, who was too busy watching Ahmad put his right hand over the left and stare at the ground to notice.

"Bismil laahir rahmaanir raheem," Ahmad said.

"It's a good thing I came," Alice went on, though her voice wobbled. "I'd never have gotten the details right. You know how you picture things one way and they turn out totally different? This canyon's a lot closer than I thought. Not grand at all, really. Confined somehow, like we're all being squeezed down a funnel. I've got a vague idea about a storyline. There's this woman, Lana, in her thirties, a kind of misfit . . ."

"It's not just me," Irene said. "No one wants you here."

In the silence that followed, only Ahmad seemed unmoved. He bent forward, parallel to the ground. *"Allahu Akbar,"* he said again. *"Subhanna rabbiyal Azeem."*

Alice stared into her plastic cup; Irene and Mary looked out over the river. Irene had outgrown fame only to pick up worse habits. Now she'd be picky about the view out her window, who her companions were. She was getting too old to waste time on people she didn't like. She'd be hungry for danger all the time, for any chance to recognize what she could lose, how much she already had. That terrier really did know everything: Happiness was a stick you had to retrieve again and again and again.

Naji had left the jet boat and come up behind them. "Irene," he said harshly.

Irene ignored her husband and marched over to Alice, who gripped the edges of her lawn chair.

"I'm not going to hit you," she said. "I'm pretty sure."

"Why don't you?" Alice said, already crying again. "Just get it over with."

Irene shook her head. "There's nothing to get over anymore. You just go ahead and stay here where everyone hates you. Plan your book, pick someone else to destroy. How about Ellis? He was nice enough to offer us his lodge for the night. You could make him a one-dimensional bigot. Drew can be your clichéd, tree-hugging liberal. Take your pick. I'm done with you."

Alice looked toward a distant plume of smoke. Ahmad stood again, then slowly lowered himself to a kneeling position, touched his forehead, nose, and palms to the ground.

"You were done with me from the start," Alice said quietly, swiping at tears. "We were never friends."

Irene blinked. It was true, but she didn't like it admitted so publicly. Dislike was something they could have danced around for years.

Mary stood as Ahmad rose to a sitting position, then prostrated himself again. Irene braced for a hand on her shoulder, a sugary voice telling her to calm down. Instead, Mary stood shoulder to shoulder with her, and Irene realized she was tall. She had never noticed before that Mary was as tall as she was.

"It was cruel," Mary said softly, looking at Alice. "I know how hard it's been for you. I know what you've been through. But you shouldn't have done this to us. It wasn't worth what you've lost, I don't think."

Alice's weeping turned ugly and loud. John dropped the stick he'd been about to throw for the dog, and Jake nudged him with his black nose. Ahmad continued with his prayer, reciting the Qur'an, standing, sitting, finally looking over his right shoulder, which Naji had once told Irene was where the angel who recorded your good deeds resided, then over his left, at the angel who recorded his sins. *"As Salaamu 'alaikum wa rahmatulaah."* The only Arabic she knew: "Peace and blessings of God be upon you."

Irene should have been thrilled with Mary's support, but what she thought instead was that everyone was leaving her. Naji would take a jet boat upriver, Alice had betrayed them, Mary was becoming as unpredictable as Ahmad, Jina wasn't even here. It had been shortsighted, not to mention foolish, to have lived so long without a plan for being alone.

"You know what's scary?" Irene said. She could have followed with any number of things—the way the gold light faded to dusk's gray just like that, the brevity of beauty, the scarceness of devotion and true friends. "This fame, the money, won't make you happy, either. You can get accustomed to anything, believe me, and pretty soon you just want more."

Alice looked up, and Irene prayed no one said the obvious: She'd have done the same thing in Alice's position. Between the four of them, she and Alice were the most alike.

Irene kicked a stick, which Jake interpreted as a new game. He ran for it as Alice's loud, hiccupy tears moved only strangers. Helena hurried from the lodge with a sweater. She wrapped it around Alice's shoulders.

"Don't cry," she said. "We talk." The old woman led Alice up to the lodge.

"Well," Irene said when they'd gone.

Mary wore satin loungewear Irene never would have guessed she owned. In addition to being taller, Mary had also confiscated good posture. She stood with her shoulders back, stomach tucked. "She had it coming," she said.

Ahmad finally turned from Mecca. Though she knew he was supposed to put the world behind him when he prayed, he said, "Too bad you're not men. You would be ruthless in battle."

Irene tapped her foot. "Your God's an egomaniac. Even I don't need that much praise."

"Allah needs nothing. Salat is for us. A perfect prayer keeps us from evil. Successful are the believers."

"Well, good," Irene said. "I believe in plenty."

Irene glanced at her husband, who looked at her with those wounded brown eyes. The problem with guilt, she thought, is that it's boring; it's not meant to last. Once you truly regret who you've hurt, you should be free of it. Once you've fallen to your knees, no man should make you stay there.

Irene raised a finger at him. "You can hate what I did," she said, "but I won't let you treat me like this."

Naji didn't flinch. He looked at her as if she was a belly-up fish spoiling the sheen of the river.

"I should not have come," he said.

He stood with his arms at his sides, unbent, inscrutable. Years ago, when boys she'd slept with compared notes, and so-called friends applauded her attempted-murder charge, Irene had learned that there were only two types of people in the world: the tiny, inner circle who wanted the best for you, and an enormous outer ring filled with billions who just might want the worst. No one in the inner circle could be replaced; if you lost someone, you staggered around with a hole where they'd been. You leaked for the rest of your life.

"If I could go back and change things, I would," she said.

Only Ahmad responded, and his tired voice surprised her, as if he'd once said exactly the same thing. "You can't go back."

Naji stepped forward, but before he could speak, Jina came flying down the trail, dragging Charlie behind her. The boy's face was bruised; tears streamed down his cheeks.

"Have you seen Danny?" Jina shouted across the meadow.

"We thought he was with you," Irene called back.

Jina reached them, breathing hard. "No. The boys went out hours ago. Charlie said they got separated."

"I'm sure he's fine," John said. "Just exploring."

"No. There was a fire and the boys panicked. Charlie fell just trying to get back."

Irene glanced at the boy, whose gaze was on the ground, who hadn't gotten those bruises from any fall. Maybe you had to be a mother to want to hear lies. She touched Jina's arm, felt more than trembling. More like a bird's body when it's dying of fright.

"I don't smell smoke," Ahmad said.

"We saw it," Charlie said. "This thing . . . this jinn started a fire."

Irene looked at Naji. His eyes widened along with the rest of theirs, but Irene noticed the fist he made. The way his gaze scanned the blue sky.

"In any case, Danny couldn't have gone far," she said.

Jina turned toward the river. They all did. You couldn't not look at it. Even when all was well and your loved ones were right in front of you, it sauntered past, a bully spooking you with the things it might do.

"We should break into groups and look," Mary said.

Jina's hands went this way and that; Irene resisted the urge to grab her.

"Let's just stay calm," Irene said. "Naji and I will go up the trail. John, take Ahmad and Charlie and head up the river path. Mary and Jina, get Ellis to take you out in the jet boat."

Everyone but Naji took off at once. He stayed where he was, head down, and in a way, Irene was thankful for his childishness. It made her feel justified kicking him in the shin. He grunted, stumbled forward. When he looked up, his mellow eyes were enraged.

"Shaitan," he whispered. "Devil."

She drew back her foot, smiled meanly when he lurched

away. "Maybe I am, but let me tell you something, Naji Saleh. I've had about as much as I can take. You want to call it quits, fine. But right now my best friend's boy is lost. Right now there's something a little more important than your goddamn pride."

She started toward the upper path, kicking rocks out of her way, thinking she might have been right to cheat on him after all. She heard puffing behind her, felt a cool fingertip on her shoulder.

"You're right," Naji said. "Of course. I'm sorry."

Irene hung her head but kept walking. "Don't you understand? The moment it happened, I was sorry, too."

There are plenty of techniques to help you survive the wilderness, but the most basic one is this: Never take a sip of anything without looking into your glass first. Wasps are wine-lovers, bees prefer cola, flies get delirious over juice. Alice had never seen such aggressive insects, dive-bombing her ears, fearlessly aiming for her mouth whenever she opened it to breathe or yawn.

She swatted the insects as Helena led her to the lodge, crying out every time she swiped a stinger or wing. Helena served her tea at the kitchen table, watched her steadily while she drank. Was Helena some agent of Irene's? Was the tea laced with arsenic? Alice detected nothing but a faint smell of peppermint, but she took small sips to be sure. She really just wanted to lie down—preferably at home, with the shades drawn. She felt eight years old, felt that stinging sensation of being hated. It rose like a rash, prickled across her skin, burned, and she couldn't remember how she'd gotten through it. The trouble with survival instincts is that they're forgotten the moment you feel safe. After she joined the sushi club, only one day a month was different, yet everything changed. She was expected; someone called if she didn't show. She filled a slot, the emotional one. There was a place for her.

The tea didn't kill her. In fact, it was good. Strong and sweet. It soothed the pain in her temples, stopped her tears at last. The room, like all the others in the lodge, was dim and calming. While it grew quiet outside, Alice finished the drink. Helena turned the cup upside down on a plate.

The old woman took her hand. Alice expected Helena to read her palm, tell her she had three breaks along her lifeline and that all her friends would leave. Instead, Helena held it tightly between her own.

"Don't be afraid," the woman said. "I see two faces on you. Someone between us. Watching you. She's like you, only older, more tired."

Alice couldn't say if her trembling was because of this bullshit or because John had not come after her. He'd sat with that goofy dog rather than comfort her, and the enormity of what she'd done sunk in. Not only had she betrayed her friends, she'd disappointed John with her writing. Her greatest success was her worst effort, and she felt as if the river was closing over her. That horrible, hungry current slamming her to a rocky bottom, filling her lungs, suffocating her.

She'd become her grandmother, taken down by words.

"A mother, maybe?" Helena asked.

"My mother lives in Florida."

Helena cocked her head. "I try to get her attention, but she won't look at me. She's a little vain, I think."

Alice snatched her hand away. She walked to the only window, which looked out on the meadow that was now empty. She heard the jet boat fire up.

"Look, I don't believe in this kind of thing."

Helena laughed. It was so unexpected, so girlish, that Alice turned back. The woman turned over Alice's cup, where the tea leaves had stuck to the bottom in the shape of a lamp, slender through the bottom, an umbrella on top. She could only imagine what that might mean—probably death or disaster. The loss of all she held dear.

"Belief," Helena said, still laughing. "Who cares? The face is still there. Narrower through the cheeks. Eyes like stones."

Alice got a chill down her spine. She thought of her grandmother. Near the end, Norma Meyer's whole face had seemed to be disintegrating, sinking, except for the eyes. Her suicide had made all the papers. Wouldn't it figure that Alice's guardian angel would be a woman who couldn't even save herself?

Helena watched her, watched belief dawning, then turned back to the tea leaves.

"I want to talk to my children," Alice said.

Helena nodded. "When Ellis gets back, he'll bring out the phone."

"I want to be happy."

"Well. That's another story."

Alice stepped back to the table, gestured toward the cup. "What do the leaves say?"

She braced herself. She remembered the way her grandmother had sat in a chair and not moved, how the last drops of joy had drained from her as if there was a leak in her heart. She thought of the realization Norma must have come to, that if you let things go far enough, you reach a point when it is impossible to fix your life.

She thought about a psychiatrist she knew. What a gift it would be to always have someone on her side.

"Lamp," Helena told her, then looked up and smiled. "A surprising revelation. Something lost will be regained."

For Mary, the jet boat was almost as thrilling as the raft. Ellis explained that they had to pick up speed immediately in order to plane on top of the water and stay clear of rocks. There was no margin for error. The channels were narrow, the boat wide; he had to steer dangerously close to boulders to make it through.

There was a sheltered seat behind the windshield, but Mary sat in the open stern of the boat. She turned her face into the spray and tried to focus on spotting Danny, but possibilities clouded her vision. After she'd seen Drew swimming with the salmon, she'd wondered what it would feel like to swim beside him, flop down on sandy beaches, kiss. Drew had come here from somewhere else, too, proven it could be done. Everything could change. A woman who'd never made plans was free to do and become anything, and Mary imagined herself as a campfire story, a canyon legend, a river nymph. A tale of such audacity, romance, and strangeness that most logical people would not believe it.

She laughed, then ducked her face to hide her ill-timed joy. Of course, her ideas were preposterous. She and Drew were nothing alike. He'd come because his father was here, because he was a man and could handle the rough conditions, because he'd found a purpose. She had no purpose; she'd come because she had nowhere else to go. Even if she wasn't imagining that Drew looked at her a little longer than the others, that his voice softened when he said her name, her future was not on the banks of the Salmon River. Her Honda sat on the street back home; her savings was tied up in mutual funds. Every fantasy she'd had since she'd gotten here was ludicrous, including the one where she appeared to be going back in time. Whenever she heard the slap of Drew's flip-flops, she remembered something else from her youth: that she'd once loved all animals, not just cats; that she'd been a giggler; that she'd been extraordinarily fast. As a child, she'd won every sprint she'd entered. In the heat of summer, when other kids withered and slowed, she'd gotten even faster. In the last twenty years, she'd spent far too little time outdoors.

The jet boat slammed through waves the size of her condominium, and she bit her lip to keep from hooting. She could fly out of this boat at any moment, and probably would, the way she was leaning over the side, strumming her fingertips through the water. Her scalp tingled, as if it were being filled with bubbling oxygen.

Jina stumbled to the back of the boat, bracing herself against the chop of the waves. "Do you see him?" she shouted over the engine.

Mary shook her head, pulled Jina to the seat beside her. Jina had stopped crying, but her body was stiff, unyielding. Her gaze never left the shore. First the right bank, then the left, right, left. Here she was, twelve years later, looking for someone else on the Salmon. How she must hate this river, this whole canyon.

"There!" Ellis shouted.

Jina turned where Ellis pointed. In an eddy near the left bank, two human forms floated on their backs. Mary's heart leapt to her throat. Then one of the forms lifted his head, smiled, and waved. Drew. He sat up in the water, shirtless, wearing khaki shorts and flip-flops, a blue bandana around his head. Ludicrous, certainly, the way her body leaned forward, every hair stood on end. As if every person on the planet was magnetized and had only to find true north. The other form got to his feet, and as they closed in, Mary saw the marks on Danny's face. A cut on his cheek, his left eye nearly swollen shut. Jina's legs buckled, but Danny was hopping up and down, blue as a fish, ecstatic. Ellis pulled the boat up beside them, jumped out, and tied the rope to a rock on shore. He breathed deeply once, twice, then turned to his son.

"That's it," he said. "You're fired."

Mary and Jina jumped into the shallows as Drew stood. The water took a dozen channels down his chest, and she watched enviously as one trickle claimed his hip, another a thigh, a third the scar on the side of his knee. She wanted to shake her mother, wanted to ask her what had scared her, wanted most of all not to think of her now.

He didn't even look at his father. "Heya, Mary," he said.

She really was going back in time; she felt a teenager's shriek at the back of her throat, a brash disregard of logic, consequences. Someone ought to have warned her that love is easier to start than stop. She'd had trouble with the very basics, hadn't come close to the hard part yet.

"Calm down, Dad," Drew said. "Everyone's fine."

"My God," Jina said. "Danny, what happened to you?"

Ellis took Drew by the arm. "You know what you put this little lady through? You stop to think about what happened to her before?"

"If you'd give me a minute to ex—"

"You don't think, that's your trouble. You and your kind. You *feel*, am I right? Bordering on queer, but I ain't going there today. You think it's all right to put a mother through hell while you fill a boy's head with talk of *fish*. You don't care that you're hurting people. People don't matter to you much."

"If you'd just listen—"

"No, I don't think I will. I tried to make it up to you, let you pass out your propaganda, get the guests all riled up. I got nothing else to feel guilty for. It was your mother's choice to leave. It was her decision. I tried to call you; she wouldn't put me through. I'm done now, you hear? I'm not putting up with any more talk of the *scenery*. This is hard land. Hell, I could fill the river with gasoline and she'd eat it for breakfast. She'll survive us all."

Drew narrowed his eyes, for a moment looked more like his father than he could have stomached. Then he took a deep breath, gently touched Danny's swollen cheek as if it was exactly the color it should be, the deep blue of the river. When he turned to his father, he finally looked his age. Slumped and tired.

"You're killing this place," he said softly.

"*Bah!* I own the river company. Remember that."

"Half."

"Fifty-one percent."

Jina splashed through the water, stepped between them. "Stop it," she said. "Danny." She took the boy's face in her hands.

Danny ducked away. "I fell. Finding my way out of the woods. Up there."

Jina followed his finger upriver, through the trees, but Mary was certain Danny was exaggerating. Surely he hadn't gone that far.

"Charlie said he fell, too," Jina said.

Danny looked up, surprised. "Yeah?"

Jina sighed. "What were you boys doing? He said there was a fire, but we don't see anything."

Danny shrugged. "I thought so. I don't know."

The air did smell slightly smoky, but the canyon was always like that at dusk. There were hamburgers and hot dogs roasting on beaches from here to Riggins.

"Probably that fire in Hell's Canyon," Drew said. "The winds are coming out of the west now."

"Nah," Ellis said. "It's the fire down in the White Clouds.

Damn environmentalists won't let them clear the dead pines. Whole thing's a tinderbox from beetles."

"And I suppose your answer is to clear-cut?" Drew said. "Just bring in the bulldozers."

"Please!" Jina said. She tried to catch Danny's gaze. "I was sick with worry."

Danny stepped back, and Mary didn't blame him. It was panic, not smoke, in the air. Too many imaginations running wild.

"Right," Danny said. "It's all my fault. Blame me for falling."

"No harm done," Mary and Drew said at the same time. She turned to him, smiled. The pressure on the small of her back was either a butterfly or his hand. "My bet is you and Charlie will be watching your step from now on," she went on. "You won't be going too far."

Danny glanced at his mother. Jina bit her lip, shifted her weight as if something was unbalanced inside her, forces driving her two ways.

"I need to know where you are," she said finally. "I don't want you leaving camp without an adult. Anything could happen."

"Yeah, yeah," Danny said, bouncing again. "Got it. You know what, Mom? You know what Drew says? There's a guy who drowned here one year and came back to life. Isn't that awesome? He's cold-blooded now. He's, like, part fish!"

Ellis shook his head. "Damn stories," he said, but Mary noticed that he kept one eye on the river, as if a man might swim past at any moment. Mary truly hoped he would. A fish-man, she thought, her heart racing. There went her imagination again. Gills for lungs, a silvery sheen to the skin, the strength to swim for miles—in fact, to never stop. She dared a glance at Drew, found him staring right back at her.

No wonder teenagers do damage. Their bodies are filled with electricity, not blood. When they start to believe they're wanted, they burn.

12

A good storyteller believes his own stories, so Naji Saleh went into medicine. He loved telling tales, but he had an exceptional grip on reality. For Danny's sake, he spoke of the branches of trees as the arms of the jinn, but he couldn't keep a straight face. He was a doctor, a scientist; how could a spirit possess a canyon? How could a tree ever, even under the most extraordinary circumstances, be anything more than a tree?

This kind of thinking made him a fine Muslim, no matter what his father and brother might think. Islam is a rigidly monotheistic religion; at best, other idols and spirits worked the fringes. The jinn, Khidr, Iblis, king of the Satans. Beautiful, scary side stories, with no basis in fact. For a while after he moved to the United States, Naji continued with the salat, praying five times a day, getting in his forty rakats. It wasn't his growing practice that sapped his faith, or Irene's desire to go places, to throw yet another party when he ought to be on his knees. No, he stopped praying because it occurred to him that God had all the makings of myth, too. He was another good story that Naji couldn't quite believe.

He heard the roar of the jet boat, the honking of the horn. Danny had been found. Irene leaned against a tree in relief, but Naji had never doubted the outcome. Danny was an American boy, and, by and large, American boys survived. He turned back toward the lodge, walked softly, while Irene flattened pine-cones, snapped branches off at the wrist. She wouldn't have stopped, he was sure, if the trees cried out, if a jinn appeared right in front of her.

Of course he had to divorce her. He was no extremist; he wouldn't shame her or enforce one hundred strokes. But neither would he live with a woman who couldn't see the obvious. He had come to the United States for the educational opportunities and stayed, quite frankly, for the money. He was a practical, mythless man, and the fact that he'd fallen in love with a fanciful soap-opera star, a flashy woman completely unsuited to him, yet the only one who'd ever made him laugh out loud, should have proven to Irene that devotion cannot be questioned or ignored. He was divorcing her not for the affairs but because she was blind. She'd never seen how happy she made him.

Ahmad would quote from the Qur'an: "It may be, if he divorced you, that Allah will give him in exchange consorts better than you." Or, from the hadith: "Wives are playthings, so take your pick." Ahmad would tell him he should have beaten Irene a long time ago. In Saudi Arabia, as long as a man stops short of disfiguring his wife, any amount of force is allowed. Ahmad would tell him a lot of things, and Naji would not listen. He loved his brother, but after Ahmad started the fire, Naji trusted very little of what he said.

All Naji had ever wanted was to become a doctor, and that self-seeking desire had shamed his father, revolted the brother who rose from the ashes of the house fire as another person—first a haunted boy beside his father's hospital bed, then, when their father recovered, a transformed, fiercely pious young man. The only time Naji prostrated himself was when he asked their father to allow him to study in the United States, and he never heard the answer. His father left a plane ticket on the table and all of Naji's belongings in a pile outside the front door. He never spoke to his oldest son again.

Ahmad had taken Naji to the airport, but there was contempt in his eyes. Ahmad said he'd only followed him to the United States to bring him home, but Naji didn't want to believe it. Every man can and should grow up to change his mind about everything. Only boys think like their fathers.

But sometimes men regress. When Irene was getting parts, away from home for weeks at a time, Naji wandered the house, lost without her. The furniture, the paintings, the rugs all looked excessive, overdone; nothing made sense for a man alone. He felt revolted by his extravagance and fell back on his roots—washing obsessively, masturbating in terror, fearing Allah's punishment for his indulgences and doubts. Desperate for solace, he wondered if salvation could be found through jihad, which promises forgiveness for those who fight for Allah. But always, thankfully, Irene came home. Furniture regained appropriate dimensions, frivolous knickknacks became, once more, cherished works of art. He admitted that he didn't want redemption; he wanted to continue committing the worst sin in Islam: the worship of someone other than Allah. He'd been fighting jihad for her all along.

Now, in the woods, Naji slowed and Irene slammed into his back. "I was shown the Hell-fire," Muhammad said in the hadith, "and that the majority of its dwellers are women." Islamic women veiled their beauty, lowered their gazes. They appeared to be kept in their place, but there'd always been a knowing smile beneath his mother's veil, black eyes that took in everything.

"What?" Irene asked. "Do you have something to say?"

It felt like he'd been talking for hours. Days.

Irene narrowed her eyes at him. They stepped into the meadow in front of the lodge, and Naji felt parched. Since he'd come to this country, he'd suffered from an unquenchable thirst. It was all those soda commercials, the marvelous sting of Coca-Cola, root beer's extravagant foam. He slipped Mountain Dew into his coffee cup so his patients wouldn't know he drank it for breakfast.

Ellis was tying up the jet boat, Danny hopping on shore like a beached fish. The sun had dipped behind the mountains, and the water looked dark as the wines Naji had also grown to love. The delicious Napa Valley merlots and pinot noirs. Ellis stomped to the lodge, grabbed his rifle from the porch. With any imagination at all, Naji would have invented a gleeful murmur following the old man as he disappeared into the woods.

Ellis had an imagination, but right now it was swamped with

visions of wringing his son's neck. He headed up the Lucky Creek trail, not bothering to chat with that movie star and her husband. He'd dealt with Hollywood liberals before— celebrities who got back to nature with a hundred members of their entourage, studio execs who demanded fresh steaks but refused to hear where they came from. A bunch of fur-covered hypocrites, if you asked him. He had no time for their long-distance causes and sentimentality. If he didn't tag enough elk in summer and fall, he and Helena went hungry in winter. Simple as that.

He cocked his rifle. Hunting seasons were for people with access to supermarkets. No slick-dressed Boisean was going to tell him elk season didn't open until September. It opened the day Ellis went out to hunt. Let Fish and Game come after him; he'd welcome a fight. It'd take his mind off bigger issues, like what he'd felt when he'd seen Drew lounging in the water, trying to turn the next generation even softer. Ellis had realized then and there that he'd have been better off not knowing his son at all. Strangers invoked far less disappointment.

He couldn't blame Drew entirely for the way he'd turned out; when he was being honest, Ellis blamed himself. Nearly forty years ago, Ellis's ex-wife got fed up with the weeks he spent on the river and took Drew, along with the good china and every last cent from their joint savings account, to L.A. No doubt she'd bad-mouthed Ellis every minute of the next thirty-five years, until Drew showed up on Ellis's doorstep and pronounced him the devil in flannel. Apparently, Ellis's son had spent his teens, twenties, even early thirties trying to be everything Ellis was not, including a vegetarian, a liberal, and a shiftless drifter. He'd gone to half a dozen colleges, switched majors continually, worked job after job only to discover that he knew only what he didn't want to be: a man a woman ran from. There was no excuse, Drew said first thing, to turn hard and mean as the land.

Ellis offered no rebuttal. For a while, he thought it was his penance to listen, to not say one word about a woman who never should have insisted she loved the mountains as much as he did, or about how sensitive the ears become after everyone you've loved has left. For a few weeks, Ellis waited for Drew to speak his piece and leave, but the farewell never came. Drew refused to sleep indoors. He lay on the beach, stared gaga-eyed at the stars, and one morning Ellis found him curled up like a baby, sobbing. Ellis expected some boy lover to come walking out of the trees then and there, for his whole world to go up in smoke. Even without a homo for a son, it did. Drew refused to leave the canyon, said he'd finally found his calling. He was going to save the salmon, protect the river, offset any damage Ellis might do. Where there was death there was life, he said, or something nearly as cockamamie. While living up No Man's Creek, Ellis had often imagined the sound of his son's voice, and it had never said anything as ridiculous as that. Until Drew came back, Ellis hadn't fully appreciated what a blessing two decades as a hermit had been.

He'd gone up No Man's Creek for two reasons: because water had started to look a little scary after those boys died in Big Mallard, and because he'd come to believe, as his ex-wife had told him, that he wasn't fit for company. They were hard years, sure, but also satisfying, humbling. Eighteen years later, he walked out the same way he walked in—with nothing but pebbles in his shoes, holding a rifle and an ax. He felt nearly hospitable, so he hiked upriver, found a level spot past Rainier, and built his moonshine shed first. He made money off his whiskey and, after he fashioned some pine-straw mattresses, from the rafters who wanted a real bed. After a few years, he saved enough for the jet boat. No woman in Salmon would have him, so he put out an ad for a Russian wife. The night Helena arrived, she looked at the makeshift cabins, the mud, and the outhouse, and, with the little English she'd learned on the train west, said, "This no New York, man." He laughed; that was her gift to him. More than he'd expected, probably more than he deserved.

Helena liked Drew from the start, the way he always got ships in his tea leaves, a fortunate omen. She was the one who came up with the idea for a river-running company he and Drew could manage together. "A truce," she said. "A meeting place." She wouldn't let Ellis say a word when Drew drained the profits for salmon recovery, when he railed against senators Ellis had voted for and admired. She kept him silent whenever Drew brought his long-haired friends to the lodge to hug the trees and cry over the fish on their plates. "He knows you're father," she said at night, her wonderful hair sliding through his lips, another gift. "You in charge."

But something had changed today, something in Drew's eyes. There was no longer an inch of give in them, as if he'd had enough, too.

Ellis stomped through the brush, up the game trail, making so much noise that he scared away any animal worth its salt. He wished it was voting day. He'd like to tighten the screws on

Drew, usher in a few more antigay, anti-salmon, anti-ridiculousness Republicans. Even when he'd lived in a shack up No Man's Creek, he'd come out to vote for the most conservative senator on every ballot, and he'd tell anyone who'd listen why. Because this was Idaho, and that meant no one in pinstripes could tell you what to do. You could be a thief back east, a serial killer from Texas, even a hippie from California, but once you got to Idaho you were the guy whose hand-built cabin could never be found by the Feds, due to neighborly misdirections. In Idaho, you got to start over, and Ellis couldn't say if that was right or wrong, only that, like many men, he'd started out here shaking and had grown, over the years, quiet and still.

Men like Drew, men who wanted to clean up the rivers and welcome the homosexuals, men who worshipped fish and Vermont governors, men who thought they were saving this state, were actually ruining it. Hell, why didn't Drew just move to Massachusetts where he'd be welcomed, where his plans would work? Ellis lowered his gun, took a deep breath. It was impossible for the young, the idealistic, to understand that sometimes nothing you do matters. Sometimes the kindest thing you can do for yourself is leave things alone.

Ellis heard the crackling of twigs, saw a flash of brown through the brush. He raised his rifle, felt a surge of adrenaline, a momentary joy. The animal's head was down, grazing, and from down the draw Ellis heard laughter, the strings of Drew's guitar. His own son didn't respect him, had built a life out of opposing him. He pulled the trigger.

Animals don't cry. Ellis scoffed at Drew's pathetic arguments against hunting—how unfair it was, how uncivilized, an archaic cruel streak only barbarians would brag about. Ellis countered that somebody had to do the killing; it was childish to pretend otherwise. Drew had never held a rifle, so he couldn't know. The joy wasn't in the killing but in the hunt. A good hunter slowed his heartbeat to the speed of the wind, let the humanness slip out of his veins as he stood still as a tree. A good hunter fiercely protected the wilderness and his right to it. He was more environmentalist than a hippie like Drew would ever be.

Ellis walked across the clearing, stepped around the bush, saw the elk. His hand began to shake; the rifle fell. He dropped to his knees beside Elvis, whose eyes were still open, whose nostrils flared. He looked into the creature's eyes and heard no music. He curled his weathered hands into fists.

Ahmad stood on a rise, watching the man kneel beside the dying elk. He felt pity for the beast but not for the man, felt things he hadn't prepared for.

He had come on this trip with Naji expecting to hate this land, hate it the way he hated the excessively ornate houses in his neighborhood, the horrors of the Castro district, the entire garish city. He had come with visions of scorching the hillsides, turning the river black with ash, yet now all he could imagine was disappearing into a canyon and never coming out. There was no denying the majesty of this place—tree-lined peaks, ferocious rapids, soil so fertile that things grew overnight. He'd grown up in a monochrome landscape, planted gardens in sand; he'd rationed water for his mother's favorite two-date palms, awoke to a layer of fine silt on his sheets. It was hard to understand Allah's thinking: The most beautiful land on the planet belonged to people who didn't deserve it.

Americans didn't even appreciate what they had; they spoiled their treasures with sewage and development, remorselessly killed animals that lived nowhere else on earth. They would be punished in the afterlife, but what right did they have to happiness and beauty now? Ahmad's father had demanded he study the Qur'an, but it wasn't until Ahmad was sixteen and his father caught him sneaking out one last time that he took Allah's words to heart. When his father beat him hard enough to crack his skull, he remembered whole sections, beginning with Qur'an 4:56: "Those who disbelieve in our revelations, we will condemn to the hellfire. Whenever their skins are burnt, we will give them new skins. Thus, they will suffer continuously. God is Almighty. Most Wise."

He sneered at the man crouched over the animal, crying over the very thing he'd destroyed. Americans were like children, stupid and rough. They ruined things, then wanted someone else to fix it. They preached peace but were bullies, while Islam was clear: "If anyone desires a religion other than Islam, it shall never be accepted of him." There are no evangelizing Muslims; there is no need to change minds. If you do not believe, you must be expelled, ignored, or defeated, and Allah reserves a special place for those who fight in His name. "If you are slain or die in the way of Allah, forgiveness and mercy from Allah are far better than all they could amass."

He had not always believed this. As a teenager, he believed in his singing voice. He believed in kissing as many girls as he could. He believed he could dance, though never in his own house, where his father would beat him for such sinful displays. He was young, naïve, so he believed he could outwit his heritage. He did not have to follow his father's rules, subscribe to such a fierce religion. He could escape through his bedroom window, and the beatings he suffered when he came back would only make him more resolute.

Which was true, until his skull cracked. Tears had slid down Ahmad's cheeks as his father dropped his hands, stepped back.

"Only Allah will not disappoint you," his father said, which turned out to be true.

He had headaches after that. His singing voice wobbled, he heard music when none was playing, and people looked at him as if he wasn't right. When he was well enough to leave his room, he lit a mound of kerosene-soaked sheets beneath his parents' bed. He screamed for Naji, pulled his mother from the room before the flames took hold; his father escaped with third-degree burns on eighty percent of his body. When it was unclear if the man would live, Ahmad got the shakes. His friends avoided him; he hardly slept. In the middle of the night, he walked stiffly past houses where he'd once danced, managed only whispers on street corners where he'd laughed. He felt as if he'd died in the fire and been born into another world—a world where men were forced to cruelty, a world where only violence worked, a world of men, unfortunately, where everyone but Allah disappointed.

When his father recovered, Ahmad bowed his head to God's will.

They never spoke of it. Beyond atrocity, they found a kind of tenderness, the stunned stillness of men who have gone too far. The beatings stopped, as did Ahmad's rebellion. When his father was released from the hospital, he and Ahmad walked out with their arms so tight around each other's waists, they looked like one man.

His father was there when Ahmad devoted his life to jihad, to warfare against the nonbelievers of Islam. It was his father who sent him after Naji, who hinted that there might be more in store for him in America than merely bringing his brother home. "Slay the pagans wherever you find them," his father quoted from the Qur'an.

Ahmad had made contacts in America, but no group, in his mind, went far enough. He wasn't sure what his mission was, but he knew it was more than a computer virus or power disruption that struck terror in no one. Even a suicide bomber was no longer the top news item of the day. Allah demanded more than that, and Ahmad required a demanding god. Otherwise, he would have no respect for Him.

Ahmad looked at the man once more, then turned his back. The deeper he went into the mountains, the more relief he got from the chronic pain in his skull. Naji belittled his interest in Khidr, the prophet, the traveler, the Green One; his brother had been so stripped of his faith, he could no longer imagine that everyone is more than they seem. Like Khidr, Ahmad had been given an affinity for nature; he'd been lifted from the realm of men to receive illumination directly from Allah. There was no more obvious sign than being led to this place, to tinder-dry forests, thousands of acres of trees weakened by bugs and decades of abuse. He reached the peak and his head was clear. He felt a surge of joy, a perfect, painless moment. He finally knew his charge: Everything must be lost in order to be gained.

On the summit, he had a view of the lodge, of the lovely

river, of his brother smoking his cigarette on the lawn. Ahmad steeled himself against emotion. Naji had tried to keep him safe all those years ago, signaling from the window when their father was waiting to beat his errant son. Ahmad had tried to return the favor, tried to bring Naji home, but Allah had willed this ending. Everything had led to this moment, when he reached into his pocket for the match.

Down the mountain, John struck a match, lit the propane light in the bedroom. He closed his eyes and imagined being at this lodge with only Alice and the kids, the whole river to themselves. They would run their own raft, sleep on white sand beaches, sit around a campfire until the stars came out, too many stars to be believed. He imagined wilderness the way most people wanted, even needed, it to be: tame and predictable, all the sights within walking distance of the campground, the bathroom, the shore, something you floated through, took pictures of, put in your pocket as a souvenir. Nothing like what was really out there, bigger than you could imagine and impossible to prepare for.

He turned to the bed, the scattered, crumpled notes, a dozen ways to say good-bye. Alice was more courageous than she realized; words were often a daredevil act. The truth was that taking risks, tearing down what he'd built, gave him no pleasure at all. He was in insurance for a reason; he knew to safeguard what was treasured most. Yet he settled on a note, folded it in his pocket, rehearsed. He'd floated a portion of the Salmon. He'd gone as far as he could.

Someone pounded on the door, and he prayed it was Alice, coming to comfort *him* for a change. He prayed for a lot of things and tried not to lose faith when his prayers went unanswered. One day, he thought, God would take a break from the complicated stuff and listen to a simple man. He'd teach John how to make his wife happy.

It was only Drew at the door. "Thought you might like to take a hike," the guide said. "The sun's down, but we can make it to the waterfall before it's totally dark."

John stepped back. "You're not fired, then?"

Drew laughed. "Probably. But my dad and I have this unspoken bargain. He pretends I'm crazy, and I picture him like some actor in an old John Wayne movie. We stay away from what's real. That's the only way we can stand it."

John tapped his pocket. "I think I'll pass on that hike, if you don't mind."

Drew nodded. Every trip was the same. Someone turned jubilant. Another cracked. Most guides prepared more for foul people than bad weather, but for five years, Drew hadn't delved too deep. His guests paid the money that saved one more salmon. If he looked beyond that, if he looked into their eyes, he got sidetracked, started thinking, as most do, that sometimes people mattered more.

He got damn good at sidelong glances, until Mary. Suddenly, he couldn't *stop* looking at her, and he got more than distracted. He got downright confused. What was it, exactly, that needed saving here? A river, a fish, maybe something as simple as a laugh. Mary had laughed so rarely, she still sounded like a child. She'd been saving all her pleasure up.

"You're leaving, then," he said.

John shrugged. Drew thought the man ought to leave. On a raft, the quickest path to disaster is uncertainty—taking too long deciding what you need to do.

Drew left John in his bedroom. He looked for Mary, felt uncomfortably rebuffed when Alice told him she'd gone to her room. Avoiding the others, he headed to the river trail, fell into a quick, agitated step. Without tourists, he tuned out the sights, didn't glance at the bear tracks he might have pointed out. He made better time alone but didn't enjoy it much.

Since he'd arrived on his father's doorstep, the river had made him feel needed, noble but never cherished, never really acknowledged at all. He was surprised at how small and selfish he still was. He wanted to save the salmon and have her *notice*. He wanted a hero's welcome every single night when he came home.

He had never considered that he might be the one who needed saving.

It was nearly dark when he reached the rapids at Rainier. A flash of silver through the trees caught his eye. He knew it was a man, but in the darkness wrinkles look like gills across a creature's neck. Creases take the shape of scales. Drew blinked; he liked a good story, but he was not the fool his father took him for. Unfortunately, exhaustingly, he knew the facts. The water in the Salmon River was grossly polluted; in the 1990s the Grouse Creek mine, applauded by the state for its environmental record, dumped cyanide into the path of migrating salmon at levels sixty times greater than those toxic to fish. Hundreds of thousands of sockeye once traveled the nine hundred miles from ocean to rivers to lakes in the Stanley basin each year; now the return of twenty-one hatchery-produced adults was hailed as a triumphant success. The thirty-five gray wolves reintroduced into Idaho in 1995 were considered nonessential, and within five years two dozen had been shot to death. He could go on and on, but knowledge like this weighed on him like a stone. When he'd first learned the facts, he'd felt as though he was being squeezed dry of hope. That was the first time he swam with the salmon, creatures that hurt no one, whose morals were pure. If they could swim to the ocean and back, certainly he could convince a few old men to make their path a little easier. Certainly, he could change one man's mind.

The man he'd heard about, told campfire stories about, stepped around a tree, came forward. "There's a fire," he said. "Maybe more than one."

Everyone knew the stories about Pearl. About this man, found in the river. No one knew the truth, so anything could be said— that Pearl had hooked him in the Salmon, reeled him in and warmed him up. She would have eaten him for dinner, except that he began to sprout legs and arms. He asked if he could stay.

"My dad thinks it's smoke from the White Clouds," Drew said.

The man shook his head. "It's close. No lightning strikes, either. Could be someone's cigarette. Or arson. Wind's still heading away. You'll be fine if you leave first thing tomorrow."

"How about you?"

The fish-man walked away without answering, walked until

he was alone. He slipped into the river and didn't feel the cold. He lay on his back in an eddy, stared at the sky. This stretch of river was crowded by Salmon River standards—three cabins and a fire lookout within three miles. Surely, someone had called the Forest Service about the plume of smoke growing in the distance. He prayed he wouldn't have to go to Ellis's and make the call himself, something he'd done only once before, when Andy had the fever.

Reluctantly, he rose from the river, headed back along the trail to Lantz Bar. After that, for miles, he'd find trails where there were none, walk the land and never get lost. He could slip into Montana and still find his way home.

Pearl had left with Andy this morning, and he was relieved to find them in the garden when he returned, harvesting the banana-sized pea pods by starlight. Their garden was the talk of the canyon, a veritable farm. He put his hand on Andy's head, kissed Pearl on the mouth. She smiled, flipped her hair. Sometimes she looked like the prom queen she'd told him she'd been before. Sometimes he admitted he was probably happier this way.

He didn't tell her about the smoke. He'd do whatever was required to keep her and Andy safe, including abandoning the cabin, taking to the river itself. He'd never told her about the cougar he'd shot after it stalked the cabin for three nights, or how close he'd come to leaving. He didn't want to worry her. She'd already plucked him from the river. She'd already done enough.

. . .

Alice was first in line to use the satellite phone Ellis retrieved from the basement. She sat at the kitchen table while Jina lounged in the living room, flipping pages in a fishing magazine that could have been the same one she'd read twelve years before.

"Grandpa's not teasing you, is he?" Alice asked her son. "Did Grandma leave a light on in the bathroom last night? Are you brushing? I miss you terribly. I can't wait to come home."

She talked for ten minutes, nearly nonstop. When she hung up, Jina heard her breathing, stilling her tears. It was exhausting, hating her. Jina had no idea how she would keep it up.

"Your kids don't care what you do for a living," Jina said. "You could do nothing, and they'd still be grateful you're home when they get off from school. They'd still feel lucky."

Alice looked at her hands, finally pushed herself up from the table. "If that's the case," she said quietly, "then Danny's lucky, too."

After Alice had gone, Jina looked at the magazine, but she'd never been much interested in fish. The satellite phone rang, but Ellis hadn't come back from hunting. Helena was out in the garden.

She walked to the phone. "Red Salmon Lodge," she said.

"Jina? Jina, is that you?"

She almost said no. She heard the river, the groan of trees. She'd longed to hear Mike's voice, but now it sounded like a scream across the quiet, something out of another time.

"Hello, Mike," she said.

"Thank God. I've been calling and calling. The phone must not have been working. Listen, it's about Ahmad. You should have told me he was going with you."

"I didn't know until the last minute," she said. "Anyway, Ahmad's fine."

"No, Jina. I don't think he is."

She shook her head. She had the most ridiculous notion that she was betraying them both: Zach with Mike, Mike with Zach. Even Earl was there, hunched over forlornly in the back of her mind. Maybe she hadn't loved any of them right. Each wanted something she didn't have, something she'd given to the others.

"Does this mean you're going to tell me something for once?" she asked. "You're going to trust me with what you know?"

She didn't know if she wanted him to. She'd complained that he never told her secrets, but now she realized she'd walked out of the room every time one might be spilled. She hadn't confused him with Zach; she'd depended on him being someone entirely different, someone safe, quiet, contained. She'd never realized just how much he'd done for her; he'd shrunk himself to the size she needed him to be.

"There's a file on him," he said. "There's a file on everyone these days. There's nothing concrete; otherwise, we would have moved already. It's just a hunch, Jina. I want you to come home. You and Danny. Please come home."

Her stomach was in knots. Mike's tenderness spilled through the phone, while in person it suffered from the yawn he couldn't stem, from a glance at the television, his odor after a day in the sun. It was disconcerting how much easier it was to love him, or anyone, when he wasn't there.

"I can't," she said. "I can't do that to Danny."

"But Ahmad——"

"He's fine, Mike. Devout, certainly, but that's no crime. It's admirable in this day and age."

She heard him clicking his teeth, holding back words. Finally, he said, "And you? Are you all right?"

She glanced out the window at the glow of the campfire, a ceiling of stars. Irene and Mary were laughing out on the lawn. "We'll see you in a few days," she said. "We'll talk then."

"Jina!"

If he'd been beside her, she'd have pressed her face into his chest. She'd have let him steer the raft or take them home, and it seemed that was the whole problem. Up until this moment, she'd let men decide what she would do.

"I couldn't bear it if something happened to you," he said.

She stiffened from surprise, realized he loved her better from a distance, too. Or with a broken proposal between them, when it looked like she was getting away.

"Oh, Mike," she said, "unless you're dead, things happen all the time."

When she walked outside, she was satisfied to note that the wind had been overrun with girl talk. Mary and Irene had taken their drinks down to the beach. Their voices matched the river, light one minute, intense the next. Alice and Helena huddled together on the porch, Alice's voice squeaking, Helena's deep and soothing, like cloud cover on a blazing day.

Jina found Danny cross-legged on the lawn, picking through a smorgasbord of rocks. She tried not to look at his face, not to guess what had really happened today. He and Charlie had both covered for the other, and that was something. That held hope.

She sat beside him. She had stayed on that mountain too long, trying to logic away Ellis bringing up Zach's name to that woman. She'd clung to the tree, told herself that of course it wasn't *her* Zach. She'd seen him floating facedown in the river. If it were her Zach, he'd have come for her.

When she'd discovered Danny gone, it had felt like her lungs collapsing, like she was caving in. It was impossible to understand the simplest things—the assurances Mary offered, Ellis's placating nods around every deserted bend. Jina had looked over the jet boat's railing and cursed the water. She'd prayed that the salmon did go extinct, that an earthquake jammed Big Mallard, that people stopped coming. Person or place, she knew a bully when she saw one.

Her son tilted forward like a miser over his treasure, sorting his rocks. His T-shirt was torn, his shorts mud-stained. His red hair was a tangle of dirt and sap, and she knew that despite finding him safe and sound, she hadn't fully recovered him. Like anyone who went into the woods, he came out as another person. At this point, there was nothing she could do.

She massaged her chest, a painful spot beneath the sternum. She'd taken too many short breaths today. She stared at the dirty, brave, enlivened creature who was like his father in so many ways except one. Danny, it seemed, would survive.

"You realize there are animals in the woods," she said.

He shrugged his shoulders, and she took his arm, pinched just a bit. "Dan?"

"I'm not stupid," he said, jerking her off.

"You could have come back with more than just a few scrapes. You might not have come back."

"Duh," Danny said. He gave her such a scornful look, she drew back. She was actually beginning to dislike him, and that was a relief. It was a normal, suburban kind of feeling. It eased the pain in her chest a bit.

"There are people in the woods, too," Danny had to add.

"Oh? Did you meet someone?" She was stunned to hear how calm her voice sounded. She could have been asking him what level he'd reached on his latest video game. She could have been talking about things of no consequence at all.

"Just some kid. He was picking raspberries for his dad."

It was crazy, ridiculous, for Zach to come to mind, to picture him so clearly he could have been standing right in front of them, his bushy hair in his eyes, his arms swinging restlessly. It was foolhardy to resurrect him, yet it seemed equally as unwise to squash his memory, never to let Danny know how much she had loved his father. Zach was part of the wilderness now, mostly inaccessible but always there.

"Did I ever tell you how brilliantly your father maneuvered through Salmon Falls?"

Danny knocked over his rocks as he looked up. "Yeah?" he said, trying to sound nonchalant.

"Oh, yeah," Jina said, sorting his rocks, finding the brightest one—a rare cobalt blue to start.

John had been restless all night, down by the river one minute, looking out their bedroom window the next. Alice attributed his unease to a sudden fear of the water, a fear she was battling herself. Near midnight, she convinced him to go to bed, and he

fell asleep with his hand on his pocket, didn't stir when someone knocked on the door.

Alice opened it to the sight of Helena with shovels.

"Come" was all the woman said.

Alice slipped on her water sandals, glanced back at John.
"Maybe I should——"

"Come now," Helena said. "Don't be put off by tears. In Russia, men cry all the time."

Alice didn't like the sound of that. Nervously, she followed
Helena out of the lodge and up the trail. The stars were
shrouded by haze. It could have been Helena's tale of a face between them or the smoke in the air, but Alice moved slowly,
suddenly wary.

"Helena," she said.

"*Shhhh.*"

Ellis crouched in the clearing over the corpse of an elk.

"So this Elvis," Helena said.

Ellis looked up, his face stained with tears. "You knew?"

Helena laughed. "I know how to use the generator, old man.
I played your records, watched those silly movies about the
beach. Too much singing, but he had nice eyes."

Alice looked from one to the other. Probably they were both
a little crazy. Two old fools alone on a river. She didn't understand why she envied them so much.

Helena turned to her. "He's impossible. Stinks. Never picks
up his socks, leaves the outhouse a mess."

Ellis looked down at the elk, laid his hands on either side of
the beast's face.

"And all this is nothing," Helena went on. "Like dust—hard to see and easy enough to fix. I wanted a new life; he gave it to me. Reached a hand clear across the ocean to grab me."

She smiled softly, put a hand on Ellis's shoulder. "He's gone now," she said. "Let him be."

She helped Ellis to his feet, gestured at Alice's shovel.

"Dig," she said.

Alice just stood there. Obviously she'd been mistaken for Irene or Jina, for someone strong.

"Dig," Helena said, softer now.

Alice struck the dirt with her shovel, hit bedrock. Her arms trembled from the backlash.

"May take a while," Helena said.

It was dawn before the hole was big enough, and when it came time to move the elk, Ellis couldn't bear to touch him. Alice turned away from the agony in his eyes. He hadn't lost what he loved best; he'd lost what he most admired—a worse loss in many ways.

"Come on, come on," Helena said.

It took all their strength to roll the thousand-pound elk into its grave. There should have been a puddle of blood beneath the bull, but the grass was oddly bare. Helena ran her hand over the dry spot.

"Humph," she said. "His spirit didn't get very far."

Helena threw a handful of dirt on the grave; Alice did the same. Ellis just stood there, looking bereft.

"Cover him up," Helena said to Ellis. "Regret will only stop you from building me that fence you promised. Believe me, old man, I'm not waiting another year to plant my herb garden."

She picked up a clump of dirt and wedged it into his palm.

"Go on now," she said. "Get over it." Then she took Alice inside for tea.

13

By morning, a thin layer of ash coated the windowsill. The air inside the lodge was slightly smoky, the way it was at home when Danny's mom forgot to open the fireplace flue, but at least here there were no sounds of panic. No one ran around, flinging open windows and leaping at smoke alarms. Danny bet there was always smoke around in summer, the constant threat of much worse. No one got worked up until they were staring down a wall of flames.

Charlie had gotten up early. Danny's mom was gone, too. Hopefully, they were already down by the raft, and they'd finally get out of this place. Danny had been ready to go since yesterday, since he saw the jinn. He didn't understand why everyone spent so much time talking and eating and sitting around. The raft was just sitting there, straining toward the river, calling to him. *Let's go. Let's go. Let's go.*

He dressed excitedly, packed his Game Boy and toothbrush in the dry bag. Then he saw the note taped to the door.

We're up the mountain with Ellis. You and Charlie stay in camp.

Mom.

"Shit," he said.

Outside, the sky was gray and dirty, and Charlie was pacing.

"I can't take much more waiting around," Charlie said.

It was creepy to think the same thing as a troll. It was even more disturbing to charge up the mountain beside Charlie, no matter what that note said. They climbed in silence and heard the strangest thing—the scratchy sound of an old 45, a love song by the King.

"Is that fuckin' Elvis Presley?" Charlie asked.

Danny elbowed him to be quiet. They reached the first summit, peeked through the trees. The adults stood around a fresh grave. Ellis had dragged a bulky generator up the hill, hooked up an ancient record player. Listening to that music was like hearing the worst kind of ghost—a man who'd had everything and let it slip away.

"I'm going back," Danny said.

He didn't care how it sounded. Let Charlie call him a wuss; he was used to it. He was going to stick to the river from now on. The woods freaked him out. There was always something he didn't expect—cabins and men where there should be only nature, or the sweetest singing voice on Earth.

One glade decimated by fire and the next spared, with no reason why.

Danny kept to the path. He wasn't about to get lost again.

"Hey!" Charlie said. "Wait. I'll come with you."

Danny glanced back warily. They both looked like shit, but it had been worth the pain and bruises just to watch the women put their fingers in their mouths and swab Charlie's scabs.

"Don't do me any favors," Danny said.

"I'm not, freak. Believe me."

Charlie wrapped his arms around his stomach, and Danny realized he was telling the truth. He was afraid of getting lost, and once you were afraid, even freaks served as friends.

He thought of all the things he could do: take off fast, dart in and out of trees, lead Charlie in circles until he sat down and cried. Like the hero of a video game, he could steal the enemy's weapons and become just like him in order to win. It occurred to him that he hadn't turned on his Game Boy for twenty-four hours, a record.

"Come on, troll," he said. "This way."

They'd walked fifty feet before Charlie said, "What'd you call me?"

Danny shrugged. "Troll."

Charlie made a fist but didn't swing it. "Freak."

When the adults returned, red-eyed, Danny and Charlie pretended they'd been at the beach the whole time. Ellis and John hauled down the generator; Drew got on the satellite phone to report what looked like a growing forest fire just over the rise. Charlie and Danny both looked toward the mountains where they'd seen the jinn.

"I didn't dream it," Charlie said.

Danny shook his head. "Me neither."

For a moment, they smiled in sync. "Bitchin'," Charlie said.

Drew came out of the lodge. "Not to worry," he said. "We live with fires every summer. Forest Service says there's already an air tanker on it."

The gear guide had set up a second camp downstream, so there wasn't much to load. The soles of Danny's feet itched; he couldn't wait to see the next rapid. The others used the out-house or stood around, talking, and he prayed they wouldn't get hungry or pull out chairs.

"Hey," Drew said. "Happy birthday."

Danny grinned. He was twelve years old today; his mom had given him a card last night, a gift certificate to Barnes & Noble.

"Come take a crack at the oars," Drew said.

Danny leapt in the raft beside Jake, who was wearing his doggie life vest and a red bandana. They were still tied to shore, but to Danny the helm of a beached raft was as good as captaining a submarine. He knew just what to do, as if some-one had spent the last twelve years teaching him to be river-worthy. One final piece of knowledge, how to find his way across land as well as water, came to him yesterday, when he cried himself to sleep in the woods and saw the man in his dreams.

It was the same man he'd seen in his room every night, his fa-ther for sure, but Danny hesitated. The eyes were different—still the blue he'd always pictured but cold and creepy. Eyes you'd see staring up at you through water. The man didn't move, didn't speak, didn't point the way home, and already as teary as a girl, Danny cried more. He wanted a dad who did *something*. Said hello, offered him a hand, *anything*. Mike would have made him forget all his fears by now. He'd have been tickling him senseless and tossing him around like a beanbag. Finally, Danny couldn't take it anymore, couldn't stand the silence most of all.

"Hey," was all he could think to say.

His dad looked at him a moment longer, then turned and walked away.

Danny opened his eyes abruptly; his father had left him alone in the woods. His cheeks were soaked, he felt groggy, hopelessly lost; all he could think to do was listen for the river. He wiped his tears, thought he heard a rumble faintly to the left. He picked a trail and took it, passed the time imagining himself guiding a raft down the Salmon, seeing other people through. Once or twice, the trail led upward again, and he feared he was going the wrong way, but finally he turned a corner and saw the river, saw Drew cleaning trash from the banks. He pumped his fist, though he felt less relieved than exhausted. It isn't always the greatest thing to find out exactly where you are. Turned out he didn't need a father to show him the way, especially one with nothing but dumb shock on his face. Turned out he didn't need nearly as much as he'd thought.

Finally the others straggled into the raft. First Irene, hogging the front again, then Naji, still cautious, but this time sitting only one row behind his wife. Ahmad looked surprisingly cheerful, while Danny's mother glanced back at the lodge as if it was the last outpost of civilization, which Danny fervently hoped it was. Charlie turned this way and that, showing off his swollen, purple nose like a trophy, and Mary dabbed orange-colored sunblock in a T-shape across her nose and cheeks. Alice came out next, stopped beside Helena. The old woman whispered something in her ear and Alice looked startled at first, then smiled.

Alice came down to the river. "John hasn't come down yet?" she said.

It was unclear who she was asking, and no one answered. Drew stepped out of the raft, and Jake hopped after him. The dog found a piece of driftwood to chew to bits. Drew offered his hand to help Alice into the boat, but she just stood there, slowly lowering one hand from her hip.

John stepped out onto the porch.

"There he is," Jina said. "Get in, Alice."

But Alice didn't move and Danny knew why. John was not dressed in river shorts and sandals but in long pants and a pair of loafers. He dropped his bag at his feet.

For a moment, they were all silent. Then Irene said, "Oh, shit."

Alice had already started crying, and more than anything in this world, Danny wanted her to stop. Danny's mother never let him see her crying. She might be falling apart inside, but she put on a show around children. Why couldn't Alice pretend that after a certain age, no one can touch you? He didn't care if it was all illusion: He wanted to believe there came a time when pain stopped.

Alice didn't care what he wanted; she bawled her eyes out. It was unbearable. Apparently, she was incapable of forward motion, so John came down, took a note from his shirt pocket. Danny mumbled, "Let's go. Let's go." Drew excused himself to use the bathroom.

Thank God for the river was all Danny could think. *Thank God it made noise when no one was speaking.*

For a minute, forever it seemed, Alice and John stood next to each other without saying a word. The fact that a man could let his wife cry like that, that it didn't turn his knees to jelly, made Danny realize that Drew was the only man he admired here. Drew, who was still half kid. John and Naji were cruel, Ellis inscrutable, Ahmad just plain scary. If only Mike was here. Mike, who chased bad guys and still came home kind.

"Is this some kind of joke?" Alice asked. Her voice shook the way it had before she became famous. The way it had shaken every time Roger proudly brought her to school, his novelist mommy, and she began her speeches not with her accomplishments but with an apology for not having written Harry Potter, for not being anyone they would have heard of yet.

John leaned forward, kissed her cheek. He'd started to cry, too, and even the troll didn't dare scoff at that. Charlie squirmed in his seat; Danny met Naji's gaze. Irene's husband looked terribly sad, the way he had this whole trip, and Danny couldn't take much more. He couldn't believe he was twelve years old and the only one who'd figured it out: Everyone will fail you, but if you love who you're given, you'll be loved when you fail them, too.

John crumpled the note in his hand. "I think I'll end my trip here," he said.

Even Irene curled forward, seemed unusually fascinated by a seam in the raft.

"I don't understand," Alice said, though she had to. Even Danny did.

"You go on," John said.

Please don't anybody else start crying, Danny thought. Jake had found a grimy animal bone, and the sound he made when he gnawed it reminded Danny of this canyon, of wilderness in general—total greediness and indifference in the face of human pain.

He couldn't take any more. Danny yanked the rope from shore and grabbed the oars. In a second he had them riverbound while Alice and John stood dumbly on the sand. Drew came running, shouting; the dog yapped in outrage. Danny's mother looked at him in astonishment and fury, while Charlie yelled, "Oh, yeah!"

"I'm the river!" Danny shouted, taking them around the bend and straight toward Rainier Rapids. And when the water rose up to strike his face, he really thought he was.

It might have been all right.

If they'd been on the other side of Rainier Rapids, they would have had an easy float to Lantz Bar where, Mary would later learn, Frank Lantz had lived, gardened, and cut trails for forty years. Past young Coy Lansbury's grave was a gentle stretch of the Salmon, easy rides past Alder and Otter creeks. But Danny was aiming for big water.

There was pandemonium, which made Danny's eyes shine brighter. Naji lunged for the oars and Jina for her son, but a twelve-year-old, a birthday boy, has a steely grip about certain things. Danny's fists were iron around the handles of the oars. He refused to budge and Mary hooted, bringing a shocked stare from Irene.

"Everyone just stay calm," Mary said. "We'll pull in after the rapids. I know Danny can do this."

Of course, she knew nothing of the kind. Danny could just as easily flip them as lead them to safety, but either way he took her breath away, his toothpick arms straining to turn the raft head-on into the waves, his face ecstatic. In a strange way, she hoped they did turn over; she wanted something, *anything*, to happen. She turned to Jina, who had let her son go, who sat stiffly in her seat now, watching Rainier come quick and fast. The raft began to bounce.

"Hold on," Mary said.

Jina shook her head but did, in fact, grip the rope along the side of the raft. Naji gave up trying to remove Danny from the helm and crawled forward toward Irene, who didn't have enough sense to hunker down. She sat on the bow, feet dangling over the sides, hands in the air as if she was harnessed beneath the safety bar of a roller coaster. Naji dragged her back, deposited her roughly on the seat beside Ahmad, who had started to pray.

The first foamy trough of Rainier engulfed them. The waves

that rose like walls on either side snatched the oars from Danny's hands. The paddles swung wildly; the raft folded in two, sliding them all toward the center of the boat. Just as quickly, the raft snapped back open and began to climb a wave. The boat rose quickly, vertically, and Mary looked over her shoulder, saw nothing but river below.

It seemed as though time stopped. Jina threw herself on top of Danny, got a hand on Charlie's life jacket. The rest of them clung to ropes and rubber, anything tied down. The rapid that flowed around them was so loud that Mary couldn't hear screaming. Or maybe no one said anything at all. Then slowly the revolution continued; the bow of the boat began to close over them. She saw orange plastic instead of sky, felt herself falling toward the river.

Funny how in that moment, when fear made sense, she felt none of it. There was only a rush of adrenaline, an instant plan of attack. Mary crawled straight up the raft, using the weight she usually disdained to high-side the bow back down into the water. She felt it responding to the pressure, sliding back the way it had come, then the bow hit the water with a smack.

Mary heard roaring in her ears, louder than any river. Only when it was over did she feel the thunder of her heart. Naji, his lips in a thin, white line, grabbed the oars. Danny's face was pale, his shoulders trembling. He'd just learned a terrible lesson: Once you're afraid, the greatest moments of your life are spoiled.

"What a ride!" Mary said.

"Mary!" Jina was on her knees, shaking. She squeezed Danny's arm as if she could pinch away all future acts of daring.

As if she hadn't seen what a life without risk had done to Mary, hadn't been paying attention at all.

"Oh, for Pete's sake, we're fine," Mary said. "Even if we'd flipped, we'd have survived. Our life jackets would hold us. That's what you've got to understand, Jina. Most times, everything turns out fine."

For a moment, Mary thought Jina would hit her. Jina must have agonized over coming back here, only to find it hardly mattered. She'd steeled herself against the memories, the old pain, when today's troubles—Danny's whereabouts, his recklessness, Mike's absence—obviously hurt more. She'd been looking back while her hopes and concerns went on without her, knowing the future, building the road she'd walk on if she only turned around.

Jina stood so suddenly that even her tiny frame rocked the boat. She looked down at Danny. "You have to know where to take the waves. You don't need your father to teach you that. I can do it, if you'd just ask."

She sat, turned away, and Mary knew it took all she had to do it, to let him be. This was not a river for mothers. Mary touched her arm while Naji steered the raft to shore. A few minutes after they tied off, Drew and Jake swam toward them in the shallows. Jake bolted up on shore, shook his fur, dousing all of them. Drew came to his feet, wearing shorts and his blue bandana.

He looked at Danny, who bowed his head. "You shouldn't have done that," Drew said. Then he smiled, turned boy again. "But, dude, sweet maneuvers."

Had the river kept him young, or would he have been the

same anywhere? As a child, Mary had never believed in Santa Claus or fairies, yet all of a sudden she wanted magical waters, time slowed or even reversed. The impossible.

Drew turned to her. "I saw what you did," he said. "You were amazing."

He touched her arm, his fingers ice-cold, delicious. She'd just high-sided a raft, but it felt far more dangerous to put her hand over his, to hold on.

They considered how to retrieve Alice. Irene asked if they had to retrieve her at all.

"Dad'll bring her," Drew said, and Mary marveled that every conversation didn't focus on the fact of him touching her. "Let's get down to the next camp."

Two hours later, Alice arrived at camp in the jet boat. She didn't eat a bite of Drew's flank steak. She went inside her tent and zipped it up.

"One of us should talk to her," Mary said, but didn't offer herself. The only evidence of fire here was a sky of luscious rainbow sherbet, swirls of orange, yellow, and pink. The only thing she could think about was Drew.

After dinner, she went for a walk. At one point in her life, she'd walked to try to drum up emotion; now she walked to drown it out. But she failed to concentrate. The walk quickly turned to a jog, then an all-out run. She was no longer a sprinter, but she covered some ground. She laughed at the slap of her feet on dirt, the sting of wind on her face. She dodged trees, flew over rocks. Only the river stopped her.

She knew when Drew was there. The hairs on the back of her neck stood on end; she gasped for air long after her breath should have returned. Tears sprang to her eyes when she real-ized her mother had never felt this: terrified for all the right reasons.

Drew moved beside her and they sat, shoulders touching, in the sand beside an eddy. His eyes softened whenever he looked at the river, and she had a brief, unselfish thought: He should never leave the canyon, never discover what he was really up against.

"Will you stay forever?" she asked.

"Forever's a long time. Before I came here, I never held a job longer than two years. I either got antsy or suicidal. I was what my mother called 'a lazy bum.'"

Mary smiled. "You were looking for your soul."

He turned to her, took her hand. With other men she'd stiff-ened; his fingers were icy relief. Every touch unwound her, twisted another limb free, untangled a jumble of bones.

"The Nez Percé Indians believe one day Coyote will destroy the dams," he said. "The salmon will return. The forests will be reinvigorated. We will all be one people."

This was the only kind of talk she wanted to hear from now on. Just legend and the best possible outcome. "What do you believe?"

He pulled her hand to his chest, and she sucked in her breath. She was coming undone, couldn't get enough air around him. What a lovely state of confusion.

"I believe you're beautiful."

He turned her body to rainbow sherbet, swirls and swirls of pastels, softness, cream.

"The salmon are more than fish," he said. "They're our spirit, what's best in us, our devotion and our perseverance. Save them and we save everything, you know? I got that, finally, when I came here. It wasn't about me anymore. You can't imagine what a relief that was. Once I had something to fight for, I felt better. I think my dad did, too. Sometimes it's an enemy that gives meaning to our lives. Sometimes it's a lover."

He made her body liquid; only her mind stayed hard, sharp. He was in love with fish and forests and wolves and dirt. He was in love with everything, and after waiting so long, didn't she deserve to be somebody's only one?

"Mary," he said, and for a moment she contained herself, resisted. "Mary."

She closed her eyes. He'd fill her head with the plight of the salmon, the degradation of the ozone layer, then send her back to a city of red tape. Or, worse, he'd turn cynical just as she took up his causes. He couldn't possibly stay this beautiful and impassioned forever, but then, like he'd said, nothing was forever. Each part of life was a stretch of river to explore and leave behind. Our only regrets are the things we don't see.

She opened her eyes. "Drew," she said, feeling crazy, feeling rash, feeling like the start of a tale that would be told around campfires for years to come. She leaned forward and kissed him. Did all men taste like the river? Their teeth knocked, and she pulled back, embarrassed. But he only put his hand on her shoulder, pulled her down on the sand.

"I'm a little out of practice," he said, and she smiled. When she kissed him again, she used her tongue, not her teeth. It was amazing how fast they learned.

. . .

Alice lay in her tent while they marveled over flank steak and Irene told a ghost story not at all appropriate for children of Danny and Charlie's age. She burrowed inside her sleeping bag while Ahmad and Naji debated haunting accounts of the jinn and their campfire made ghostlike shadows on the canvas walls. She lay until everyone went to bed and all was silent, until she heard her name. It was just a faint murmur, accompanied by a rustling in the bushes behind her tent. Someone stood just outside the flap, an arm raised as if beckoning her.

"No," she said, but her voice rose, as if the word was in question. Without John, she realized she was down to two choices: She could go to pieces, or she could become someone he might want back. She knew how to create characters; perhaps she could be one. The kind she used to write, the brave ones, the ones who fought for someone or something else. The heroes she'd been proud of.

She unzipped the tent. No one stood outside; the campfire was down to embers, though the air was thick with smoke. The wind had turned. The air whizzed with panicked insects and ash. The only light came from Irene's tent. Naji spent his nights with his brother. Alice hurried across camp, crouched down.

"Irene?" she said. "I heard something."

There was silence, then the zipper moved. Irene poked her head out. "And?"

Alice looked at her hands. Her French manicure was ruined,

the white tips filled with dirt. "Isn't it enough that I've lost everything?" she said.

Irene smiled meanly. "Nope."

"Irene——"

"You said yourself we were never friends. So why do you care what I think? Why does it matter so much?"

Alice stepped back. Could Irene really be that blind? Even lousy friends matter. Whether you're a popular girl or an outcast, you suffer the same fate: After a while, no one new begs for your company. You have to make do with the people you already have.

Alice wouldn't be here if she thought it could be any different. She wouldn't have written the book if she'd had other stories to tell. Her imagination was shot. She wrote what she thought people wanted to read, what might sell; she hadn't written for herself in years.

"Go to sleep," Irene said, zipping up the tent.

"Please. I heard——"

She heard a rustling again, right behind her. She whirled around, but the campsite was empty. The last log crumbled into ash.

Irene blew out her light, refused to answer. There was a tangle of red and blond hairs near the open flap in Jina's tent, but no one stirred. Mary's tent hadn't been set up; Alice had no idea where she was.

Alice shivered. In the daytime, the lighting of a bird on a branch is delightful; at night, it's the crash landing of dread. The day's falling pinecone is the night's vampire. She was afraid of what was out there, but at this point she was more afraid of staying put.

She had loved her husband, but not enough. She adored her children, but they were marvelous, separate, often indifferent creatures. They were not in charge of her happiness. It was terrifying, worse than darkness, to realize that only she was.

She waited for the rustling, heard it again through the trees, away from the river. She took one step, then another. She jumped at every snap of twigs, but she jumped forward.

Even through the smoke, without a moon, there were shadows—malevolent silhouettes through the trees, shades stalking the bushes. The woods were a whole other country at night. She lost her footing and steadied herself on a tree, but the pine bark came off in her fingers, soft and moist. She heard a rumble, a low growl, and above her head an owl took flight. Even the line of sweat down her back was skittish, darting right and left.

Still, she followed the rustling, swore she heard her name again. She climbed a steep trail, emerged on a false summit, with a taller, steeper ridge beyond. She looked down toward camp, toward the river, where the smoke sneaked in, low and thick. When Danny had launched the raft without her, John had taken her hand, held it so gently she'd thought he was going to relent.

"I wish you'd never been a writer," he said.

She'd bowed her head. She had often wished the same thing, but wishes alone don't change much. Her head was full of drama, of poetry, not sense. She struggled for ideas, agonized over first drafts, cried over rejections, but somewhere in between, when the plot grew solid and the characters rich and complex, she read one perfect sentence, and the hairs on her neck stood on end. She felt like the luckiest person on the planet, someone who could create one grain of perfection, someone who could pick up a pen and make friends. Her eyes raced across the page, anxious to find another gem, and she lost track of time. Her body swayed. Sometimes she sang out loud. For an hour, maybe a whole day, what she'd done was good enough.

"It's my passion," she said. "I never said that was the same thing as joy."

She followed noises, headed into another valley, up another ridge. The smoke thinned and the moon poked through. Her grandmother stood in her path.

Norma Meyer was nothing but a shadow now, her features dissolved into black. The old woman stepped forward, held out her hand. The creature was a horror—red, knowing eyes and a body that had collapsed. The ghost of misery—a woman praised for her profundity who couldn't solve the simplest puzzle in her own life: how to feel sated, how to love. Alice stumbled back. She *had* done better than her. She'd had the guts to say she was sorry. She'd told her children that she loved them. Even if the worst happened, they'd know it wasn't that.

"No, Grandma," Alice said.

The creature cocked its head, and Alice tapped her foot in exasperation. Like her grandmother, death had tempted her a time or two, but wasn't life the real siren—beautiful, irresistible, always sweeping her toward one rock or another? The only problem was expecting too much from it—adventure, high seas, happily ever after. When your head is full of stories, the simple act of living can seem dull. Just going on hardly seems a fitting ending for a hero, but then, Alice had always been hard on her writing. She'd been hard on herself.

"Go away," she said.

She was stunned when her request was granted. Just like that, her grandmother disappeared.

She smelled the scent of rain, raised her palm to see if it was falling, and a man caught her arm. She screamed, and he put his hand over her mouth, then quickly released her.

"I didn't mean to frighten you," Ahmad said.

He wore black and smelled of smoke. She looked where her grandmother had been, then into his eyes.

"What are you doing here?" she asked.

"I should ask the same thing."

"I heard something."

He raised his eyebrows. "I saw you leave camp. I was worried. You shouldn't be out here alone."

Alice wrapped her arms around her waist. Ahmad had not said two words to her this whole trip, but that wasn't what bothered her. It was the fact that she smelled not only smoke but lighter fluid. His cheeks were marked by soot.

"Is the smoke getting worse?" she asked.

His teeth flashed in the darkness. "It's the Waugh Ridge fire. At night, the winds change and bring smoke into the valleys. It might rain, though. That will help."

He'd hidden his hands in his pockets. She glanced once more where her grandmother had been.

"I thought . . . Did you see someone there?"

He took his hands from his pockets, and they were not blackened as she had imagined, but clean, his fingernails well trimmed.

"You see things in darkness that can't possibly be there during the day. I used to slip out at night. A long time ago. I'd fall asleep in school."

She met his gaze. She had trouble imagining him young, imagining him anything other than a stranger, no matter how much time she spent with him. Yet he had come after her, which was more than her friends had done.

"I'll bet your parents weren't too happy with that," she said.

He looked at his hands. "No. Not particularly."

She started back toward camp, but he quickly closed the distance and took her hand. She stiffened, but his eyes were kind, his voice like the whisper of trees.

"Alice," he said, "you're going the wrong way."

She looked around. Indeed, she'd stepped deeper into the forest without realizing it.

"Oh," she said. "I thought . . ."

"Come," he said. "I'll walk you back."

He held tight to her hand and guided her home.

They hiked around Lantz Bar, to the old blacksmith shop and up Little Squaw Creek to the water tank. Frank Lantz had liked corn whiskey and dogs, and he'd been able to judge people in a heartbeat. Irene walked the grounds, relieved that he was no longer around to look into her eyes and tell her what kind of person she was.

Alice pummeled Drew with questions about the site and

Frank's wife, Jessie, who apparently loved life on the river. Jessie had planted a garden, brewed beer, relayed radio messages from the fire lookouts.

Something had changed in Alice. Irene watched her for an hour, trying to figure out what it was. When Jina returned from Coy Lansbury's gravesite, she gave Irene the answer.

"She's stopped crying," Jina said. "She's done."

Drew let Irene take the oars through Devil's Teeth Rapid, and it was a wonder she didn't kill them all. She took them sideways to the waves, dropped over a ledge, slammed into one of the devil's molars. She didn't care if their faces went pale; Danny's and Charlie's were shining. Her best acting job, it turned out, was the one she didn't do. She didn't act her age, and that appalled adults but thrilled their children. It made her wonder what other talents she might have.

As Drew directed, she pulled to the right before Salmon Falls so he could scout the best hole to run. He whooped when he saw the whitewater, but Jina grew quiet. Even Danny didn't dare comment on the size of the water pouring through the narrow gaps between the rocks. They were heading into Black Canyon. Irene gawked at the huge granite walls that dwarfed this slender part of the river, then across the raft at Naji. Alice slid to Jina's side.

"You and Zach weren't stupid," Alice said. "Maybe you didn't think through all the worst-case scenarios, but that's lovely if you think about it. You didn't waste one second you had together. I didn't put that in the book. I'm sorry, Jina."

They were all still, then Jina reached over and took Alice's hand. "It's all right."

Alice pressed her cheek to Jina's shoulder; Mary put an arm around them both. Irene contemplated pulling the raft loose and taking them helter-skelter through the falls. Some scenarios, she ought to tell them, *are* worst-case. Some wrongs can't be undone.

Jina was still holding Alice's hand when Drew came back and told them he would run the left slot. She held it all the way through the rocks and rolls of Salmon Falls and the dark canyon beyond. Held it past the aeries, and the place Jina said Zach went over.

"I'm so sorry," Alice said.

Jina nodded, touched Danny's shoulder. "He was born to run rivers," she said.

They leaned over the side of the raft, lounged in the quiet water before Barth Hot Springs. Naji lost his perpetual grimace and even laughed, occasionally, when Ahmad doused him. Irene was sorry to see the camp at Sunny Bar.

Still, she applauded the impressive display of wines Drew brought out, the fine look of him in cutoff jeans and no shirt.

"I can't believe no woman has scooped you up yet," she said.

Naji and Ahmad sat in camp chairs, smoking pipes. Irene could still feel the river, her body bouncing one way, then another.

"I'll start with the merlot," she said.

She fixed Drew with one of her TV smiles, pressed in close when he offered her a glass. His eyes widened, but otherwise he didn't take the hint. He went to the beach to set up the kitchen.

Mary sat down beside her, stretched out her legs. Jina and Alice had gone off to talk.

"Still expect to hear banjos?" Mary asked.

Irene laughed. Mary had darkened to the color of Danville brown, but out here it was a beautiful color. Her fingers danced across the arm of the folding chair.

"You love it here, too," Irene said.

Mary nodded. Faced with true wilderness and two-story rapids, who'd have thought they'd be the ones to become brave?

"What if I go home and nothing's changed?" Mary asked. "My condo and job will be gone, but otherwise I'll just have to pick up where I left off."

Irene shook her head. "You've changed. Listen to you. Your voice doesn't twitter. Don't take this the wrong way, but I actually like you now."

Instead of taking offense, Mary laughed so loudly that Drew looked up from his kitchen and smiled.

"We should make a pledge to come back every summer," Irene went on. "Maybe we could bring along a boatload of city kids who've never seen wilderness. Can you imagine? We'd give them an adventure they can take back to the projects. Show them how much more there is than what they see."

Mary turned to her. "You're really thinking about that."

Irene shrugged. "It's the mountain air. I'm thinking about everything."

Drew brought over a platter of crackers and smoked cheese. "Here you go, ladies," he said, though he looked only at Mary. "I'll feed the boys later. They're not very hungry."

Four sunburned feet stuck out of the raft. As Drew turned, Irene's hand reached out almost of its own will. She encircled his wrist, ran a thumb over the freckles that flanked either side of a wide, blue vein. She held on even when Mary sucked in her breath and Jina and Alice returned with red-rimmed eyes, their arms around each other's waists. When Naji got up and walked away.

"You're a fool," Ahmad said, turning the contents of his pipe into the fire ring. He stood to go. "I do not say this lightly: My brother is a good man."

As Ahmad walked away, Irene let go. Drew blathered some quick excuse to escape; Irene hardly heard it. She stared at the white flakes on the back of her hands, the nail polish down to a few specks near her cuticles.

Mary scooted her chair beside Irene's. "Actually," she said, "believe it or not, Drew picked me."

Irene began to cry. "Oh, shit," she said. "That's wonderful."

Jina and Alice brought chairs, formed a circle. Just like that, they were a foursome again, and Irene didn't have the energy for outrage. In Naji's country, women receive one hundred strokes as a punishment for adultery; hardly anyone mentions that men get eighty. From any perspective, in any culture, with any excuse, unfaithfulness is unacceptable. She couldn't keep blaming Alice. The one she'd never forgive was herself.

"All right," Jina said. "Details."

Irene dried her tears, straightened. "Yes. I want a perfect picture of that man's body."

Mary laughed, and Irene noticed that she'd lost weight on this trip. Just enough to whittle a hollow beneath each cheekbone, to carve an S-curve into her waist.

"I still can't believe it," she said. "This whole trip has been surreal. I'm telling you, that river grabs you and takes you where it wants to go. Have you looked at him? He wants *me*. Does that make any sense to you?"

Irene looked at the brightness in her eyes. "Actually, yes. But don't waste our time with feelings. How does he kiss? Where does he kiss? How big is it?"

Jina grabbed the wine. She filled their cups, drank hers in long gulps, like it was root beer. She closed her eyes when Mary spoke.

"His hands shook. My God, I made a man's hands tremble. Did you ever feel like everything in the universe is shaking, and this one man is all that keeps you still?"

Down the beach, Drew turned on his radio, bopped his head while cleaning up. Where had Naji gone? Why did Mary have to point out the obvious—that they were all at the mercy of who and what they loved?

"It's all going to come crashing down around me," Mary went on. "Isn't it?"

Irene finished her wine. "Maybe."

"It'll be worth it," Jina said. "It was with Zach." Her eyes were open now, staring at the river.

"That's the first time you've said his name on this trip," Irene said.

Jina shrugged. "It doesn't sound real. I've dreamt about him, but he still makes love the same way. I can't picture him old."

Irene waved an arm. "The past is a teenager, easy to make pretty. Face it, we're middle-aged women now. How do we look in the mirror and feel good about what we see now?"

When they said nothing, she set down her wineglass and stood. "Do you realize we might all end up alone?"

They recoiled, silent, and Irene shook her head. It wasn't really a question, anyway, at least not for a sushi club or a friend. It was what you asked yourself when a man died or left or merely disappointed: How do you feel whole when you're just one person? She never had. Ironically, she'd only felt strong enough to be alone when she'd been with Naji.

She walked out of camp. Beyond the ridge was a trail down into a narrow valley. She zigzagged through trees, crossed a dry creek bed, and found Naji leaning against a boulder, watching a coil of smoke snake toward the eastern horizon. She stood beside him. They couldn't hear the river here, and she was amazed at how silent it was otherwise.

"It's glowing now," he said.

She followed his gaze to the eastern mountains, which were indeed an ominous orange. A plane emerged from the smoke, turned around, and went back into it.

"Naji," she said. "There's no excuse for it. Ahmad's right about that. Nothing I can say will make amends. I see that now."

He said nothing. She spread her palms on the boulder, was amazed at the heat it held.

"I was just a dollar sign to most men," she went on. "Their five minutes of fame, a story they could tell the boys. After a while, I learned to take what I could get. At least they made me feel pretty. Maybe you can't understand this, but when you're young, when all you've ever been is nice to look at . . . I knew what I had to offer. I knew why you married me."

He shook his head. "You must not tell me why I married you. Why would I do such a thing? Marry a crazy American girl. Know that I can never be enough for her."

Most of all, she missed the right to touch him. He'd promised to love and honor her, but even more fundamentally, he'd pledged his body—his fingers for pleasure, his chest for warmth, his arms for safety.

"*I* wasn't enough for me," she said honestly. "It didn't matter how many men I slept with, I never gained any ground."

He nodded, which scared her more than the silence, or yelling. As if he'd already let go, distanced himself, come to terms with what he had to do.

"You were a crazy American girl," he said. "Pretty but hollow, yes? A paper doll."

She began to cry again. Really, the tears were getting out of hand. She'd end up like Alice at this rate.

Naji always had a handkerchief. Even here, he took one from his shirt pocket, dabbed her cheeks. "But you are stronger now," he said. "More like cardboard, maybe?"

She didn't dare look up. She knew she was greedy; she was a California girl and, thus, wanted everything: good looks, a fabulous man, a fulfilling career, money, friends, and gorgeous scenery. She wanted time back, the past erased, and access to Naji's brain so she could know whether she stood a chance, if lovers could forgive as well as friends.

He sighed, put his handkerchief back in his pocket. "There are female jinn," he said. "One met a friend of Muhammad's on the street. She pressed him down, forced him to utter three verses of poetry. Thereafter, he was a poet. This is women, yes? Demons even while acting as muses. There is no telling what women will do."

"Naji—"

"We're done with this conversation, yes? We're sick of it?"

She looked up, swallowed. "Yes," she said.

He shook his head at her new line of tears, took his handkerchief back out. "We need a new topic," he said, swiping another tear from her cheek, leaning in to kiss the spot dry. "You pick."

14

They say in Idaho if you don't like the weather or your life, wait five minutes. Rain will relieve a sweltering afternoon, snow will give way to fair skies, something is bound to change. At the campsite on Sunny Bar, a caravan of clouds motored in over the western mountains, and the muggy, thick heat became a light rain. The smell of smoke vanished, and fog covered what might have been seen—defiant flames on a distant ridgetop, an expanding crown of white smoke.

Drew built a campfire at three, and by four it was dark as dusk. Naji went into Irene's tent; the others brought chairs beside the fire. Jake pawed the soil, nudged a pine cone, circled three times, then lay down. Jina cracked open the Baileys Irish Cream.

Danny and Charlie prowled the edges of the woods, impervious to the rain. They couldn't find their shirts, or so they said. Jina imagined there'd been some furtive toss overboard, and downriver they'd see Tony Hawk's face caught on a snag. Their denim shorts sported torn hems and fringe; around their heads, they wore Drew's blue bandanas. Despite the layers of suntan lotion Jina had doused them with, both had burnt along their noses, darkened to honey everywhere else. Danny's freckles had disappeared.

They used sticks as weapons. Danny lunged forward, thrust his stick-spear into an imaginary neck. He raised his fists in victory, and Charlie howled, more animal than the animals they pretended to hunt. Jina gripped the edges of her camp chair, suddenly aware of how lucky the mother of a gamer really was.

Drew threw a tarp over the kitchen. There were hours until dinnertime, time for even a river guide to rest. He joined them by the campfire, touched Mary's knee as he reached for the liqueur. She looked shocked for a moment, as if she'd forgotten she was now one of the lucky ones, then she smiled clear to her eyes. When they were safely back in Danville, when the photos came back, Mary would have to believe it: The coils of her hair had become exotic river weeds, her arms smooth and brown as tree limbs that had been riding the river from its headwaters near Stanley.

Something rustled in the bushes, and Charlie and Danny went still. Jina recognized the scrambling of squirrels, but the boys retreated to the campfire, pretended to be cold. She turned to hide her smile. Jake raised his head, watched the bushes steadily.

"Could be a bear," Drew said, poking at the fire with the tip of his river sandal. "Or moose. Those are the most unpredictable. They'll ignore you one day and charge the next. Maybe a bobcat."

"A cougar was living in the Malibu Colony," Charlie said. "They shot it."

He jabbed his stick in the fire until the tip flamed.

"Sometimes animals and men don't mix," Drew said. "Sometimes men are worse."

Jina leaned to avoid the smoke. Ahmad put on another log, poked the fire until the smoke vanished and the flames rose straight and orange.

"Everything from man to beast to river submits to God's laws," Ahmad said. "Choose the right path and no harm will come to you."

The rain was light as mist, the fog spilling like a slow-motion avalanche down the mountain.

"So you're saying everyone who's ever drowned or been murdered by a madman had it coming?" Jina asked.

Ahmad studied her awhile before answering. "I am saying everything happens as it should. There is no point in imagining it could have been otherwise."

He rested his hands on his knees, watched the fire. Jina liked to think she could read people, but Ahmad was inscrutable. Irene didn't trust him, but Alice said he'd guided her back to camp. He held himself apart, then offered comfort when no one else dared. Some people have midlife crises and go wild, but like Ahmad, she'd prefer to go still. Instead of buying a convertible, she'd please the neighbors and tame her yard. She'd put in a new lawn, flower beds of bright geraniums, even a fountain. Make the outdoors as safe as within—an accomplishment only an adult can appreciate.

"I was telling Danny about the fish-man," Drew said, smiling at the boys. "It's quite the legend around here."

"Fish-man," Ahmad scoffed.

Drew turned to the boys. "It all started when the river fell in love with a man. She dragged him down to join her, but he fought for his life. He loved someone else and swore that even if the river trapped his body, his heart would never be hers. Spurned, the river tossed him from her belly, gave him gills and fins as a parting gift. They say he lived; but he could never go far from the river after that. He had to return daily to cool his scales, to drink from her. By the time the woman he loved came for him, he was beyond recognition, more fish than man. She passed right by him without knowing who he was."

Drew paused, looked where the mountains hid behind the fog. "It was a mile or so upriver that Pearl found her husband on the bank," he went on. "Right where the legend says a fish-man was born."

"Awesome," Charlie said. "Fish-man."

Jina glanced at Danny, who had copied Charlie's lead and was setting his stick on fire. He waved it in circles, painted trails of light. At some point during this trip, he had stopped being haunted and she had started. Without Mike to ground her, to tell her what was logical, or even what was right, she inserted Zach into every story. She imagined him at the end of a trail that led to Pearl's place.

"Pearl walked around a bend and there he was, lying face-down in the sand," Drew said, looking at her. The guide was uncanny; most river guides are. They know how far to push you, how much you can take. They bolster your confidence with relatively easy runs like Gunbarrel and Rainier, and before you know it, you're taking chances, aiming for the biggest holes.

"Carted him two miles by wheelbarrow," Drew went on, "straight up over Black Ridge, or so they say. Spent a month draining the water out of him, trying to convince him to live."

Jina had known that even though the raft was heading forward, she was going backward. Like a woman at the end of her life, she was hardly cognizant of her deathbed visitors while she reminisced with ghosts. She remembered everything now— how Zach had smelled like the river, the way he'd leaned across her body to block the worst splashes, the brightness of his eyes when the water was coming fast. How light love felt at that age, as if it filled her with air rather than substance, as if she could fly.

"Why didn't he want to live?" Alice asked.

Jina looked across the campfire at Alice. Her betrayal still stung, but, in the end, Jina understood that stories needed to be told, needed to be read, savored, wondered at, then set down at the end of the evening. Even writers had to put them away.

"That's a secret between him and Pearl," Drew said. "For a long time, no one even knew he was here, her cabin's so well hidden. She's protective as hell of her son."

"Andy," Danny said.

They all turned to look at him, but he was oblivious, swordfighting Charlie with a blazing stick.

"That's right," Drew said. "You met him when you got lost. Pearl brought her son here when Andy was still a baby. When it was obvious . . . She drank. That's what people say. She was a party girl in Salmon. Pretty as a picture. A prom queen. She went off with a group of Colorado boys on their way to the river, and things went wrong. She never pressed charges, never named names, but she came back quiet. Some people said she got what she deserved. Others, well, I guess it was hard to pity a girl with so little sense. No one helped her much when they found out she was pregnant. Her parents turned their backs on her. She wasn't welcome in church. Had to drop out of high school, live in her car. She drank her way through it, and there was not much surprise when Andy was born the way he was."

"Fetal alcohol syndrome?" Alice asked. She reached into her pocket, then slid her hand out, empty. For a moment, she had that glint in her eye that meant she was crafting stories, then she turned aside, sheepish, as if writing was some shameful addiction she couldn't shake.

"Looks that way," Drew said. "She had a hard time in Salmon, but people on the river have a different take on things. As long as you survive, you're given a dose of respect. We appreciate what it takes to get this far. It was an amazing thing Pearl did. Packed up her baby and a few belongings. Drove to the end of the road, abandoned her car, and started walking. This was no rough-and-tumble man, remember. It was an eighteen-year-old prom queen. She took over an old miner's shack up Corey Creek. Never asked for help again."

The campfire spit out embers. Danny snuffed his stick in the sand and said, "I could do it."

"Yeah, me, too," Charlie said. *"No problemo."*

Drew laughed. "Sure you could."

Jina stood, her back to the trail that led to Pearl's place. She walked to the river. Three days left. Seventy-two more hours was all she had to get through, then she could go home, talk to Mike, try to work things out. She wondered why she felt so heavy, like her limbs had filled with water. Drew came up beside her.

"It's about a three-mile hike," he said. "Pretty rugged terrain. To Pearl's place."

"Have you seen him?"

"Me? Sure. He pulls snags from the river. Keeps the lanes safe for the rafters. Warned me about the fires just yesterday. He's tall, strong as an elk. Quiet. He and Pearl . . . They're a good match. A backcountry couple."

Jina flinched. "What does that mean?"

Drew reached out his hand, then dropped it. "It means anything they feel for each other comes after they finish the chores. Hunting, trapping, fishing, gardening, clearing the river, maintaining the cabin. It's still standing, which means they get things done. You can't know what they feel for each other; you never can, in any relationship. But I'll say this: No one on the river can imagine one without the other. Zach's not much for talking, but he takes care of the boy. Loves him. Anyone can see that."

Jina blinked. All she had to do, of course, was eat dinner, go to sleep, and leave first thing in the morning. Get up, pack the raft, and float past the point of no return. All she had to do was act like the weakest river and go forward. She'd never realized before how difficult and admirable a task this was.

"I know you don't want to hear this," she said. "But sometimes, after you lose everything, you manage to go on. You want to break, but you don't."

They both heard the scream of the engine. Jina stepped ankle-deep in the water to see upstream, was the first to spot the jet boat and its passenger leaning precariously over the bow, the first to see the improbable.

Mike had come to Sunny Bar.

Mike led her up the trail, though she seemed more skittish with every step, as if in four days she hadn't yet learned how to walk on dirt. He, on the other hand, was surprisingly steady. His skin tingled; his body still rose and fell though he'd been off the water for an hour. He heard jet engines in his ears, knew he was shouting but couldn't help himself.

"You should have seen it," he said. "Right over the drop in Salmon Falls, not two inches from the rocks. I'm telling you, Jina, I thought I was dead at least twice."

He laughed. He couldn't feel his toes, and he didn't know if this was from the water in his socks or because the rest of his skin was on fire. His hands danced. He'd been going over the things he would say to her for the last twenty-four hours. He stopped and reached for her shoulders.

"I've got something to tell you."

She shook her head. He couldn't understand how she'd gotten paler. The rest of them were tanned and disheveled, dressed in torn shorts and bandanas, looking like happy river rats, while she wore chinos and a button-down shirt. She was actually sallow.

"Mike—"

"No, listen. I'll be quick. I've rehearsed."

He smiled, hoping to woo her, to transfer some of his exhilaration to her eyes. He was so light on his feet that he barely touched the ground. He hadn't eaten for twelve hours, and maybe that was all it took to defy gravity. A half-day fast, one bold move, and anything is possible.

He'd marched into the office yesterday and announced he was ready to resume field duty. Of course, it was more complicated than that. Papers had to be signed, half a dozen men convinced, but the first step had been taken. He didn't have to overcome fear, he just had to overlook it.

Whether he hid in his office or opened the door, it made no difference. Men would do what they were going to do. A terrorist intent on doing harm would find a way to pull the trigger, but he would also be a slave to the very thing he hated, shackled to what he thought of most, a lifestyle he couldn't tolerate or a religion he despised. Already captured, in a way. All the good guys had to do was wait.

"I talked to my boss, told him I was ready to start field work. When I heard Ahmad was here—"

"You came after Ahmad?" she said. "You came after him and not me?"

She had no idea how much he loved her; that's how bad at this he was. His heart beat on mute. He only sang at the top of his lungs in the car, when no one could hear him.

"No," he said. "Jina, I came for you."

She shook her head, walked up the path. He had to talk now, and fast. Talk the way the sushi club did, thinking all their secrets were safe even though Alice had proven that they weren't. Trusting one another not because it was a wise thing to do but because they couldn't stand it any other way.

"I had a partner," he said. "Ben. I always went in first, but that day . . . I had to take a call. There was a girl, explosives strapped to her chest, just a kid. She detonated. Ben couldn't have felt a thing. That's what I keep telling myself. But it's kept me up at night. I don't sleep much. I'm tired all the time."

She stared at him and he realized his voice was shaking. It had been wobbling while he'd been convincing men to take a chance on him again, while he'd been making reservations and, ironically, asking the waterfall neighbor if he'd watch the house while Mike got on a jet boat, flew down the Salmon River, and told a woman yes.

"Oh, Mike," she said.

"It's all right to get scared," he said, "but you can't shut down. I see that now. Ben would have been furious with me for retreating behind a desk. You must have been furious when I couldn't give you a sure sign that you were adored. But you are, Jina. There's only one thing that scares me more than death, and that's losing you and Danny."

He had not expected her to fall into his arms, but he had hoped for some kind of forward motion. A smile, perhaps a few tears. Instead, she stared for what seemed an eternity into nothing more than a thicket of trees, a turn in the path. Finally, she faced him.

"I don't know what to say."

"Don't say anything. It's all history. We don't forget the bad things, but we don't have to live like they're still happening.

You know what I'm saying? You know when things get blurry, and you can't tell which story you're in?"

She shook her head as if his words were some other language, as if he'd waited too long to say them. All decisions of the heart need to be made without pause or analysis. Love is only muddied by logic.

"They have this legend here of a fish-man," she said.

He knew, as soon as he laughed, that it was a mistake. Things like ghosts and revelations, destiny and intuition, are drop-dead serious. Those we love must be believed.

She turned her back on him, started quickly down the path. He caught up only after they'd cleared the trees and were in clear view of the others. He lowered his head, spoke in a whisper.

"Please," he said. "I came to say yes."

She closed her eyes but cried anyway. He'd ridden down the Salmon River imagining death in every rapid, celebrating life with every success. He'd ridden with visions of their passionate reunion, but now he'd settle for the power to make her stop crying.

"I need time to think," she said.

She went inside her tent. On the ride down, Ellis Cantor had given Mike the rundown on John leaving Alice, on the death of an elk named Elvis, on everything except the fact that everyone had changed. Alice's eyes were dry; Irene and Naji held hands; Drew, Mary, and a bandana-wearing dog looked like a contented family, until they approached Ellis and he turned his back.

Ahmad was nowhere in sight. Mike knew he ought to find

him, but instead he walked across camp, knelt beside two boys with the obvious bruises of a fistfight on their faces but who still stunk of fish and happiness. He had a fully charged, brand-new Game Boy in his pocket that he didn't bother to take out.

He ran his hand gingerly over Danny's swollen cheek. "I missed you," he said.

Charlie scoffed, but Danny looked up. Mike had gone to a shrink after his partner died. For six months, the woman told him that change took time, that he'd have to work on his fears for years to come. Certainly she was right about the fears, but she was wrong about change. People transformed themselves in a heartbeat. They came to their senses during one long, lonely night; they grew up between the rise and fall of a wave.

"Hey," Mike said. "You want to sleep under the stars with me tonight?"

"Really? Just you and me?" Charlie stopped scoffing, dropped his stick in the fire. "You, me, and Charlie?"

Both boys turned to him now. Mike laughed, ruffled their hair. "You got it," he said. "Just us three."

The call connected, but Alice had to scramble for reception. It was light here until ten, but an hour's rain had turned the evening to shadows. The kind of night, in Danville, when she pushed the button on the gas fireplace, plugged in a video, and cuddled her daughter while Belle transformed a beast. The kind of night made for just one purpose: to send you inside with the people you love.

She zigzagged through trees, climbed rocks, even shimmied

up a canyon crevasse, trying to hear their voices, even cherishing the way they fought over the phone.

"So, Mom?" Roger said, winning out as he usually did, muscling the phone from the hand of his six-year-old sister. "Can I get a GameCube? I tried it at the mall and it's way better than Xbox. Danny already told me he'd give me his old games."

Alice breathed deeply. Look how lucky she was: She had the money to give her son what he wanted. Her biggest challenge would be not to give him everything, to stop short of buying him back.

"Tell you what," she said. "When I get back, let's see how much allowance you've saved. Maybe if we put our money together . . ."

"*Yes!* I *knew* you'd say yes. And Mom? Guess what Dad said. Guess."

Alice didn't dare. "I don't know. Tell me."

"He said you and me could go on the raft next time. Are they letting Danny steer? How about August? School doesn't start until Labor Day."

Alice breathed deeply. "Has your dad talked to you at all?"

" 'Bout what?"

"Nothing, hon. Listen, we'll talk about rafting when I get home. I'm cutting the trip short."

"What? Not you, too! Is, like, Bigfoot out there? Zombies?"

Alice laughed. "No, honey. Nothing like that. I just miss you."

"Jeez." He paused. "Me, too."

Roger handed the phone to Sue, who told Alice she was never staying with Grandma and Grandpa again. "They gots no peanut butter," Sue said. "No chocolate stuff to put in the milk."

"I'll buy double on the way home. Sue, can I talk to your dad?"

The static got worse as John came to the line. Alice looked up the crevasse, but the rock was slick, the slope too steep. There was nowhere else to go.

"You got home all right?" she asked.

"Fine. I had a four-hour layover in Boise. They've got a decent McDonald's in the terminal. A milkshake never tasted so good."

His voice was just the same. He might hate her, but he'd never yell. He was a man who'd never gotten credit for the things he didn't do.

"John, I've asked Ellis to take me out tonight. I'm coming home."

He was silent. He might not want to be cruel over the phone but he also couldn't offer kindness. Either way, she thought bleakly, he's done.

"What about your research?" he asked.

She laughed harshly. "Oh, for God's sake, who cares? You left me, John Aberdeen. I'm standing in the middle of this godforsaken wilderness alone."

The static worsened. Alice scrambled down the crevasse, headed toward a clearing in the trees. She could make out only the tail end of the words. ". . . ed . . . it . . . on . . . ove." She started to run. It was urgent, suddenly, that she understand him, that she not miss another word.

". . . wouldn't want that for them," John was saying as she reached the clearing. "Not in a million years."

Wouldn't want what? Her children to become the products of divorce, or to suffer a mother like her?

"I love them, John," she said.

"I know you do."

"I always tried to protect them, to not let them know what I was feeling, but that only isolated me more. I got so wrapped up in . . . me. It was like living in a tunnel, and everything I said came echoing back at me, and it was so dark."

"Alice . . ."

"I know. I'm writing again. Listen. This place is different. Didn't you feel it? So many more things matter here. You lose yourself thinking about them. You can't help but get swept up."

A shiver struck her, and she realized she was soaked through. She hadn't been turned into a fish, but the river had still come to get her. She might have to move closer to the bay when she got home. Or up near the lazy rivers in Sonoma County, the countryside John had always loved.

"I didn't pay enough attention to you," she said. "I'm sorry."

She heard him breathe in, heard the whistle he always made through his teeth. She closed her eyes. "I want to come home," she went on. "Take a break from writing. I don't expect anything."

He laughed softly, and she didn't care if it was physically impossible, she knew her heart flipped. For a moment everything she wanted and needed was up in the air. For a moment, she was entirely at his mercy, and she knew exactly how fortunate she was to have someone whose life purpose was to catch people when they fell.

"I'm surprised at you, Alice," he said. "Where's your happy ending?"

"Oh," she said, content to leave it at that.

When she got back to camp, Mike, Danny, and Charlie were lying in sleeping bags beside the campfire. Ellis waited by the jet boat, her bags in hand. He hadn't said hello to Drew; in fact, he'd kept his back to all of them, standing stiffly and looking up-river where, once the mist lifted, the last of the long day's light glowed red. Everyone had turned in early, which was just as well. Not everything could and should be tied up at the end; she'd learned that after book three. You have to leave space in a reader's mind for a character to go on.

As Alice turned to go, Jina and Irene emerged from Irene's tent. Jina had on Irene's small fanny pack. She avoided Mike's gaze, her sights already set on the path up Black Ridge. Alice hurried to meet them at the trailhead.

"Don't," Alice said.

Jina didn't flinch. "Irene loaned me her gun. It'll be dark soon."

"Jina—"

"What if it's him?"

Alice knew it wasn't only writers who had to be bold with their stories. Friends, too, had to dare to speak the truth. "Then he doesn't want you to find him," she said.

Irene's eyes widened; Jina looked stricken. They were cruel words, and sometimes those were the only kind that worked. Sometimes.

Jina straightened her spine, suddenly seemed much taller than she was. "Damn what he wants," she said.

She flipped on the flashlight, started up the path. Alice took a step after her, but Irene grabbed her shoulder.

"Let her go," she said.

Alice turned back. "She'll only get hurt."

"Then she'll get hurt. It won't kill her."

"I wish I could—"

"Alice, *go*."

Naji called out for Irene, and she dropped her hand from Alice's shoulder. Her whole face changed. She hurried across camp, turned back when she reached the tent. "Next book," she called out, "no cats. You hear me?"

Alice breathed deeply. "I hear you."

Mike heard her, too. He sat beside the campfire, staring at the trail Jina had taken. Alice tried to walk past without turning him into a character, without imagining where he'd go from here, but she couldn't help herself. She'd never written anyone like him: a man who acted most nobly when he did nothing at all.

She stomped to the jet boat, nodded to Ellis as he turned over the engine. Wouldn't it figure that the day she gave up writing, her head filled with heroes and plots? She felt the pen against her hip as she climbed in, got an itch there as they sped away. By the time the sky was darkening and they were half a mile upstream, it was a stone she couldn't deny. She snatched the pen from her pocket, grabbed a wrinkled paper from the floor of the boat. She felt compassionate and ruthless at once, a pirate. Writers, she thought giddily, are liars and thieves.

Beware.

15

Sex, Lies, and a Smoking Gun

Jina had been walking for an hour when she realized the trail was no longer there. It was dark now. Her flashlight illuminated only pine needles, underbrush, a particularly dense stretch of trees. She couldn't find her own footprints behind her. No broken shrubs or familiar boulders, no lover's thread to guide her out. Her fingers had gone numb clutching the flashlight. The light dimmed, then went out.

She laughed, it was so predictable. She was acting like a teenager, so why shouldn't she slip into one of their movies? She refused to imagine repercussions. She had rock songs in her head. The river was cursed, all right; it made everyone feel as though they were eighteen. Out here even mothers played Truth or Dare.

"I dare you to keep walking," she said out loud, and took a step in the dark. Truth: It felt *good* to walk out of camp, as if she was recovering pieces of herself dropped twelve years ago——an affinity for night, her own desire, expectation, fearlessness, pride.

She retraced what she thought had been her steps and found the path hiding beneath pine boughs. She looked back once, then headed over Black Ridge.

She walked three miles an hour in Danville, but on mountain trails, in darkness, it takes longer. She reached one false summit and saw the descent into the canyon, the beginning of a narrow switchback trail. She whistled at the steep grade; something—— an owl, she hoped——called back as she started down.

At least the smoke was gone; the sky was a Pollock painting, a splattering of stars. After half an hour of steep descent, the path leveled off in a narrow canyon. Cliffs became obstacles, and the trail was forced to crisscross a knee-deep stream. She followed the path someone had carefully laid——a set of three boulders across the water, a log bridge smoothed of its splinters. The trail was well tended, the pine boughs cut to a man's height. The landscape turned vertical, daunting, decadent in its beauty, and it came to her, all at once, that she would not have stayed. If she and Zach had finished the run, if he'd asked her to follow him to some remote cabin, she would have said yes instantly, then regretted her decision more each day. She would have planted a garden, lived without friends, without art and ambition, and hated him the way she'd hated Earl——the way you hate anyone who doesn't understand who you are and what you need. She'd have left in the middle of the night, and it all would have turned out the same way anyway.

Jina took her first deep breath in four days and it smelled glorious, something she would like to bottle and put on her nightstand at home. She might have laughed out loud if she hadn't walked around the turn and hit her toe on a granite slab laid as a footpath.

She looked up and saw the cabin. It was no more than a shack, tin-roofed, tiny. A pile of neatly stacked firewood easily outsized it. She'd lost track of time, but it couldn't have been much past eleven. There were still flickering lights in the windows. A shadow passed the glass, and Jina stepped back. It was impossible to tell if the silhouette belonged to a man or a woman.

She looked at the large garden guarded by tall wire gates. In the darkness, she could make out little beyond spinach leaves, a tangle of beans, the frilly tips of carrots. There were fruit trees beyond, probably apples, pears, plums. A canal had been cut to bring water from Corey Creek, and was kept in check by a series of wooden floodgates, a farmer's invention.

That one deep breath had been the briefest gift. When a boy laughed, she had trouble taking in air. She realized how brave it was for a man to say he loved you when there was no longer any clear indication that you loved him back. She thought of the steps Mike must have taken—resetting his career, getting on a plane, finding Ellis, jet boating downriver—just to reach her. She knew Zach never would have gone as far.

Maybe the sincerity of her proposal shouldn't have been

trusted, but neither should Mike's rebuff. Both of them, it seemed, had spoken too soon.

She stepped back. There was a clanking of dishes, another laugh, a shadow that passed the window, then came back. Someone looked out into the garden, and Jina felt a rush of coldness. She thought of Naji's jinn, but she wasn't afraid of spirits coming to get her. *She* was the menace in the darkness, the devil come to ruin everything. She turned her back to the cabin. She would have left, she told herself later, if the door hadn't opened just then.

She heard a footfall, a scrape. *I dare you to go*, she thought, as her feet just stood there—no better than a child who knows what's good for her and, so, does the opposite—unable or unwilling to control herself. Truth: You don't get anywhere when you're looking back.

She looked over her shoulder. It was the woman who'd come to Ellis's. Pearl. She had a boy in tow, a frail thing with pale blond hair and slack, angelic features. Jina grabbed the gate, crouched down to let the dizziness fade. She knelt beside a strawberry patch, big, fat berries left for friends to pick.

The woman said something to the boy, who moved to the end of the porch. Pearl stepped onto the path alone. She was so hearty, Jina swore the ground vibrated when she walked. The woman wore a paisley skirt, a blouse with blue bonnets printed all over it—pretty clothes, the kind you wear to parties and Sunday brunches.

It was hard to remember that she'd done nothing wrong. Jina forced herself to stand; even so, she had to tilt her head back to look into Pearl's eyes, the way she did with most men. Pearl blocked her view of the cabin.

"Well," Pearl said.

"Please," Jina said, extending a hand, then dropping it. "I'm sorry."

Sorry for coming, sorry for trying to look past, where she swore she heard another, heavier footfall on the porch, a footfall that couldn't possibly belong to the boy.

Pearl raised her hand and Jina flinched, sure she was going to be struck, but Pearl merely swiped something from Jina's cheek, then looked heavenward.

"Smoke's gone," she said. "It'll be cold tonight. Perhaps you'd better come in."

"Pearl—" Jina grabbed her hand. She wanted the view blocked a moment longer, wanted one minute more. None of this was real. This was what happened when you tried to force fate: It got twisted, convoluted, wrong. You got what you wanted and felt sick inside, impure. Now was the right time to speak to Mike, to pour her heart out. Right now, when she stood somewhere else.

She squeezed Pearl's hand, as if the woman could guarantee solace and peace of mind the way she'd guaranteed, with sheer will and strength, a quiet life for her son.

Pearl snatched her hand away. She had deep gray, almost pewter eyes—the sturdiest metal. "I'll be inside," she said.

Pearl returned to the cabin, took her boy's hand, and said nothing to the man standing on the porch, holding the railing as if he might fall otherwise, as if he might drown again. She went inside and slammed the door.

Then it was quiet, except for the trickle of the stream, a faint whistle of wind through the trees. *You would sleep like a baby here*, Jina thought. *Sleep your life away.*

"Jina?" Zach said.

The key to life in a river is dead things. The mountain streams that flow above the tree line look pristine but are lifeless. Blue and cold. On the other hand, creeks that originate in forests, where fallen trees, crumbling wood, and rotten leaves collect in the water, are teeming with life. Insects bore into downed logs. Mold grows, fungi softens the wood, earthworms eat to their hearts' content, and eventually the tree becomes soil, a feast for bacteria and larvae, which are breakfast for beetles and dragonflies, which are dinner for salmon and trout.

From the moment he opened his eyes in what he thought was heaven but turned out to be Pearl's cabin, Zach knew what he'd become—another dead thing to nourish the river. He hurt so bad he figured pieces of him were still floating in the Salmon, a feast for coyotes and bears.

Death was shockingly painful, not at all the peaceful conclusion he'd been promised at the First Presbyterian Church in Kimberly. His body would not warm, his head wound pulsed, his broken bones refused to heal. Human sounds hurt his ears; even Pearl's softest whispers pained him. For weeks, he lay by the open window and focused on the chatter of the blue jays, the endless questions of winter owls, the bugling of migrating elk. He thought death would be autumn eternal—everything falling, fading, going to rot—but instead, winter came. The snow fell two feet deep outside the door, and his body shivered and recovered. The cabin filled up with wood smoke, and he realized, with great regret, that he wasn't dead at all.

He stumbled out of the cabin three months after he'd been dragged into it. He plowed through thigh-high snow, got all the way to the river, before Pearl found him and showed him Jina's wool coat and life jacket, and told him his wife was dead. Dead in Big Mallard, which shattered their scow. Her body had been recovered and flown out, and the rescuers were long gone, having given up looking for him. Dead, she told him. No one knew he had survived.

So this woman on the path in front of him was a phantom, a phantom who, apparently, could age. This Jina was a few pounds heavier than his spindly young wife, with splashes of gray in her hair. She wore the loose, comfortable clothes he remembered, still styled her hair in that childlike pageboy cut. She looked like Jina, not at all pale and transparent but with an angry blush to her face. Not even slightly diaphanous, but with her fists balled up, her tiny foot tapping the ground in fury.

"You son of a bitch," she said and, unlike any ghost he could dream up, began to cry.

Zach clutched the porch railing he'd replaced last year, using bolts he'd salvaged from the mine a quarter mile up the draw. He struggled for breath. Long before this haunting, he'd had trouble breathing. Air never reached his lungs; no amount of water quenched his thirst. Sometimes he swam clear to Nixon Bar, six miles downstream, then turned around and swam back up. He could outswim the current and that scared him. It wasn't natural, a man feeling more comfortable in water than on land, a man with no fear of drowning or the cold.

He blinked and Jina disappeared into the forest. Andy's voice drifted from the cabin, squealing with delight when he picked Queen Frosting's card. He played Candy Land with Pearl a dozen times a day, never caring if he won or lost. Whenever someone reached the castle, he put his blue game piece back on start.

Andy had been such a quiet baby, Zach hadn't noticed him for weeks. The boy made a kind of chirping sound when he was hungry, and Zach mistook him for a bird. It wasn't until Pearl had to chase a porcupine from the living room that she thrust the child into Zach's arms. The baby was the first thing that didn't stink of the river; in fact, he smelled like candy. Like peppermint, though they had none of the herb in the house. Andy hadn't cried, though surely Zach's cold, scaly body must have shocked him. The boy had eyes the color of trout, perfectly placid eyes that accepted stillness and current alike. Zach put his bandaged hand on the back of the boy's neck, held it there gently until they both fell asleep.

Now Andy laughed, and Zach reached for the door. This was all a test, or Pearl's horrible idea of a joke, or simply illusion. It was the dream he'd had a thousand times and never told—Jina come back to life, whole and happy, and this half life, this waterlogged life, abandoned.

He never turned the knob. Zach had seen everything from avalanches to wildfires, but he had yet to see a ghost. He stepped off the porch, caught up to Jina beyond the garden. She sat on the ground, her ankle twisted oddly around a root, pounding her fists in the dirt. Less a spirit than a furious, forsaken girl. He crouched down, wondered how he could be so unsteady at his age, after so much. It was almost as if, the older you got, the less secure you were about things, the less you knew. His hand shook so badly that he couldn't touch her, couldn't lift her chin to see if it was really her. Still the brave one, she threw back her hair, stared him right in the eye.

He gasped harder, a fish out of water, fell back on his heels. He'd insisted on combing the river even after Pearl told him Jina was dead. Months after it was over, he took to the banks each morning, followed faint footprints that petered out in rocky moraines. A couple of times, he saw the old man, Ellis, roaring past in his jet boat, but Zach ducked behind trees, avoided him. He couldn't bear to be found, exposed for what he was: at best, a careless husband; at worst, a murderer. He avoided everyone but Pearl, and sometimes even her. In spring, he left her cabin and slept by the river. Lulled by the current, he became oblivious to hunger and cold. He never would have moved if Pearl hadn't shouted for him, if she hadn't flown through the woods with Andy in her arms, the boy's tiny body giving off steam—if he hadn't been faced with the thought of someone else dying under his care.

"Oh my God," he said to Jina. "You're real."

He buried his face in his hands. The last thing he remembered was celebrating how far he and Jina had come. They'd been on an easy stretch of the river, and he'd taken off the ill-fitting life jacket, imagined them living there for the rest of their lives. He thought it was Jina who knocked him over. As he fell into the water, he was laughing, planning to pull her in after him. He must have hit his head; he felt a quick, sharp pain, and when he opened his eyes, another woman was expecting him to respond, to drink her soup, to get up. For a month, all those things were so impossible that he didn't speak a single word. He didn't trust his own hands or his voice; he craved death. He feared he could only do harm.

"You . . . left . . . me," Jina said. "You left me here to die."

He dropped his hands, saw the tears all down her cheeks, the horror in her eyes. "No," he said, everything flooding back. All the sleepless nights, the pain that was excruciating but never bad enough to knock him out, to drive her from his memory. "No. I never would have. Pearl found me. She told me . . . I thought you'd drowned."

He could see she didn't believe him. She shook her head, and one of her tears landed on his arm, stung him. "I searched," she said. "You have no idea. The woods. The cliffs. I looked everywhere."

"Jina—"

"It doesn't matter the reason. You left me to die."

He leaned back. He couldn't deny this. He'd brought her on the river, on his river, and abandoned her. He'd acknowledged his guilt the moment Pearl brought him Andy's feverish body and he took the boy to Ellis's. He came out of hiding, delivered his own sentence: He went on.

"How did you find me?" he asked.

She shook her head. She pulled her ankle inward, massaged it, stood. She was wobbly on her feet, and he stood quickly, reached out to help, but she jerked him off, glared at him.

"How could Ellis not tell me?" she asked. "How could he not track me down, let me know you were alive? He knew I called the sheriff for months, until they insisted your body would never be found. How could he not, at least, tell you the truth? He was the one who found me. Him and your father."

Zach stared at her. His father had been here, searching. He squeezed his eyes shut. He couldn't tolerate the thought of the old man turning over rocks, looking for all that was left of him—his pocketknife or an empty can of peaches. Whenever Andy stayed in the woods too long Zach envisioned catastrophes. He was frantic until they found him. He could only imagine what a father felt when the search went on for days, when it never ended.

But Ellis never got the chance to father Drew, which was why he could let some men stay lost. When Zach brought Andy to Ellis, the old man showed only a moment's shock at his resurrection, then put a hand on top of Zach's head as if he was the one on fire. It was the only time Zach cried.

"The river," Zach said. "This canyon. People protect each—"

"Don't you dare," she said, her eyes so furious that he wouldn't dare anything. He could hardly look at her. "Don't you dare tell me he kept quiet to protect you. I went home with your father, Zach. He died thinking his only son was lost."

Zach dropped his head, began to rock like Andy. This couldn't be real. At any moment, Pearl would nudge him awake. She'd put her cool hand on his forehead, shush him, give him a welcome list of things to do.

"Apparently, everyone knows about you," Jina went on. "You're a legend on this river. The fish-man. The man the river drowned and spit back out. Believe me, my mind is eased now. I'll sleep well, knowing you've always been just fine."

She limped past him, as volatile and rash as she'd been twelve years ago. Still a girl, really, which seemed impossible, considering how much he'd aged.

"So that's it?" he shouted after her. "You show up in the middle of the night like some ghost, then disappear again? That's what I'm . . . what our marriage is worth to you?"

She whirled around. "Our *marriage*? A few soulful looks and one ill-conceived adventure? Does that really count? I had no idea what I was doing back then. My God, do you realize how frightening that is? I fell in love with the idea of you. I had no clue I couldn't give up everything, and that someone who really loved me wouldn't ask me to."

"You can't have been alone all this time?" He formed it like a question, though he knew that it wasn't.

She stared at him. "No."

He looked through the trees to the lights of his cabin. He couldn't hear them now, though he imagined Pearl working the cards to make sure Andy got all the candies, landing in mud puddles on purpose.

"I've thought of you every day," he said softly.

He could see, right away, that she hadn't. He tried to be glad for that. It was the very least he could do—wish that she'd gotten over him quickly, that she'd found someone more suitable to love.

"I don't care," she said. "Thoughts mean nothing."

"Not out here they don't."

She tried to glare again, but he could see the fury slipping from her, her shoulders settling down. Mountain air did that. You had to catch your breath in the middle of fighting, take a break from crying, just to get enough air. You couldn't keep it up.

"You got what you wanted after all," she said. She waved her hand toward the cabin, and beyond it at the black cliffs, the monstrous wilderness. "You got to stay."

He crossed the path, put his arms around her before either of them could give him all the reasons why he shouldn't, before he added up the years that had passed, and all the ways their minds and hearts and bodies had changed. He buried his face in her hair as if he'd let go of her yesterday and all that had happened in the twelve years since was nothing but a blink of the eye, an aberration. She felt the same, still tiny but invincible. His knees went weak at the wonder of holding her, knowing she was all right. Whatever happened next, she was all right.

"My God," she said, crying, clinging to him now, touching his back, his arms, as if she couldn't believe he was all there. "What kind of life is this? Why didn't you just leave?"

He kissed her head, finally had the right answer. "I'd never leave without you."

He walked as if there were streetlights, as if it was daytime. Jina used to have to race to keep up with him, but thankfully he'd shortened his stride in twelve years, slowed down. He led her past a thicket of elderberry bushes to a surprisingly lush plot of grass. The green tufts were curled over with too much growth. She smelled dampness and moss yet heard no stream.

"It used to drive me crazy," Zach said, his shoes squishing

across the moss, "trying to figure out where all the water comes from. In August, the snowmelt's done and it never rains. Didn't you ever wonder how the river goes on?"

She hoped he would tell her, in long, slow paragraphs. Take the whole night to explain the origin of creeks. She'd missed his voice most. She'd pictured his face, recalled his smell, slept in a shirt she'd taken from his closet, but Zach's voice remained distant, temperamental. It only came when it wanted to.

He took her hand, pulled her down on the grass. She thought he would kiss her, but he swiped her palms over mounds of wild peppermint and moss. He poked her fingers into a tiny, wet pucker in the hillside.

"This," he said. "One drop of moisture rising from the earth. A teardrop, right? The smallest thing imaginable. Yet it slides downhill and all along the slope, other tears are sliding, too. Eventually the teardrops meet, start a creek, one of hundreds of creeks. It's sorrow that fills the river."

Had he searched for her at all? Had he dreamed of her, too—made her into more than she was, never let her fail him? Did he love Pearl? Where would they go from here? Each question was another tear in the hillside. It was impossible to know where to begin.

"The scow," he said. "You must have—"

"I jumped out. I tried to catch up to you, but you were already gone."

He looked away. "Sometimes I dreamt it. I saw myself floating, useless. Just leaving you there."

Jina felt the moisture seeping through her pants, knew the truth now. "There was nothing you could have done."

He shook his head. "Of course there was. We didn't have to come at all. I could have kept you safe in Kimberly. I could have kept on the life jacket."

"After you fell out, I thought I saw you on the bank," she said. "Maybe that's when she got you. I might have been a split second away."

He said nothing, and she couldn't bring herself to ask what Pearl meant to him. What would happen now that he knew Pearl had lied?

"I wanted to keep looking for you," Jina went on, "but I realized the only way out was up. I broke my leg on the moraine. Elvis—you remember Elvis—stood guard over me. Ellis and your father found me. He died two years ago. Or maybe you knew."

She'd assumed the eyes could not change, but his had. In place of the bright blue of an Idaho sky, they were now murky and green. His whiskers were silver. His breathing was bad.

"I didn't know," he said hoarsely. "Ellis became . . . he took ownership of the secrets. He could stand it, and he did. He didn't interfere; that's what the men of this canyon value most."

"I went to your father's funeral. He'd been waiting to die for many years. He wanted to catch up with you."

She didn't know whether she wanted him to fall apart or leave. Each moment they sat there must have felt like a claw in Pearl's skin.

"Tell me about Pearl," she said.

He leaned back, ran his hand over the stubble of a beard, through the hair that was unchanged, still a tangle of red weeds. He couldn't get his fingers through it.

"She found me. She'd been here only a few months then. She had Andy. I know it was awful what she did. I won't deny that. But out here, you have to take what you need. There's no valor in letting your child starve while a stranger's garden grows rampant. It's a different kind of virtue."

Jina stared at her hands. "You forgive her," she said.

Zach shook his head. "Forgiveness takes too long. I understand. Andy needs so much. He needed even more in the beginning. But he's something, Jina. I thought it was the woods that would keep me, but it was just a boy."

His eyes lit up, and when Jina felt the pulse of jealousy, she knew she'd waited too long to leave. She couldn't hear the river from here, but she stood. The path was somewhere to her left, through the trees, hidden.

"I wasn't going to fail them, too," Zach said softly.

She sighed. "You didn't fail me. It was an accident."

When he started to cry, she looked at the sky. She tried to imagine how anyone had ever plotted their course on so little information. It was like asking a man to marry you before you were sure you wanted him to say yes.

She knelt beside him, put her hands on either side of his face. She kissed his tears. He still tasted like the river. At least that much had not changed.

She knew it was her imagination, the remnants of Drew's campfire story, but in the darkness, his skin gleamed. She saw a flash of iridescence, ran her fingers over gill-like ribs. He touched her arms, and the scales of his palms tickled her flesh; she couldn't see through the gaps between his fingers, as if the skin there was webbed.

When she kissed him, she heard the river again, though it was miles away. She tried to hold him, but his skin was so slick that he kept slipping through her fingers.

She pulled back. "I was pregnant," she said. She put her head on his chest but couldn't hear a heartbeat.

"No," he said.

She had never liked fishing. Had always thought humans the cold-blooded ones, and all their tactics unfair. "His name is Danny," she said. "He's here."

16

Pearl lost twice in Candy Land, then tucked Andy into bed. She read from his favorite Magic School Bus book, the one about electricity where the Frizz takes her students inside wires and into people's televisions—a story made even more incredible because Andy had never seen a TV. He liked the part when the kids got stuck inside the vacuum cleaner, and he liked Arnold, who was always scared. The science itself mystified him, but Pearl insisted that they read every word. Some people in the canyon went mad from solitude; lack of stories got to her. More than soda pop or hair dryers or soap operas, Pearl missed having a place to go. When Ellis discovered them and brought that first delivery of books, along with batteries, a sack of flour, and an old but functional Walkman, Pearl kissed him in gratitude, then went into the cabin and shut the door. She finished four novels in three days, including *To Kill a Mockingbird*. She pretended that Atticus Finch was her father and that most people, in the end, did right.

She read according to Ellis's tastes. Three books on the intricacies of fishing lures, half a dozen westerns, two volumes of classic Shakespeare. Ellis brought her cassette tapes, too, rock groups he thought she might like. Nirvana and The Red Hot Chili Peppers—city bands that drowned out the river. Pearl put on her headphones and sang out loud, as militant as a rock star, as impassioned as anyone. She remembered that in some fortunate circles, more than survival mattered.

Andy thumbed ahead to see which dress the Frizz would wear next. He liked the one patterned with tornadoes. He wished he could go up inside a cyclone, be blown by a hurricane clear across the Atlantic. He loved summer storms, and his eyes lit up whenever he heard rumbles of thunder. She still found it amazing that she'd brought him somewhere dangerous and he mistook it for the safest place on Earth.

Pearl kissed his cheek, brushed a lock of hair off his forehead, hair so pale and easily faded that by the end of summer, only she would see it. Her bed stood two feet away, and she'd never wished it farther. Andy had rarely cried as a baby, but when he did she only had to reach out. Zach had said he'd put in a bathroom, save her the cold trips to the outhouse, but Pearl wasn't about to change a thing. She missed parties but not much else. She brewed her own beer, shot her own food, found a man in the middle of nowhere. Everything she needed had been hiding at the ends of the Earth.

She blew out the propane light, slid into bed. As Andy fell asleep, she hummed; she didn't want to hear anything else. She could tolerate quite a bit, but even she had limits. The night she went with those boys, she was as drunk as they were, until the sixth one's turn. By the time he took her from behind, her mind was crystal clear. When he shoved her face in the dirt, she hardly felt the pain. Some people live in fear of some terrible thing that might befall them, while she got it out of the way early. It was over, even when all eight boys went another round.

When her parents called her a whore, she packed her bags. She lived in her car, drank too much, but that didn't make her a monster. After Andy was born, she kissed the cheeks and forehead doctors were already calling abnormal, deformed. She listened to their diagnoses and didn't panic. When someone instantly becomes your whole life, knowing you won't survive without them is something of a relief.

As fall approached, the car got too cold. Girls she'd known her whole life snickered when she nursed inside. Pearl's hubcaps were stolen while she and Andy slept, and the next morning the policeman who lived two doors down from her parents told her she was upsetting people and would have to park outside the city limits. Pearl drove to North Fork, kept going until she reached the end of the road at Corn Creek. She put her son in a backpack, loaded up with diapers, flashlights, and her father's revolver, and walked into the woods. She and her baby ate roots and slept on beds of pine boughs until she stumbled on this miner's cabin, which had a rusted wood stove, a moldy mattress, and half a roof. When it rained, water sloshed around her ankles, but by then, Pearl couldn't feel it. She was immune to everything that wouldn't kill her. She wrapped her arms around her child and realized that she was the first girl she'd liked in a really long time.

Now she heard a woman's cry, a man's whisper, a brush of wind. Zach's body had appeared on shore like a man dropped from heaven, and she'd done what she had to. Like repairing the roof with sticks and mud, or shooting a man who appeared at the cabin door one night with madness and desperation in his eyes, hoisting Zach's river-cold body into the old wheelbarrow and carting him two miles was survival and nothing else. He stayed, at first out of sorrow, and then from duty. He slept on a bed of straw by the door for three years, and every night for three years she assumed he would be gone by morning. Then one day she came in from the garden he'd fenced in, with an armful of the wild sorrel he'd started from seed, and found the straw gone. He sat on the edge of her bed, his hands on his knees. His hair had grown wild; after those first weeks when she tended him, she rarely saw his face.

"Pearl," he said.

Andy began to cry. She got him a glass of milk, a luxury thanks to the goat. The goats Ellis had given them while Zach sat there, like a deer frozen in headlights. Pearl chopped up the sorrel, made a salad dressing from homemade almond oil and apple vinegar. She waited until Andy took his afternoon nap before sitting beside Zach.

"We can survive without you," she said. "You can walk out that door, and we'll be fine."

He looked up. People like Zach, like her and Andy, were supposed to vanish, to stop upsetting people with the fact of their existence. They were meant to be forgotten, yet even the forgotten had a place. Wilderness saw to that.

"I don't deserve you," he said.

She smiled, still a bit of a belle. "Well, of course not."

He lifted his hand tentatively, set it back down. She sighed. In high school, she was thought too pretty to touch. All the boys were petrified of her; she wasn't asked for a single date until the rumor began circulating that she'd go all the way.

She picked up Zach's hand, held it between her own. Under his tutelage, she'd learned to shoot straight. She'd bagged elk, deer, moose, and she'd put on weight, all muscle. The long hair boys had buried their noses in and said smelled like apples was shaggy now and speckled with pine sap. Instead of heels, she wore boots handed down from Helena; she hadn't shaved her legs in three years. But when she kissed Zach, she could have been on the roof of a skyscraper, on a crowded dance floor, anywhere. She was every girl who'd initiated a kiss; she hardly breathed, waiting for him to give some sign it was what he wanted.

It took him long enough. Her heart raced, her hands slipped from his, she wondered if she should have left him by the river, the water's cold lover. But finally he slid his hand behind her head, parted his lips. His skin was so cold, it took all night to warm him, and every night since had been the same. He came to bed cold as a river and she had to use all her will, every drop of feminine charm, to make him human again. He slept with his stomach to her back, pressed tight against her warmth, so that she never knew for sure if it was love or need that kept him there.

She stared at the ceiling. Men turn strange in the backcountry, but women grow strong. She and Helena not only chopped their own firewood, they survived when men left. Ellis had hiked out one snowy day in December and stayed away until spring. During those five months alone, Helena continued to welcome the snowshoers who stopped at the lodge. She kept the woodstoves burning, butchered a cow, and sent the steaks downriver to Pearl. On the first of each month, she showed up on Pearl's doorstep, her Russian parka wrapped around her, a bundt cake and a stack of wonderfully ridiculous fashion magazines in her hands. When she and Pearl sat down to coffee, she said what she always said. What they all said.

"I married the river more than the man. It's all the same to me."

Those words helped at every hour but this one, when Pearl's eyes wouldn't close and the sound of footsteps outside the cabin didn't stop at the door, and her boy took deep, easy breaths. Women on the Salmon skin their own meat and don't beg. So Pearl did it secretly, under the covers.

"Please," she said.

Ahmad walked past the cabin door. He'd followed Jina for three miles, watched her leave with the man. He knew there was only a woman and child inside, no one to stop him. He'd heard the boy's laughter, didn't dare let it slow him down.

He crept to the side of the cabin, the generous wood pile. On the horizon, his fires glowed feebly. Though he'd heard the hum of air tankers, the damage thus far was minimal. Even his nightmares were ineffective—every forest he burned magically regenerated itself, every infidel he destroyed rose up stronger through his children. Like Khidr, he felt closest to God in the woods; he guided the lost home. He'd followed Jina as he'd followed Alice, and she'd led him to this tinderbox, a perfect combination of kindling and canyon winds, isolation and slope. So what did Allah want from him? To destroy the only place left where He was truly evident? To sacrifice people for God, or God for people?

Irene was a shaitan, a devil, but he liked the other women he'd been riding the Salmon with. Now it was Naji who infuriated him. His brother had gotten everything he wanted; he'd gotten away. Ahmad had begun to shake at night.

He felt steadier when he took the lighter fluid from his pocket. It had been the same all those years ago beside his father's bed. Assault is self-defense from another angle. At least he acted when another man would see no hope.

He heard the woman now, moving around inside, then going still. It was too much like a movie here: big sunsets, breathtaking scenery, blustery, brave characters who would seem cartoonish anywhere else. He was ashamed to admit he'd gotten wrapped up in it, walked out surprised to find it day instead of night. Anything the woman and her son felt were petty, he reminded himself. They lived in their shack and thought it the universe— one well-lived life as important as a hundred of them.

He no longer felt clean enough to perform the salah. Dirt clung to his hands no matter how hard he scrubbed; his hair sported bits of sand and fish. He faced Mecca, though at night, with so many mountains surrounding him, he worried that he might be turning west instead. His voice was a whisper the woman inside would mistake for an owl.

"*Allahu Akbar,*" he said. "*Allahu Akbar. Allahu Akbar. Allahu Akbar.*" God is great. God is great. God is great. God is great.

Jina pulled her knees to her chest. Zach stomped across the birthplace of a creek, failing to recognize the damage he did. Jina imagined a whole series of caverns and waterways beneath the soil collapsing, tears plugged, the river going dry.

"You were pregnant," Zach said.

She regretted it the moment she told him. The thoughtlessness was a leftover, a last youthful puff of smoke; kissing him was just as naïve. She could close her eyes and make them both twenty, but a woman made love with her eyes open. She saw flaws; she saw what was really there.

"I named him Daniel," she said.

He swung his head like a caged bear. Right, left, neither direction a way out. "Daniel," he whispered.

"He just turned twelve. He's a whiz at Game Boy."

He looked up quizzically. A man trapped in time, pre–Game Boy, pre-father. The world had gone on without him.

"Daniel" was all he could say.

"He has red hair. I could never comb it." She hadn't realized she was crying until he lifted her from the ground.

"Daniel," he said, a sigh.

The waterway she'd thought collapsed found a new route. The serenity of the woods was all illusion. Water never stopped; somewhere a tree fell, an earthquake rumbled, another mountain was born. Even with all their dramatics, humans were dull in comparison.

"Somehow my dreams spilled over," she said. "He saw you, Zach. Every night. Even though I never told him what happened to you, he knew about this place. Did you . . . did you ever dream about him?"

Zach pulled away. "How could I have? I didn't know about him. If I had . . ."

She rose on tiptoes, wouldn't let him lie. Not even to himself. When he quieted, she fell back to the soles of her feet, stepped away.

"Your life is here," she said quietly. "You wouldn't have left."

He lowered his head. She heard her heart beating inside her chest, a branch falling, and the flight of startled birds.

"You're the love of my life," Zach said.

He closed the gap between them, lifted her off her feet as if she might run. But she wasn't going anywhere. Not once he kissed her.

"Daniel," he said into her ear, and she wanted to tell him to call him Danny. He liked to be called Danny. But by then he'd put her down.

"If we leave now," he said, "I'll be there when he wakes up. We'll go home together."

He squeezed her hand, smiled like the man, the boy, she remembered. She felt giddy, hopelessly young. It's so easy to be happy; just take what you want. Don't think for a second about people or consequences. Don't think. She imagined walking back hand in hand, kneeling beside Danny, kissing him awake. There would be tears, another man's heartache, a majority of happiness, three-quarters' joy. They'd finally float out of the Salmon River canyon together. She'd bring Zach home.

She put her arms around him, held on tightly to stop her body from shaking. The trembling was as bad as it had been af-ter delivering Danny. Her jaw chattered, her body shuddered with adrenaline, with the shock of what she'd lost, and what she'd gained as a result.

"Jina?" he said, holding her tighter. He must have felt her tears on his chest. He ran his hands up and down her back, thinking her cold.

Like Alice, she'd been given her heart's desire too late, after she'd learned to live without it.

I dare you to let go, she thought, and she did.

"You can't leave this place, Zach," she said. "You know you can't."

The boys fell asleep, then awoke around midnight when Mike got up to stoke the fire. Charlie lifted his head, followed Mike's gaze toward the path.

"You hear that?" Charlie whispered.

Mike turned his back to the path; he knew for a fact that nothing was there. "Relax," he said. "It's just us. Look at the stars." He pointed out the constellations he knew—Orion, Ca-nis Major, the Big Dipper. When he ran out of knowledge, he made more up.

"That's Dalmatian Retching," he said, pointing south. "See the vomit coming out of his mouth."

Danny and Charlie laughed, and Mike returned to his sleeping bag, put his hands behind his head. There was a rock beneath his spine, but Danny snuggled up against him, and he wasn't moving for anything.

"How about Barbara's Boobs?" Charlie said. "Over there."

Mike checked out the double halos to the west. Indeed, the boy had a good eye. He couldn't scold him for that.

"Chicken Peeing," Danny said.

The tents were quiet, the campfire white-hot and warm. Mike had not slept outside since he was eighteen. He'd made excuses, said his back couldn't take it, but as of this moment, he was in no pain at all. Apparently, his spine was meant for the shock treatment of jet boats and bedrock. He hadn't felt a twinge since he'd set foot in Idaho. He liked the view straight up. A boy who'd seemed a baby when you were standing over him was actually, when lying beside you, nearly full-grown.

"Mike?" Danny said.

A strange thing happened after Mike stepped on Ellis's boat. The first rapid terrified him, but by the second he was imagining Danny's face as he crested a wave and came speeding down the other side. The river was a trail of bread crumbs that Danny had left for him. He imagined himself the man in Danny's dreams.

"Yeah, Dan," he said.

The corners of Danny's mouth still sported traces of marsh-mallow. Mike hadn't asked him to brush his teeth before bed, and he wasn't going to. If he got the chance, he'd be a horrible disciplinarian. He swore it.

"I don't see him anymore."

Mike brushed the hair from Danny's eyes. "Your dad, you mean?"

"Yeah. I thought. . . . I dreamed him once more, but then he left. He's gone."

Mike nodded. "Dreams don't tell us much. It's what happens when you're awake that counts. I'm sorry, Dan."

Danny shrugged; Charlie was snoring. Danny made a circle with his thumb and forefinger and peered through it, as if this would bring the heavens down closer. "It's all right. You're here now."

Mike breathed deeply. The smell and sound of the river were so strong that they nearly overpowered the littler things. The changing scent of a twelve-year-old boy, for instance, from sugar one minute to sweat the next. The swishy sound of a son settling into his sleeping bag, surrounded by wilderness, safe and sound.

"You bet I am," Mike said.

Jina went to him, tried to hold him.

"Zach," she said.

He jerked away, stalked so deep into the trees that she feared he was leaving her again. She opened her mouth, closed it without calling out. She remembered this from before; shouting accomplished nothing here.

Zach returned, his face angry but his hands out before him, like a man begging for his life.

"It's over now," he said. "You're all right. You're here. I can come home."

The trembling in her body was beginning to subside. Jina

could only imagine what had come loose inside her, a lung fallen to her abdomen, a hip bone disengaged and sunk. She had pains in the strangest places, between the wings of her shoulder blades, in the soft spot below her ankle, behind an ear.

"This is your home," she said.

He looked stricken, and she had to turn away, had to squeeze her eyes shut to keep from seeing in his face a mirror of her own desire. They *deserved* this. All that shaking was her body screaming. That shaking was what was left of her youth.

"You can't tell me I have a son, then expect me to stay away," he said. "You can't do that to me."

She opened her eyes. "You can see him. Meet him. But you're not the kind of man who abandons his family."

They stood there for what seemed like hours, though it was probably only seconds. A foot apart, both pleading a case they didn't fully believe in, both taking the side they couldn't bear. They stood until the sky lightened to gray, Zach's shoulders sunk, and Jina knew, with despair, that she'd won.

"I could bring Danny here in the summer," she said. "It'll take time for him to adjust to the fact that you've always been . . . In the end, I'm sure he'll be thrilled to come. And you could visit. We have a house in the suburbs."

Zach stepped back and something even more elemental, like the right side of Jina's heart, fell. He was a boy in the woods; he'd never grown up. He was still afraid of settling down, of turning out like his father, of someone ruining his plans.

"Ah," she said, rubbing her chest where it burned. "You're not going anywhere. You're happy with things the way they are."

"Happy," he said, laughing harshly. "Let me tell you something. Sometimes you have to pretend that nothing can ever change. Sometimes that's the only way to go on."

She understood then the secret of how he and Pearl had survived. They adapted in a heartbeat, stitched their hearts to what worked.

"A son changes everything," he said. "Even Pearl would understand that."

He didn't dare look at her. There was only one fantasy left. A cruel escape during the night, the three of them slipping east into Montana, where they'd find their own river. Danny would learn to hunt and fish. This could be their decision now, not a destiny imposed on them. All Jina had to do was lean in the direction they could go, weaken until Zach had to carry her. She merely had to need him more than Pearl and Andy did.

She balled her fists, took a deep breath, stood straight. And Zach must have remembered that pose, because he held up his hand. "All right," he said. "All right."

It was nearly morning; a light ash had begun to fall. He stepped forward, and she knew if he kissed her once more, she'd curl up on the forest floor and weep.

But all he said was, "Will he hate me?"

She grabbed his hand. "Of course not. Danny's always adored you. Somehow he's always known who you are."

"Jina," he said. His eyes were filled with tears. "Does it matter that I love you? Does that matter at all?"

She heard a voice from the cabin, perhaps Pearl getting up—birds, branches, a distant plane returning to the fire. She heard Zach, too, but it was only one of many noises, and that was both a loss and a relief. That was just the way it was when you grew up.

She took him in her arms. "It matters," she said.

His crying was terrible. His pain made it hard to breathe. "You're not invisible anymore," she went on. "I know you're here."

Zach nodded mutely, buried his face in her hair. His body had grown cold again. She rubbed his back furiously, but her touch seemed pointless, like trying to warm a whole river with the heat of one body.

He pulled back. "They'll be worried about you."

She thought of Mike, allowed him back in. She knew he wasn't sleeping, knew he must be thinking she'd proved his fears correct. She'd figured out who she loved and who she didn't.

And she had.

The trail was beyond the cabin. They walked back and Zach dropped her hand before they came into view. They heard nothing but birdsong, then the sound of a man's chant.

It scared the birds away. Zach crouched down, grabbed the largest stick he could find.

Beside the cabin, Ahmad was on his knees. He looked heavenward, despite the falling ash, and smiled. Zach stepped without making a sound, but Jina landed on a pine cone, cracked the spine. The chanting stopped; Ahmad turned. Jina saw the empty cans of lighter fluid, the puddles on the woodpile adjacent to the cabin, matches lined up in a row. She saw, in her mind, the cabin engulfed, flames too furious to get past, Pearl and Andy opening their eyes, briefly, as their blankets exploded.

By then, Ahmad had lit the first match.

"Hey," Zach said. "Hey."

Ahmad rocked; the sway of his body made the match go out. Zach lunged, got within ten feet before Ahmad lit the second match and tossed it on the woodpile, into a puddle of lighter fluid.

"In Sha'Allah," Ahmad said, as the flames whooshed.

17

The most dangerous things are often the most beautiful: the inside of a tornado, the eyes of a desperate girl. It takes fire to make the best sunrises, and the beginning of this one looked like a field of red poppies, flowers and colors too bold to be believed.

Irene hardly glanced at it. She sat cross-legged on the beach beside Naji, the terrier's nose in her lap. She'd confiscated Danny's Game Boy when no one else seemed interested, had been playing Mario Kart most of the night while she waited for Jina to return. She grimaced as she jabbed the tiny buttons, and the dog raised his head.

"You try," she said. "It's fucking impossible."

Naji had not slept, either. He looked over her shoulder at the game. *"Oooh,"* he said, as she cut off two virtual drivers, moved up to sixth place. "Good move."

He noticed the rafts before she did. Six of them, their guides humorlessly bringing them to shore. Irene turned off the game. She'd seen this company behind them at the put-in, everyone splashing and screaming, a Labrador running around, but they were quiet now. The dog didn't lean over the bow but rested inside, head down.

Irene realized it was still an hour before sunrise. The light was a wall of flames, two ridges away.

"Dudes," the first guide said. "You've got to go. They closed the river behind us. Man, it's bad. The whole canyon's on fire."

Irene turned to Naji, her stomach turning. "Jina's not back. Oh, God, Ellis. Helena."

"We heard the blaze was small," Naji said to the guide. "Going the other way."

"It's not just one fire. Blazes were set all over the canyon. Winds blew them up last night."

Naji took Irene's hand. "Someone from one of our boats," he said.

The guide nodded. "Looks like it. Can you believe that? We bring these people through, set up their fucking tents, feed 'em lobster, and they torch the place behind us?"

"I'll get Drew," Irene said.

She ran up the slope. The boys were still asleep by the fire, Mike percolating coffee over the flame. Irene hurried to Mary's tent.

"Drew," she said. "You'd better get up. There's fire."

Drew emerged shirtless, instantly alert; he and Mike ran to

the beach. While Mary dressed, Irene glanced at Ahmad's tent, already knowing what she'd find: the flap open, the sleeping bag rolled up, unused. She'd had no trouble thinking the worst of Ahmad; that was not only Mike's job but any adult's. Her problem was not saying it outright: They'd brought a madman along.

Mary emerged from her tent as Irene took the coffee off the fire, ripped out tent stakes. A few minutes later, Naji came up behind her. He leaned against her shoulder; for a moment, Irene had to support his weight, and this was an easy task for her. This was what she'd been waiting for.

"He's gone," she said. "Probably all night."

Naji nodded. Drew ran back to camp, already throwing gear into piles. Mike didn't hesitate. He headed straight to the path over Black Ridge.

"Mike!" Drew shouted. "You can't go. We've been ordered out. God only knows what's happened behind us. My dad . . ."

Mike stared up the path. He swung his head, clenched his hands into fists. Irene watched the horizon, which wasn't a field of poppies at all but spilled ink. The wind had picked up even while they stood there. She could smell the air—an almost pleasant aroma, like a backyard barbecue, the first strike of a match.

"I'll find them," Naji said. "It's my responsibility."

"Naji, no!" Irene said. "God knows what Ahmad's thinking. What he'll do."

Naji took her chin in his hand. "This is my fault. I could have helped him. Last time, I didn't help him. I should never have brought him here."

"I'm not leaving without Jina," Mike said. "How long is the hike to Pearl's?"

Drew shook his head. "Three miles. You'll never make it."

"Of course I will. Naji, too. It's not even dawn yet. You've got to give us a couple of hours. You can try to reach your father on the cell phone, or at least reach someone who can get to him from the other end. And call this number." He grabbed his dry bag, took a card from the wallet inside. "It's my boss. I'm sorry, Naji. He'll need to know. We have no idea the extent of this. There may be others involved."

Naji turned aside. "I don't think so. Ahmad has always been alone."

"It's possible you don't know everything about him."

Naji ignored the statement, turned to Irene. "You and Mary can watch over the boys while we're gone."

"Don't be an ass," Irene said. She squeezed Mary's arm. "When the boys wake up, tell them we'll be back soon. Don't tell them how bad the fires are."

There were tears in Mary's eyes, but she agreed.

Irene went for her gun, then remembered she'd given it to Jina.

"I'll lead," she said, and started up the path.

Zach charged the porch, screaming for Pearl and Andy.

After that, everything seemed to happen at once. Jina heard shouts behind her: Naji's voice, Mike's. She saw Ahmad striking another match and moving where the wood and kindling lay against the cabin walls. She fumbled, getting Irene's gun from the pack, but once she aimed she didn't hesitate. She'd never fired a gun before, and the recoil sent her flying backward. She realized she'd heard more than one shot.

Mike grabbed her, and she saw a flash of silver before he put his own gun back in its holster. Pearl stood on the porch, a rifle clutched in her hands. It could have been any of them; perhaps, in the days to come, that would help her sleep. Zach ran to the garden, sunk a hose into one of the canals he'd dug to bring water from Corey Creek. He raced to the woodpile, siphoned water through the hose until the flames settled down and the wood began to steam.

"Did he think he'd get away with it?" Pearl said to no one in particular. "This is Idaho, for God's sake."

Naji ran to his brother, made clucking sounds Jina could hardly bear. The wound in Ahmad's chest was tiny, but the ground beneath him dark red. His eyes were unfocused. No, he hadn't intended to get away with it. He'd thought only what he'd been told, that this precious life was meaningless, that terror changed minds rather than turning them resolute, that God was as mean-spirited as men. He hadn't had much imagination; that was his trouble. Even with all his prayers, he'd suffered from a lack of faith.

Ahmad looked past his brother to the sky, his gaze panicking a bit, moving right and left, as if he ought to be seeing something else by now.

"Allah," Ahmad said. "Allah, I'm afraid."

Irene ran toward them. She looked at no one but Naji, who

was trembling so badly, he couldn't hold Ahmad's head still. She knelt beside him, gently pushed her husband aside, and cradled Ahmad in her own lap. Her body rose and fell like the wind. Her knees were quickly covered with blood.

"Look where you are," she said, nearly out of breath, nearly an echo. "You're home."

Ahmad closed his eyes. Andy giggled, and it sounded absurd under the circumstances, absurd and wonderful. Jina swayed, and Mike was there. His arms came around her, warm to the touch. She buried her face in his chest until Ahmad went still and the flames of his fires licked at other cabins, at the dens of wolves, and choking black smoke billowed up over Corey Ridge.

"We have to go," Mike said.

Naji looked up. "I can't leave him."

Pearl went to the shed and came back with a shovel. "I'll bury him with my goats," she said. "He doesn't deserve it, but I'm no tyrant."

Zach continued to pour water on the woodpile as smoke billowed over the ridge, and he watched Jina and Mike.

"What about you?" Jina asked. "The fires . . ."

"We'll be fine," Pearl answered for them. "If the cabin goes, there are others. There's always the river to protect us."

"Zach?" Jina said. "What about Danny?"

He made sure every last flame had been put out. Jina thought he stooped as he walked toward her, but it was hard to tell through the smoke and steam. It was hard to know anything for sure.

"There's no time now," he said. "You have to get out." He reached into his pocket, came out with his knife. "I'll try to catch up to you, but if I can't make it, will you give him this?"

She blinked, took the knife. "Of course."

Mike looked at Ahmad, but he was speaking to Zach. "There'll be people coming. Agents. There's no way I can help that."

Zach nodded, his arms stiff at his sides. "All right."

Jina glanced at Ahmad's body, at Andy playing on the porch as if everyone lived in the path of a wildfire, and finally at Mike.

When he took her hand, she changed her mind, realized that a few precious things can be counted on. Kindness in the face of cruelty. The optimism of boys. Love. Some things are fireproof.

Mary and the boys were building sandcastles when a fire helicopter swooped in.

"The fire's just over the ridge," a voice boomed from a bullhorn above. "Two hundred thousand acres. You have to leave now."

Mary put her arms around the boys' shoulders. She leaned toward their ears but still had to shout to be heard. "We're ready to go. We'll give the others a few more minutes to get back. They'll make it. Don't worry."

Drew raced down to the beach, tossed the cell phone angrily into the raft. There was a curve to his back that would probably never leave him.

"The Feds are coming," he said. "No one answered at the lodge."

The wind from the helicopter blades whipped sand into their eyes. The boys got in the raft; Drew untied the ropes.

"Now," the man in the helicopter said.

Mary ignored the orders from the helicopter gestapo, stared up the empty trail.

"Mary," Drew said.

She held up her hand. "Wait."

They came five minutes later, running down the path. Mary's eyes burned, but she turned to the boys.

"See?" she said, as if it had been a trick.

The boys' eyes widened at the bloodstains on Irene. There wasn't time to ask where Ahmad was, but Danny whispered to Charlie, "Another one bites the dust."

"All right," Charlie said. "This beats L.A."

Flames crowned the trees on Corey Ridge as they hit the river. The boys oohed and aahed; Mary put a hand on Drew's knee. There's no way to stop a wildfire; you just try to contain it. You wait it out. The real terror, as Ahmad must have known, is not violence itself but uncertainty. Not knowing what will happen next. She felt the muscles in Drew's legs straining as he rowed them toward the center of the river, felt him tremble every time another tree went up with a whoosh.

Only the boys cheered through the rapids of Bailey and Split Rock and Big Mallard. Naji remained white-faced; Irene held tight to his hand. Despite the somber mood, the river carried them quickly downstream, away from the blazes, to clearer skies and safety. Jake leaped out first at the Whitewater Ranch, splashed through the water, happily fetched the stick Danny threw.

Mary knew it was the last bit of quiet they would have. Once the FBI arrived, they all would be detained, interrogated. Zach's cabin, if it still stood, would be searched, Ahmad's body recovered. Zach's existence would be revealed, Pearl's son exposed to the spotlight, their hideaway put on the evening news. God only knew what would happen to Naji. Perhaps Mike's word, and Naji's twenty years of lawful American citizenry, would be enough to keep him from a place like Guantánamo. Perhaps not.

Drew led the group to the ranch to check for news. Mary stayed on the beach, walked into the river, walked until the water was right up to her thighs. She reached through the water, sorted rocks until she found a flat one. She didn't have much practice with wishes, so she started at the top, wished for peace and joy and courage and passion, for something more stable and lasting than her own fickle wishes—a chance, perhaps, to make someone else's wishes come true. She slung the rock sideways, watched it bounce across the water once, twice, three times.

By the time Drew came to tell her that agents were flying in from Boise and there was no news of his father, Mary refused to come out of the river.

"Mary?" Drew said.

"Let's not go any farther."

He looked lost, while she knew exactly where they were: at the beginning, at the start. He seemed stunned that he could love his father, someone he hated, this much, while she knew that love, and life, were at their best when they made no sense. Just look at her. She had a car payment due Wednesday, a gym membership going to waste. Who said these things mattered? Who made those rules? Did anybody really expect her to walk away from the man who had breathed her to life, who was better at saving things than he realized? She might be inexperienced, but she was no fool. Anything could happen next; that was the beauty of it.

He'd never grown up; she'd started out old. They were fire and water, elemental. She stepped out of the water, the river nymph now, and he went to her, buried his face in her shoulder. Even acts of terrorism can't destroy everything. Someone always survives to tell the tale, to inspire others, to forgive. There's always something left; this was what she could teach him.

"Just stay?" he said, and Jake, who was always listening for chipmunks to chase or a reason to celebrate, perked up his ears.

Mary pulled Drew into the river with her, sat him on a shallow shelf, kissed his tears, held him. When the salmon came again, they'd still look homeward, color-blind. They can't see fire at all.

Jina stood beside Mike when he got the call from Riggins. Twenty agents were there, amassed almost instantly from four western states. They had talked to a number of jet boat captains and agreed to come upstream to meet Mike and the others at Mackay Bar.

Jina watched Mike's shoulders fall as he set down the cell

phone, watched him avoid Naji's gaze. He took a deep breath, turned to her. Now that they had a moment to talk, she didn't know where to begin. It was as if their raft had flipped in one of the rapids upstream and pieces of their cargo were still flying by. There went their baggage, their tender beginning and subsequent lack of effort, all the things they should have said. They'd been shipwrecked, without resources, and she felt a wriggle in her stomach, a new thrill. Now, at last, she was alone with him.

She reached out, hesitated. He looked different with the sun on his face.

"You came," she said.

His gaze softened; he pressed his forehead to hers. *"Duh."*

She laughed, slipped her arms around his waist. What fools they'd been, starting out like an old married couple. Determined to skip the scary parts, even if those were sometimes the best. But it hadn't happened that way. They'd spent all their time backtracking, unlearning each other's habits, growing more and more unsure. And now look at them: flustered by the very idea that they might have met someone who could be the one.

Danny swam on his back around the raft; Charlie lounged inside, across two seats. It was silent until Irene said to Mary, "Didn't I tell you to take that offer on your condo?"

Jake danced around them, as if dogs have ambitions, too, and sometimes achieve them.

Mike got another call, and Irene pulled Jina away. Mary came up beside them.

"I wish we could all stay," Irene said. "We're just getting good."

"We'll come back," Jina said. "Who needs sushi? We'll be the salmon club. The second-chance club. The river mamas."

Mary looked at Drew, who still faced east, toward the fires, toward the Red Salmon Lodge. Jina knew any news but the best would fall on deaf ears. He wouldn't abide hopelessness. He was lovely that way.

"I'm terrified," Mary said. "It's wonderful."

Jina put her arms around them, knowing that the sushi club was broken, over, knowing nothing would ever be the same, which led to a host of surprisingly pleasant imaginings: a couple of mismatched canyon castaways, happy as clams; a faded celebrity who realizes she's better at other things; grasses and wildflowers emerging on scorched hillsides, pine saplings shooting up everywhere, thicker than before; the man in her dreams the same one she wakes up with.

Another one coming through the trees.

Mike closed his cell phone; Jina whirled toward Danny. He was still floating, looking skyward, but even before he saw the shadow on the water, he felt Zach's presence. He always had.

Danny came to his feet slowly. Jina hadn't had time to plan how she would tell him his father was alive, but she knew it wasn't like this. She rushed forward, her hands out in front of her.

"Let me explain," she said.

Before she could, Zach was there, crouching down, eye level with his son. He looked over Danny's red hair, the wide stance that kept him stable in water, the eyes that, when it counted, didn't show fear.

"Hey," he said.

Danny glanced at Mike, who smiled, urged him forward. Jina blinked back tears. She really wanted to hate this place, but it was too hard. The canyon kept bringing out the best in the men she loved.

"Hope you don't mind," Zach said. "I hurried so I could see you. You know who I am?"

Danny nodded, balled his hands into fists. Charlie peeked out over the side of the raft.

"Your mom said you can visit," Zach went on. "Every summer, if you want. Andy would like that. I'd . . . like it."

Of course he didn't mention Pearl. Jina saw a flash of pink through the trees, heard Andy's singing somewhere up on the ridge.

"Danny," she said. "I just found out. I don't know what to . . ."

Her words fell away when Danny stepped forward, touched the bones in Zach's wrist, tested the solidity of his skin. "I knew it," he said.

Zach didn't move, as if it was a hummingbird perched on his hand.

"I wish I'd known," Zach said.

Danny blinked. Sometimes wishes *were* enough. "Do the Lymonds have a cabin around here?" he asked.

Zach nodded. "Sure. Back by Lucky Creek."

"You notch trees for a trail?"

Zach nodded again. "Helps to find your way when the snow's deep."

Danny removed his hand, slowly began to smile. "Bitchin'," he said.

The river was quiet here, slow and mild until Elkhorn. Of course, life was exactly the same. Miles and miles of flat water, then a flurry of rapids and rocks, a hole or waterfall where it wasn't expected. Another tragedy or victory, followed by stillness once more. She used to live for whitewater, but she was done with that.

"We have to go," she said. "I'm sorry, Zach. We have to meet the FBI at Mackay Bar."

He straightened.

"My mom said you were born to run rivers," Danny said.

Zach balled his hands into fists, too. He pretended he was cold and rubbed his arms when they shook.

"She told me the same thing about you," he said.

Danny glanced at her. "Yeah, I'm pretty good. You should have seen me in Rainier. Could still use a few pointers, though. What to do when you turn sideways. Maybe you could teach me that."

Zach's teeth flashed, and in that moment Jina knew she'd have to battle to keep Danny home even a day each summer. She'd have to battle a daredevil, a hero, a legend, and accept, as all mothers eventually do, that she'd never compare.

"Oh, yeah," Zach said. "I can teach you that."

He reached out, his hand hovering for a moment above Danny's head before he touched his son's hair. Jina felt Mary's arm sliding around her waist, Irene coming from the other side.

Finally, Zach stepped back, put his hands in his pockets, headed toward Mike. "He's buried in the meadow," he said. "I'm taking Andy and Pearl downriver for a while, until the fire passes. There's a cabin up Churchill Creek. You can find us there."

Mike nodded, but as Zach walked away, he called out, "You said Cow Creek?"

Zach turned back. "No, I said——"

"Cow Creek," Mike finished for him. "You said Cow Creek. That's what I heard."

The men stared at each other, then Zach bowed his head, disappeared into the trees. Danny watched the last place he'd seen him, as if there was still a remnant there, a spirit only he could see. Then suddenly he smiled and looked back at Charlie.

"Told you," he said.

He launched himself into the water. A split second later, Charlie cannonballed in beside him, came up with his eyes wide open.

"Bet he can teach you to breathe underwater," Charlie said.

"You think?"

"A fish-man for a dad," Charlie said, and whistled. "Fuckin' cool."

Irene pinched Jina's waist. "Too bad nothing happens around here."

Jina laughed, felt the air finally returning to her lungs.

Later, they got into the raft; Drew untied them from shore.

"We'll stay here until you bring the Feds," Drew said. "But I'm warning you, we might be delirious with happiness. There'll be no point interrogating us at all."

Drew and Mary stood on shore as Mike rowed the rest of them toward the center of the river.

"Idiots," Irene said, but there was admiration in her voice.

Jina didn't say a word when Danny and Charlie took turns at the oars. Charlie spun them through Elkhorn; Danny launched a backward dive through Growler. Even Naji smiled at the surprise of his survival.

A flotilla of jet boats and agents was waiting at Mackay Bar when they arrived.

Mike squeezed Jina's hand, looked at Irene and Naji sitting silently in the front of the raft. He tossed a rope to Patrick Bergowitz, who might be a master at locating terrorists but didn't have enough sense to wear shorts. He sweated in blue jeans and a button-down shirt. Even Naji had to smile.

"Mike," Bergowitz said at once, "you shouldn't have let anyone bury him. You know that damn well."

Jina noticed how the agents stepped forward when Naji emerged from the raft, the handcuffs one carried, how tightly Irene held her husband's hand.

"A man had just watched his brother die," Mike said. "Besides, there was a fire bearing down on us. There may be no evidence left, except what was buried."

Bergowitz swiped a hand across his forehead. One of the jet boats fired up. "Donahue's in charge of interrogation. No one's going anywhere until we know everything. No one's leaving."

Charlie and Danny jumped out of the raft; Charlie hooted. Danny shushed him with a kick, but he was smiling. They'd be sketchy with details, Jina was certain—unbearably slow to open up.

One man searched Naji, frisking him roughly down the torso, between his legs. Another opened the handcuffs.

"You can't be fuckin' serious?" Irene said.

Mike stepped forward, but Bergowitz grabbed his arm. "Mike. You know I have no choice. He's the man's brother. He brought him here."

"Naji's guilty of nothing more than having too much faith," Mike said. "He loved his brother, but he never once held me back when we set out after Ahmad. He was a great partner. Reminded me a lot of Ben."

Bergowitz said nothing.

"He's not going anywhere," Mike went on. "For God's sake, look around. He's not going to swim away. Aren't we all just a little too afraid?"

"No, Mike," Bergowitz said. "We're realists." But he gestured toward Donahue. "If he so much as breathes in the wrong direction, put them on."

Mike shook his head, but at least the handcuffs disappeared for the moment. Still, the men encircled Naji, hardly let him see daylight. Donahue took out his notebook and tape recorder. Irene held up a hand when they fired the first question.

"It's better as a story," she said. She cleared her throat, flashed her Hollywood smile. God help them. "Where Naji comes from, there's the legend of the jinn."

Bergowitz took Mike aside. "You'll have to guide us upriver. Where's this cabin? Who owns it?"

Jina slipped forward, took Mike's hand. Bergowitz frowned at her, but she merely smiled back. She wasn't going anywhere.

"Well, now, that's the thing," Mike said. "Hard to say who owns what around here. Mostly, people just show up for a time. Do some gardening. Move on."

"Someone stayed long enough to bury him."

"That's true. But they had to escape the fire, too. Last I heard, they headed up Cow Creek to another cabin."

"We'll send Douglas and Pierce that way. You'll lead us to Ahmad's body."

Mike stared at him. "I'll lead you. And I'll help you bring out a body that'll tell you nothing. You and I both know that, Patrick. You can't see hatred on a dead man's face. Can't see love, either."

"Let's get to the boats."

Bergowitz rushed off, but Mike lingered. He held Jina's hand, brushed a finger over her knuckles.

"It'll be all right," he said, and she knew he was talking about more than the retrieval of Ahmad's body. He was talking about the two of them starting over, about Zach and his family staying safe, about Naji going free and Mary and Drew creating a life on the river and Danny taking on the strength of two fathers and Alice turning John into her next hero, and all the fires going out. He was devoted to all kinds of optimistic unlikelihoods.

"Duh," she said.

His whiskers tickled her when she kissed him. He was still smiling as he got in the jet boat with Bergowitz and took off upstream.

Jina watched them until they were out of sight, then reached into her pocket. She glanced at Irene, who seemed to have caught the interest of the agents, all of whom flinched when she reached over her shoulder to grab the jinn on her left. Then she walked to Danny, handed her son the knife she'd first seen on the belt loop of a young man who didn't belong on a cruise ship, a knife that had helped whittle the scow Zach thought himself devoted to, not yet knowing the meaning of the word.

"It's from your father," she said.

The river worked its magic once more, turning his gaze toward the mountains, then upstream, turning out the best in him. "Which one?" he asked.

Readers Guide

The Secret Lives of the Sushi Club

Christy Yorke

1. The author begins *The Secret Lives of the Sushi Club* by relating the legend of the Salmon River. Its moral is "be careful who and what you love." Would you say that Jina, Alice, Mary, and Irene are careful in matters of love?

2. Alice is taken aback at her friends' reaction to her novel. What is her justification? Are you sympathetic to it?

3. As each character's private life is exposed, they react with anger, sadness, self-loathing, and other powerful emotions. In your opinion, which of the four friends suffers the most? How would you react in the same situation?

4. At one point it's suggested that when you put four women in a room together, someone is bound to get hurt. Discuss the power hierarchy within the Sushi Club, and how it evolves over the course of events that take place on the Salmon River.

5. The challenge of confronting and moving beyond one's past is a major theme in *The Secret Lives of the Sushi Club*. For Jina, the challenge becomes very literal. How does it manifest in the other characters' lives and the lives of their children and spouses?

6. Alice's husband John was a writer and an activist in his youth, but he gave it up to become an insurance agent so that Alice could continue to pursue her writing career. According to Alice, John's biggest mistake was asking her to be happy. According to John, Alice's mistake was continuing to write even when it had a negative effect on her personal life. Do you agree with their assessment of each other? How do they reconcile their differences in the end?

7. There are strong forces of creation and destruction at work in Yorke's story—not least among them the power of Alice's writer's imagination and that of a young boy's visions. What is the connection between these forces and the ones that affect the character's physical world? Discuss the author's use of fire and water imagery.

8. Irene's husband Naji and his brother Ahmad are very different even though they share a past. How does the nature/nurture debate play out in the context of their relationship and the disaster that befalls them? Is sibling rivalry a factor?

9. Each member of the Sushi Club forgives Alice in her own time. At what point does Alice begin to forgive herself? Who helps her move on, and how?

10. Jina's son Danny eventually comes to understand that the father he has is more precious than the one he never knew, yet he also embraces the adventurous spirit inherited from Zach. How does his decision reflect the story's overarching theme?

11. Based on the following quote, discuss how each member of the Sushi Club deals with her inner demons: "Alice had spilled all their secrets but one, the one nobody talked about: All four of them were for sale. Jina for one more whiff of the past, Mary for a different future. There is a price at which every person will sell her soul, and for Alice and Irene it was heartbreakingly low. Just a bestseller and a part in a soap opera, then they were left with nothing but yearning, with the devil, a jinn, inside them." (pp. 120–121)

12. The wilderness often attracts a variety of eccentric and strongminded people. On the Salmon River, the characters meet and are challenged by others who hold opposing points of view. What are each of the characters fighting for? Who has sacrificed their relationships for the sake of a cause or moral stand? What ideals, if any, do you believe are worth fighting for?